EMPIRE

THE EAGLE ELITE SERIES #7

by

RACHEL VAN DYKEN

Empire
Eagle Elite #7
by Rachel Van Dyken

This is a work of fiction. Names, places, characters, and events are fictitious in every regard. Any similarities to actual events and persons, living or dead, are purely coincidental. Any trademarks, service marks, product names, or named features are assumed to be the property of their respective owners, and are used only for reference. There is no implied endorsement if any of these terms are used. Except for review purposes, the reproduction of this book in whole or part, electronically or mechanically, constitutes a copyright violation.

DEDICATION

to twirling

EMPIRE

Noun: *Organization, Kingdom, Business. To rule or have power or authority. Command, control, dominate. EG: He built an Empire—he refused to see it crumble beneath his feet.*

PROLOGUE

MARCH

Frank

THE GLOOMY DAY matched my dark mood. Merciless rain pelted my umbrella and cascaded off the edge. I adjusted my grip on the polished wooden handle. Arthritis had crept in and it was sometimes hard to tell when I had a secure hold on something. Age had never been a friend of mine. The clock, it seemed, never stopped ticking, the seconds going by faster than I could have ever imagined, the years disappearing like sand through an hour glass.

The spongy ground sank beneath my feet, pieces of grass stuck to my black Valentino loafers.

I kept walking.

My stride strong.

My purpose even stronger.

The grave was marked well, I'd made sure it would be. After all, it seemed the least I could do — give my brother a proper burial, when it was me, his most feared enemy and in the end most trusted ally — who'd had a hand in watching him die.

It wasn't my fault.

I hadn't pulled the trigger.

But I knew the dangers in what we did.

I knew the cost of our chess match.

I just wish it had been me — instead of him.

A few more feet and I stood in front of the large gray stone. I'd known Luca wouldn't have wanted something elaborate — after all he'd made his way through the world being the silent one, the death blow you never saw coming, until it was too late.

I licked my cracked lips and shook my head as I read the tombstone. "Loving brother, fearless leader..." My voice cracked. "Blessed father." I closed my eyes as the sting of tears burned.

Father.

And only two people here knew.

Phoenix and myself.

"I'm so sorry, brother..."

Would I have done things differently? All those years ago when I made Luca into the man he was, when I forced him into the Nicolasi family, when I stole the woman he loved and turned him against the world.

Knowing what I knew now... would I do it all again?

"For what it's worth old man..." I pointed to the gravestone next to his. "I'd like to think... that at least in the afterlife — you'll have her."

I'd buried my wife next to him, where she belonged. Where she had always belonged.

Every night I prayed that they were finally united in heaven.

While I was cursed to roam the earth without my

brother — without my wife, and in charge of four mafia bosses who were younger than I was when I had taken over.

The empire I had built was changing, morphing into something I no longer recognized.

With a sigh I made a cross over my chest and mumbled a prayer.

"Well this is depressing," came a low voice behind me.

I didn't need to turn around to know it was Phoenix De Lange, newest boss to the Nicolasi family — handpicked by Luca himself.

"Did you bring it?" I kept my eyes trained on the gravestone.

Phoenix let out a curse, "Yes."

I held out my hand.

"Are you sure you want to know?"

"Yes."

"Maybe we should talk to Tex about this before—"

"Give it over damn it, I'm your elder."

"Don't pull the age line, old man. You can still take me down, and you know it."

I smirked and kept my hand firmly in the air. The minute the folder touched my fingertips, I snatched it away and held it tightly against my chest.

"They aren't going to like this…" Phoenix growled.

"They don't get a say."

"The hell they don't." Phoenix let out a bark of laughter. "But sure, if it helps you sleep at night." The rain started to pour down in sheets. "When do you leave?"

"As soon as possible."

"Safe travels."

"Always."

"Does anyone else know you'll be gone?"

I turned and offered him a sly wink. "Secrets, secrets, secrets, what else do I build my family on?"

With a slight shake of his head, Phoenix took a step back. "I can't protect you if this goes badly — especially if I don't know where you are... at least bring one of the men."

"No." I glanced at my watch. My flight would leave within the hour. "Don't think I will."

"Damn it, Frank."

"Don't 'damn it, Frank' me..." I held out my hand. "Now, leave like a man before I have to remind you who's older... and more experienced."

Phoenix offered a sad smile and shook my hand. "Be well, Frank."

"Be well, Phoenix."

CHAPTER 1

A Midsummer Night's Dream, it takes me away to a place where everything is beautiful — and alive.

—Valentina

SIX WEEKS PREVIOUS
JANUARY

Valentina

"SORRY!" I STUMBLED out of the way of an athletic blonde in a pencil skirt and Nikes power walking her merry way along Fifth Avenue. Business professionals and customers shuffled past me, I nearly collapsed onto the sidewalk, barely managing to dodge the intense foot traffic before my face made an imprint onto the cement.

Nobody acknowledged my apology, nobody really even acknowledged me. Then again, it *was* New York. I could be breathing my last breath, and the chances of someone actually stepping in were one in a million. Pretty sure I saw that in one of my Freshman Psych classes. It wasn't that New Yorkers were mean or rude like people assumed. They were just busy.

And busy meant they didn't have time to stop on the sidewalk and help an eighteen-year-old girl to her feet because she looked like she was about to get smothered against the nearest window.

I took another deep breath. This was stupid.

I *was* stupid. It was a bank. How many times had I walked by this exact building and thought nothing of it?

My stomach clenched. Today was different.

I felt like one of the girls I'd read about in my romance novels, the ones who had adventurous lives, were pursued by drop-dead sexy men in full body armor. Hah, yeah that was so not my reality.

I tugged my coat tighter around my uniform just as my phone buzzed in my purse.

Probably one of my uncles checking up on me to make sure I was on my way to the store.

Now or never.

The letter had been burning a hole in my pocket for weeks, and I wasn't the type of person to ignore things, especially weird things, things that actually made my life seem less normal, less boring. For the last eighteen years I'd gone to school, tried my hardest to get good grades, and worked at my family's flower shop.

Oh, and I read.

I had no specific talents, unless you could actually count reading, which, is apparently frowned upon when you're applying for college. I could still hear my Uncle Gio's laughter. "Reading is a hobby, Val, not a talent."

My phone kept buzzing.

I clenched my teeth, then pulled it out of my purse

and answered it. "Yes?"

"Val?" Uncle Gio's thick accent wrapped around me like a warm hug. "Are you sick?"

"No." I glanced helplessly at the glass windows of the skyscraper. "I'm on my way."

"You will be late." He stated it like a fact, didn't ask.

"Maybe." I said distractedly. "Traffic is... bad."

"But you walk."

"I have to cross streets, Gio."

He was quiet and then. "Did you eat?"

"Gio!" I groaned, already feeling my cheeks burn with embarrassment, when would I ever be an adult to them? "I ate, all right?"

More silence and then. "I don't believe you. I brought extra cannoli, just in case."

If I ate any more cannoli someone was going to have to start running to work instead of walking. "Fine, I just — I need to go, it's hard to hear you."

"Where are you?"

"Close!" I lied. "See you soon, Gio!"

"Love you, little Val."

I held my groan in. I would always be little Val.

Always.

I straightened my shoulders and shoved my phone back into my purse. Little Val would back away; little Val would have burned the letter I was currently carrying.

Little Val would probably have told her overprotective uncles and brother.

But I didn't want to be little anymore. I was a woman.

I reached for the door handle just as another body bumped into me propelling me through the doors with an *umph*.

The crisp smell of papers and too much floor cleaner burned my nostrils as I turned a few circles. Where the heck was I supposed to even go?

I stepped out of the way and pulled out the letter.

Bank of America
Safety Deposit Box 36

There was no return address, and it wasn't even in typical handwriting, but typed out. Maybe I should have said something to my uncles.

But, and here's the creepy part, the part that led me to the bank the minute they opened. The part that had me lying to my uncle for the first time, since… forever.

At the very bottom of the page was a quote from Shakespeare.

The course of true love, never did run smooth.

It was one of my favorite quotes. When I was five, I'd stolen one of the old books from Gio's library and snuck chapters when I could. Again, I was an odd child, so if you knew me, you'd know it wasn't particularly strange for me to devour words like they were bread and butter.

I'd been obsessed with A Midsummer Night's Dream ever since then, and that very book was still placed under my bed at night.

I had it memorized.

Geez, I was lame.

"Miss?" A drop-dead sexy guy approached me. His black suit barely moved as he walked, like it was glued to every muscle in his body. The black tie atop the black shirt screamed "danger!" The high end sunglasses hanging out of his front pocket said casual but not careless. My mouth must have dropped open, because a small smile curved around his lips as he ducked his head.

"Are you..." I turned around. "Oh, I'm sorry were you talking to me?"

"You talking to me?" he said in a perfect De Niro *Taxi Driver* accent. "You talkin' to me?" He laughed a bit.

I joined him, realizing how ridiculous I was being. I was in a bank, looking like a lost child, and he was in a suit. Clearly he worked there, though his name tag wasn't visible. I frowned.

"May I help you with something?" he asked holding out his hand, his smile was easy, but something about it had me hesitating. Silky black hair lay against his olive skin, he looked Italian but his stormy blue yes... there was something predatory in their depths. I felt like I should know him, but I didn't, nor did I really want to know a man who had such a calculating smile. His grin deepened, my legs itched to turn around and run away.

"No." I said quickly. "I just... wrong building."

"I'm sorry." He grabbed my arm gently. "Did I scare you? I didn't mean to. I work here and you were staring down at a paper and you looked lost, I put two and two together..." As his voice trailed off, he tilted his head, one eyebrow raised.

Tension eased its grip on my body. "Sorry, I'm just..." I waved into the air. "Long night reading vampire novels, didn't get much sleep."

"Tell me, how is Edward?" he joked, a half smile tugging up one side of his gorgeous mouth.

"Still with Bella, damn him." I fired back quickly.

He burst out laughing. "You're going to do just

9

fine."

"Do?"

"Now, what did you say I could help you with?" He was already reaching for the paper. I let him have it because I didn't want to be rude. That was my biggest downfall — my niceness. Let's just say it was basically impossible for me to pass a homeless guy without giving him every single bit of spare change I had, even though I knew that he'd most likely spend it on something bad.

The man scanned the sheet and then handed it back.

"Weird, right?" I said jokingly, a bit embarrassed that he'd read the whole thing and now probably thought I was insane or had escaped a mental institution.

"Eh." He shrugged. "I've seen weirder." His smile faded. "You have no idea."

"I believe you," I croaked out.

"Safety deposit boxes…" He turned on his heel and started walking, and I followed mutely. "…are right over here." He scanned a key card over some metal thingy and walked me to the farthest corner of the building. "Go down the hall and find your number. Some have keys, some of the high profile deposit boxes use a thumbprint."

I held up my hand and then dug through my purse, finally locating the key and lifting it triumphantly into the air. "Key."

"Fantastic." He nodded once. "Stay as long as you need."

"Thanks." I bit my lip in nervousness, I was really doing this. Holy crap. My heart slammed against my chest as I walked down the quiet hall.

"I hope you find what you're looking for Valentina,"

he whispered after me. "I truly do."

My steps faltered.

I'd never told him my name.

Shaking, I quickly turned around.

But he was gone.

I nearly toppled into another lady on my way out of the hall to find him.

"Miss?" She was juggling about a million papers. "Can I help you?"

"A man," I blurted. "He just left down the hall and—"

"No." The lady frowned. "I would have seen him, I'm sorry, maybe… you imagined it?"

"Right." I swallowed the dryness in my throat, my heart really going to town threatening to crack right out of my chest and start thumping across the floor.

"You look lost?" she offered with a tilt of her head, she was pretty, and appeared a bit young to be working at a bank, but what did I know?

"Nope." I clenched the key between my fingers, sweat pooling around the metal. "I have a safety deposit box to look at."

"Well," she said, nodding, "let me know if you have any questions. My name's… Emiliana."

"Okay." I took two steps backward then turned on my heel and made a beeline for the boxes, they lined both walls.

Finally, I located number thirty-six, and without giving myself time to chicken out, shoved the key in the lock and turned it.

Had I known then what I know *now* — I would have ran toward the bank, shoved my way through the fires of hell, and done just about anything legal or illegal to get to that box.

Shaking, I pulled the box out and went into one of the private rooms and closed the door behind me.

CHAPTER 2

All is lost. Romance. Love. Stories. Endings. All. Is. Lost.

—Sergio

Sergio

"Hey." Frank nudged me with his elbow, and I glanced at the newspaper rolled up in his hand. Ink smudges lined a few of his fingers. "I need some coffee, did you want anything?"

I shook my head and sank lower in the uncomfortable metal airport chair, unable to concentrate on anything other than the pounding of my own heart, and the sweat that was starting to trickle from the back of my neck.

I flexed my hand into a fist and kicked my feet up onto my suitcase, pulling my beanie so low it nearly covered my eyes.

It had been two months.

Two months since she was taken from me.

Stolen.

The ache in my chest grew. I couldn't drink it away. I'd tried. And then felt so damn guilty for trying to drink her away that I spent the very next day sobbing my eyes out, thinking how disappointed she'd be in me. And how disappointed I was in myself.

Why end my life?

When she would have done anything — anything.

To keep hers.

"Mama!" A little girl in a pink frilly dress reached up for her young mother. The woman had dark hair that matched the circles beneath her eyes. "Please, pretty please!"

The woman sighed then slowly lowered herself to the little girl's level. Something about their moment was tender, something drew me to them, a yearning in my chest, a desire to see something beautiful.

Andi's death had been beautiful.

But since her death, I'd been struggling trying to find that beauty in the realm of the living.

The world was no longer filled with color. Just blacks and grays.

And it was slowly killing me, eating away at my soul.

"Mama!" The girl giggled, her blonde curls bouncing across her shoulders. "Please just once?"

The mom sighed again, then grinned and held out her hand. The little girl took it.

And twirled.

My entire body seized as the world around me ceased to exist. All I saw was that blonde little girl, face lifted up toward the ceiling, giggling with abandon. With one arm spread, one hand clinging to her mother for balance, she twirled again then fell into more fits of laughter.

I saw Andi in that twirl.

Felt her in the laughter.

My dead wife.

My Russian Mafia princess.

My vodka drinking terror.

I was afraid to close my eyes, afraid that feeling of peace would leave me as quickly as it had appeared.

Sadly, nothing lasts forever. Nothing.

The girl stopped twirling. The mom grabbed her hand. They walked away.

The world faded to black again.

My heart, once beating wildly in my chest, slowed to its normal rhythmic pace. I breathed in and out, because that's what you did when you didn't know what else to do anymore.

You simply *existed*.

You inhaled. Exhaled. Smiled when you were supposed to. Asked all the right questions, gave all the right answers.

With trembling hands I pulled out the silly list Andi, my wife, had made when we got married.

It was a honeymoon list, but basically she'd just written down a whole bunch of stupid shit she wanted to do before she died.

Lucky for me — a ghost of a smile tugged at my lips — I was part of the plan. And I spent my nights holding her, making love to her, living for possibly the first time in my life.

Days were filled with laughter and tears.

I was in the mafia; I knew better than anyone how short life could be. My enemy had always had a face, a gun, always pursuing me. Wanting to end me, so I ended them first.

But, time? Time can be an enemy too. Its face is never

intimidating, but the sound of the clock? Probably the most gut-wrenching sound in existence. One I still couldn't stomach.

The only clock left in my house was the one on my phone for that very reason.

"Hey." Frank swatted me with the old newspaper he'd been carrying around for the past few hours and sat. "You look sick."

"Tired," I grumbled.

"Me too." He nodded sagely. "Me too."

I snorted. "You're old, you have an excuse."

"We're both old," he said after a few beats of silence. "My body is old… your soul? Maybe even your heart? Much older than mine. Much, much, older Sergio."

I didn't know what to say to that. Wasn't sure I even wanted to acknowledge the truth of his statement.

"You may want to study up before our next flight." He handed me the newspaper roll. "I'm going to shut my eyes for a bit."

"Great, I'll just protect both our asses."

With a chuckle he waved me off. "Why would we need protecting? I'm just a feeble old man being escorted by my favorite grandson to my birthplace, New York." He looked positively giddy. "I can hardly wait to smell the trash."

Right. If Frank Alfero, mob boss to one of the oldest families in Chicago was old and feeble, then I was a priest.

Shaking my head, I unrolled the newspaper and frowned as I pored through the first three pages. After the fourth, I paused where my thumb had landed on a picture.

I let out a curse, because the girl in the picture was

the very one I was supposed to be meeting in a few hours — saving. And according to my deceased wife's wishes — marrying.

Apparently I wasn't going to be doing any of the above — since she was just newly engaged.

To Frank Alfero's cousin.

CHAPTER 3

One sees more devils than vast hell can hold
                    —A Midsummer Night's Dream

Valentina

"Are you insane?" I yelled. I never yelled. I blinked my tears away as Gio started mumbling a prayer under his breath while Papi and Sal looked on with tense, wrinkled faces.

I'd just decided to take a break in the back room when I was attacked by the uncles. Of course, since they all walked with limps, I saw them coming.

I snapped the stemmed roses in my hands then dropped them onto the counter. It was a slow day.

"Take a break!" Gio had said.

"Have some cannoli!" Papi'd encouraged.

"And while you're at it, sit down, we have news." Sal spread his arms wide and announced. "We have found you a young man!"

The breath whooshed from my lungs and all the blood left my brain. Maybe I really did need to sit down.

The cannoli rolled around in my full stomach, threatening to pop back up and make a second appearance all over the roses I'd just spent hours arranging.

Roses that apparently were going to be decorating our house that evening for my engagement party!

Italians!

"Look," I began, trying to sound stern. Why couldn't I have been born with more of a backbone, like my twin brother Dante? People stared at him and whimpered. They stared at me and went *aw, how cute!* "I just barely turned nineteen! I have years before I need to get married, and I can easily pick out my own husband, thank you very much!"

"But you do not date." Sal rubbed his bald head, his shoulders hunched over as if he was in pain, maybe his arthritis was acting up again? It wasn't as if my uncles were spring chickens; they were in their seventies. "And we worry for you."

I narrowed my eyes and then jumped out of my chair when a realization hit me. "Are you guys sick? Is someone dying? Just tell me now and get it over with so we can come up with a plan." I mentally started crossing off all the things we'd need to do if they were, in fact, sick. I could take care of them, I mean, it was my job, they were like my parents. The three stooges, but still, all I had!

Confusion clouded Gio's expression. With his round black hat propped proudly on his balding head, he looked like a train conductor. "Doctors. Who goes to doctors?"

"Normal people," I said through clenched teeth.

"Bah!" Papi finally spoke up. "We are Italian."

He thrust his fist against his chest as if that proved his heritage, which, in a way, it did. "We are healthy, virile, men!"

"More wine?" Gio poured a few more generous glasses as they all slowly passed them around.

The shop was still dead.

Clearly they weren't sick if they were drinking and offended at the notion of even seeing a doctor.

"You know what you guys need?" I sat back down. "You need a hobby. One that doesn't involve my love life."

"But you could *learn* to love Nico!" Gio spread his arms wide. "Yes?"

"No!" I argued. "I don't even know Nico!"

"Of course you do!" Gio said as my uncles joined in laughter. "You used to play together as children."

I gave them my best blank expression. "Then by all means, we shall be married at once! I mean, we played together so…"

My sarcasm was completely lost on them as they giddily nodded their heads in agreement.

Groaning, I covered my face with my hands. "I'm not marrying Nico."

"He will be so disappointed." Papi clicked his tongue. "His mother was elated to get him off her hands."

"And into mine?" *Do not yell at your uncles.* Nice, nice, nice. I gripped the sides of the wooden chair so hard I was afraid it was going to crack. "Are you guys insane?"

"We would not know." Gio laughed. "We do not go to doctors, remember?"

"Impossible," I grumbled under my breath. "No." I

stood. "My answer is no."

Sal hunched over even more. Oh, dear Lord. "My arm."

"No!" I fought the urge to smile. "Stop it! Your arm is just fine. Sal! I mean it, stop pretending like you're hurt. That's cruel and unusual punishment." He put on a good show of shaking his wine glass as he lifted it to his lips. "Uh huh, careful not to spill any of that wine, Sal."

Gio made a cross over his chest as if the very idea was a sin against the church.

"Fix this." I held up my hands. "I love you all, but… you need to ask me before you start finding me strange men and engaging me to them! And announcing parties and—"

"Don't forget putting it in the newspaper," Papi coughed out.

Groaning, I closed my eyes and managed to take a few soothing breaths. "Don't suppose you'll share that wine?"

"No." They said in unison while Sal quickly swiped it from the table and hid it in his coat.

"Nice." I nodded. "Real nice, Sal, you used your bad hand."

He switched the wine back to his other hand muttering, "Damn it," while Papi smacked him in the back of the head with his rolled up newspaper.

I untied my apron with a sigh. "I'm gonna go across the street and visit Dante. Consider this my break."

Each of them blew me kisses.

But still no apology.

Then again, they were Italian. Controlling. Managing. Temperamental. Shoot. I was going to have to fix it myself. If I didn't do the breaking up, I would end up married to a stranger that most likely had a unibrow and liked his women in the kitchen — where they "belonged." Blah! I knew the type. And I refused to be tied down to it. Besides, had they missed the point that I was nineteen? Who got married at nineteen?

They had.

All three uncles.

Who survived their wives.

And now had nothing better to do than meddle in my life and drive me insane!

I ran across the street and pulled open the door, thankful that my twin worked so close by.

Then again, my family basically owned the entire block. We had a cleaners, where two cousins worked, a bar, and the flower shop.

Though it had always seemed strange to me that, besides the bar, we weren't ever really busy yet were able to completely stay afloat in a down economy.

My uncles said they were fantastic at investing.

And I left it at that, besides, it wasn't my place to ask questions.

"Whoa, there." Dante smirked as I made a beeline for the bar and pulled out a seat then, in dramatic fashion, threw half of my body against the bar top and let out a huff.

Dante leaned over so we were nearly nose to nose and whispered, "Rough day, sis?" His knuckles were taped — they were always taped, because he was always getting in fights, but I was too exhausted to argue with him about the blood currently dripping down on the wood bar.

"They're driving me insane!" I threw my hands

into the air and stood. And then decided the only thing left to do was pace back and forth.

Dante chuckled and rapped his knuckles against the bar like he was knocking. "I take it you found out about Nico?"

I stopped walking and shot daggers in his direction. "You traitor! You knew?"

"Hah, they told me last night. Laughed my ass off, told them that maybe they should ask you first, and you know what they said?"

"No, what?"

"They said, 'We know what is best for our niece.'" Dante used his best Italian accent as he pressed his thumb and forefinger together in the same gesture Gio was known for.

"Of course they did. Of course." I crossed my arms. "Do you know Nico?"

"Oh, I think you know Nico, too. You just don't, you know, *know* Nico."

"Huh?" I wrinkled my nose and stared at him.

Dante smirked. "Third pew at mass. Wears enough cologne to actually render someone devoid of the ability to smell for at least three hours after contact, and last Sunday his suit was purple. Head to toe. I think his jacket was velvet."

I sucked in a breath. "Nooooo. That's him? Gross! He shook my hand after church! Dante, his palms were sweaty."

The bell on the door jingled. We both turned to see an elderly gentleman make his way toward us. He looked around Gio's age, maybe seventy-two? But he wore it well. His three-piece suit was clearly Italian. Thick, wavy gray hair was styled perfectly. He screamed money.

Old New York money, the type you get illegally, if you know what I mean. I took a cautious step toward Dante even though he was on the other side of the bar. I don't even know why I was intimidated other than the stranger's clear blue eyes seemed to see right through me.

Did I know this man?

"Hello," he said in a lightly accented voice, and then he smiled, instantly transforming his face into friendlier territory. "I was looking for Sal Alfero?"

"Alfero?" I repeated, sharing a look with Dante who'd suddenly appeared to have swallowed something sour. His face was completely white, his jaw tense as he flexed his fingers into a tight fist. "I don't know—"

"No Alferos here," Dante said in a completely detached and hollow voice. "Sorry." His fists tightened even more as fresh blood slid down his wrist.

The man's smile turned to a scowl. "Are you sure?"

"My uncle," I interrupted. "His name is Sal but his last name is Grecco."

The man turned his full attention to me. "Grecco." His laugh was deep, intoxicating, warm. "Interesting, thank you, my dear."

With a tilt of his head, he politely excused himself and left.

"Huh, that was weird," I muttered to myself.

Dante swallowed. "Yeah. Weird."

"You okay?"

"Yeah." He recovered quickly as if he hadn't just looked ready to kill someone. A mixture of sorrow, confusion, and anger crossed his features again, before he grabbed a cup filled it with ice, and added in some Coke. "Drink up, sis. It's going to be a long day. You've got a man to break up with."

"I hate you."

"You know, that's the meanest thing you've ever said to me?"

I made a face.

"Hey, that's a compliment! You're nice. It's a good thing."

"I'm a pushover." I reached for the glass and slipped a straw inside, greedily sucking down the soda. "There's a difference."

"Val." Dante reached for my hand then brushed a kiss over the top of my knuckles. It was his thing. He was a true Italian gentleman, and my friends went crazy for it. Let it be known that at six-foot-five, Dante Grecco was a lady killer through and through. With icy blue eyes and strong, solid features, he could easily model. Muscles bulged beneath his shirt as he moved around the bar and started prepping for the evening service — once happy hour hit he had to go back to waiter duties since he wasn't twenty-one yet. "I love you." His back was still turned to me. "We've got each other, yes?"

"Yes," I said automatically, my eyes honing in on the injuries to his hands. For how long? That's what I wanted to ask. Because I wasn't that naïve. I knew what people whispered about behind his back — that he fought for money, that he was good at it — that at nineteen he was dangerous, uncontrollable, an animal.

"Good." He turned back around, placing both of his hands on the bar top. "We'll get through anything, as long as we have each other."

"Even Nico?"

He burst out laughing. "Yes, even Nico. Poor little jackass is gonna have a rough night."

"Me! I've had a rough day! Think of my night! Besides, I was late for work so I'm sort of behind on arranging—"

"You?" Dante interrupted, his expression concerned. "Late?"

I couldn't exactly say yes, because I received a top secret letter from an unnamed source and went to the safety deposit box only to discover another letter addressed to me, one I hadn't yet read, since Gio texted that he was going to call the police if I didn't show up in a few minutes.

Ugh, never late. Always nice. Total yes girl.

Maybe I should just marry Nico.

"So?" Dante snapped his fingers in front of my face. "You were saying? Late? Everything okay?"

"I'm supposed to marry a cologne commercial. No I'm not okay." I grit my teeth. "Keep 'em coming." I slid the soda toward him, he filled it up, and I spent the rest of my break laying my head against the countertop wishing for an alternate reality, or at least a love story better than I had.

But those love stories?

The truly epic ones?

They usually belonged between the pages of a book — not with the girl who works at the flower shop every day but Tuesday. The girl who spends her days off in the park reading. The girl who cries during Broadway shows and once asked her uncle if she could be a princess when she grew up.

No, those epic stories.

They weren't for girls like her. Like me.

CHAPTER 4

My soul is in the sky

–A Midsummer Night's Dream

Frank

I MUTTERED A curse under my breath as I re-entered the brisk New York air. She looked... so much like him.

And her.

Getting shot hurt less than seeing my flesh and blood and knowing without a doubt they did not even know who I was.

Did not know the circumstances of their birth.

Or how much they were loved, despite what they might think.

Grecco? I had not given Sal permission to use that name. Granted, all of my dealings with New York had been less than hostile.

The minute Luca took over the Nicolasi family.

All hell broke loose in mine.

Leaving me to pick up the pieces.

A divide had occurred between the ranks. Several of my cousins decided that their loyalty would be better served with the Nicolasis, while others were appalled at what I had done to my own brother — basically selling him to another crime family. Never mind that he was successful, or that it was because my father wished it.

I did what I had thought best.

I had been young.

Stupid.

Completely hell-bent on following through with my father's wishes, unaware that by following through with his instructions, I'd break one of the strongest crime families that ever existed, allowing the Abandonatos to take their rightful place.

Not that I was bitter.

The Abandonatos were better being the leaders of the Cosa Nostra in the United States.

Just like the Campisis were best at running things overseas, and making sure every family was kept in check.

I patted the inside of my jacket, my old fingers fumbling with the letter from Luca, his dying wishes.

For me to find his children.

And establish them within the Family.

But I had to wonder.

By doing what he asked — would I push my family further away? Because a dead man's wish... was a fickle thing. A slippery slope.

And if things went correctly....

I sighed again as I eyed the black Mercedes waiting.

Sergio.

The first chess pieces had already been moved.

Now.

I would wait.

"Oh, Luca," I whispered. "I wish you were here. I do need your guidance, more than ever."

The breeze picked up, whipping a newspaper around my legs. I kicked it off and made my way over to the waiting car.

Sergio looked up.

His face was pale.

He was a good actor, making his friends and family believe that he was doing fine. That his wife's death was making him a better man — and in a way, it was.

But he was also mourning.

He was more than devastated.

He was lost.

I knew the look well.

For it was in my own lonely reflection every day.

Dear God, don't let him turn out like me.

I clutched the silver chained cross in my pocket and said a prayer to the saints, a prayer to Mary.

And hoped.

That was all I could do.

Pray.

And hope.

"It's their move." I said once I was inside the car, the door slammed after me. "I have established my presence. We will see how they accept us this evening."

Sergio frowned. "This evening?"

"A party." I slapped him on the thigh. "So try not to look like your wife just died. Even though I know she did. Whatever it takes. We get the job done, do you understand?"

"Yes," he snapped, his eyes focusing for the first time in hours. Sergio did well under pressure, under orders, control. The kid didn't need a hug, he needed a good ass kicking.

I was just the man to do it.

I'd like to think Luca knew that.

Which is why, if Dante and Val wanted nothing to do with us, it would be Sergio taking my place.

Sergio leading my family.

I needed him strong.

My gut clenched as my past unfolded in my head… Funny, I had said that exact same statement over thirty years ago, as justification, of what I did to Luca, forcing him away from the only woman he had ever loved, faking his death.

Keeping them apart.

"Hey, you all right?" Sergio elbowed me. "You look like you may be sick."

"Eh." I waved him off. "I'm old. I'm always in pain."

He rolled his eyes and let out a small laugh.

I tried to join in.

But my chest pained me.

For regardless of what people assumed, I did still possess my heart. And when I thought upon my sins, the direct result was a physical pain that refused to leave me.

A pain that reminded me.

I wasn't just playing with lives.

But shaping destinies.

And I was the least worthy of them all to be doing such a thing.

CHAPTER 5

If the shadows have offended think but this, and all is mended, That you have but slumbered here, While these visions did appear, And this weak and idle theme, No more yielding but a dream.

–A Midsummer Night's Dream

Valentina

"Just try to be nice," Sal encouraged in a stern voice. "We bought a dress!"

"Yes," I said dryly. "I can see that."

It was a pink monstrosity that had puffed sleeves and ruffles around the middle; it looked like something a first grader would wear and, even then, she'd probably still get made fun of. I half expected to see ankle socks with hearts and little black shoes. My first heels! Yay!

"Val." Gio yawned and motioned to the dress with his cane. "We thought you would want to feel special on your special day."

It was sweet.

They had great intentions.

Wrong intentions.

But their hearts were in the right place.

I gritted my teeth and pointed to the dress. "Thank you, but I actually, I um… Dante." I fabricated the lie as quickly as my mind would work. "He actually helped me pick out a dress, and you know how Dante gets when he doesn't get his way."

The uncles nodded gravely.

Dante's temper was infamous.

Though, for the life of me, I had no idea where he got all the anger. After all, my uncles were the tamest men I knew.

As if to prove my point, Gio yawned loudly while Sal reached into his pocket and pulled out a hanky.

I rolled my eyes. If a spider crawled across the floor, they'd most likely rescue it and wave a tearful goodbye as it crawled down the front steps of our brownstone.

Papi leaned heavily on his cane as he entered the room. "There is not enough room for the pig."

"Pig?" I repeated, dumbstruck. I'd left work with the three of them in tow and marched into my brownstone ready to call every last person who had been invited to the party, only to discover it was going to be nearly impossible to cancel on over forty people.

Forty.

People.

So the only choice left was a public shaming of Nico. Either that or going through with the party and letting him down easy afterwards.

"I told you!" Sal shook his head as his furry eyebrows crinkled toward his nose. "We only need one pig! But no," He slapped his hand against his thigh and stood. "'Two pigs, Sal, they will not go hungry under this roof!'"

"Well," I shrugged. "At least they won't..."

All eyes fell to me.

I sighed. "You know what? Why don't you three go deal with the food situation while I get ready."

"Yes." Gio ushered them out like a mother hen and hesitated at the door.

Frowning, I walked over to him and placed my hand on his arm. "Gio? What's wrong?"

His eyes filled with tears. "You are my life, my little Val."

With a grin, I tugged my lower lip between my teeth as warmth spread through my chest. "I know, Gio."

"I am sorry for the trouble tonight. I only meant to protect you from—" he hesitated and finished. "The world."

I laughed. "And Nico is the man to do it? What? With his cologne?"

Gio thumped me lightly on the foot with his cane. "He is a big strong man!"

"According to Dante he wears velvet suits."

"Dante talks too much," Gio grumbled. "I worry." His eyes filled with tears. "About your future."

It was my turn to get emotional as I pulled him in for a tight hug, he smelled like cigars and wine. "Gio, I love you. And I promise, you have nothing to worry about. I have the best uncles in the world taking care of me. What could possibly go wrong?"

He didn't answer.

Instead he paled and broke eye contact. "Oh, Val, a great many things." He sighed as if the weight of the world had just been placed on his shoulders. "But first, I check the pig," he mumbled in Italian while I frowned after him. Why was he suddenly so worried about my safety?

I worked in a flower shop.

And my best friend was my twin brother.

Hardly the troublemaker, the worst thing I'd ever done was lie to them once and go to the safety deposit box, which they didn't even know about.

My pocket felt suddenly weighted down with that lie. The door creaked as I quickly shut it. My room was on the second level of the brownstone so I didn't have to worry about anyone peeking through the window.

With shaking hands, I pulled the heavy envelope from my pocket and sat on my bed.

Valentina.

My name was printed across the letter with wide black block letters as if the person took great care in drawing each letter out.

The envelope wasn't sealed.

I tugged the sheets of paper out.

It had been thick because the paper was thick.

Expensive.

And it smelled…

Like a boy.

No, that wasn't right. Boys didn't smell like a mixture of cedar and peppermint. A man, it smelled like a man.

I lifted the thick paper to my nose and inhaled as the scent of paper and a thick, sensual, spicy cologne swirled around me.

Yelling erupted downstairs. The words "pig" and "bastard" were tossed around like a volleyball while I continued sniffing the letter like a crazy person.

Finally, I opened it up completely and stared down at the beautiful cursive writing. Funny, it smelled masculine but the writing was too neat to be by a man.

He was so beautiful. The type of beautiful that made a woman ache, in all the best ways. To find a flaw in the prince would take an eternity and the princess would spend an eternity trying to discover that flaw, because the excitement was in the discovery. Never begrudge the journey, Valentina, for it is the journey that makes the ending happy.

Read a page a day. That is all I ask. One page. Every day. You'll know what to do when there are no longer any pages.

The truth is around you.

Love, after all, is eternal.

All my love,

R.

With trembling hands I set the pages on my bed. I didn't count them, I was afraid that if I pulled each individual sheet apart, I'd ruin the surprise and gorge myself by reading every last one.

As a reader, I'd never had self-control. I wasn't so horrible a person as to read the ending before the beginning, but I rarely started a book and finished it a week later. I absorbed the words like they were my lifeline, as if the lives I were reading about truly existed.

I repeated the words in my head... about the flawless prince, wishing for once it was true. Wishing that my current reality wasn't putting on a velvet suit in hopes of marrying me while forty of our closest family and friends watched on.

Was it so wrong to wish for a flawless prince over Nico? Did that make me selfish? Reading gave me high expectations. Sometimes that was depressing, and sometimes it was the only thing that got me through boring days at the flower shop where I'd watch handsome men buy flowers, where they'd write cards that gushed about love and beauty.

Maybe that was what had attracted me to *A Midsummer Night's Dream*. The poetry, the sheer beauty of everything around the faeries.

An abrupt knock on the door interrupted my thoughts. I didn't have time to answer before Dante came strolling in.

"Hey!" I quickly hid the sheets under one of my pillows. "I could have been naked!"

He gave me a knowing look. "After being walked in on by the uncles, you asked for a changing screen, I would have seen shadows."

I eyed the flimsy screen across the room. I'd found it at a garage sale and begged Gio to buy it for me. He'd blushed a billion shades of red, mumbled out a sorry, since he'd been the last to walk in on me before dinner, and quickly handed the woman a hundred dollar bill.

She responded by trying to give him more stuff, which he took, because we were Italians, and gifts were like food; you accepted, you always accepted, even if you were full, you accepted.

Dante snapped his fingers in front of my face. "What? Huh? Did you say something?"

"No, but you did just spend the last thirty seconds gazing into thin air with your mouth wide open. Not a great look, Val."

"Shut up." I stood and shoved my hands against his bulky chest. "I really do need to change. Did you need something?"

"The pig." Dante's eyes twinkled with amusement. "It is not big enough! We will run out of food!" He mimicked Gio's voice perfectly. "I've been sent to get another."

"Nooo!" I wailed. "He said only forty people."

Dante snickered. "He lies, he always claims the family dinner will be small. Remember last week when he said he was inviting a few colleagues over?"

I shuddered. We'd had more than twenty men in suits dine with us. I hadn't liked it. Papi had said they were old friends.

But none of them had looked friendly to me.

They seemed too… polished.

A few of them were young.

Too young.

Young enough to be my age, which was silly because, well, who was that successful at nineteen?

Their accents were funny as well.

Not quite Italian, not quite American… yet.

Not New York.

A mix of Chicago and Sicilian, I assumed.

"You're doing it again," Dante said in a bored voice. "I just wanted to warn you that this party's about to get a little bigger. Oh…" He grinned and let out a low laugh. "Also, Nico just arrived, and he asked about his fiancé."

I growled.

"Just think of all the tiny cologne babies you can have, I bet we can even find a few miniature suits. They'll look just like their papa."

"Out!" I shoved against his chest with a laugh. "And thanks for the warning."

"Any time," he called behind him as laughter erupted from downstairs. The party wasn't even supposed to start for another half hour, but that's how Italians were. They didn't just come to the party on time, they came early to help. Meaning, they came early to drink wine, they came early to buy more wine, and they came early because they almost always brought enough food to feed a small country. Just a little something they cooked up just in case.

Just in case anyone starved.

It really was a miracle nobody had to push me around in a cart because of my inability to walk — I did enjoy my cannoli.

With one last look at the door, I rushed over to the pillow and tugged the papers out, slid them back into the envelope, then shoved them under my mattress, taking special care to cover the side of the bed with a blanket.

Nobody would look there.

Because I was little Val.

I didn't take chances.

I didn't hide things.

And I certainly didn't live on the wild side.

"Valentina!" Sal called from downstairs. His yell was followed by loud laughter.

Sighing, I reached for my simple black dress and closed my eyes. I should have been thinking about rejecting Nico.

Instead.

My thoughts lingered on the pieces of paper.

And the mysterious prince.

Who had no flaws.

Yeah. Right.

CHAPTER 6

Lord, what fools these mortals be!
—A Midsummer Night's Dream

Sergio

I WAS SUPPOSED to look like Frank's grandson.

Anyone would see through the lie in seconds. How stupid were his cousins? That's what I wanted to know.

Ever since Andi's death, I'd been working out harder, and had somehow managed to put on a few more pounds of muscle. Maybe it was because every night when I laid my head on the pillow... I still smelled her.

And it wasn't that I didn't want to remember her.

It was more this need to... actually sleep. Frank still commented on the dark circles as if I wasn't painfully aware I resembled a zombie more than a human being.

My dark jeans hugged my legs as I tucked in the last of my white button-up and pulled my jacket tight around my body. My blue and black scarf wrapped twice around my neck, giving me a false sense of comfort. I hoped I looked approachable enough, because the only warning Frank had given me was that we were going to a party.

I asked if it was the type where we used guns.

And he only winced.

Which really couldn't be a good sign.

"How long has it been?" I asked once we parked across the street, our black Mercedes blended in quite well with the rest of the Lincolns and Audis.

Frank frowned. "A while."

"Well, that's descriptive, thanks."

He let out a low chuckle. "Just, don't pull your gun. They'll be offended."

My eyes widened. "No shit? So if I pull a gun, I'm going to offend them, but they're more than welcome to pull a gun on me?"

"You've been shot before." He shrugged. "Just duck."

"Wow." I let out a low whistle. "For a loving grandfather, you kind of suck with the sentimental stuff."

He chuckled as I got out of the car and then abruptly pulled me into his arms for a hug, slapping the shit out of my back at least three times before kissing both of my cheeks.

"What the hell was that?" I whispered, not sure if I was more amused or uncomfortable.

"That—" he pointed back at the house "—was for the men that I know without a doubt are watching us. They need not know of your identity just yet... but mine? They will know me. They do not need to know your name. Listen very carefully. Here you are not Abandonato. Here you are a business man."

Well that was easy. I *was* a businessman. I owned

several businesses, but they were all *Abandonato* businesses.

"Do I have a different name too?"

"Sergio." He grinned as the wind picked up blowing his thick wavy grey hair away from his face, it made him look younger. "Just Sergio."

"Yeah, I give them five seconds to see through that."

"Eh, people see what you want them to see. You know that as well as I."

I gulped and looked away as his point aimed straight for my heart and dug in. I'd been feeling guilty about putting on a good show for my family back home in Chicago. Frank was the only one who knew it was all complete bullshit.

That I was lost.

That I felt like I would *be* lost forever.

And the fear that came along with it — the fear that I'd found my home, only to lose it, along with the comfort that I'd never feel that way again.

Ever.

"Let's go." He slapped my back one last time as we walked across the street and made our way up the stairs to a neat brownstone. It was old, but well kept. The brick clean, the door displaying a nice knocker, and the mat in front of the door said *Welcome*.

Hah, if they only knew...

Frank raised his hand to knock.

But it wasn't needed.

I knew it wasn't needed, he knew it wasn't needed, but for appearances, he did it anyway.

The door swung open.

A tall man with dark hair stood blocking our view. He had shots of gray woven through his hair, and he was holding a glass of wine, his lips pressed together in a tight frown.

I stood my ground. Ready to take a bullet for the Alfero boss if need be — the last thing I wanted was to be held partially responsible for the killing of the last of the legends.

Because that's what Frank was.

A legend.

"You." The man seethed.

Frank's cold stare had me wanting to chuckle. Damn the man was a bastard when he wanted to be. He tilted his head to the side and said. "Aren't you going to invite me in, Gio?"

"Go to hell," Gio whispered. "They are safe. I have kept them safe."

Another stare down took place.

We really didn't want to be standing in the street, our backs exposed, our necks popping out like a dart board just waiting for the darts to come flying.

"Gio," I repeated the name and held out my hand. "I'm Sergio, Frank's... grandson."

He stared down at my hand then narrowed his eyes. "You're no more his grandson then I'm his aunt."

I took his half outstretched hand and squeezed. "And you have a very odd way of welcoming your family into your home..." I peered around him. "Roast pig? Sounds delicious." I shoved past him and entered the house, as he cursed behind me.

I expected a party.

Something small.

Like a birthday party.

I might come from a big family, but the bosses and wives, we mainly kept to ourselves, because we couldn't trust anyone.

So a party would include, what? Twelve of us?

Though I remembered years when I was younger, when parties occurred every night, when the entire neighborhood would drink wine and laugh.

Suddenly I was transported back to my childhood.

Back to a simpler time, when Andi would have been alive.

When I was a child and innocent in the ways of the world.

In the ways of the mafia.

Women laughed loudly while they piled plates of food, men smoked cigars in the corner, their gestures big and loud.

And then, as if an announcement was made.

All talking and laughter stopped.

I was used to people staring.

So I straightened my shoulders and glared through every face, armor firmly in place. Just try it; seriously, my finger was itching to pull a trigger. I needed to get the aggression out somehow.

Frank's hand gripped my shoulder. "Allow me to introduce... my grandson, Sergio."

Men literally parted like water as we walked through the house, some ducked their heads, others nervously looked away while cursing under their breath.

But the women.

Appeared pissed.

More than pissed.

As if they knew Frank's entire story and were just itching to scratch his eyes out.

Huh, no wonder he never visited home.

Not one friendly face.

But at least no guns.

I had to admit, I was disappointed.

"Eat." A woman approached us, swallowing slowly as her eyes darted between the two of us. "We have two roast pigs."

"Must be some celebration," I spoke, careful to keep the slight accent from my voice. Andi had always said it came when I was either really emotional — or in bed. I pushed at the painful memory, but it clawed itself back into my consciousness, when the woman in front of us smiled warmly and handed me a plate.

She pressed a hand to my wrist and whispered, "Eat."

Because that made my wife not dead.

Food?

Italians.

The plate felt foreign in my hands and, for a minute, I was disoriented as if I truly wasn't aware of the purpose it served.

"You put food on it," Frank muttered under his breath as he moved past me and started pulling at the pork.

The woman's smile turned into a frown. "Are you... vegetarian?"

And again all talking ceased.

God save me, you'd think she just asked if I'd denounced the Italian flag and didn't go to mass.

"No." I forced a smile. "Just... really jet lagged."

"Oh." People around me exhaled all together and then started chattering; I wondered if they would kick me out if I said I preferred soymilk?

There was so much food I didn't even know where to start. Huh, was that how Phoenix used to feel when

I made fun of him for not eating? Back in the day, he'd thought that he didn't deserve any kind of pleasure, that even tasting chocolate or wine would cause him to relapse into the sexual predator that he'd convinced himself he was. Asking the man to eat a grape was a life or death situation — or it had been. Until he was saved.

Damn it.

I didn't want to be saved.

No saving was needed.

Because the truth of the matter was, I wasn't really lost. I was just... empty.

The truth hit me so hard, I sucked in a breath. My chest cracked, just a bit as I mindlessly started piling food onto a plate that I knew within five minutes would be dumped into the trash.

"So..." The woman's eyes were too intelligent for my liking. Her black hair was pulled back into a low ponytail, and her face was smooth and clear. It was nearly impossible to tell how old she was, but I knew she was at least pushing sixty. I frowned. Or maybe younger? She was beautiful, but clearly old enough to be my mother. "You do not like food then?"

I pressed my lips together in a tight smile and was about to answer, when Frank wrapped a strong arm around my shoulder. "There has been a loss."

"A loss?" she repeated taking a step back from me.

I didn't know what to say. What the hell was he doing?

"He has lost himself."

The woman nodded sagely as if she hung on every piece of shit that flew out of his mouth.

"But he will find it." Frank squeezed my shoulder.

"Because if he doesn't, I imagine she would be disappointed, and the last thing a man needs is to disappoint the one he lives for. Isn't that right, grandson?"

Pissed that he was bringing up something that was real in front of a complete stranger I jerked away and muttered, "Bathroom?"

The woman pointed down the hall. I made a beeline around the table heaped with food, careful to keep my eyes averted lest anyone actually recognize that they were the same as Nixon's, as the Abandonato boss, as the one family who had basically crushed any dreams the Alferos had of being the leaders of the Cosa Nostra.

Hell, they'd probably shit themselves if they knew who they'd just invited into their home.

The Abandonatos and Alferos in Chicago had buried the hatchet a year ago.

But something told me the Alferos in New York were still fixating on a mistake that had happened long ago, when a family turned against itself and blamed the easiest target — the Alferos.

They were powerful — but they'd never recovered.

After going down a maze like hallway with doors on both sides, I finally found the bathroom and was just about to knock on the door when it swung open.

A girl about the age of eighteen let out a little gasp. "You."

"Me?" I frowned. "I'm sorry, I don't believe we know each other."

As if horrified, she took a step back then placed her hands against her cheeks, it did nothing to hide the red tinging the outer corners of her sharp cheekbones. On second thought, she looked older than eighteen.

And then it hit me.

It was my turn to take a step backward.

"Valentina," I whispered her name as fresh pain sliced through my entire body causing every single muscle to tense with anxiety. "You're Valentina."

The one that was meant for me.

The girl who, months ago, I would have married, had it not been for Andi. Not that Valentina was even aware of her father's matchmaking. But that was what the mafia was built on, power, power, and more power.

She looked different than the pictures.

Older.

Andi's words haunted me. *"You'll love her, Sergio."* I tensed even more, my fingers digging into the door frame. *"She needs you... needs you to push her. She loves reading."* Andi's voice died in my head.

Just like in real life.

And I was struck with such resentment that the only reaction I was capable of... was anger. "Are you going to move?"

Valentina jumped a bit, her hands clasping in front of her as if she was afraid to touch me. Then, with a slow nod, she moved out of the way. It wasn't until she left that I was able to breathe again.

But when I did.

I really wish I hadn't.

She smelled...

Exactly like Andi.

CHAPTER 7

Jack shall have Jill;
Nought shall go ill:
The man shall have his mare again, and all shall be well.
—A Midsummer Night's Dream

Valentina

Tears of embarrassment stung the back of my eyelids, making it impossible to see straight as I ran away from one of the most dangerous and sexy men I'd ever encountered in my life.

He'd been perfect.

Until he opened his mouth and basically demanded I move.

I'd never actually been spoken to that way before. Did that make me soft? Or maybe just stupid. Maybe I was so ridiculously sheltered that I couldn't go to the bank by myself, and I stared at complete strangers with such rapture that I basically blocked them from being able to take care of a basic human function.

Ugh… more embarrassment came as I cringed and slowly unclenched my hands. My nails had made actual imprints into my palms.

He was just a guy.

A really good looking guy. So gorgeous that, when he made his entrance into the party, I'd nearly stumbled backward into the dessert table.

He came in with the same man from the bar.

Both of them were of the same transfixing beauty. One was older, rougher, while the other was probably in his late twenties, with haunting dark circles beneath his eyes and a strong jaw. I couldn't even comprehend how a man could appear so beautiful yet so masculine at the same time.

Full lips had pressed into a hard stare as he silently dared anyone to say something to him. And he didn't march into the room, he seemed to glide, as if he owned the entire house, as if the house was no longer a house but a castle and us his servants.

Had someone bowed I would have thought he really was royalty.

It was unfortunate he was so rude.

Then again, I had been blocking the way. Oh no! I stomped my foot. Had he been talking to me that whole time and had I done the whole stare off into space thing that I often did when Dante talked to me? Bad enough that I'd escaped to the bathroom to add more perfume, perfume one of my best friends had gifted me with before basically disappearing out of my life forever. That's so not what I needed to be fixating on.

"Shoot," I grumbled then started basically tearing off my thumbnail with my teeth.

"Bella," Nico said in a heavily accented voice. It was the first time that night I'd actually heard him before I smelled him, so either he'd showered or I was becoming immune to his scent. A shudder rippled through me. That couldn't be a good sign. The last thing I needed was to be used to his musk. "You look so stressed! You should be celebrating with me!" He let out a low chuckle then, kid you not, licked his forefinger and thumb and patted down his own eyebrows.

Was he for real?

His suit was black velvet; he wore a red tie.

I wanted to strangle him with it.

He was the reason I had been hiding in the bathroom in the first place. I'd seen the two men enter, and he was as transfixed as everyone else, so I'd quickly bolted as fast as I could to the nearest bathroom, only to remember, as I was halfway out the window, that my uncles would be sorely disappointed in my behavior, even if all of this was really their fault. Then my eyes had fallen to the perfume, and a hair tie, the rest was history.

"Nico," I said his name curtly, like I was ready to give him the speech, when all of a sudden he looked behind him, then backed me up into the corner and tried to kiss me.

I wasn't tall, not by any means, so when I shoved him, it only made him chuckle and try to kiss me again.

Wanting to puke, I tried turning my head as his lips landed on my neck.

"I knew you would be so soft." He licked me. The bastard licked me!

I was just getting ready to knee him in the balls as a total last resort when I heard a throat clear.

Nico backed away.

And the same guy, who I'd just embarrassed myself

in front of, took a step forward.

"I don't think she wants you to kiss her," the man said in a very calm, yet coolly detached voice that had me wondering if he even had a heart in that chest or just a soulless box that collected dust.

"But she does," Nico argued.

"She doesn't," I argued right back. "You were hurting me, and I don't even know you!"

"We are to marry!" he announced loudly.

"Oh, dear God, save me," I moaned. "What's my middle name?"

Nico appeared perplexed. "We do not need to know such things to make babies."

"Joyce," the man next to me whispered. "It's Joyce."

"Who are you again?" Nico demanded to know as he puffed up his chest, it only made him look more stupid, if that was even possible.

The gorgeous man smirked. That was the only flash of amusement I saw before he put an arm around my body and said in a completely lucid voice. "I'm her fiancé."

I nearly choked on my tongue as Nico sputtered and thumped his chest. "I am her fiancé!"

Something flashed in the guy's eyes as he reached for Nico's jacket and, literally, lifted him two feet off the ground then slammed him into the nearest wall, a few pictures crashed against the floor, glass went everywhere. "And now, you're leaving. Touch her again, and I'll reach into your weaselly little chest and pluck out your ribs. One... by...one."

When Nico was released, he tugged on his jacket and pretended he didn't look frightened. "We'll see about that."

He marched off.

Leaving me with a clearly angry and slightly insane stranger. Didn't matter if he was gorgeous, he'd just claimed me as his fiancée, and he knew my middle name.

"Hah, know my social security number too?" I joked out loud to break the tension.

He didn't even flinch when he said. "Why? Did you forget it?"

I laughed nervously and backed away. "I get it. You have one of those dry senses of humor or something like that?"

Still. Nothing. Though his lips did twitch a bit.

"A man of many words."

This time he let out a low chuckle. "I'm more of an action kinda guy."

No, he was more like perfect.

To look at that is.

Not one flaw.

Not even a scar.

Nothing.

How was that even possible? Especially if he was as violent as he appeared to be.

The letter I'd just read drifted into my consciousness, what were the odds?

"So." Suddenly chilled, maybe from the shock of all the violence, I rubbed my arms. "Thanks for the save. I guess I'll get a broom so I can clean up all the glass."

"I'll do it," he said, swiftly walking by me. Then he paused, his shoulders tense. "Stay here."

I wasn't stupid enough to argue. He had just lifted a guy into the air like he was a toothpick.

When he returned he quickly swept up the glass

into the dustpan, and then went back toward the bathroom, I'm guessing to dump the contents.

"Sorry about the pictures." He lifted the worst of the two and frowned as another picture fell to the ground, one that had been behind the main picture.

"Hmm, that's weird." I bent down and picked it up and stared into the face of a vaguely familiar man. He was holding two small infants and smiling.

Memories flickered as if someone had turned on a movie, but before I could conjure up anything, the man ripped the picture out of my hand.

"Hey!" I reached for them.

He shook his head. "Your uncles will want to re-frame them. We have no idea how old they are. Imagine what a shame it would be if they were ruined."

I guessed he was right, but still, how important could it be if it was hidden?

"Some of the most important treasures are ones we haven't yet discovered," he said in a whisper.

"So." Something about him was definitely off. "Who are you?"

This time he did smile. "Your fiancé."

I laughed. "No, seriously."

He tilted his head as his eyes slowly inspected me from head to toe. "You're extremely young."

"And you're rude, and, it appears you have an anger problem."

"Hah!" He burst out laughing. "Valentina, you have no idea."

"Val," I corrected. "Everyone calls me Val."

"And who's everyone?" He held out his arm, so I looped my hand through it and walked with him back into the main room.

"My twin brother, my three uncles, all my nonexistent friends…" I leaned in and whispered. "My goldfish…"

His lips did that sexy twitching thing again, and then he turned his ice blue eyes in my direction. "You don't seem like a goldfish type of girl."

"Fine, I don't even have a goldfish, but if I did."

"He'd be a lucky fish." He smiled, his straight white teeth were almost blinding in their impact. Geez, he shouldn't flash those things around. Maybe that's why he didn't smile. He was afraid women would simply give up on life and fall at his feet in worship. His unruly hair kissed the back of his neck.

It should look ridiculous.

Instead, it looked hot.

I really needed to stop reading so much and actually find a boyfriend, or even just a man who wasn't family.

Ugh, my lameness had never been so clear.

"What's your name?" I asked. I needed a quick subject change so I didn't suddenly fall into his arms and beg for a kiss or do something equally as embarrassing.

"Sergio." His tone changed from warm to chilly, and then when I looked into the eyes of Papi, Sal, and Gio, I knew exactly why.

They'd blocked the way into the main room.

They looked ready to kill.

Who was this guy?

And why were my uncles so mad?

Of course, they'd always been fiercely protective, but this seemed like something more.

"So." Gio's voice was hard. "You have finally come to claim them? After all this time?"

Them? Who was them? Confused, I frowned and looked to Papi. He was reaching inside his suit jacket, probably for another hanky, while Sal stood straighter as if he hadn't just been hunching over.

As if they'd just turned into transformers of the human variety, every single one of my uncles stood to full height and glared. What the heck was going on? They'd never appeared so... dangerous.

"Val," Sal said in a clear angry voice. "Get your brother."

"No need," Dante said from behind me, and then I was shoved behind him and out of Sergio's reach, as his muscled hand thrust me backward. "I heard there was something going on."

"Guys," I said in a pleading voice. "It's an engagement party, have you all lost your minds? Besides, Sergio saved me from getting groped by Nico!"

All the men's heads turned toward me, including Sergio's. His face was a mask of complete indifference. I would have expected him to look smug, but instead, I couldn't read him at all. Clear blue eyes blinked at me slowly. Geez, he really was attractive.

I shivered.

"What the hell!" Dante roared. "You left her alone? With that idiot?"

"Eh." I shrugged. "Nico's harmless."

"I meant him." Dante sneered in Sergio's direction.

With a mocking smirk, Sergio said, "Why... I'd almost say you were... afraid of me."

With a violent curse I'd never heard my brother utter — ever — he charged Sergio, only to be held back by all three of my uncles.

"Val," Sal barked. "Leave us."

"But—"

"Leave!" All of the men yelled in unison. All but Sergio. He gave me a brief glance and then a nod of permission.

And oddly, it was like I needed to know it was okay.

That everything would be fine.

Because when Dante had moved.

I'd seen a flash of a knife in his hand.

And it broke my heart.

What had my brother gotten into?

And were the strangers part of it?

Did this have to do with the blood on his knuckles? Had he finally taken things too far?

I left with a sinking stomach, legs heavy, I moved down the hall and walked back into the party, wondering if that was the defining moment of my life.

Where everything was about to change.

They were fighting. Hardly rare for my family.

But something about the way they all stood.

And the way Sergio's eyes drew me in.

Something was different.

Something was changing.

Nico glanced at me from across the room, and I had a brief moment of insanity where I was tempted to flip him off then throw cake in his face.

Which wasn't me at all.

Huh, maybe I had some of Dante's anger after all. Maybe, somehow, I'd inherited that as well from our dead parents.

Strength.

The thought made me smile to myself.

CHAPTER 8

So quick bright things come to confusion
—A Midsummer Night's Dream

Sergio

HE KNEW.

That was my first thought.

The second?

Holy shit, he was huge for a nineteen-year-old.

And finally, the third?

A horrifying lump in my throat — because he looked exactly like Luca. Hell, the bastard even stood like him. God help me if I had to kill him, because it was like I was staring into the face of one of my mentors.

Even though my emotions were going into overdrive, I kept the smirk in place, and of course didn't hesitate to make sure Val escaped unscathed, without knowledge of the dark. I at least owed her that after treating her like complete shit. She didn't deserve my anger.

And the last thing I wanted was for Andi to be upset with me — she did say she'd haunt me if I was an ass, and I wouldn't put that past her.

Nobody moved as Val left the room and walked down the hall.

It was quiet, but the air was electric, like someone had just released years worth of tension in that tiny space.

I had to give it to them; the uncles had appeared feeble, until they were forced to quit the little act.

Old and senile, my ass.

They looked powerful.

And angry.

So very angry.

Well, good news, folks! I knew anger well, and I wasn't beyond kicking some old man's ass just because I saw him using a cane ten minutes ago. I had to be angry, to be indifferent, to get through the next few days, or, God help me, weeks, in a constant state of dark emotions, because the minute I let in the light...

It hurt.

Damn it.

Everything hurt.

Years of training with the FBI and my own crime family kicked in, I hit Dante's forearm with my hand, the knife fell to the floor as I shoved him against the wall and pulled both hands behind his back, rendering him incapable of doing anything except giving me a backward head butt.

"Let's speak plainly, hmm?" I slammed him against the wall harder. "I will not hesitate to end you. Really, you should take it as a compliment. I have over 40 kills to my name. I am a trained assassin. I will not hesitate. I never hesitate. You're a damn child, a pawn in a man's war. Pull a knife on me again in front of your sister, and I'll use that same knife to cut out your tongue. Piece. By. Piece."

Dante didn't flinch, but he did smile.

And I, honest to God, wanted to slit his throat for it.

"Don't test me." I grunted releasing him from my grip. "I've killed people for less."

His eyes finally averted as he stepped away from me, briefly touching the spot on his throat where I'd placed the blade.

It wasn't two seconds before I felt the tip of a gun pressed against my back.

"Nobody comes into our home and threatens our blood!" I wasn't sure which of the old men it was, but I was sure of one thing.

Frank.

He was watching.

And laughing.

What the ever loving hell?

"I really don't want to send you into a nursing home, old man." I shook my head. "Put the gun down."

Frank crossed his arms and leaned casually against the wall. Should I offer popcorn? The bastard was enjoying every minute of the show!

The gun pressed harder.

"What do you think, Frank?" I nodded toward him. "Six seconds?"

He grunted. "You losing your touch?"

I shrugged. "I was trying to be humble."

"Hah." His shoulders shook with laughter. "You don't wear humility well, son."

I grinned. "Don't I know it."

"One." I elbowed the man in the ribs and ducked to my right as I pulled the gun over my shoulder and flipped him over my body, he fell against the ceramic tile just as I slid my foot across the floor taking another one of the men down. Dante surged toward me. With another kick and then a punch to his jaw he was down.

"Four!" Frank called out.

"Kinda busy!" I yelled, as the last man charged me. I used his momentum against him; the minute he hit my body with his, I slammed my hands against his chest then lifted him into the air and threw him to his back on the floor.

"Five." Frank nodded, approaching on my right. "Impressive. But next time, try harder."

"Maybe next time you can help," I snapped.

Frank cracked his knuckles in front of him. "Arthritis is acting up."

"My ass."

"What was that?"

"Nothing." I rolled my eyes as the groans of the men filled the room; I had to give them credit, they were already starting to get to their feet, ready to die for their own damn pride.

"Stop this." Frank held up his hands. "We came to discuss family matters."

"The hell you did!" Dante yelled. "You don't come into our home, attack my family and—"

Frank held up his hand again. "This was merely a... demonstration of what will happen if you refuse to listen. Listen, and we'll be on our way. It's as simple as that."

The old men helped each other to their feet and shared thunderous looks before one limped forward and nodded. "We agree, but first." He pointed to me. "Who the hell is that? Because we all know he isn't your grandson."

Frank smirked and slapped a hand on my back. "Why, I thought after the last few minutes you'd have simply put two and two together, apologies." His voice lowered. "This is Sergio..." He paused dramatically, the freak. "Abandonato."

Cursing followed.

And I could have sworn each of them clenched their fists.

Because if there was anything the Alferos of New York hated more than Frank and the rest of the Chicago crew... it was the Abandonatos, the family that owned Chicago, that forced them away from their homes.

The family that took over when they had lacked the ability to do so.

I should duck my head.

Offer my sincerest apologies.

Possibly shake one of their hands and say something nice.

Instead, I responded with, "And if things don't go well... your future boss. I'd show the respect I'm due. Starting now."

CHAPTER 9

A sweet face man a proper man, as one shall see in a summer's day

—A Midsummer Night's Dream

Valentina

IT HAD BEEN an hour since my uncles had disappeared, I was worried. I was trying not to be paranoid, but they loved parties. The last time we had a party — which was last week, mind you — it had raged until two in the morning. There had been several cases of wine, and somehow, during the party, a goat was brought in while someone offered to slaughter it for more food.

More food.

As if they didn't already have enough.

I later found out it was owned by one of the party goers who lived in Upstate New York, a gift, he said.

My uncles politely asked for the goat to be dead first.

The man begrudgingly agreed — and after a few glasses of wine, added in a chicken for good measure.

To say our parties were legendary... well, that

would be an understatement, but this one, it felt... off. Like everyone was sitting on pins and needles just waiting for something horrible to happen.

Even Nico was in the corner whispering with his parents.

They raised their voices above the music. Nico took one look at me, then stomped over to where I was standing. "We cannot marry."

Hey, wasn't that supposed to be my line?

"Um, okay." I tried to look upset, when really I was elated. But why the sudden change of heart? "Can I ask why?" Not that I wanted him to go back on his proclamation, but he seemed angry for some reason.

"You are bad blood." He sneered. "We cannot have bad blood in our family."

"Bad blood," I repeated. "I'm one hundred percent Italian."

Again, why was I arguing with him about this? The amount of cologne that man had on was staggering. I took a step back just so I could breathe.

He finally locked eyes with me. "You are bad blood."

Yeah, you said that freak show.

"Okay then." I folded my arms across my chest. "Sorry for being... bad?"

"It is all right." His shoulders sank. "You cannot change the circumstances of your birth."

For some reason, his insult made me want to pluck out his eyebrows and feed the hair to the chickens.

"Well," I said in a shaky voice. "I guess that's that."

He backed away. "Abandonato Scum," he muttered under his breath, and then he joined his parents on the other side of the room. I saw Dante speaking to them.

He looked — afraid.

Dante never looked afraid.

I motioned him over.

He looked directly at me. Recognition flared in his eyes. Then he turned to the crowd. Mouth open, I stared. He'd just ignored me.

Another thing he'd never done.

He turned down the music and whistled. "Party's over, we have..." His eyes locked on mine. "Business."

The surrounding people nodded their heads and started cursing in Italian as if they knew exactly what type of business he was talking about.

Still confused, I watched as every last person left our house.

"Dante..." I swallowed back the fear in my throat. "What's going on?"

"War," he whispered.

"America's at war!" I screamed. "Oh my gosh, do we even have a bomb shelter?" I started running around in circles, I needed to grab a book or something, or my notes. Crap! I needed my letters!

"Val!" Dante yelled.

"I need—" I was hyperventilating, but I couldn't stop "—to go to my room and get—"

"Val!" Dante roared, gripping me by the arms so that I was forced to look into his icy blue eyes. "Not that kind of war. It's... business."

"Business," I said dumbstruck. "Is war?" I shook my head. "You're not making sense. *None* of this is making sense!"

"Good." He looked relieved. "That's... good."

"Dante?"

"Val," Gio barked my name as he limped into the

room; his lip was bleeding. Sergio wasn't far behind.

I charged toward Sergio. "You hurt my uncle! You bastard!" Sal and Papi followed, all of them bloody.

They were the least violent men I knew.

And Sergio, well, he screamed violence! It was in the very air he breathed, the way he carried himself.

Dante tried to pull me back, but Sergio lifted up his hand. "It's okay, let her. It will make her feel better."

So for the first time in my life.

I hit another human being.

Because I was afraid.

I hit him in the chest, and when he didn't move or even make a noise, I hit him again and again and again as the confusion of the night washed over me, and when I was done, I realized, he was hugging me.

"Where is her room?" he asked, not seeming to address anyone in particular.

Someone must have pointed because nobody answered, and he picked me up in his arms and carried me up the stairs and into my bedroom where he gently placed me on my bed and sighed. "You're young."

"Yeah, you keep saying that," I said as tears streamed down my face. "Why did you hurt my uncles?"

"Would you believe me if I said they hit me first?"

"No."

He chuckled. "They may seem old — they can pack a punch."

"My uncles would never hit a person." The idea was almost laughable. I probably would have laughed if I wasn't so scared.

"Okay." He sounded like he didn't believe me. "Val." He used the name I'd told him to. "Sleep."

Yeah, right, because sleep was going to come so

easily. A snort of disbelief escaped as I glared. "And things will look better in the morning?"

He hesitated, those gorgeous lips pressed into a firm line. "No."

"That wasn't very encouraging."

"Would you rather I lie?"

I swallowed the thickness in my throat; it felt like I'd swallowed a golf ball and was trying to cough it back up. "I'm not sure."

Sighing, he reached out and touched my cheek, then jerked back as if he couldn't believe he'd just touched me. Abruptly, he stood and turned his back to me.

It was a nice back.

Muscular in all the right places.

I just bet that shirt had a hard time staying on.

I had a sudden image of him ripping it over his head then mentally scolded myself. He was the enemy, he was the reason something had happened — was happening — tonight. Everything in me screamed danger.

And yet, I was stripping him in my head.

Yeah, I was losing my mind.

"I used to believe it." His voice was barely above a whisper. "The lie, the one that says all you need is a good night's sleep, and things will look better in the morning, feel better, be better." He hung his head. "Now I know the truth."

I swallowed. "And what's that?"

He turned, just enough for me to see his striking profile, the tick in his jaw as he clenched his teeth into an almost grimace. "Regardless of what surrounds you, the blanket of darkness at night, or the warmth of the sun during the day, circumstances remain.

Sadness… remains, anger… remains. Sleep promises rest — I haven't rested in a very long time."

I leaned forward. "If the next word out of your mouth is that you're a five thousand year old vampire, I'm probably going to jump out my window."

His lips broke into a tense smile. "Sorry to disappoint. I'm human. So very human." He frowned as if the thought actually upset him. "I bleed just like everyone else."

"Clearly." I pointed to his knuckles. "Sergio?"

He crossed his arms and faced me again. "Val?"

"Who are you?"

"Don't worry about who I am, worry about what I'm not."

"A vampire?"

"That." He grabbed the blanket from the foot of my bed and placed it over me. "And… I'm not your friend, Val."

The comment stung.

The golf ball in the back of my throat swelled, stretched wide and spread down my chest as I fought for a breath that didn't hurt.

"Okay." I finally squeezed out, my voice weak. "No false hope and all that?"

"I don't do hope," he snapped, and then he whispered under his breath. "Not anymore."

He walked with a jerking gait over to the door and left, shutting it behind him, leaving me to wonder… if he wasn't my friend…

Did that make him my foe?

CHAPTER 10

A lion among ladies is a most dreadful thing
                    —A Midsummer Night's Dream

Sergio

I'D BEEN FIELDING texts and calls from the crew back in Chicago all night. Tex was losing his shit. He even went as far as to ask if Frank shot my sorry ass. I replied with a middle finger emoji and moved on.

Nixon was next.

Followed by Chase.

Even Phoenix decided it would be in his best interest to play therapist. God help us all if the darkest mob boss out of all of them, the one with the most secrets, the worst past, started sending me motivational texts about teamwork.

Actually, it was more along the lines of, keep your head out of your ass, you can't see the sunshine when you're poking your head where it doesn't belong.

I didn't have the energy to respond. Not after dealing with all the Alferos, damn it. A little warning from Frank would have been nice. Then again, that wasn't really Frank's style.

He was more of a toss the person into the snake pit and, if he lives, give him a promotion sort of guy.

My neck hurt, my knuckles were scabbed over with a mixture of blood and torn skin.

And the night was young.

We'd left the Alfero house with plans to have a meeting the following day, which was good, all things considered.

They wanted to talk that evening.

But I knew the last thing the innocent girl sleeping upstairs needed was to wake up and truly see her entire existence altered. Granted, you couldn't run from reality, from your truth — if you could, I'd have done it.

God knows, I'd tried.

The truth would find her soon enough — and the happy girl who offered easy smiles and doted on her uncles like they were senile retirement home members, would be gone.

Replaced by the harsh reality that only the mafia brings.

Death.

Blood.

Destruction.

Repeat.

"Don't be gone long," Frank said once the car stopped near Times Square.

"Aw, you gonna miss me, old man?" I tried joking, even though my voice was gravelly, foreign. The night had taken its toll already.

Frank rolled his eyes. "Try to stay alive."

"I'll do my best."

He snorted as I slammed the door to the Mercedes and leisurely walked toward Broadway.

Blood roared in my ears as I hit Broadway and looked at all the signs proclaiming a variety of shows.

With shaking hands I pulled out the honeymoon checklist Andi had given me and looked down at the scribble that said, Go to a Broadway show in New york and sing along even if it sounds horrible.

I didn't have much to choose from since it was getting so late. I finally decided on Beauty and The Beast, maybe because I felt like the beast, only in the end, I wouldn't turn into the prince.

Then again, it always boggled my mind. The prince had lived so long as a beast, how was it possible for him to go back to his royal status? And what was the purpose of all of his suffering if he was left with no reminder of the way he looked toward people on the outside? It would fade. And in my mind, it was only a matter of time before the prince became spoiled and discontented, because that was life.

That was the *real* human condition.

Save me today, and I'll live for you tomorrow.

Fix it and I'll do anything.

Just this once! And my life is yours.

We say a lot of words we don't mean.

And yet, I would say all of those things again and again, if it would bring her back to me.

With lead-filled legs, I went to the box office, purchased my ticket and sat in the farthest row back I could.

It was packed; then again, it was Friday.

My phone buzzed in my pocket.

I pulled it out.

Nixon: *Are you dead?*

Sergio: *I'm texting you back, does that answer your question?*

Nixon: *You need backup?*

Sergio: No.

I turned off my phone and slid it into my pocket just as the lights dimmed then lit up again only to dim one last time. As the music swelled, I closed my eyes and hoped to God, one day, one day I'd be free.

SUNLIGHT STREAMED THROUGH the curtains, landing square on my eyes. I hissed out a curse and tossed a pillow in the general direction of the window.

We were staying at a boutique hotel near Times Square, the more people around us, the merrier. It meant we didn't have to worry about getting shot at. My money was on the uncles staying up all night trying to figure out how to order a hit on their own family and the single Abandonato in a sea full of Alferos.

Four loud knocks on my door had me leisurely getting out of bed, grabbing my Glock, and holding it behind my back as I peeked through the peephole to see who was there.

Dante.

He didn't appear armed.

Didn't mean he wasn't.

Sighing, I pulled the door open. "Either I'm going to be your first kill, or you want to talk." I scratched my head with the gun in my right hand. "My bet's on the latter."

"You're a real arrogant prick, you know that, right?" Dante observed in a calm voice.

"I'm very aware of my accomplishments, yes."

Rolling his eyes, he shoved past me.

"Yes, please, come in. I wasn't sleeping or anything."

"Men like you don't sleep, too much blood on your hands."

"Jaded for someone so young."

"Nineteen isn't young, not in this world. How old were you when you first killed someone, when you took someone's life?" His blue eyes locked on mine. They saw too much, just like Luca, damn it.

"Fourteen," I answered in a deliberately bored tone. "Though I was only ten when my father forced me to shoot the family pet at point blank range. Then again, it was either shoot the pet or my own cousin. I chose the dog."

Dante didn't flinch, but he did avert his eyes.

"I don't need your pity," I snapped.

"Good." He sneered. "Wasn't offering it."

"So that's it? That's what you wanted to know? How old I was before I sold my soul to the Family?"

"No." His shuttered expression cracked, revealing something I recognized well — fear. "I wanted to talk about Val."

"What about her?"

"She doesn't know."

77

"No shit."

"Would you just listen? And stop with the sarcasm, damn it. Do you realize how annoying you are? Or how emotionally draining it is just to be in the same room as you?"

"I'd like to think it's part of my charm."

He took a deep breath and walked over to the window, keeping his back to me. Stupid move. I could kill him without hesitation.

But maybe that was the point.

He was trying to show he trusted me.

By showing his back.

I nodded silently. I respected that.

So I lowered the gun to the table and crossed my arms. "I'm going to assume that when you say Val doesn't know, what you're really trying to get across is that she doesn't know you know."

His shoulders tensed.

"And you've been keeping it from her... how long?"

He didn't answer.

"Dante."

"My whole life," he whispered. "Gio, Sal, and Papi made a promise never to reveal anything to Val. It would destroy her, the truth. The promise included me... until things went wrong."

"You mean until you were sent away, and the families started their little war?"

He nodded, still staring out the window. "They trained me. I swore I'd never tell Val but now..." His shoulders lifted and fell as he released a heavy sigh. "Now she's going to find out."

"She won't hate you."

"She will."

"Val seems like a forgiving person."

"Hah!" He turned and met my stare. "And you know her so well?"

"I'm about to," I muttered, sitting on the bed. "Look, for what it's worth, there isn't any part of this situation that makes me comfortable. My family is perfectly happy in Chicago. The Cappo runs things from there as well as Italy. We finally have peace because of what your father has done, because of the Empire he has built. I'm not here out of any selfish ambition. I'm here because I owe it to him to follow through with his plan, from the very beginning, so even if that means I have to eat shit — literally, I'll do it. That's how much I respected Luca. I would consider it the greatest compliment of my life if someone said I lived the way he did."

Dante tensed again. "If he was so great, why did he leave us?"

Playing therapist wasn't my strong suit.

Why wasn't Andi with me?

She'd always known what to say.

When to make a joke.

When to be serious.

When to offer wisdom.

I had my gun.

And scars on my body.

That's all I had.

"This life," I started slowly, struggling to choose the right words, "is not the one he wanted for you. Had he not died, we wouldn't be having this conversation. But he did die. That leaves us with only one choice."

"I haven't decided yet," he whispered.

"Neither have I."

He frowned. "What do you mean?"

I smirked. "I haven't decided if you've got the balls for the job yet, cupcake. It's going to take a hell of a lot more than trying to sucker punch me in the face to prove your worth."

"Yeah well, I'm young, not stupid, I figured with your training the easiest way to shock you was to charge you like a bull."

"It probably would have worked if you hadn't yelled before you ran at me."

Dante laughed softly and then a bit louder. "Yeah, I'll work on that."

"Mafia rule number one." I nodded. "Don't let them know they're dead until they see their own blood on their hands."

"Morbid."

"Life."

"I feel like I need to go to Disneyland after talking with you. Happiest place on earth, Sergio... I need happy if this my future."

"I can't promise you'll find it in the fold."

"Yeah. But one can hope, right?"

No. Wrong.

There was no happiness in death.

There was only finality.

And silence.

"You drive?" I changed the subject.

"Yeah, why?"

"You're taking me and Frank to the meeting."

"So now I'm your chauffer?"

"Even made men have to start somewhere," I called out as I made my way into the bathroom. "Oh, and touch any of my weapons, and I'm going to decapitate

you before you can utter a sorry."
He held his hands up. "Got it."

CHAPTER 11

To show our simple skill, that is the true beginning of our end

—A Midsummer Night's Dream

Valentina

HE WAS RIGHT.

I hated that he was right.

Because the morning came.

And I still felt angry and confused.

My mornings used to be filled with laughter and teasing. Instead, we all sat around the small coffee table and waited in silence as the clock on the wall ticked off the minutes.

I was almost afraid to move.

Afraid to breathe.

Dante wasn't there.

And I was worried.

Worried that we were in trouble — or that we owed money to someone. After tossing and turning all night, that was the only conclusion I could come up with. We owed money to some very bad people, and they needed us to pay them back.

It finally made sense.

How the flower shop and bar were able to stay open through the economic downturn.

Why, even though we were never busy, we never struggled to pay bills.

Dante's bloodied hands! The whispers about his fighting.

I felt so stupid.

So naive that I hadn't seen it before.

And, if I was being totally honest, I felt a bit betrayed that my uncles hadn't confided in me about their financial struggles but put my own brother in some sort of underground fighting gang. Guilt gnawed at my chest. There were so many things I'd asked for in the past few years that I never really needed.

Things that I couldn't sell now.

I'd already done a Google search for extra jobs, but everything available was, basically, either dangerous like a bike courier or they wanted more experience than I had.

One thing was for sure.

I wasn't going to college — probably ever.

The screen door opened and then slammed shut. Footsteps echoed across the worn hardwood floor, and then Dante, Sergio, and the older man — Frank, was it? — all appeared from down the hall.

They shuffled into the kitchen where I sat at the table.

My heart sank even further.

We were going to get killed in front of the pancakes. I just knew it.

Because everyone's expressions were grim, as if a

death just happened in the family, only I knew it was probably going to be mine.

"Please!" I shot to my feet. "Please don't kill us!"

Frank and Sergio shared a look while Dante closed his eyes as if he was in pain.

"Whatever we owe!" I kept talking, the words tumbling over each other as they spilled out. "I have some money in savings, and I'm sure we can figure out a payment plan or something. Just please don't kill us." I was bordering on hysterics as big hot tears rolled down my cheeks.

Sergio slowly made his way over to me and grabbed my hand. "Nobody's going to die."

"Yet," Frank muttered.

My knees buckled and I sat back down while Sergio spat out a curse under his breath. "Was that really necessary?"

Frank shrugged.

Dante rushed to my side. "Are you okay?"

"No!" I jerked away from him. "I'm not okay! Just tell me what's going on! And what we owe, and how to fix it!"

"That's going to be difficult." Dante stood to his full height then backed away. "We don't owe any money... What we owe is more..." A pained expression formed on his features. "...personal."

"What do you mean?" I searched the faces of my uncles, but every time I tried to get them to make eye contact they looked away.

I felt like I had no one.

And yet, there was Sergio, right by my side.

"Show her," Gio barked.

Frank stepped forward and pulled out a black

folder.

It had my name on it.

But I'd never broken any laws.

I didn't even jaywalk.

So, a folder with my name, it had to be a bad sign right? A really bad sign.

With trembling hands I opened it.

The first page was a birth certificate, with my exact birthdate and my full name, but the last name I didn't recognize. It wasn't Grecco, it was Nicolasi.

"Valentina Joyce Nicolasi," I whispered. "But my last name…" I didn't finish because my picture was on the next page. It had to have been taken a year ago, because I was wearing the coat I'd gotten for Christmas. What. The. Hell?

What followed were pictures of me as a child. I recognized some: my first trip to the City, me carrying a giant stuffed dog, and swinging in the park with Gio — how old had I been? Four? Maybe five? The earlier pictures didn't make sense to me, I was in a city I didn't recognize, holding mans hand.

And finally, the most recent, me and Dante in the park laughing, both of us wearing smiles while someone in the background watched, a man, a man I recognized, his smile wide, his eyes hopeful.

It made my chest ache.

His smile was familiar.

As if that smile used to be directed toward me.

I let out a gasp and covered my mouth, then whispered between my fingers. "Is that… our father, Dante?"

He nodded, his expression grim.

Wasn't this a good thing?

"Where is he?" I yelled, jumping to my feet. "Is he here? Is that why you guys are all acting weird? I thought he didn't want anything to do with us, and—"

"My brother," Frank said softly, "is dead. I'm sorry."

I fell back against my chair as bitterness washed over me. So that was it? I finally got to see truth, and the rug was ripped out from beneath me?

"Keep reading," Dante urged.

Sergio was as still as a statue next to me.

I turned the page and saw my name again.

It was a contract.

Between the Abandonato family and the Nicolasi family.

I hereby swear upon death that if it is within my power to join Valentina's hand in marriage to Sergio Abandonato, I will make it so, or let my soul burn for an eternity.

"I'm BETROTHED?" I yelled, looking up.

"Not just betrothed." Oh, *now* Gio speaks up? "You are promised to Sergio… to—" he swallowed "—one of the most powerful Mafia families in the Cosa Nostra. If Dante does not take his rightful place, you will be marrying the new boss to Frank Alfero's Empire."

I burst out laughing.

Nobody joined me.

My laughter faded. "You can't be serious!" I pushed to my feet. "Is this a prank? Mob boss? Cosa Nostra?" I scanned the room for hidden cameras, because, come on! Mafia? Did that even exist anymore? The idea was laughable. Why was everyone still sitting? "Guys! The joke's up, come on, whose idea was this?"

Nobody moved.

Finally, Dante spoke, "Val, it's real."

I frowned. "Dante, seriously…"

"Damn it, Val!" Dante's voice rose. "Our father was Luca Nicolasi! One of the most lethal mob bosses in history! Frank is your damn uncle!" He pointed at Frank who managed to look at least a bit sad.

The lines in Frank's face drew into a scowl. "You could have said that better, Dante."

"Better she know than assume it's a joke. I wish." He put his hands on his head and turned around in a circle then faced me. "Val…" His nostrils flared. "I kept it from you to protect you, all right? I would never purposefully—"

"All of you?" I stumbled back, jerking away from him. "All of you knew? This whole time? And I was in the dark?"

Choking on a cry, I stared at each of my uncles, none of them could look me in the face, even Frank had averted his eyes and pinched the bridge of his nose.

Dante swore and punched a hole in the kitchen wall.

Dust settled at his feet.

And Sergio simply stood there. In the same spot. Staring.

"How long have you known?" I directed my question at him.

"Eight weeks."

"And you've waited that long to tell me! What kind of person are you? You could have at least given me warning! Oh look hi, I'm Sergio, I OWN you!"

"My apologies," Sergio said in a tense voice. "I must have been too busy taking care of my cancer-ridden wife. How selfish of me." He moved toward me with a cat like grace, predatory, like he was going to pounce.

"You're right, I should have texted you the minute she died and told you the good news."

"I—"

"Say you're sorry and I won't hesitate to shoot something."

I lifted my chin as tears clogged my throat. "Shoot something. Just make sure it's not a human. And I *am* sorry. There, I said it. Because as much as this sucks…" It was nearly impossible to keep the tears of sadness and frustration away, and I finished in a whisper, "That's worse."

His lips parted a bit and then he turned on his heel and stomped out of the room.

"Is he really going to shoot something?" I asked the room.

"Probably," Frank answered then held out his hand. "Val, let's go for a walk, shall we?"

"Am I safe with you?"

"I'm a wonderful shot."

I narrowed my eyes and assessed him. "I bet you are."

He offered a polite smile. "You're my niece, I would protect you with my life."

At least he was willing to give me something. My uncles were still staring daggers into the table as if it was going to come alive and start spouting Shakespeare. "Fine."

"Good girl." He kissed my hand. "I promise, it's not so bad as it seems."

"Oh?"

"Actually…" He winced. "I'm afraid it's worse."

CHAPTER 12

And though she be but little, she is fierce!
—A Midsummer Night's Dream

Sergio

CEMENT.

Gravel.

Pavement.

Streetlights.

I exhaled slowly, the shaky breath staggering in puffs of white in the freezing air as I leaned against the brick wall in the narrow alleyway. The winter chill should have been powerful enough to choke the life out of me, but I felt nothing.

Except a keen numbness that had me, once again, wondering what the *hell* I was doing in New York. I wasn't making things better. I'd already beaten up a few old men, threatened to shoot people in front of a girl who'd never seen violence a day in her life, and that was with me *trying* to control myself.

God help us all if I truly lost my shit.

I wiped my face with my hands then focused on a

tiny crack in the wall. Life was easier that way — it was the only way I knew how to handle the tumultuous emotions surging through me, focus on small, don't think about the bigger picture.

So I focused on pieces.

I focused on cracks in the pavement.

The dust of a few scattered rocks the cement at my heel.

It was the same way I looked at Val. My efforts, so far, had been working, ignore her body and face as a whole, but hands? Yeah, I could stare at her hands, she had three scars on her pointer finger, I assumed it was from thorns in the roses she often arranged.

She had a dimple in her right cheek that, on first glance, looked like another scar, but really was just a really deep indent that made her appear even more innocent than she was.

Her hair was dark brown.

But, when she tilted her head at different angles, shots of gold shimmered.

She was short.

Not as short as Andi, but short enough that I knew my presence would be extremely intimidating to her.

Pieces.

I looked at pieces.

Never her smile, only her teeth.

Eyes were fine, as long as she didn't lock gazes with me too long and, really, I was confident that even if she touched me for a prolonged period of time, I'd be okay.

It wasn't that she wasn't striking — she was Luca's blood through and through, she had his hazel like ghost eyes, so light that they almost seemed white at times, and she had Joyce's smile.

I'd bet it killed Frank.

And that's when it killed me — this wasn't just his niece, this was his wife's daughter.

Damn me.

I'd been outside having a near nervous breakdown over the fact that I had to marry the girl — a mere eight weeks after my wife's death, mind you — and Frank had just met his wife's son and daughter.

His brother's children.

The last thing he needed was my emotional baggage to go along with it. I kicked the wall one last time and was just about to turn the corner when I saw Frank and Val on the porch of the brownstone.

I held back.

They sat down in the cold, Frank on the top stair, Val, too, but as far away from him as possible, nearly underneath the railing, her arms wrapped around the post as if it was enough to protect her from a man like him.

"You're upset," Frank said in a bland tone.

I rolled my eyes. No shit she was upset, old man! She'd just been told that her family was mafia royalty, what normal, innocent girl wouldn't be upset when you exchanged their iPhone for a gun and told them to make sure they always sit in booths when going out to eat?

Once you knew your own blood, it was impossible to go back.

The chilling knowledge of her heritage alone would make sure of that. She'd always watch her back from here on out, never stand in line at Starbucks, and, when she walked home at night, she would always think she was being followed.

Mafia breeds paranoia.

As well as insanity.

They go hand in hand, but they also keep you alive.

"I'm in shock," she finally said, her eyes meeting his. She tucked a piece of hair behind her ear and ducked her head, staring down at her shoes. "My whole life is a lie."

Dramatic, but true.

I frowned as she chewed on her lower lip, sucking it into her mouth only to release it.

A strange mixture of anger and lust jolted through me like lightning.

The wrongness of the emotion started a cold sweat as I continued to eavesdrop.

"We thought it best to protect you. Luca was a very dangerous man. He was also convinced you could never live a normal life if you lived under his roof. He knew something must be done. You were raised until the age of five in Italy. I'm sure you remember fragments." He sighed, his breath swirled around his head. "There were two death threats against you and Dante... I'll never forget the night my brother called me to say he needed to put you both in hiding. The only people I could think of..." He glanced back at the house. "Were also, at the time, not my biggest fans."

"At the time?" She joked.

"Yeah well..." Frank chuckled. "Blood is blood. They had no choice, and they adopted you as if you were their own." He angled his head and studied her. "You have been happy, no?"

After a few seconds, she nodded.

"And you've been well taken care of?"

Another curt nod.

"Believe me when I say, the last thing I want to do is ruin your future, but it was your father's dying wish that you not only know him, but that you join the Family. By joining through marriage you are automatically—"

Val covered her mouth with her hand and laughed.

Frank frowned.

I stared harder. Had she just laughed? At Frank Alfero?

"I'm so sorry!" Val laughed harder. "I laugh when I'm nervous. I just... it's kind of funny right? I read, Frank. That's what I do."

"I don't think I understand."

"My excitement in life." She smiled again to herself. "Was reading, mainly historical romance. Women had no power in Regency England. They couldn't even own property. Did you know that once they were married both the church and crown only recognized them as property of whomever had wed them?"

Frank shook his head.

"Marriages were formed based on wealth, power, protection, prestige." A wry smile curved her lips. "Are you telling me the same thing, Frank? Am I supposed to marry Sergio for all of those reasons? Or is there more?"

Frank shifted on the step.

I waited to see what he would say. Because there was so much more to that story — to the real reason we were here, to why it was imperative that they join the ranks.

"Sergio doesn't need you, not emotionally, not financially, not physically."

She jerked back as if she'd been punched but kept

her mouth shut.

"He has more money than he knows what to do with, used to work for the FBI, is an expert hacker, and now that his wife is dead..." He shook his head. "...he honors her memory by staring at walls."

Thanks, Frank. Glowing review.

"The last time I saw him laugh it was forced, and I fear I have already lost him. Then again, nobody ever had Sergio — nobody but his wife, because even before her, there was an emotional detachment in his killings and dealings. He is not a safe man, nor a sane one, Val."

I curled my hands into fists. What the hell!

"But," continued Frank, his gaze growing intense, "he will protect you with his life — and more importantly, he will protect you with his name. For someone to make a murder attempt on an Abandonato is to invite the Cappo and the rest of the five families to wipe out that person's entire existence, and not just the person foolish enough to try... but the rest of the blood line, and the best part?" He paused. "Our Cappo, he thirsts for blood. He's like a lion, barely tamed by his wife, only able to stay trapped inside the four walls of his house for hours if she keeps him..." He coughed. "Occupied."

She stared at him for a long moment. "What's a Cappo?"

Frank chuckled to himself. "I forget you know nothing." He leaned back against the stairs. "I guess in your world that would be like our Godfather, though it pains me to say it, considering Tex is only twenty-five, hardly my elder."

"Twenty-five?" Val repeated. "How old is everyone else?"

"I'm the oldest." Frank's voice was grave. "The last."

"The last?"

His posture stiffened. "Of the Original bosses." He turned to her. "And so help me God, I will leave this earth seeing my promises made to my dead brother, do you understand? Run away, I will find you. Fight it, you will lose. Listen carefully, because this is the only situation where my love for your father trumps my love for you — because I owe him, more than you'll ever imagine — you will marry Sergio, you will join the Family. You will do it with a smile on your face because you are a Nicolasi, you are our future, and you will make your father proud."

CHAPTER 13

Hell is empty and all the devils are here.
—A Midsummer Night's Dream

Frank

I WAS BEING too direct. Too cold.

I didn't know how else to be.

Trace would be disappointed in me — but I could not find it in myself to do anything more — or to offer Val an escape, away from the promises made.

Promises owed.

Blood promises, that's what those papers in my folder held. After all, Sergio wasn't the only one with a list, checking off tiny little boxes, exhaling in relief each time he did so.

I too had my boxes.

My list.

My bag of tricks.

I would not stand by again and watch The Alferos fall.

There is a certain finality, a harsh realization when you age, when your reflection in the mirror starts to truly appear the same way you feel in your chest.

Legacies are like the wind, you may not see them, but they are there, constantly altering the course of the weather.

Joyce had always said that I was a cold bastard when I wanted to be, and she was right. I was.

But it was time — my time.

A man feels these things in his bones. Hell, I even felt it in the air as I left Val alone on the stairs and made my way back into the house, my footsteps announcing my arrival into the kitchen.

"She will marry two days from now," I announced. "But first, mass tomorrow."

Gio's eyes locked on mine. "Why do you do this, Frank?"

"It is what he wanted."

"She would have been safer not knowing," Papi chimed in. "We can keep her safe."

Time for the cold heartless bastard.

"Gentleman." I pressed my hands against the table and leaned over it. "Our time, it is coming to an end."

Silence.

"A new generation is here."

"We have heard rumors," Gio whispered. "Rumors of the wars between families…"

"Vito Campisi was shot by his own son in the chest." I sighed. "Nixon Abandonato has been boss in Chicago for three years now. Chase, his brother, helps Mil De Lange run the De Lange family, and the Nicolasis?"

"Phoenix De Lange," Sal said in reverence. "A man of many secrets."

"A man you don't want to piss off," I said. "My point is this… it is in the wind, it is no longer our time, and we can no longer sit idly by." I glared at all three of them. "Sit on our own secrets, and refuse to help the new members as they rise up and take control of the families. We have the heritage of our families to think about. Do not fight me on this or you will have a very unfortunate accident that the coroner will no doubt excuse as old age, capiche?"

"Capiche?" Sal coughed while Gio and Papi muttered and crossed their arms.

"Now..." I sat and exhaled. "Where is the wine?"

Papi chuckled. "It is ten in the morning."

I simply stared.

Gio nodded. "I forget this about you, Frank. Real men drink at ten, this is why I do not kill you."

Sal stood, walked over to the cabinet, and pulled out a bottle. "One or two—"

"Three," Frank interrupted. "It's going to be a long weekend."

CHAPTER 14

The lunatic, the lover, and the poet, are of imagination all compact.

> –A Midsummer Night's Dream

Valentina

WITH SHAKING HANDS, I read the next letter.

I'll continue the story about the prince. I know you enjoy reading. It was really the only way I figured you would get it or truly understand. Again, only one page a day, and you'll know what to do when there are no more pages.

There was a certain wildness about the prince. He was at times cruel, turning his beauty into a beast, and yet, he had moments of such tenderness that the princess wanted to cry. Was he simply wild in need of taming? No. Do not do it. Do not tame the beast. Allow him to be wild. You do not tame a lion, but it is possible to befriend it, to lie down next to it and know with a certainty that the lion will protect you while you sleep. Let him be fierce. You need fierce in your life, Valentina. Today, is a new day, you have many challenges ahead, do not forget to enjoy the simple things — like dancing in the rain.

All my love,
R

I re-read the letter over again.

It made no sense.

Who was this mysterious R, and why was she — since I'd already decided it was a girl — writing me about this prince? I had to admit, after today, it was a much needed distraction, it was just... weird.

An authoritative knock on my door made me jump. I quickly shoved the letter under my mattress and stood. "Come in."

Sergio swept in the room, his look thunderous.

I fought the urge to cower in his presence. He had times where he appeared so... fierce. Like the lion I'd just read about.

"Yes?"

"I wanted to set the record straight." His voice was cold.

"Okay." I licked my lips and braced myself for the impact of his words.

"Wait." He frowned. "What the hell are you doing?"

I looked down. "What do you mean?"

"You're all—" he waved his hand in front of me, irritation creasing his brow "—rigid."

"Oh." I nodded. "I'm preparing myself for your roar." I laughed at my own joke. He didn't. Eh, tough crowd.

"Roar?" He looked so confused, poor guy. "Am I suddenly an animal?"

"Well you're manners are less than perfect, but no, I just mean, I'm ready for you to be mean, get angry, do the whole intimidating thing you typically do, and then you'll march off without making eye contact, and I'll spend hours trying to figure out why you were so mean. Because I'm a girl, we do that. And I'm a girl who has way too much time on my hands." I took a breath. "So whenever you're ready."

He opened his mouth then closed it. "You're kind of...quirky aren't you?"

"Yes." I nodded solemnly. "Almost like a princess locked in a tower... the only time I ever go to the movies is if all of my uncles and brother come. Once — once I tried to go with a guy and found them all in the back row. Naturally Gio was yelling because they didn't serve wine at the theater."

Sergio moved across the room and stared out the window. "Tell me more."

He wasn't looking at me, but he seemed more relaxed.

And stories I could do.

I lived and breathed stories.

"Well..." I sat on my bed. "I couldn't figure out why no guys ever asked me out in high school. On the last day, someone must have finally felt like they could break their silence. Dante had threatened many lives... and you've seen him. He's got serious anger issues. Was Luca like that? Our father?" It felt weird asking, but I assumed they had been close, and I was desperate for some sort of connection with the man who had left me — the man who had left both of us.

Sergio hung his head. "He was... terrifying."

"I didn't inherit his terror."

Sergio's shoulders shook. I thought he was trembling until laughter bubbled out of him.

It was beautiful.

The sound.

Just like him.

Of course it would be.

"Are you making fun of me?"

"You have a dimple." Sergio turned and crossed his arms. "I'm sorry to be the one to break the news to you, but you're the least terrifying person I've ever met."

I stuck out my tongue.

"You just made it worse."

I chucked a pillow at him.

He moved out of the way then slowly walked over to me and sat on the bed, careful to keep at least a foot of space between us.

"Talk time?" I asked.

He nodded. "Gotta admit, I had a really scary speech for you, it was pretty heartless, cruel, the type that makes grown men cry."

"Lucky me."

"I can't do it," he admitted in a stunned voice. "Maybe it's the dimple."

Heat washed over my face as I reached up and touched one of my cheeks.

"One day..." He sighed. "You'll find someone who makes you blush just like that, someone who's just like the guys you read about in books, you'll find a man worth fighting for." He shook his head slowly. "That man... isn't me."

His words stung, and I had no idea why. We were strangers, but rejection is rejection.

"Please don't try." He swallowed and looked down at his hands. "Don't try to get me to fall for you. Don't try to get me to fall in love with you. No seduction, no angry tears when I don't kiss you goodnight — I can't... I just..." His voice trembled. "Promise me you won't ask for something I won't ever be able to give you."

106

My body was suddenly so heavy — tired. And I'd discovered in the past few days it was possible to FEEL anger in your bones, to feel it wash over you, right along with rejection. I hated it. "You said please."

"I'm working on my bedside manner."

"It shows."

He smiled.

I cleared my throat and glanced down at my hands as I twisted them in my lap. They were clammy. Then again, he made me nervous. Just being around Sergio was like jumping head first into dark water — it was terrifying, yet at the same time still refreshing. "Is it because of me?"

Sergio exhaled a curse as his body tensed next to mine. Our thighs brushed, and I shivered. "No."

"That's very... reassuring, please go on and on about my many attributes." I said dryly.

He laughed again. "Are you always this sarcastic?"

"Yes." I nodded seriously. "I'm extremely sarcastic in my head."

"You're fine."

The comment stung.

"And," he continued, licking his lips, "I'm sure you could make any man happy..."

"Is that why you never look at me?" I asked. "You're not very convincing, because right now I feel like the Wicked Witch of the West minus the magic."

He didn't move, but he clenched his jaw, and the muscle twitched as if he was grinding his teeth together. Slowly, he turned toward me, his blue eyes finally locking on mine.

The look he gave me was too much.

And yet not enough.

He didn't look through me the way other people did.

It was as if, with one simple look, he was able to strip me down to the raw reality of who I was.

To make eye contact with Sergio Abandonato was to know both pain and beauty simultaneously.

I was afraid to speak.

The moment was tense.

Finally, he reached out and cupped my face with both of his hands, then leaned in and kissed my forehead. "You're very pretty."

"And here I thought you were going to say young again." My voice shook, I couldn't help it. He was still touching me.

With a sad smile, he dropped his hands to his sides and stood. "I'd never forgive myself if I allowed you to believe that you were the issue... I'd rather kill someone at pointblank range then be the one to make a girl feel insecure about her own beauty."

Was he real?

What guy was concerned about that?

Only perfectly haunted ones who wanted nothing to do with me. Fantastic.

Sergio stood, thrusting his hands in his pockets.

"What was the other speech?" I asked once he reached the door.

Without turning he said, "Try to kiss me, and I won't hesitate to kill you. Ask me for my love, and I'll do us both a favor and make your death look like an accident."

I burst out laughing.

He didn't.

"You're being dramatic right?"

He left.

"Right?" I called after him.

Chilled, I rubbed my arms and then marched over to the door and closed it. I eyed the lock for maybe four seconds before turning it.

It was the first time I'd locked my door since I was six.

I wasn't sure if it was because I was trying to keep the monster out.

Or if it was to keep me in.

Because guys like Sergio made girls stupid.

He had wounds.

Scars.

Emotional baggage.

And he killed people.

The last thing he needed was to be saved.

Maybe. I walked over to my bed and sat. Maybe he just needed a friend.

CHAPTER 15

I'll follow thee and make a heaven of hell, To die upon the hand I love so well.

—A Midsummer Night's Dream

Sergio

THERE WAS NO time for actual wedding plans.

I refused to participate, regardless.

And I knew I was being an ass, but history was repeating itself. I just wanted to get the job done then drown myself in a fifth of whiskey — as many times as possible.

It wasn't her.

It was the situation.

Val was just fine.

Fine.

Hah.

I'd ruffled her feathers — completely unintentionally, but girls like Val were dangerous. She was completely unaware of her own beauty. What was worse, she was innocent.

I'm sure she made many a man want to corrupt her.

Because for two seconds, maybe a half a second, I'd thought about it. That's how pathetic I was — I assumed one night of hot sex would make me feel better.

Even though I knew it really wouldn't.

I was like Phoenix now.

Completely unable to think of sex without shaking like a drug addict. I couldn't think about sex without thinking about my dead wife.

She'd said to move on.

She'd said she understood in her letter, understood what I'd have to do, and for some reason it almost made it worse, that when she was lying next to me in bed, she had known the clock was ticking.

She had made love to me... knowing that she wouldn't be the last.

She had kissed me... knowing that I was promised to another.

Every moment.

Every touch.

I was her last.

But she wasn't mine.

How could she have still loved me? Knowing that? Knowing what my future held?

It gave me a headache thinking about it.

Ever since leaving Val's room the day before, I'd been completely unable to focus on anything. My concentration was shit.

And I wanted to blame her.

Because I'd hurt her feelings; I'd looked at her.

I'd looked at her and thought about kissing her.

Then wanted to strangle her for being the cause for it.

I was a danger. To myself. To Val.

But I couldn't tell her that. I couldn't march upstairs and say, *Surprise! Your future husband thinks about your murder — anything so he won't have to touch you.*

Not the best wedding gift.

Like putting a noose in a fancy box and telling her to go crazy.

I poured more wine and stared into the fire.

I was doing that a lot lately, just randomly staring at things, searching for answers in all the wrong places. I poured more wine and stared into the fire. I could handle the flame, not the whole fireplace, the whole fireplace somehow translated into much more meaning to me, meaning I wasn't ready to face.

The air shifted, a shadow crossed briefly in front of me, the footsteps were heavy, solid. "Dante."

"How the hell did you know?" he asked in a defeated voice as he joined me on the couch.

"Practice." I drank more wine.

"So..." Dante coughed into his hand then crossed his arms.

"Spit it out, man."

He leaned forward and placed his hands out in front of him as if he was going to give me a huge speech. I really didn't want to talk about his sister.

"I'm just gonna come out and ask it, all right?"

"Probably a good call, I'm not a patient man."

"No shit," he muttered then rubbed his hands together. "I want you to train me."

"Huh?" I set the wine on the coffee table and turned to face him. "Train you? How, exactly?"

He gulped. "I want to know how to fight better. I'm a good shot, but I could be better. I have anger issues, and I don't know why — at least, I know I struggle with my temper. I was just thinking, since you're here, and since... I guess I have no choice now..." His voice trailed off.

"You realize what you're asking me," I stated in a quiet voice.

"I think so."

"You *think* so?" I sneered. "Thinking is the same as hesitation. You don't think, you know. If you want me to train you, I'll train you, but do you really think you're ready? To laugh death in the face? To end someone's life? Do you even realize the innocent people I've taken from this world? Are you ready to do that? To kill someone who doesn't deserve it? Because it seems to me that you may be under the impression we only kill the bad guys." I let out a heartless laugh. "I wish."

"You kill innocent people."

"I kill." I nodded. "Period. A job's a job. But loose ends? We don't do loose ends. If we have a rat and he has a family, a wife, kids, and we suspect them..." I shrugged. He'd figure it out.

He was quiet for a minute then whispered, "Has that happened before?"

"More times than I'd care to admit."

"Did Luca ever hesitate?"

"He hesitated when necessary. He knew how to time everything, he was.... strategic."

"That." Dante nodded, his lips drawn into a grim line. "Teach me that. Killing must be the last option, but outsmarting people? That I know I can do."

A weight lifted off my shoulders, because the last thing I wanted to do was teach Luca's son about murder. But intelligence? Yeah, I could do that with my eyes closed.

"Yes."

"What?" He frowned.

"I said yes. I'll train you."

He exhaled. "Thanks."

"I don't do hugs though." I held out my hand; he gripped it and shook on it.

"Dude, I hug my sister. That's it."

"Good to hear it."

"How is she?" he asked, changing the subject.

And I was back to staring into the fireplace, reaching for my wine — anything to take away the churning in my stomach. "Good."

"Will you ever be able to love her?"

I thought about it for a while. Could I? Not in the way I loved Andi, but I imagined I could learn to love her like family, and that was better than nothing. "Like a sister... I can love her that way."

"Hey." Val knocked on the wall, announcing her arrival. "The uncles are gathering in the kitchen. There's wine, there's yelling, and I heard something about Chicago? Can you guys come help?"

Dante rolled his eyes and stood. "When are they not fighting?"

"Right." Val held up her hands in innocence. "But they never fight if they've already finished three bottles of wine."

"Girl has a point," Dante muttered as he moved past Val.

Her eyes darted to mine, uncertainty and hurt laced every angle of her face. Damn it.

She'd heard.

The dreaded sister word.

At least now she knew.

I'd protect her with my life.
I'd love her like I would any family member.
But she would never share my bed.
Or have my heart.

CHAPTER 16

Now I am dead. Now I am fled.

–A Midsummer Night's Dream

Valentina

HE DIDN'T EVEN apologize or at least explain himself. It was rough, the entire situation was rough. It was like being told you're good but not good enough.

I realized in that moment, when Sergio stared me down, refusing to go back on what he said about me being like a sister, that I'd been more than coddled and sheltered. I'd been straight up locked inside a box with only one window looking out on the world.

I straightened my spine and gave him a half smirk even though I didn't feel it. "If I'm your sister that means you'd pull a Dante and go to the movies with me, doesn't it?"

He looked confused and extremely uncomfortable. "I guess."

"Good." I nodded. "Because I really want to see this horror movie, and Gio gets nightmares, so I guess that means you're up!"

"You want me to go to the movies with you?" he repeated, his shoulders slumping in defeat.

"Yup!" I nodded. "I'll just go get my purse. Brothers also pay and get extra butter on the popcorn but make it look like they're ordering it for themselves, so it looks like I'm still eating healthy." I paused to take a breath. "Also, I like Sour Patch Kids."

"Should I be writing this down?" he asked in a defeated voice. "Or will you remind me when we get there?"

"Soda." I tapped my chin. "I mix coke and Dr. Pepper."

"That's blasphemous!" he gasped, joked, and finally relaxed his stance, though his version of relaxed still looked like he had a stick up his ass.

"I live life on the edge. What can I say?"

"Rule breaker." He took a step toward me. "Does Dante sit by you?"

"Nope." I sighed. "He sits behind me. So basically you're like my body guard, lucky you."

"So I'm a human shield?" he asked, his blue eyes doing that twinkle thing that made my knees weak.

"Think you can handle it?"

"I'll do my best."

I turned around and ran up the stairs.

When I got back Sergio already had his jacket on.

I shoved my phone into my purse and quickly put my brown leather jacket on and then wrapped a scarf around my neck. "I just need to go tell the uncles."

"Done." Sergio opened the door. "You're welcome."

I hesitated and then walked through. "Th-thanks."

"So…" Why did he have to be so nice to look at? A light wind picked up, causing his wavy hair to whip against his strong cheeks. "Do we walk or take a taxi?"

"Taxi." I held up my hand. "It's too cold to walk."

"Is it?"

"For those of us who have hearts," I said under my breath.

He paused and then burst out laughing. "Holy shit, was that a dig at me?"

I shrugged as the taxi pulled up.

"Damn, and you're not even apologizing."

"It was more of a passing comment under my breath..." I got into the taxi and slid across the cold, worn vinyl seat. "But true."

Sergio slammed the door after him. "And here I thought I was making a good impression."

"You offered to kill me if I kissed you."

The taxi driver frowned into the rearview mirror.

"She's kidding," Sergio reassured him.

I refused to let him get off that easy. "You also look at me like you want to throw up."

Mr. Taxi Driver's nostrils flared.

"Uh." Sergio laughed uncomfortably. "I just have a lot on my mind."

"The wife."

Taxi Driver's eyes looked like they were going to bug out of his head. Yeah, this was probably the best entertainment he'd had all day.

"I don't talk about it," Sergio said in a drop-the-subject voice.

"Maybe you should."

"I have enough money to afford a therapist, thank you," he said through clenched teeth.

"Money doesn't buy happiness," I fired back.

Sergio released a string of pithy curses. "Did

someone spike your milk this morning during show and tell?"

"Lactose intolerant."

"Sorry. Your Kool-Aid." His eyes narrowed. "It's like you're trying to piss me off."

Bingo. I smiled. "Funny, that's what Dante says to me all the time. Just think of all the things you get to look forward to. Isn't that what you said you wanted?"

Sergio looked ready to strangle me. "No. I don't believe I asked for an annoying little sister, but if that's what you're offering, please don't let me stop you. Just know, I won't hesitate to put you over my knee if you get out of hand."

The minute the words left his mouth. I froze.

He froze.

The taxi driver stared little laser-like holes into the rearview mirror.

And Sergio leaned toward me.

I swallowed as tension swirled around us.

He gripped me by the chin and turned my head to the side, his lips brushing my ear. "It's like you have a death wish."

"You wouldn't do it."

He pulled back as both of his eyebrows shot up, and then he looked down, like something had caught his eye.

I followed the direction of his gaze and let out a little gasp as a gun dug into my stomach.

"It's been directed at you for the last four minutes," Sergio said through a practiced smile. "I meant what I said. Listen well. I keep my word. Kiss me, and blood will be spilled."

"Y-you're a crazy person!" I hissed, shoving at his

chest. "And I wasn't going to kiss you!"

"Sure you weren't." He put the gun away. "Good talk though, right? Oh look, the movie theater."

To say that I scrambled out of the car like a kid running away from her kidnapper would be a gross understatement, but the minute my feet hit the pavement, I paused.

My body told me to run.

The guy had pulled a gun.

On me.

I didn't even watch violent movies, I'd just panicked and said the first thing that popped into my head!

And I was about to go to the theater with a guy who probably showered in blood on a daily basis and by the looks of it — got off on it.

Shivering, I forced myself to take a deep breath and wrapped my jacket tighter around my body.

That was the thing about men like Sergio, or maybe just loyalty in general. He'd promised he would keep me safe, but I wondered if that promise was only extended until I was more trouble than I was worth.

I was safe, not because of what I was to him.

But because of who my dad had been to him.

I was nothing.

And yet, a part of me still yearned to be... something.

Anything really.

Pathetic.

"Change your mind?" Sergio's smooth voice interrupted my thoughts. He was the type of man you felt even when he wasn't speaking. His presence was impossible to ignore, kind of like his ridiculous good looks.

Weren't mafia guys supposed to be old?

Fat?

Chain smokers who bought Cuban cigars and sat behind large desks while counting money and ordering hits on people who pissed them off?

"No." I finally found my voice. "I was just thinking...."

"About?" His hand touched my back, ushering me forward, but not pushing, almost as if he was giving me the option of still saying no.

I increased my pace so that I couldn't feel the warmth of his fingertips. "Popcorn." I turned and winked, hoping it would hide the fact that my body was shaking.

Maybe I was the crazy one.

Because he was armed.

The man was *armed*.

And he had no qualms about pointing his weapon at me whenever I got too close.

Huh, we'd have a happy marriage.

I guess we'd never argue, since I liked living.

And, you know, breathing.

It would suck not to make my twenty-first birthday because I didn't fold the towels just right.

And again, I froze.

Was he that neurotic? Or was it just the closeness?

"On a scale of one to ten..." I was proud of the way I kept the shaking out of my voice. Why was I so scared? Oh right, because he'd pointed a gun, no, shoved a freaking gun into my stomach and done it with a smile on his face. "How OCD are you?"

An easy laugh escaped him as he glanced around the movie theater lobby and then back at me. "What makes you think I'm OCD?"

"Things." I gulped then forced a smile that I didn't feel. How was I supposed to go through an entire movie knowing he was one uncomfortable conversation away from losing it? "So?"

"What can I get you?" A teen boy looked at Sergio then smiled wider when his eyes fell to me.

Immediately, Sergio wrapped a protective arm around me, basically forcing my body to curve into his warmth. "My wife and I will have two buckets of popcorn, two packs of Sour Patch Kids, and a bottled water."

I didn't correct him about the water.

"Wait." Sergio held up his hand. "Sorry, Dr. Pepper mixed with Coke."

The teen scrunched up his face then rung us up. His eyes fell to me again then back at the register, like he was trying not to look but couldn't help it, which was comical, since I didn't really think I was anything to look at.

When he handed Sergio back his change I could have sworn I heard a growl from my "husband."

As it was, he jerked the candy so hard out of the kid's hands that I was surprised he didn't do a front flip over the counter.

"He's a boy," I whispered under my breath. "No need to shoot him too."

Sergio glanced down at me, muttered a curse. "He was staring."

"He looked about one science project away from solving world hunger via his mom's basement... hardly the type of guy that I'd date."

"Date?" Sergio said it so loudly the people in front of us waiting to show the attendant their tickets jumped and then turned around. "What the hell do you mean date?"

Crap. I'd messed up again.

My palms went sweaty while my face felt numb with fear. Regardless of how pretty he was to look at — I was finally fully aware of how dangerous he was to me.

To everyone around me.

Sweat trickled down my lower back as I gulped down more soda and shrugged. "I just mean, he's not my type."

"No shit he isn't, because you don't get a type anymore."

"Right." I licked my lower lip, pretending not to be scared, pretending to be the brave person I wasn't was wearing on me.

By the time we made it into the theater I was dizzy.

It was too much all at once.

"So..." Sergio's voice was in my ear. I jumped a foot. He frowned as if he couldn't figure out why I'd be so jumpy. "Dante sits behind you, right?"

"Right." I exhaled in relief. I forgot. It wasn't a date. It was a challenge. He'd called me his sister, so therefore he was my brother, right? Hah. I relaxed a bit as I pointed to a seat a few rows back and quickly stole the goodies out of his hands then made my way to my own seat before he could object.

The credits started rolling.

And I found myself ducking in the chair.

The hair on the back of my neck stood on end.

As if I was being watched — because I was.

Ten minutes into the movie, I was so stressed out, I almost burst into tears. My back was to him.

Wasn't that a big no-no? My back was to the dude with the gun.

Even though he was supposed to protect me with the gun, all bets were off now.

Sweat pooled in the palms of my hands.

The music rose as one of the actresses ran down the stairs screaming.

I couldn't take it.

And then, a body sat down next to me.

Sergio gave me a suspicious look then put a seat between us.

I exhaled.

But it wasn't relief.

At least I knew where he was.

And where the gun was, he was right handed, so there was that.

I finally allowed myself to relax enough to watch the movie when I saw Sergio's right hand duck into his jacket.

I gripped the plastic arm rests, my fingers digging into the cheap sticky plastic material as he slowly pulled something out.

He turned.

And I flinched so hard that there was no mistaking what I thought he was doing.

Even though he had grabbed a black cell phone.

The damage was done.

My entire body shook as a big fat tear escaped, I tried to wipe it away but I wasn't fast enough.

"S-sorry." I shoved past him and ran.

But my body was too scared.

Too tired

To make it very far.

I ran into a trash can and nearly tumbled against the wall when strong arms came around me and pulled me into one of the theaters that wasn't showing a movie.

Darkness engulfed us.

And an electrical charge that warned me to run, yet again, filled the air.

But it was Sergio.

So I stayed.

Because I was that stupid girl.

The one who believed that everyone had something good — right?

"Look at me," Sergio's whisper was urgent, harsh, as he held my face between his hands. "Val, look at me."

I shook my head. "I think — I'll just... not."

"You'll just not," he repeated softly. "Val, please."

Slowly, I lifted my eyes to his, unable to stop the fact that the longer I stared at him, the more they filled with big, fat, ugly tears.

"Damn me to hell," he muttered and then pulled me in for a tight hug, one that felt safe, even though I knew better now. I knew better.

I tried to pull away.

But he wouldn't let me.

So I turned my face into his chest.

It was hard to breathe.

But at least he wouldn't think I was trying to kiss him.

Even though the car ride hadn't gone that way, if anything, he'd leaned forward like he was going to kiss me, I'd simply reacted to his reaction.

Cause and effect.

Not that I'd argue it.

"Val…" His words went from English to Italian then back again as he cursed himself and this life. "I'm sorry."

"For?"

"Stupidity doesn't work on you." He sighed. "And I mean that as a compliment… but for your sake, I'll say it." He pulled back so that his face was inches from mine. "I'm sorry for threatening you in the cab, but most of all, I'm sorry for making you feel like you aren't safe with me, when the exact opposite is true. I would die for you. Val, a gun is all I know…" He shook his head. "Knew. It was all I knew until someone showed me more… sometimes, it's just easier to revert to old habits. It's easier not to think."

"Okay." I tried to pull away. Needed to get away.

"Val, you're not even listening to me."

"Heard you loud and clear." I tried to look convincing. "You're sorry, and I shouldn't be scared. Got it!" I made a beeline for the door.

Well, I tried, but he was freakishly strong and kept me paralyzed against the frame of his huge body.

"You may have heard, but you don't understand." He cursed again. "Words… were never my strong suit."

"No?" I laughed nervously, still trying to peel myself away from him. "Because you were pretty clear about your intentions the other night."

He frowned. "I've literally never had a woman pull away from me. Ever. I'm also not used to doing things… delicately."

"Kinda caught that," I said mouth dry.

"Shit." He pinched the bridge of his nose. "A little help here."

127

The screen in the empty theater lit up with a preview, who knew they still showed the movie even if nobody was in there?

A girl ran across the screen in the rain and then she turned back to the guy and yelled. "A kiss to make it better?"

Sergio's eyes widened a bit as he glanced from the screen back to me.

And without hesitation.

Placed his mouth across mine.

CHAPTER 17

Lovers to bed, 'tis almost fairy time
—A Midsummer Night's Dream

Sergio

HER LIPS WERE soft.

It was her first kiss.

It had to be.

Because she wasn't doing anything.

At all.

It was like kissing a soft wall.

One that smelled really good — too good.

Memories assaulted me, and then finally, I licked the seam of her lips. With a gasp, her mouth opened. I hadn't planned on kissing her at all, let alone kissing her the way I was.

But, damn it, she wasn't kissing me back.

And I was proving a point.

And she was ruining it by not responding.

Her soft moan was all I needed to hear and, when she pressed her fingertips into my biceps, I knew she was enjoying herself. Kissing another woman wasn't

129

as painful as I thought it would be.

It felt different.

But not bad.

Not like cheating.

Then again, I was too confused about everything and too upset that I'd scared her to even feel anything but relief that she wasn't running away screaming. I was used to dealing with strong women. Women who knew how to fight back, even physically if need be.

Hell, if I pulled a gun on Trace she'd probably shoot me first.

Mil would laugh while kicking her spiked heels into my forehead, and Mo would slit my throat before I could even apologize.

And Andi.

Andi would have tried to tackle me to the ground and choke me out.

Val was just starting to respond, her tongue tentatively touching mine, when I pulled back.

Andi, Andi, Andi.

What the hell was I doing?

Val still looked afraid.

And the kiss had affected me in ways I wasn't ready for.

My lips buzzed while my body craved the nearness her soft curves promised.

Damn it, I was a changed man. A man who finally knew what it was like to have someone to share the horrors of life with — and a woman who had no choice but to say yes to me at the altar.

"Sorry." I apologized again. "I was just..." I refused to let her think it was more than me proving a point, so that's exactly what I said. "Proving a point. See?

No gun." Except for the one in my pants, what the ever loving hell? When had that happened? My dick strained against my jeans as horror and astonishment washed over me.

With a gruff curse, I motioned to the door and muttered, "We good?"

With a confused stare, Val opened her mouth then pressed her fingers to her lips and gave a mute nod. Pieces of dark hair whipped across her cheeks, and I stared longer than necessary at her lips. Again. And then at her face, which was a really bad idea, because I was looking at the full picture, the lips with the eyes, the cheeks, the innocent bow-shaped cherry lips.

Damn it.

"Great." Just freaking great. How the hell had a simple kiss turned me on?

It was wrong.

So horribly wrong.

Yet my body was ready — and screaming about the rightness of it all.

Hell.

"We should get back to the house, unless you wanted to watch the movie?" *Please don't want to watch the movie.*

"House," she said in a hoarse voice. "House sounds good."

We sat a foot apart the entire taxi ride back to the neighborhood, and when the car screeched to a stop, she jumped out and ran inside the house, slamming the door behind her.

Which left me on the doorstep after I paid the driver.

With no choice but to call the guys and see if they could make sense out of the mess I'd created.

"I'm a piece of shit," I blurted the minute Tex answered with his gruff voice asking who I killed and if I needed cleanup.

Tex burst out laughing on the other end of the phone. "This may be my favorite conversation we've ever had. Please continue. Should I be recording this? Hold on, I'm putting you on speakerphone."

"You son of a bitch! You said you were alone!"

"He's the Cappo, he lies for a living," came Chase's amused voice. "So, you're a piece of shit, and...?"

The phone crackled like they were playing hot potato with it, taking turns listening to my embarrassment.

Funny, the rage wasn't even present in that moment.

I was too damn confused and irritated to feel even the slightest bit of anger, which, if I thought about it too long, made me feel even more unsettled.

Anger had always been available.

And now, it was out of reach.

Because of a stupid kiss.

And the words that had followed.

I groaned and slammed my hand against the cement stairs, my palm stung as little pieces of cement stuck to my skin. "I pulled a gun on her."

"And?" Nixon asked.

"You too? Really?" I rolled my eyes and looked up to the sky hoping like hell Andi was enjoying the show. Grab popcorn, sweetheart, it's about to get much worse. I could almost hear her laughter ringing in the air.

And for the first time in a while.

It didn't make me want to commit suicide.

Progress?

Or maybe just insanity.

I'd take either. Both?

Over the confusion, I felt in the pit of my stomach as though I'd just marched into completely unfamiliar territory and lost the map that told me how to get back to the safe zone.

"Was she in trouble?" Chase asked.

"If those Alferos are giving you shit, we'll take the next flight out. Son of a bitch, I knew it!" Tex started barking orders while I waited for someone more sane to interrupt him.

Naturally, the sane one would be Mo, his wife, who was the next to speak. "Wait, you pulled a gun *on* her? Not *for* her?"

Silence.

I looked at the phone. Yeah, still connected. I sighed.

"In my defense, we had a moment." Oh hell, someone just shoot me and get it over with. A moment? Seriously? Was I eighteen again?

"Gasp!" Chase yelled. "No shit, Serg, a moment, huh? Better notify the CIA. Better yet, bomb New York. God forbid you have a moment with anyone."

"I'm setting you on fire next time I see you," I growled. "Fair warning and all that."

Chase laughed. "Losing your touch, since the last time you tried to hurt me you used the element of surprise, who's a bitch now?"

"Still you," I fired back.

"Wait, wait, wait." Another feminine voice piped up.

I sighed. "Hey Mil."

"Yo." Something crunched on the other end of the phone. "Bee's here too."

"I think it's safe to just assume..." Nixon chuckled.

"...everyone's here."

"No shit," I muttered. "And my humiliation's complete."

"Let us be the judge of that," Tex said. "Now, you pulled a gun on her because you had a..."

"Moment." Chase finished for him.

"Right." The bastard was probably using every ounce of control he had to keep himself from laughing. "And so you pulled a gun on her to scare her away from your... hidden treasure?"

"Maybe his—" he coughed "—treasure doesn't work anymore." Chase snickered. "Like it's hidden but no map can find it..." He burst out laughing. "Serg, be honest, was there ever any treasure in the first place? We won't tell."

"Forget setting you on fire, I'm gonna take a sniper's shot, coward's way out and all that, hope you don't mind."

"Eh." Chase laughed again. "I'll duck."

"He's good at that," Mil offered helpfully while Chase started yelling so loudly I had to pull the phone away from my ear.

"I really don't know why I called," I said mostly to myself. "I'm just trying to keep her away, all right? My wife just died. Oh, look a freaking elephant, I think I just shot it in the ass." I huffed out a breath and kept talking so I wouldn't lose my nerve. "Look, it's fine, I'm here on a job, the only problem is she's my job and, as of yesterday, she didn't even know the mafia existed outside of TV shows."

I was met with absolute silence.

"Shit, you're serious?" Nixon asked, his voice laced with disbelief. "I mean, we assumed she'd at least not be ignorant."

"She works in a flower shop," I interrupted whatever else he was going to say. "And she thought it was a hidden camera show! And then she accused me of being a loan shark."

"Hah, if the shoe fits," Chase muttered.

"Wait," Bee piped up. "What does this have to do with the kiss?"

"Keep up!" Phoenix snapped. "They had a *moment,* and he panicked because she's innocent."

"Kind of." I frowned. Was that why I freaked? "More like, I panicked because I don't want her, not like that."

It felt wrong saying those words out loud.

Like I was hurting her even though she wasn't even there.

But I couldn't want her.

Not like that.

And I couldn't give her anything she deserved.

But I could at least keep a promise. Right?

"Harsh," Tex coughed. "So after the gun what did you guys do?"

"Watched a movie." I might as well tell them everything. "And I noticed that she couldn't even look at me without shaking, so I tried to make things better and asked for a sign, you know, because clearly I'm losing my sanity, and a preview came on about kissing and making things better so I just... went for it."

"And when you say you went for it?" Tex's voice held amusement.

"I kissed her, and forced her to kiss me back, then told her it was to prove a point, and she slammed the car door and the door to the house in my face, and now

I'm freezing my nuts off sitting on the cement talking to you bastards, no offense girls, and most likely fulfilling a lifelong dream of Chase's by allowing him to play Doctor Phil."

"Love that guy, he's a genius," Chase whispered reverently.

"Tex, I say this in all seriousness, come down here and put a bullet in my head, it will be easier that way. Please."

"Okay!" Tex answered. Yelling ensued as more noise made it impossible to hold the phone to my head. "What!" Tex yelled about the dropping of plates and crashing. "He said please! He never says please! He's desperate! Mo, get off!" Mo started yelling in Italian while Tex asked, "How you want it?"

"Oh I'm not picky, head, clean exit, you know, the usual."

"So you want to look good for the funeral? Cool." Tex sounded frighteningly excited about being able to end my life. Then again, he'd been waiting for years, ever since I basically made him believe I'd slept with his wife before they were together, but Tex had never been good at forgiving old wounds, no matter how happy he currently was.

"Nobody is killing anybody," Nixon said in a calm voice. "Look, Sergio, have you thought maybe about… more finesse in this situation?"

"Hah!" Trace burst out laughing. "Oh, sorry, sweetheart, go ahead, talk to Sergio all about finesse, I'm all ears."

I couldn't help but grin. Nixon was the last person who should be talking about any sort of romance. The man thought with his gun first. Always first.

"Look, it was a mistake calling you guys. I just…" I didn't finish what I was going to say; maybe the silence was all it took to get the message across.

Because at the end of the day, they were family.

When Andi died.

The guys had cried with me.

When I needed help with the funeral, they jumped at the chance to make sure I had everything I needed.

And when I didn't want to get out of bed, it was Phoenix who kicked my ass and told me to go for a run.

Without them, I probably *would* be dead.

Because I already felt halfway dead, and they'd done everything in their power to breathe new life back into me.

"Thanks," I finally said. "I think I'll just keep powering through."

"Maybe." Nixon sighed. "Try not pulling a gun on a girl who isn't used to violence."

"No violence." Tex cackled. "Does he even understand how to use words?"

"Very funny." I rolled my eyes. "All right, I'm going to go face the firing squad also known as the Alfero uncles. Wish me luck."

"Those bastards are big dudes, don't let the limping fool you," Tex added.

"Could have used that advice yesterday when I nearly got taken out by all three, thanks for the help!"

"You got in a fight!" Chase whined. "It's so boring here."

"Yeah, well…" I glanced back up at the brick building. "At least you aren't being forced to marry a child."

"I married Mil, so…." He didn't finish. I assumed she hit him in the balls.

Laughing with them for first time in a while, I hung up the phone and reached for the screen door, only to have it open before I had a chance.

"You have a horrible habit of eavesdropping." I slid my phone into my pocket and crossed my arms while Val glared.

"And you have a bad habit of constantly telling others how much you hate me."

"It's not hate," I fired back. "Believe me, I know hate. You have absolutely no idea what that word even means, so I'd appreciate if you didn't use it as if you did."

"I hate you," she said it softly. "I really do."

"No, you don't." I reached for her, but she pulled back. "Your feelings are just hurt, maybe your pride, but you'll get over it."

"You're right." She shook her head. "You suck with words."

I smiled. "We get married in less than two days. You have two more days of freedom."

"And what will I have with you?" Val asked. "A prison sentence?"

"A life with me?" I looked down as the anger resurfaced, because she was right to hate me, even though she had no clue how much a human could hate something — I hated cancer, I could never hate a person, no matter how much I tried, I hated things that destroyed people, not the person itself.

Humanity was too frail.

To hate.

And it bothered me, that she flippantly tossed

something around without realizing the power behind its intensity — its truth.

She was young.

Naïve.

But who was I to judge her hatred?

No one.

Just her future husband.

"Two days," I said it again, maybe for both of us. "And then you're mine, and this whole hate business? It ends then."

"Says who?"

I took a threatening step in her direction and reached toward my jacket, I didn't pull my gun, but the threat was there. "I say."

Her lower lip trembled.

Shit. Old habits really died hard.

With a cry she shoved past me and ran up the stairs to her bedroom, the door slammed, knocking a picture onto the floor by my feet.

One step forward.

Twenty steps back.

Because of my inability to connect the hurt, the pain, the confusion, the anxiety, I couldn't link the feelings and make sense of them.

So I defaulted.

To what did.

My numbness.

My anger.

And for the first time that afternoon... I once again felt the sweet comfort of nothing.

Only this time...

I hated it.

Hate.

A strong word.

Too strong for my lips.

And just like that, I thought of Andi and her inability to hate anything, even the ugly.

Because to her, even the ugly was beautiful.

I needed to find beauty in my situation.

Instead, all I saw was the reflection of the ugly, the deep wallowing pit of despair, that nothing in my life, or Val's, would ever be the same.

Because of choices made long ago.

We were already… dead.

Swirling in a sea of endless hate.

I did hate something more than cancer.

I hated words.

I hated contracts.

I hated the situation.

But most of all, I hated that she would never look at me the way I secretly craved — with the opposite of hate — love.

CHAPTER 18

The more I hate, the more he follows me
—A Midsummer Night's Dream

Valentina

I WOULD NOT cry.

Not over him.

That was twice.

Twice in one day that he'd either told me he thought of me as a child or as his sister, and he was telling other people, consciously saying the words out loud over and over again, unaware that each time I was within earshot.

The words stung so badly.

More now, because he'd kissed me.

He'd kissed me.

I'd done nothing, too terrified to move, afraid he'd pull a knife on me, or worse yet, change his mind.

His lips had been so soft, pliant, and if I were being completely honest with myself, wicked, like he knew how to please women. I had been one kiss, one caress away from exploding beneath his touch.

I was *that* easy.

And then, just when he was starting to press his hard body against me, he'd pulled back and muttered something about proving a point.

I was so embarrassed that I wanted to cry.

Rejected again.

I'd rather he hate me than give me little glimpses of the man I thought he could be only for him to hide them away again. I'd rather he leave me the hell alone.

Instead, I felt like a toy.

A toy that was convenient to play with when he was finally in the mood to let down his own walls.

I don't even know how long I sat in my room.

Wanting to believe that I truly hated him, but knowing it was useless in the end. Knowing that I needed to be the mature one, accept fate, marry the guy, and just move on with my life.

Life. Huh, whatever that meant.

My uncles had given me the next two days off at my request.

They hadn't asked about the movie.

But they did ask where Sergio was.

Business, always business these days. I'd gone to get him only to hear him laugh about being married to a child.

I looked down at my clothes.

Nothing about what I wore was womanly.

Maybe that was the problem.

I was in jeans and a T-shirt, hardly sexy.

Was that what he wanted?

If only I could see what his wife had looked like, maybe that would help. I made a face. Or maybe it would fill me with such insane jealousy that I'd hide under my bed for the next few hours and slit my wrists.

I bet she was beautiful.

Just like him.

It killed me a bit to know that he was always going to compare me to a woman I would never measure up to.

How was that fair?

A knock sounded on my door.

"Who is it?" If it was Sergio I was going to lose it.

"Dante."

"Come in. You always do anyway," I grumbled, wiping at my cheeks and then pinching them to make sure that I didn't look as horrible as I felt.

Dante walked into the room with a package in his hands. He was frowning, it aged him, and at the same time made me more aware of the weight he'd been carrying all these years.

"What's that?" I tried to keep my voice chipper; the last thing he needed was to keep holding the weight on his own.

Dante tossed the box in my direction. "No idea, it's from Neiman Marcus. Been shopping?"

I laughed. "Yeah right, like I could afford Neiman Marcus."

He didn't say anything. Which was weird.

"Dante?"

"Hmm?" His head snapped up. Was his jaw swollen. "Are you okay?"

"Yup, just... tired." He faked a yawn, the little liar, then started slowly backing out of the room. "Oh hey, how was the movie?"

I swallowed the thickness in my throat as the distance grew between me and my twin, but, maybe it had always been there, he'd just hidden it from me out of concern.

He was all I had.

Him and my uncles.

And now it felt like I had nobody.

"Good," I lied. "It was... awesome."

I didn't even remember what movie we went to.

"Good, sis." He exhaled in relief. "You deserve to be happy."

"So do you."

"What makes you think I'm not?" he snapped.

"I didn't say that." What was happening to us? To my family. "You're right, you seem tired, go lie down."

He mumbled something under his breath and shut the door quietly behind him while I sucked in the last of the tears I had and stared down at the brown box.

Curiosity got the best of me and then, as I opened one part of the box I started to panic. Was there a bomb inside? Holy crap! Boxes always had bombs! With a shriek, I tossed it to the floor and pulled my feet onto the bed, as if somehow *that* was going to keep me from getting killed.

The door flew open as Sergio made a hero-like entrance. With his gun held in the air, he shouted, "What happened? Are you hurt? Is someone in here?"

Suddenly feeling stupid and horribly embarrassed, I tried to think of a lie, but what was I going to say? Sorry, I screamed because I saw a spider? Lame.

"You're going to think it's stupid." Heat danced across my cheeks.

"Try me." His eyes narrowed as he put the safety back on his gun and tucked it into the waistband in the back of his jeans.

I pointed at the box. "I didn't order anything from Neiman Marcus, and that box is addressed to me and… I just panicked."

Sergio slowly made his way over to the box then picked it up. "Can I ask why?"

Yeah, he was going to think I was an idiot. "Well, don't bombs come in boxes?"

Thankfully, he didn't burst out laughing; instead, he smiled down at the box in his hands and gave it a hard shake.

"No!" I ran at him, then swatted the box out of his hands. "It could be like, live ammo!"

"Live ammo?" he repeated, his grin widening. "In a box?"

"Yes!" I put my hands on my hips, "You know like live… wires and… such."

"Wires and such?" His eyebrows knit together. "Is that what makes bombs these days?"

I scratched the back of my head. "Yes."

"You're sure?"

"Absolutely." Whatever, I was holding my ground, even if I was wrong; I was going to go down in flames.

"Or…" Sergio knelt down and picked up the box. "It could just be a gift."

"How do I know the difference?"

He handed me the box. "Live on the wild side, Val." He stood to his full height. "Besides, do you truly think, after all these years, we'd let a Neiman Marcus box take us out?"

I sighed, and some of my tension eased. "Man's got a point."

He chuckled. "Val, just open it. I'll wait just in case."

"Promise?" I liked him this way, he made me forget

he was a horrible human being, he made me forget the hate… when he smiled.

"Yup." He held out a knife and pressed it against the tape. "Any last words?"

"Oklahoma."

Sergio pulled the knife away. "What the hell kind of last word is that?"

"It slipped!" I said defensively, and looked down. "And it was my safe word when I was little… you know, like when you get scared, you're safe—" I frowned. "Why are you laughing! This is serious!"

"Holy shit. Do you know what it means to have a safe word?"

"Yeah." I nodded slowly. "Like a word you use when you're in trouble, why do you keep laughing at me!"

He full on belly laughed.

I felt his laugh everywhere.

And knew it was a life changing moment, hearing Sergio laugh, hearing him really laugh.

Maybe people like him lived their lives in darkness so long that they forget what it meant to lose yourself completely to the insanity or humor of a moment. Maybe in darkness a lot of us were just waiting for something to make us feel — something to make us laugh.

"Okay, what, why is it funny?"

"Never mind." Sergio seemed to gain control of himself again. "Go ahead, open the box."

"I'm asking Dante." I started for the door.

"The hell you are!" Sergio raced after me and blocked the door. "If you mention safe word around Dante, you'll never live it down. I can promise you that."

Warmth rushed my face again, and I knew I was turning red, but I wasn't sure why. "Okay, fine, so tell me what the real meaning is, and just for your information, I'm right too!"

"You are... kind of." He licked his full lips, and smiled brightly, like it was the best day of his life. His eyes roamed around the room, until he must have located what he needed. He reached for a piece of rope that I'd turned into a fun, wrap bracelet, and then quickly grabbed my hands. Before I was aware of what he was doing, he'd tied the rope around my wrists.

"Um, what are you doing?"

"Pay attention," he whispered, his lips pressed together as he tightened the rope and then tugged me toward his body. I swayed a bit as he gently pushed me back onto the bed.

Confused I looked around. "I'm tied up."

"Right." He nodded, crossing his arms. "Remember your word?"

I looked down. "Oklahoma?"

A feral smile twisted his lips. "Good. Now only say it if you mean it."

"Okay?" My voice warbled.

You'd think I had just told him the funniest joke known to mankind. He burst out laughing then turned around with a flourish, tugged his T-shirt over his head.

I let out a gasp.

So many muscles greeted me that my vision went blurry.

My palms were pressed together, creating a clammy sweat that ran between my wrists. The sight of the bonds had me nearly panting on my own bed.

He stalked toward me, his muscular body moving with precision that I'd only ever read about.

When he was in front of me, he kneeled, then tugged me up and with a grunt flipped me onto my stomach, pressing his body against my back, his lips tickled the edge of my ear. "Safe word... Get it? You're tied up. Safe word is your word for when you get scared during... BDSM."

"BDSM?" I repeated, my brain not exactly firing on all cylinders since I had almost two hundred pounds of muscle pressed against my backside.

"Bondage..." he whispered, his breath fanning across my skin. "Discipline..." He brushed his nose against my neck and inhaled deeply. "Submission..."

My breath caught. "Oh. OH!" I was so stupid. "Safe word."

"You can say it now." He chuckled darkly.

My heart raced. "What if I'm not scared?"

He sighed, his weight pressing harder into me. "You should be."

"Why?"

"I wouldn't be good for you..."

"And yet, we're stuck together."

"We are."

He didn't move.

I was afraid to breathe.

"Open your gift, Val, and if you scream Oklahoma, know that I'll come running, but be prepared to answer for yourself if you're still alive; I take safe words very, very seriously, and you wouldn't want to give me the impression that you're willing to be at my mercy."

He pulled back, his hands quickly untying my

wrists. Wordlessly, he put on his shirt and left the room, shutting the door quietly behind him.

Meanwhile, I couldn't even remember my own birthday.

Because he might talk a big game.

But he'd just revealed a chink in his armor, in his tough exterior.

He was still a man.

That much had been evident when he pressed against me — all man. He was all man.

CHAPTER 19

When in that moment, so it came to pass, Titania waked, and straightaway loved an ass.

–A Midsummer Night's Dream

Sergio

I WASN'T EVEN sure how I made it down to the kitchen walking in a straight line.

What the hell had I been thinking?

I'd tied an innocent girl up!

And nearly... kissed her. Again. Only this time it wasn't to prove anything but that she felt good, and I wanted good so damn bad.

I was so tired of feeling sad and angry.

But she'd made me laugh.

Actually laugh so hard I'd had tears in my eyes.

And like a long lost memory, that small feeling of rightness surfaced, showing me that, yes, it was possible to be happy, and that maybe, just maybe, it was okay.

But my happiness didn't last for long as arguing erupted in the kitchen the minute I was within earshot.

"What's going on?" I asked in a calm voice.

Gio looked worried while Papi and Frank continued to argue. Sal shoved a note into my hand.

Frowning, I looked down at it.

"The dynasty dies with the twins," I read aloud. "Or we kill them ourselves. Your choice."

Just when things were calming down.

I slapped the note onto the table. "Where did you get this?"

Sal shook his head. "It was in a box."

Huh, didn't see that coming.

"With the signet ring of the Alferos burned against a charcoaled hand." Frank added, twisting his own metal ring around the finger of his left hand. Every boss had a crest that signified what family they were from; the rings held power because they held the blessing of the boss.

"Dramatic." I sighed, taking a seat. "Frank, any of your men losing their shit lately?"

He took a long sip of wine. "Years ago, the Family split, I am still in control, but there were a few that I... may have upset."

Sal coughed and Gio made the sign of the cross with his hand across his chest.

"How upset are we talking?" I asked the table.

"There are a few in New York who feel slighted, as if they were kicked out of the Family the minute Frank went into hiding... but if I were to guess..." Sal looked at each of the men. "...I would say it is Xavier who would feel... slighted. After all, he ran most things while Frank was in hiding."

"Xavier can rot in hell." Frank slammed his fist onto the table.

152

Dante and I shared a look before I yelled, "Well, who the hell is he?"

"Not Italian." Sal spat onto the floor then slammed his foot onto the ground. "Damn man."

"You didn't use your own family?" I frowned. "What the hell were you thinking?"

"I was thinking I had nobody I could trust at the time, so I trusted Xavier, I refused to trust blood. Blood had betrayed me. This — this decision was strictly business."

"Frank…"

"Russian." Frank looked away. "He is Russian."

"God save me from more Russians." I wiped my face with my hands. "Does Nikolai know?"

Papi slammed his hands onto the table. "You have been doing business with The Doctor?"

"Saved his life a few times too," I added. "So I'd stop throwing stones. He's a good man."

"He's a dangerous man." Papi made another cross motion.

"Nikolai knows what he needs to know. The point is, if Xavier was given a copy of the Alfero crest, the ring, my ring, to make decisions. If he is still using it…"

I held up my hand. "Yeah, got it, if he's still using any of your power as you, we could be shit out of luck. Great. Just. Great. And you were going to tell me this when?"

"I had my suspicions, but…" He spread his hands and shrugged.

"If he means to kill Dante and Val, that means he's coming for you, too." I glared at Frank. "And me."

He said nothing.

"Just another day in the life." I shook my head.

"Well, first things first, we keep the twins safe, and then we deal with the threat like always." I reached for my phone.

"What are you doing?" Sal asked.

"What Frank should have done the minute he found out." I eyed Frank with a bit of irritation. "Calling the Cappo."

"Sweet Mother." Papi started muttering prayers, "Campisi?"

"Tex?" I barked into the phone. "I need the five together. Now."

"United. In one place?"

"New York. I need you all here. Now. We need to scare the shit out of some people."

He chuckled darkly. "Serg, you just made my day twice. How can I ever repay you?"

"Just don't get in a plane crash."

"Hah."

"And don't shoot me."

He said nothing.

"Tex."

"Fine." He let out a heavy sigh. "We'll arrange for a red-eye just in time for Mass."

"Bless us Father..." I whispered under my breath. "All of us at mass has to be a sin."

Papi was still praying, Sal had joined in, and Frank looked more amused than pissed that I'd gone over his head.

CHAPTER 20

...And think no more of this night's accidents, but as a
fierce vexation of a dream.

–A Midsummer Night's Dream

Valentina

I OPENED IT.

There wasn't a bomb.

But there was a card. It was typed out, making it
impossible to decipher if the handwriting would have
been more feminine or masculine.

The instructions were simple. Weird, but simple.

It was almost like I had a fairy godmother — you
know if that sort of thing existed. Then again a few
days ago I wasn't even aware the mafia was alive and
well.

I re-read the instructions again.

**Read the next letter, before opening the
rest of the box.**

The only letters I had were the ones from the safety

deposit box, so whoever had arranged all this had gone to a heck of a lot of work.

With a sigh, I pulled the letters out from underneath my mattress and grabbed the one for that next day.

Princes, like beasts, are meant to be in the wild. Allow them to unleash their fury, for their fury is what keeps the princess safe along with the rest of the land. But there is always time for tenderness. For the prince's fierceness must be matched by his tenderness and his love for the woman he desires. But, how can one tempt a cold-hearted prince? One so broken. One so confused he isn't even sure he wants to be fixed? Easy. She puts on a dress. And twirls.

Your wedding dress.
Something old.
Something new.
Something borrowed — he's more than on loan.
Something blue.
Blessings on your special day, Val.
All my love,
R.

Who was this person? It had to be someone I knew. Nothing else made sense. I was too curious *not* to open the rest of the box. I tore through the tissue paper and gasped.

The simple white dress was absolutely gorgeous. The tags were still on it. I nearly had a heart attack when I saw the name brand and dollar signs behind it. Who paid over six thousand dollars for a dress that would only be worn once? And who would buy one for *me*?

Something about holding the white satin in my

hands felt wrong.

Like it was someone else's dress entirely.

And I was a sad imposter for who should have been wearing it.

I peeled back another layer of tissue paper.

The shoes looked worn, but only slightly; they were a silvery white, with a spiked heel. Grass stains and dirt were noticeable on the heel, but only barely. Frowning, I picked up a sliver of grass and examined it.

The shoes still had grass on them? Like they'd been in a field or something. A piece of blue satin material was stitched across the toe.

Maybe that was my something old and blue?

The last object was even stranger.

A baseball bat.

Seriously?

A note was taped to it. *"Trust me, you'll need this."*

I was even more confused than when I started.

My head hurt from the long day I'd had.

And my clock seemed to be screaming out every second that ticked by as if to remind me that I only had two days until Sergio and I said I do.

Shivering, I tucked all the gifts back into the box and crawled into bed. Maybe one day the clues would make sense, but tonight? They just made me wish that I really did have a fairy godmother who would take me away and tell me everything was going to be okay.

With a sigh, I closed my eyes and tried to get into a comfortable position. About twenty minutes later my body finally relaxed into the mattress.

I inhaled deeply and then froze as the sound of something scratching the outside of my window paralyzed me with fear.

It was my imagination.

It had to be.

But the scratching continued.

Slowly, I reached down the side of my bed where the box was. My fingers searched for the bat, but kept coming up short every time.

Terror gripped me as the scratching stopped only to be replaced by something opening my window.

A gust of wind hit me full force.

I was going to die if I didn't find that bat and make a run for it.

Finally, my fingers grabbed onto it, with a yell, I waved it in the air and ran for the door.

A figure dressed in all black chased after me.

A leather-gloved hand pressed over my mouth covering my scream.

I smacked the bat behind me, coming into contact with the intruder's body, and kept hitting until the door burst open.

The intruder stumbled backward and dodged for the window.

"I don't think so." Sergio grabbed the guy by the back of his shirt and tossed him against the door. He stumbled backward.

A black mask covered his face and mouth, even his eyes were blacked out.

Sergio stretched his neck, and it cracked before he exhaled then took his time to approach the guy before kicking him in the side.

I could have sworn I heard the sound of bone cracking.

Terrified, I stumbled back to my bed, trying to get as far away from them as possible, but my legs tangled in the sheets, trapping me in place.

Crack.

Another sound came from the man's body as Sergio kept kicking him.

And then he leaned down and pulled the mask off the guy's face.

The man spat at Sergio.

Sergio uttered, "Bad choice," before punching the guy across the jaw, blood spewed everywhere. It was nothing like I'd seen on TV.

It was messier.

And loud.

So loud.

I could hear the guy bruising, breaking, the metallic smell of blood filled the room as Frank burst through the door followed by my uncles and finally Dante.

"Recognize him?" Sergio asked in a detached voice.

"No," Frank said. "You?"

Sergio shook his head.

Sal, Papi, and Gio exchanged concerned looks before the man grabbed a knife and surged toward Frank.

Sergio was on him in seconds, using the guy's own knife against him and stabbing him in the throat, then with a quick movement of his hands, snapping his neck in half.

He fell to the floor in a bloody heap.

And that's when I started screaming.

With a curse, Dante was at my side, pulling me into his arms, but I didn't want Dante. He wasn't my comforter anymore. I might as well have been hugging a wall instead of my twin.

I didn't know who I wanted.

No one?

Maybe I just needed to be alone.

I was able to suck in a deep breath and stop screaming, which was good, because the only thing scarier than someone else's scream — is hearing your own but not registering that it's your voice until a few minutes later.

"Shh, Val it's okay, you're safe." Dante whispered reaching for my body again.

"Clearly!" Who was that yelling? Not me. I never yelled. I wasn't the type. But there I was, losing my mind! "Was I safe ten minutes ago?"

Nobody would look at me in the eyes.

"How did you guys even hear him come in?"

Again no eye contact.

"I was worried," Sergio whispered. "There have been a few veiled threats so I was coming by to double check your window when—"

"—you saved my life," I finished for him, unwilling to break the stare down we both had going on.

He didn't nod or even acknowledge the fact that he'd just done something so heroic.

Not that snapping a man's neck won him a medal or anything.

Which brought on a whole different issue.

I started to hyperventilate. "What about the police? We need to call the cops and—"

Frank laughed. My uncle actually laughed at me and then sobered. "Sorry, it's been a while since I've been around someone outside of the Family. We do not need cops."

"But." I frowned. "You have to report a crime."

"There was no crime," Frank said in a smooth voice.

"Tomorrow they will find his burned body in a car along with several murder weapons that tie him into a drug dealer of our choice and, to add to the effect, I'll toss in a few bags of cocaine."

"C-cocaine," I whispered. "You have drugs?"

Again silence.

"Right." I nodded. "I um..." I was mumbling again, I moved past every man in the room on lead filled legs and kept on walking. I remember touching the stairs because my naked feet were cold against the hardwood.

I went to the kitchen but everything was... foreign.

So I walked from the kitchen into the living room and sat Indian style in front of the fire, pulling my knees up to my chest, as if that was going to make the fact that Sergio had just snapped someone's neck in half okay.

As if it would make the whole idea that there were drugs and no cops and happy accidents where murder was blamed on others... okay.

I had no idea how long I stared into the flames of the fire. It was long enough for the log to turn to char, long enough to feel the first bit of a chill inching into my bones.

"Get up."

"What?" I shook my head then turned around. Sergio was towering over me, his face indifferent. "Are you serious right now?"

"Get. Off. Your. Ass."

Terrified, I scrambled to my feet then was so overrun with anger at the situation, I slapped him across the face.

Which of course meant he was going to kill me,

right?

Gasping, I stumbled backward.

Only, Sergio burst out laughing.

Hard.

Irritated, I lunged for him again, but this time he caught my wrists with his hands and set me aside. "Good to know that you won't back down in a fight."

"I…" Embarrassed, I looked down. "I'm sorry."

"Don't be," he whispered. "Do it again."

I narrowed my eyes. "What?"

"Hit me."

"I'm not going to hit you."

"You're a spoiled rotten little child, who's a danger to herself and should be given her own curfew along with a glass of juice every damn night. Slap me."

So I did.

He winced, then took a step back and rubbed his jaw, his fingertips tapping against the spot I'd just hit. "That's good."

"You were mean."

"I'm always mean."

Man had a point.

"Slapping is fine for girls." Sergio crossed his arms. "But we need to teach you how to escape. Had I been two minutes later, had I hesitated and gone to the bathroom, grabbed a glass of water, answered my phone — we wouldn't be having this conversation. So I'm going to teach you how to survive, and you're not going to bitch about it, and you sure as hell aren't going to cry. Got it?"

There was something terrifying about the way he spoke to me, about how he was able to get under my skin, but made it seem like the most normal thing in my world.

He made violence look easy.

He made it appear necessary.

He made me believe I needed it.

"Okay." I nodded probably five times, trying to convince myself that agreeing with a guy who, about ten minutes ago, was snapping a dude's neck, was a stellar idea.

"I'm going to come at you." Sergio held out his hands. "I want you to fight me off. I don't want you to worry about hurting me, believe me when I say, I've had the worst of the worst, so..." His smile mocked me. "Do your worst, little girl."

He'd just called me "little girl."

I wanted to stab him in the throat.

AH! Stupid effing mafia.

I couldn't even say more than effing.

It made me blush.

If I had trouble *cursing* in my head, how was I supposed to attack... that?

I choked on my spit, trying to swallow and take a breath at the same time, then waited while he charged me.

His muscled arms grabbed my body, pinning mine to the side.

All I had were my legs.

So I stomped on his feet.

He didn't even move.

So I kneed him in the balls. He dropped like a stone, his face stark white as a garbled sound squeaked past his tightly drawn lips.

Breath whooshed out as he made a gargled sound then yelled, "Fucking hell!" He touched his face. "What was that for?"

"You said you've had the worst of the worst!" I shot back. "And that I needed to escape!"

A pained laugh escaped. "I deserved that, I think."

"You did." I smiled proudly.

"Help me up?"

I took his outstretched hand, only to have him tug me down the floor and as he stretched out on top of me and whispered. "Survive."

"That was a mean trick."

"Necessary," he murmured. "Because the minute I was down, you should have run like hell."

"Oh, good idea. I'll just run back upstairs to the room with the *body* in it! That seems like a really poor life choice."

"It's dead." His eyes did that weird searching thing as he gazed down at me. "What could it possibly do to you?"

"Well..." I licked my lips. "Turn into a cocaine addicted zombie?"

"Nice imagination there, Val. Is it going to force you to do drugs too?"

"Yes," I stammered. "And I listened in school during the drug talk thank you very much."

"I bet you did." He seemed to find humor in that as his lips twitched. "Straight A's? And let me guess, you got one of those shiny certificates they give out for having perfect attendance."

My cheeks burned.

"You're blushing," he pointed out. "So it must be true."

I said nothing. What was there to say? He seemed to know everything already.

"Did you even go to prom?" He picked and prodded at every insecurity I had — swear.

"Can you get off of me now?"

I wasn't sure what I'd said but he suddenly looked horrified and then smug.

"What? Why are you giving me that funny look?"

"Was I your first kiss?"

"Sergio." I kept my voice firm. "You're literally crushing my body right now."

He lifted his weight off but kept me pinned, straddling me and then slowly moved his hands to my face as he tilted my chin toward him. "Answer."

"I've never met someone so demanding in my entire life. And I live with three overprotective uncles and a twin."

"Just answer the question, Val."

I wanted to look away but his gaze held me. "Yes."

"Yes, what?" he prompted.

"Yes," I yelled. "All right? You were my first kiss. And now that my humiliation is complete I'd REALLY like to sleep on the couch and try to forget the fact that you probably still have blood on your hands.

"Washed," he answered gruffly, and when I gave him a doubtful look he pulled one hand up and showed me. "I know how to get blood off my hands."

"Well if that isn't the most uncomforting statement…"

"How was it?" He licked his lips again, this time leaning in.

"Bloody." I refused to suffer more humiliation.

"Val," he said my name slowly, drawing it out, like he wanted to say it, like I wanted to hear a man say it. Which was so stupid, but when you're in the moment, when you have over two hundred pounds of muscle straddling you, and looking at you, not through you, how are you supposed to respond? It's not like I could swoon, I was already lying down and I wasn't the type, I was more terrified of him than I was attracted.

Mostly.

His blue eyes flashed.

Okay, so not mostly.

But he was violent.

Snapped a man's neck, snapped... a... man's... neck!

His hand moved from my chin to my hair and then to the back of my head as he gently pulled me until we were about a half an inch away from tasting one another. "I can do better."

"Don't," I whispered.

He jerked back a bit. "Don't kiss you?"

"Please." I was ready to plead with him, like he held my life in the palm of his hand, when really, it was just my heart, but just as important to a girl who needed to build a fortress of concrete and locks around it. "Don't toy with me."

"Kissing is just kissing." He didn't believe a word that came out of his mouth. I knew it, he knew it.

"Not for me," I said urgently. "Please, Sergio, please get off of me. I'm tired."

Surprisingly, he moved off of me and helped me to my feet, but the minute I tried to go back up the stairs he tugged me back. "You're stuck with me tonight. Don't worry I'll sleep on the floor, Frank has a cleanup crew coming in a few minutes, so it looks like I should add another few logs to the fire. You take the couch."

"But—"

"For once in your life, try not arguing when someone is doing everything in their power to keep you safe, yes?"

"Yes." Properly scolded, I grabbed the afghan from the chair and wrapped my body in it like a little mummy then lay down on the couch.

Watching him stoke the fire was probably a bad idea, a very bad idea, because the outline of his body in the firelight was beautiful.

It made a girl want to throw caution to the wind.

He was going to be my husband.

And the sucky part.

He would never actually be mine.

"Stop sighing," he said without turning around. "It's stressing me out."

"You? Stressed?"

"Me," he said in a clipped voice. "Stressed. I am human you know."

"Hmm."

"What? No snarky comment?" Another log was tossed onto the fire sending sparks flying into the air. "Nothing?"

"You can kill someone in less than one point two seconds." I shivered.

"You counted?"

"Not the point." I turned on my back so I'd stop staring at him like some freak. "The point is, maybe I should learn not to poke the ninja bear."

"Ninja bear?" he repeated. "I think you can come up with a more bad ass name than Ninja bear."

"Nope, Ninja bear it is." I felt somewhat satisfied that his nickname bothered him. "Goodnight."

"Val?"

"Yes?"

The crackling of the fire was starting to grate on my nerves only because it made me more tense. My body was going to be sore from all of the tightening of my muscles on that stupid couch.

Well, that and the fact I probably had a Sergio sized bruise on my front side from him lying across me.

"Don't be scared."

"I won't." My answer was quick, swift, because at least I knew that if it came down to me or some random guy who broke into our house, he'd choose me, every time.

And then a thought occurred.

What if his wife was still alive?

Would he choose her or me? Who would he keep alive?

Her.

Every.

Single.

Time.

"Don't fall in love with me," he'd said.

Well, don't worry, I can't compete, I probably never could.

"Hey, Sergio?"

He turned off the lights and was rustling next to the couch. "What?"

"Tell me a story."

Groaning, I heard a curse and then. "I'm exhausted, Val."

"You were the one who said I was a child, and children get stories, I'll wait…"

"Pain in my ass."

"What was that?"

"So this grumpy prince..." He yawned. "Lived in a castle and was mean to everyone, including his royal subjects, what they didn't know was that the beast thought that by being fierce he would earn respect. One day a fairy visited—"

"Are you re-writing beauty and the beast?" Familiarity washed over me, it was a coincidence, nothing more, that he was talking about Beauty and the Beast.

"Are you interrupting story time?"

"Sorry."

"Nobody understands the beast," Sergio murmured. "Beasts lash out because they are taught only violence, and yet it's this huge shock to everyone when things go awry. Beasts are fierce because they protect what they love. Fierceness has nothing to do with being bad, and everything to do with honoring the good..."

He was convinced about it.

Like he was the beast.

"I don't think you're a beast, Sergio."

"Some days... I think I'm both beast and prince... I just know how to hide it... but the tipping point is always there, and just because the beast protects, doesn't mean *he's* good. Don't confuse my purpose with other emotions. You'll only get hurt."

"I'm well aware of your purpose."

"Oh, yeah?"

"Sure." It was my turn to yawn. "Protect the princess in the tower, give her a kiss, and lock her back in."

He didn't answer.

But maybe it was better that way, because at least then I could imagine a world where his answer was to break me out of the tower, carry me away, and profess his love.

That's how stories were *supposed* to end.

I had a sinking feeling in the pit of my stomach that mine wasn't going to be anywhere near a Happily Ever After ending. It was time to grow up.

Time to accept my fate.

As a woman.

CHAPTER 21

...But I will wed thee in another key; with pomp, with triumph, and with reveling.

–A Midsummer Night's Dream

Sergio

I WAS IN the clouds.

There was blood on my hands.

A gun in my right.

A knife in my left.

"Where am I?" I wondered aloud.

"Mafia heaven." Andi appeared in front of me, dressed in white, just like on our wedding day.

I fell to my knees and hugged her body, burying my face against her full skirt, but tears wouldn't come.

"All dried up? How DARE you!" She laughed and then pulled away and twirled a few times, only to stop and stare at me. "I'm happy."

"Good." I choked on the word. "I'm not."

Her face fell. "And whose fault do you think that is?"

"I hate this dream."

"Dreams are simply our brains' way of processing

emotions, life, stress." She shrugged. "I'm in your dream because you're still processing, that's okay, but so is she..."

"She?" Confused, I looked to where she was pointing. The couch appeared in front of me where Val hugged her body, and a tear ran down her cheek. I reached for her but she disappeared.

"You know you're doing a shitty job when her tears outnumber her smiles."

"Hell." I wiped my face with my hands. "She's not you."

"Right." Andi nodded. "Because if she were, that would mean you were screwing a ghost. Gross, Italy"

I reached for Andi again but she stepped away and danced in front of me. I could watch her for days — years.

"I miss you," I whispered.

But it was as if she didn't hear me. She just kept dancing around in front of me, and then she paused and glanced over her shoulder. "I'm gone, Sergio."

"I know but—"

"Ashes to ashes, dust to dust..." She started to disappear in front of my eyes. "I'm gone."

And then when I couldn't see her anymore the wind whispered.

"But I'm whole."

I jerked awake in a cold sweat, tears running down my cheeks. I furiously wiped at them then caught a movement from the corner of my eye. Val sat up with a wide-eyed stare.

And then without saying anything, she slowly moved from the couch to the floor and held out her hand.

I stared at it.

With a huge sigh, she reached for my hand and picked it up, squeezed, and didn't let go.

I was still staring at our hands pressed together when she tugged me down to a sleeping position, still beside me.

Too upset to sleep, I stared at the spot just above her forehead where her pretty hair parted to the side.

"Tell me about her," Val whispered.

My eyes stung with unshed tears.

"She was... brave." There was so much more, but the words wouldn't get past my lips.

Val didn't respond. I thought she was asleep, but when I glanced down, she was staring at me as if to encourage me to go on.

So I did.

"And beautiful, and irritating as hell, and freakishly loud, and extremely violent." It was like once I started talking I couldn't stop. "She held me at gun point more than I'd like to admit, kicked my ass twice, and liked to wake me up at six a.m. just to piss me off. She made me promise not to cry over her, and here I am waking up with tears. God, I hate weakness."

"So she kicked your ass?" Val smiled. "And she irritated you?"

"You would fixate on those two things."

"Well, the tears are depressing."

"True."

Somehow I'd pulled her closer, and it felt good, comforting. Damn, I'd been too long without comfort, like a man making his penance in the Sahara without food and water. I clung to her like a lifeline.

"I'm not her." Val shrugged. "And just because I'm saying yes, doesn't mean I'm taking her place."

"I know."

"No." Val smiled sadly. "You don't. But that's okay.

Just know that whenever you want to talk about her, I'll listen."

She tucked her head into my shoulder and closed her eyes.

And just like that, one of the broken pieces from two months ago floated up off the ground and found its rightful place in the corner of my heart.

One piece.

Out of a million.

But it was a start.

I woke up pressed against Val. Unlike Andi, she wasn't a violent sleeper, but apparently, Andi had left that gift with me. My arms were sprawled all over Val, and somehow I was halfway on top of her, pressing my head between the valley of her breasts.

Like a teen trying to motorboat a stripper.

Shit.

I backed away slowly so I wouldn't wake her up, only to see her eyes lock on mine.

Awkward didn't even begin to cover it.

"You done?" she asked, her breathing a bit heavy.

I opened my mouth then closed it.

A pan, or something that sounded like one, dropped in the kitchen. Laughing commenced and the moment disappeared.

I scrambled off her and stood. "Thanks, Val."

I didn't want to add *for last night* because that made

it sound sordid, like we'd done more than just slept together, and I was about five seconds away from doing the walk of shame back to my hotel room.

"Anytime..." Her pretty smile grew. She was beautiful, not just pretty but beautiful. I wanted to hate her beauty. Her beauty meant I had to stay away. Instead, I found myself staring at her, really staring.

"Sis!" Dante charged into the room. "Your hair looks like a bird took a shit in it."

I fought back a smile as Val's hands moved to her head and with a gasp she tried pulling the pieces of golden brown into a ponytail.

It just made it look worse.

I honestly hadn't even noticed her hair.

Just her face.

Her gorgeous full lips and wide innocent eyes.

Damn me.

With a curse I turned around and called back, "I'll see you guys at church."

"Church!" Val yelled. "What time is it?"

"Late!" Dante answered, and running commenced right before I left and slammed the screen door behind me.

The New York City air was brisk, cold, the perfect chill to get rid of the fact that I'd been aroused when I'd awakened up with Val's soft body pressed against me.

Which was the exact opposite of what we both needed.

To confuse our relationship more.

And her place in it.

Business arrangement — never a real marriage.

Hah, I'd said that before, and look where it had gotten me. Sobbing my eyes out in my dreams.

175

I decided against taking a taxi and walked.

Three blocks away from their house, I noticed a man tailing me, only he was being completely obvious about it, so obvious that it had to be on purpose.

Sighing, I ducked into a nearby Starbucks, ordered two black coffees, and grabbed the newspaper.

He arrived three minutes later and sat across from me.

I slid the coffee toward him without looking up from my paper and spoke. "I didn't add cream but feel free."

"You're good."

"I'm an ex-FBI informant and from one of the most powerful mafia families in the US. Of course I'm good. And you're too obvious, so what do you want. Who has sent you?"

"Right down to business." He chuckled.

I set the newspaper down and met his gaze. Dark brown eyes, wavy hair with threads of silver and, a gold cap on his right canine tooth. He appeared around six two, but not a muscular six two. "Yes, well, it is what I do best."

"Xavier." He took a long sip of his coffee. "Would like a meeting with the Cappo."

Why the hell would the person Frank had left in charge want to meet with Tex? Only one reason. To either ask for protection or challenge the Cappo.

"That can be arranged, but riddle me this, what does a Russian want with the Cappo?"

"That question should be directed to him." The man stood and offered his hand.

I didn't shake it.

With a chuckle, he put it away. "We will be in touch,

yes?"

"I'll find you." It was a veiled threat. "Either way."

Paling, he took a step back and then narrowed his eyes. "You are not as tough as you think you are."

God, save me from such idiots. If he even knew how many kills I had, what I'd done with the very hand he'd wanted to shake.

I stood, revealing that one hand had been in my pocket the whole time, and that pocket held a gun.

His eyes narrowed as he looked down.

"Don't make me do my job today. I'm off the clock." I smirked. "Then again, overtime pays—"

He held up his hands. Luckily, the Starbucks' customers weren't paying attention. "Sorry."

"For?"

"My insult."

"Do it again…" I took three steps toward him until we were chest to chest. "…And I'll rip your throat out and put a mirror in front of your face so you can watch."

He nodded.

"Like I said, I'll find you either way, now run along. I've gotta get ready for church." I slapped his face twice, dismissing him. With a glare that was probably supposed to intimidate, he turned on his heel and hurried out of the Starbucks, while I made a beeline for my hotel. Mass was in an hour, and I still smelled like Val.

And Andi.

But her scent, Val's scent, was something… softer.

At first it had seemed the same.

Now it was separating.

It could be the actual perfume was different, or that

the same scent was unique on each person.

Either way, it was another reminder.

"I'm not her," she'd said.

No. She wasn't. But maybe… that was good.

I'd been given the exact opposite of Andi, meaning, I couldn't compare them, because they were nothing alike.

I turned around again to make sure dip shit wasn't following me and took the long way to the hotel only leaving myself a half hour to shower and get changed.

I'd only barely stepped out of the shower when my phone buzzed.

Chase: *The Eagle has landed.*

Sergio: *You're an idiot.*

Chase: *Where the hell is that damn middle finger emoji? Whatever, I'm middle finger emojing you right now.*

Sergio: *Repeat what you just typed. Out loud.*

Chase: *Still doing it.*

Sergio: *See you guys at the house?*

Chase: *Hell no, see you at church!*

Well, either we were going to all burn in hell — or God would be forgiving. One could only hope it would be the latter.

CHAPTER 22

Moon take thy flight, now die, die, die.
—A Midsummer Night's Dream

Valentina

"HE'S NOT HERE yet," Dante said in a bored voice as the priest raised his hands above his head.

I scowled and stood with the rest of my family. "Glory to God in the highest…" I moved my lips, but I wasn't singing, I was too busy wondering where Sergio and Frank were. Regardless of what Dante thought, it wasn't because I liked Sergio.

At least not fully.

It was more the idea that he could be in danger.

Or dead.

My stomach dropped.

Was that my future? Whenever he was late, I'd wonder if he was bleeding out in an alleyway?

Shivering, I wrapped my arms around myself and sat with the rest of the congregation.

The priest pressed his hands in front of his chest and opened his mouth, but no words came out.

A sudden tense chill filled the air as the door to the cathedral opened and then shut with a loud clang.

The priest's eyes were riveted on the doors.

The low buzz of whispering filled the air and then footsteps, several of them, loud, purposeful. Slowly, heads began to turn, mine included.

"Holy shit," Dante breathed.

Sal elbowed him in the ribs.

My mouth dropped open.

My mind shrieked.

Danger, danger!

Run!

Words I should listen to.

But I didn't.

The first man looked vaguely familiar, but I couldn't place him. He was wearing a black suit, expensive. Aviators covered his eyes, and his brown hair had shots of red in it, he was also as big as a giant.

On his right and left were two guys that matched him in muscle, not in height. One had a lip ring and wore a T-shirt, as if he couldn't care less that he was in church. Tattooed sleeves lined both arms, at least he was in dark skinny jeans and boots, but there was clearly a gun in his right hand.

Both of the guys who flanked the giant were so attractive that I couldn't stop staring. Even the one with the tattoos was captivating.

The one on the right had longer dark hair that was combed to the side, nearly touching his other ear. His gun was at least tucked into his jeans, though, I got the distinct impression it wouldn't take him long to have it out and lethal.

Three.

Three men.

And another right behind them.

A man who looked haunted, his eyes bloodshot but clear, as if he could see right through you, see all of your fears and make them happen with a simple snap of his fingers. He didn't have as many tattoos, and he wasn't packing — at least that I could see. But his face, there was something about his face that told me he had nothing against breaking someone in half for looking at him wrong.

He scared me.

More than the others.

Yet he was the only one that made eye contact with the congregation, as if searching for someone, and then, when he locked eyes with me...

He smiled.

It transformed his entire face.

I gasped.

"Friend of yours?" Dante said under his breath.

"I highly doubt that man has many friends."

"Probably killed them all," Dante said in a low voice.

Frank and Sergio brought up the end of the group.

And, just like that, everything snapped into place.

These weren't normal guys.

They were mafia.

But with the way everyone was staring, they weren't just any kind of mafia, they weren't familiar at all.

"So it begins," Sal said to my left. "And so it begins."

"Sal..." I tried to keep my voice down. "Who are they?"

He seemed to pale on the spot as he looked down at his lap then back up at me. "Judge, jury, and

181

executioner."

That wasn't very helpful.

The only pew that was empty was behind us.

Meaning, the men shuffled loudly into the seats behind us and sat with a loud thump.

One of the guys spoke. I wasn't sure which one because I promised myself I wouldn't turn around and openly gape anymore.

"Sorry we're late, father." The guy's voice was deep, commanding. I shivered. "Please, do continue."

All eyes went to the priest as he lifted his shaking hands into the air and whispered, "Let us pray."

Hah, let us pray indeed.

I FIDGETED IN my seat as the priest droned on and on.

"So," a voice whispered in my ear. "You're her."

Sal glared at me then at the guy behind me.

I turned, just slightly and came face to face with crisp blue eyes and soft lips. He smelled really good. Of course he did because he couldn't just walk around with a face like that and smell horrible right?

"Chase..." The giant shook his head slowly. "Control yourself."

The guy with the tattoos rolled his eyes and then pulled Chase back by his jacket. "We don't let him out much."

"Shh!" Frank hissed from farther down the pew.

The giant held up his hands in innocence while

Chase winked at me.

Sal elbowed me hard in the side. I quickly turned back around and tried to pay attention, which was basically impossible. What did he mean I'm her?

"...Holy Communion." The priests words blurred into obscurity as my mind searched for possible reasons why the men behind me were suddenly in New York.

And why Sergio didn't tell me.

I had no right to be hurt.

But I was just the same.

And I had no idea why!

We weren't married yet.

And I knew nothing about his world. This just proved, yet again, how different our lives were.

The elements were blessed, more prayers were said, I yawned, and then it was finally time to get out of my seat. My butt was falling asleep so I welcomed the change, at least mass was almost over.

Usually the rows were dismissed from front to back.

Going out of order made absolutely no sense.

Instead, nobody stood with me. Frowning, I looked around, and finally behind me.

All of the men stood and made their way out into the main aisle.

"Come." Sal stood with me. "It is time."

Time for what?

Communion?

Because it felt like something else was going on, something important.

The giant moved to the very front and knelt in front of the priest.

"It's okay." The man who had the terrifying look

in his eyes squeezed my hand. "It will make sense one day. All of this."

He was the last person I assumed would comfort me.

Where was Sergio when I needed him?

He was a few men back, I peered around the scary guy to look at him, but when I did, he ignored me and looked away.

As if we hadn't shared any sort of moment this morning.

I was back to square one.

The ignorant child that he couldn't care less about.

"I'm Phoenix." The guy placed a hand on my shoulder. "Now, it's time to watch."

"Watch?" I whispered back.

"Look." He pointed to the priest and the giant.

The priest held his hands above his head and started chanting in Italian. I didn't know my own language, but it was beautiful. I understood certain words, like "blessings" and "our leader."

"*Capo di tutti capi, amen.*" The priest kissed the giants forehead and then his right hand.

He repeated the gesture for the tattooed guy, only he didn't say as many words, simply kissed his forehead and his right hand.

Every man that had come in late received some sort of weird ritualistic blessing.

And then, they were presented with communion, leaving me, Dante, Sal, Papi, and Gio standing by ourselves in the aisle while everyone watched.

When the priest was done with Sergio and Frank, he looked to Gio and held out his hands.

"It is time." Sal's voice sounded heavy, sad.

Time for what?

Gio went first.

Then Sal.

Papi was last.

Leaving me and Dante.

Nobody was speaking.

The church was deathly quiet.

Phoenix, the one who'd been nice, walked forward and stretched out his arms in front of us. *"Sangue del mio sangue. Sangue dentro fuori. Questo sangue simboleggia la famiglia."* He turned over his right hand, palm open, then whispered, "Your right hand please."

Trembling I gave him my right hand.

He pulled a knife from his pocket and with the sharpest point of it, pricked my finger and squeezed. Sudden, sharp pain in my finger reminded me of the stab from a rose thorn. A drop of blood welled.

The giant made his way toward us, holding out something that looked like a single playing card that had been removed from the rest of the deck. Phoenix squeezed until six drops of blood fell against the card.

He released my hand, moved over to my brother, and repeated the same words and actions, using the exact same card. Tears pricked my eyes as my body trembled. I brushed my thumb over the spot that had been pricked.

"Tu vivi dal sangue, si muore dal sangue, Benvenuti alla famiglia Valentina e Dante Nicolasi."

The church stood and repeated the entire phrase word for word, in Italian.

Nicolasi.

It was my father's last name.

The giant kissed my forehead and then Dante's.

Dante trembled next to me, as though he fully understood what was taking place. But I was still in the dark. Tears blurred my line of vision as heaviness settled into my chest.

I wasn't sure if I was scared.

Or if, for the first time in my life, I finally felt the rightness of belonging to something greater than myself.

The priest motioned to us. "Come forward, daughter and son of Luca Nicolasi, and receive your blessing from God."

Dante grabbed my hand in his and led us the few steps to the priest.

The altar was set with the Eucharist, and yet, we weren't taking communion.

We were getting initiated.

"Will you receive?" the priest asked us.

"Yes." I could barely hear my own voice as he placed one hand on my head and one hand on Dante's and repeated something similar to what he'd said over the giant.

When he released his hands, he addressed the congregation.

"May God bless the Families."

"May God bless the Families." They answered back in unison and stood. Then slowly, one by one, they approached the front to kiss each of our hands.

Over one hundred people.

When the last person left and the door slammed shut, I slumped against Dante, exhausted, hungry, extremely confused, and more than a little upset that Sergio hadn't warned me.

He could have at least said, *Hey by the way you should*

probably wear comfortable shoes for mass.

Without thinking, I kicked off my heels, nearly impaling Phoenix in the thigh with one of them.

"Oops." Warmth invaded my cheeks. "Sorry."

"Eh, desperate times." He gave me a kind smile while Sergio glowered at him. "Now you get territorial?"

Territorial?

"Back off," Sergio snapped, still not looking at me.

Hurt must have been evident on my face because Phoenix shoved Sergio and pulled out a knife. "You could have at least warned her."

"I refused to take the chance that she would run," Sergio said in an even tone as all eyes fell to me.

Somehow, I found my voice, or maybe just the last bit of bravery I possessed. Because I stood and glared in his direction. "See, that's the thing about friendship. You learn how to trust someone. You give them information, fully aware of what they'll do with that information based on the relationship you have with them. So he was right to question me, since he's done nothing to prove that he's anything but a babysitter out to make sure I get in bed on time." I swallowed back tears and nodded to Gio. "Please take me home, now, Gio."

With sad eyes, Gio reached for my arm and led me out of the church, past a furious Sergio.

When the doors were nearly shut behind us, all I could hear was colorful ways to say the word ass.

CHAPTER 23

Love can transpose to form and dignity.
Love looks not with the eyes, but with the mind;
And therefore is winged Cupid painted blind.
Nor hath Love's mind of any judgment taste.
Wings and no eyes figure unheedy haste.
                                    –A Midsummer Night's Dream

Sergio

I PUT UP with their shit the entire drive back to the neighborhood. In five minutes I was going to have to face her, yet again, and feel nothing. It was unfair to ask her to go back to the way things were.

Where I was mean, cold, available, but distant.

We'd made leaps and bounds that morning. Hell we'd made leaps and bounds since the movie theater, but seeing the guys again reminded me of too much pain.

All that progress simply dissipated when Chase and Tex started bickering, because it reminded me of *her*, damn it. Everything they did reminded me of her. She'd fit in perfectly with them.

She'd been like one of the guys.

And Val wasn't.

She was soft. Scared. Vulnerable.

She was the exact opposite of what I needed.

If Tex pulled a knife on her she'd pass out.

Andi would have stabbed him in the throat then asked where the popcorn was.

I was being unfair, comparing them, but that was what you did when you'd already had love and lost it — there was a giant measuring stick that nobody could even stand next to because you knew, even before they did, that they'd come up short every time.

We pulled up to the house, I unbuckled my seatbelt but Nixon slammed a hand against my chest.

"Stay." His teeth snapped into a tight clench that hinted at how pissed he was.

Everyone got out of the car except for Chase.

Nixon let out a groan. "Really, man? Don't make me shoot you. Just go, I'll give you details later."

"Kill joy," Chase muttered then slammed the door behind him leaving me and Nixon in a super fun tense silence.

I just loved being alone with him and his twitchy finger. Hell, he probably had three guns on him and, at least two of those, magically trained on me just for shits and giggles.

"Cousin?" I licked my lips. "Do we have a problem?"

"We?" His eyebrows shot up. "You're a piece of shit, you know that right?"

"Fully aware but it's always nice to hear compliments from family."

"And a jackass." He pounded my chest with his hand, shoving me against the seat.

"Noted."

"And an idiot."

"Yup."

With a sigh, he released me and ran his tattooed hands through his unruly hair. "My wife's pregnant. I don't want to be here. Phoenix is one phone call away from needing to fly a red-eye back to Chicago because Bee's in her last trimester, and I had to physically restrain Mil to keep her from hopping on a plane to kick you in the nuts."

"We needed one boss to stay behind."

"Right, you say that to her and see where it gets you."

I smirked.

"None of this is funny. They're initiated, fine, they're in, the blood's been spilled... but we need a decision, and we need to get them out of here, and we need to do it in a way that doesn't seem like we're putting them back in hiding. Add in your whole 'Xavier wants to meet with Tex' information you dropped on us this morning, not to mention the irritating fact that the very girl you're supposed to be helping looks like she wants to put a bullet between your eyes, and well..." He leaned his head back against the seat. "Hell, Frank needs to stop keeping information from us."

"More Phoenix than Frank."

"Damn Phoenix."

"Nixon, this job is mine, not yours."

His mocking laugh wasn't helpful. "And you think you're doing a bang up job? A promise is a promise, you need to marry her."

"I know that."

"And the other part?"

I stared down at my hands.

"Sergio, you've told her the other part, right?"

I bit down on my lower lip and looked out the window at all the ignorant people who passed our car. If they only knew.

"She deserves to know what she's getting into, Sergio."

"And she does."

"But does she know what else Luca said? What he demanded? For her protection?"

My chest was so tight it was hard to breathe. "No."

"She thinks your marriage will be in name only." Nixon said it like a statement. "Doesn't she?"

"A simple business agreement." I felt numb, from head to toe, numb.

"Aw, hell, Serg, your days are numbered, man."

"I was going to tell her after we were married."

"So she could kill you in your sleep?"

"She's not violent."

Something white fluttered out of the window and landed on our car.

I blinked, my mind struggling to make sense of what my eyes were seeing.

A wedding dress.

That had been shredded with scissors.

"Not violent, hmm?"

"Son of a bitch." I punched the leather seat with my fist and reached for the door.

"Sergio, tell her before we leave."

"Tonight?"

He nodded.

"And Xavier?"

"Tex means to poke the bear. We bow down now

or later, he chooses later. We'll deliver a message and gauge his response."

"What kind of message?"

"Sorry, Frank already called dibs."

"Nixon!" I groaned. "You know it would be helpful if I shot something."

"Shoot Chase, he's still a pain in my ass, but this demonstration is all Frank's. Besides, it's his mess. Let him clean it up."

"Fine." I opened the door just as a shoe box fell directly in front of my face colliding with my boots.

The heels popped out of the box.

I froze.

They were Andi's

I'd recognize those shoes anywhere.

Barely noticeable grass stains marred the spiked heel, and a piece of blue fabric had been sewn across the open toe.

Without thinking, I gathered them in my hands and charged into the house, ready to toss Val over my knee if that's what it took to get a confession.

Maybe I'd shoot something after all.

Her.

For wrecking yet another memory of my dead wife.

CHAPTER 24

How can these things come to pass? O, how mine eyes do loathe his visage now!

> –A Midsummer Night's Dream

Frank

SERGIO DAMN NEAR took off the door. His aggression was palpable, the air tinged with his bitterness, his anger. I let out a sigh as he rushed past me and took the stairs two at a time.

The rest of the men communed in the kitchen.

I stayed back.

The sound of wine pouring and Sergio yelling at Val filled the air.

I leaned against the stairway, wincing. My bones ached. There used to be days I would go without sleep, where the sunlight and darkness melted into one another in consecutive hours, time slipped away.

And now, time it seemed, was doing the exact same thing.

"Bless him, Father," I mumbled under my breath. Was that my sin then? To bear the weight of poor choices on my shoulders, while Luca toasted to Andi in heaven?

It was as if each jagged piece I tried to pick up and put back together again embedded itself into my skin. I bled, I bled, I bled some more, and then the piece would finally attach itself. The process would repeat.

Because where there was pain.

There was also healing.

I shut my eyes just as Phoenix rounded the corner. "Do you hear that?"

"I hear everything. I'm not deaf." Not that old either, but I was tired of arguing my point every damn time one of the young ones opened their mouths to bitch.

"He's yelling—" Phoenix's voice lowered "—at an innocent girl."

"That's life." I opened my eyes and stared him down. "That's her lot in life, Phoenix. Sometimes we yell, not so others will listen, but because we hurt so deeply within — screaming is the only option."

"It's a shitty option." Phoenix's eyes were wild. "She can't defend herself, not like Andi did."

"She isn't Andi." My voice was calm, because even I, the eldest, the one who had seen the most death was, still, in my own way, mourning a life that Luca had deemed worthy of the Family, a life was still a life, and it meant something, even to me. "She will never be Andi."

Phoenix pointed up at the stairs. "But does he know that?"

"Of course." I slapped Phoenix on the shoulder. "It is why he yells."

He swallowed, looking away as the weight of my

hand pressed into him.

We were silent.

I was often silent with Phoenix.

He wasn't a man who talked through things, but, oh, how he thought. He thought with the best of them, his brain calculating, his judgments swift.

"Do you remember?" A sad smile started at the corner of his right cheek and spread across to his left, the motion making him look more human. "All her little... tasks?"

I chuckled, and removed my hand. "I remember she was a pain in your ass as much as she was a pain in mine."

"Frank!"

I stood, trying to escape, Phoenix gave me a helpless look as Andi breezed into the room carrying a giant box, papers fluttered out of it. "Shit!" She stomped her foot and grabbed the papers then nearly fell across the table until Phoenix rescued her and sat her in the chair. She was losing strength too fast.

When you loved someone, you wished for death to be swift, not slow with uncalculated highs or lows that the human brain couldn't possibly keep up with or manage.

"Okay, so here's the deal." Andi stood, even though she should be resting, since she'd just gotten out of the hospital. "Sergio's kind of a jackass."

Phoenix rolled his eyes. "Yes, let's keep making true statements all day long. That sounds like fun."

"And..." Andi said, holding up her hand. "...he's going to revert to his jackass ways once I'm gone."

Phoenix opened his mouth then stared at me as he whispered, "I'd rather not talk about you... being gone."

"Tough shit." Andi punched him in the shoulder. "Now,

open the box and let me explain."

I eyed the wine, Andi caught me staring and, with an over-exaggerated sigh, she poured us both two healthy glasses and then whispered, "It's going to be epic."

"What is?" Phoenix asked. Brave man.

"His story," Andi whispered. "His love story is going to be epic."

I rejected the thought.

And then I saw the tears well in her eyes. To be peaceful about one's death, to plan for your spouse's happily ever after, knowing you would never get one.

It took guts.

It took bravery.

And I vowed right then and there, I would do everything in my power to help her.

Until I was killed.

Or God took me from this earth.

Because finally, I'd found something worthy to live for.

Funny how it had been staring at me all this time without my knowledge. Joyce would have laughed at me. Luca would have said something cheeky about knowing all along.

I was going to fight.

Not for my own love.

But for his.

Because, God, if anyone on this earth deserved it...

It was Sergio.

"You can't say a word beyond what I tell you..." Andi pulled out a journal and began to write. "From Russia, With love."

"You okay, Frank?" Phoenix frowned. "You look a little, pale."

"Memories," I said in a gruff tone. "It appears they age me."

He let out a snort. "They age us all."

Sergio's voice rose again. I nodded in the direction of the stairway. "Give him a warning, enough to jar him out of his insanity, don't kill him."

Sergio yelled louder.

"You sure about the not killing part?" Phoenix reached for his gun.

"Are you?"

Phoenix gave an eye-roll. "Fine." He took the stairs slowly.

CHAPTER 25

For in the temple by and by with us, these couples shall be eternally knit.

–A Midsummer Night's Dream

Valentina

"WHERE THE HELL did you get these?" Sergio's voice was so loud I was surprised my mirror didn't shatter.

With a huff, I turned around and nearly swallowed my tongue. He cradled the shoes in one hand. In his other hand, he gripped a gun leveled at my head.

"Are you really going to shoot me?" My voice shook. "Over shoes?"

"That depends." His nostrils flared. "Are you really willing to take the chance… over shoes?"

"Neiman Marcus." I clenched my fists. "The box you told me to open, so I can only assume they're either from you or Frank."

"Not me." His teeth snapped together. "I would never give you something so precious."

"I'm not even worth a pair of used shoes!" I yelled. "You're such a bastard!" He was still pointing the gun at me, but I was done. Done with his attitude, with his ability to string me along and then cut that same string, only to mend it and try all over again.

It was cruel and unfair. I started for the door.

"No!" He dropped the gun to the floor and grabbed me by the arm, wrenching me back. "You don't get to leave. This conversation isn't over."

"It is! I'm done!" I yelled struggling to get out of his rock hard arms. "I hate you!"

"And you think I like myself?" He sneered. "You think I want to be this way? How stupid are you?"

"Really stupid." I kept struggling. "Because every time I let you in, you destroy everything!"

"Oh, so it's my fault?"

"I'm sorry about the shoes! Okay?" I stopped struggling and slumped to the ground, basically sitting at his feet. "I'm sorry that I threw them, that I allowed my anger with you to overshadow the fact that I was given a gift and didn't accept it."

Sergio's face fell. "They weren't from me."

"I know. Because I don't deserve shoes." I looked down at my bare feet. I didn't even get pedicures.

Never had I felt so young.

Or ugly.

Or just... worthless.

"Heard some commotion so—" Chase knocked on the door and let himself in part way, I could see Phoenix close on his heels, gun drawn.

In one fluid motion, Sergio grabbed the gun off the floor and pointed it at Chase. "Leave."

Chase's eyes narrowed as he glanced past the gun to my sitting position on the floor. "Are you okay?" He held his hand out, stopping Phoenix from barreling in the room. As it was, Phoenix looked ready to rip someone's head off.

"Yeah." I found my voice. "Maybe he'll get lucky and accidently shoot me so he doesn't have to marry me."

Chase's face transformed from one of concern to complete rage. His movements were quick, precise as he jumped into the air, and punched Sergio in the face, and then threw him onto the floor. Phoenix watched, fists clenched. "Shoot her, I shoot you, and we both know your face is all you have since you've never been guilty of a shining personality."

Sergio was on his back, but I knew he was better than that, almost like he wanted Chase to kick his ass because he wasn't able to do it to himself.

"Got it," Sergio whispered.

Chase released him and eyed me. "He won't hurt you."

"I know."

"Do you? Really?" Chase reached around to his back and pulled a gun from his jeans. I jerked, I couldn't help it. Guns were dangerous, they were violent. I had been taught to fear them.

He handed the heavy object to me and motioned to Sergio. "If he gets feisty, point at his leg and shoot, can't really hurt much — and if you hit his dick, you get a prize."

I laughed through my rage and nervousness. "What kind?"

"A big one, for hitting the smallest target." Chase held up his hand for a high five. I hit it, he saluted me and left.

I quickly put the gun on the floor, careful to set the

pointy part away from my body just in case. Wouldn't that just be ironic? I shoot myself instead of the bully.

"I deserve it." Sergio didn't move, just kept laying on his back, staring up at the ceiling. "You know, if you shoot me in the ribs my lungs will collapse, that would be fun to watch. Or you can hit my heart. It stopped working anyways. Hasn't since...."

"You're a dramatic... ass... hole."

Sergio leaned up on his elbows. "Did you just swear?"

"You bring it out in me."

"That's not a compliment."

"Nope."

I kicked the gun farther away from me and hugged my knees to my chest. "The shoes came in a box, no return address."

"No note?" he asked.

I had to lie. I didn't want him to know about the letters. "No note." Because letters were different, right? "They came with the dress."

"They aren't yours."

"Clearly."

"No, I mean, they were hers." Sergio moved to a sitting position and grabbed one of the heels. "When I packed away all of her things, they were still there, I saw them, I held them, I don't know how the hell they made their way to New York."

"Frank?"

"He's never at my house," Sergio said more to himself than to me. "She wore them on our wedding day."

"Something old, something new, something borrowed—"

"—something blue." He finished. So many warring emotions crossed his face, like he was waging his own personal war. With trembling hands he reached for my right foot and slowly slid the pump on. And that's when it clicked. He was the something borrowed. Sergio. It had been his wedding day, he was the groom, on loan. Until when? We both died?

I shivered as my foot stretched against the shoe.

The perfect fit.

Like Cinderella.

Only this wasn't one of those stories.

Not even close.

I almost wished that they hadn't fit because that would have made sense, the fact that Sergio and I didn't fit.

"They never fit her," he whispered.

Well there went that happy thought.

"But she loved shoes, so she wore them anyway."

"Sergio..." I didn't even know why I was trying. Maybe I liked pain and suffering; maybe I was more mafia than I gave myself credit for. "They're shoes."

"I know."

"Do you?"

He grabbed the other. "I have to tell you something."

"Okay."

He twirled the shoe in his hand a few times. "I married her to protect her. We weren't in love, not right away. In fact, I hated that I had to marry her... because I knew she was dying *before* I said I do."

I sucked in a breath and covered my mouth with my hands.

"Cancer's a heartless bitch." He chucked the shoe at the door. "And the harder I fell, the more it spread.

My love didn't save her, she was too far gone." His voice shook. "She told me about you after she died."

That wasn't weird. Or creepy.

"I knew her?"

"No, I don't think so. If you'd met her you'd remember her." He sighed.

"I'm sorry you had to go through that."

"Me too."

I didn't know what else to say, what else would make it better. There were no words in existence in the human language that could adequately heal his soul — and make him whole. When it came to cancer, words failed every single time, because it stole without warning, like a thief in the night, like the very devil and, if you were lucky, you escaped. If not...

You waited in the dark for your rescue.

A rescue that never came.

"I'm telling you this, not so you feel sorry for me, but so you understand, that twice it's been asked of me to marry. The first time, it was only six months, I fully planned on divorcing her until I fell in love with her."

"And, this time?" I was afraid to ask the question that I knew I needed the answer to. Hadn't he said that one day someone would love me the way I deserved? And look at me with adoration?

I wanted that day more than anything.

To feel needed.

Wanted.

Beautiful.

"Never." His eyes locked on mine. "Luca's wishes were clear. There will be no divorce and, as a way to keep you in the Family, his instructions were... painfully detailed."

My heart thumped against my chest. "I don't understand."

"His greatest desire was for grandchildren."

A choking sensation washed over me, paralyzing my breathing to a shallow wheeze. "Are you saying that we have to... sleep together, can never get divorced, and that I'm going to be stuck in a marriage where every time my husband touches me, he thinks of someone else? Because it sounds like that's what you're saying."

Please be wrong. Please, God.

He swallowed, his eyes filled with pity. "Yes. That's what I'm saying."

"And if I run away?"

"I'll find you. Or someone else will."

So many questions pushed to the forefront of my mind, but one still remained. He rarely looked at me, mainly looked *through* me, and the few brief moments he did stare at me, I couldn't read his expression.

Was that it?

He wasn't attracted to me?

Was I that vain?

That I at least needed him to say, *It's not you it's me. You're beautiful, I'm just sad.* Was that so hard?

I glanced down at my leggings and sweatshirt. It wasn't like I was dressed to kill.

"Can I ask you something?

"You're not crying."

"No." I frowned. "I think I gave up on tears. They change nothing."

"Believe me, I know."

We were a depressing pair.

"Is it me?" I knew I'd lose my nerve if I looked

at him so I stared at a spot on the floor. It was pink, dyed from the spilled nail polish that I'd gotten on my twelfth birthday. Back when things were easy and all I wanted was to have pink nails like the girls on Disney channel. "Do you think, maybe if I looked different, wasn't scared all the time or wasn't so — young?" I almost choked on the word. "Do you think it would be better?"

Cursing, Sergio made his way over to me. His heavy body leaned against mine, and then his hands were on my face. "Look at me."

With a deep breath I looked up.

His eyes penetrated.

They searched.

They *yearned*. "You are beautiful. Young, yes, but still beautiful to any man who's lucky enough to have his sight. I would change nothing about you. Because you're perfect just the way you are."

"I'm scared of guns."

"I guessed that."

"I don't even watch violent movies." I confessed, embarrassed that I'd even asked him to go to a horror movie only out of a need for distraction.

"Not a shock."

I just kept talking as he held my face. "I'm insecure."

"People who appear confident usually suffer the most from insecurity."

"I don't know how to fight."

"All humans are born with the basic instinct of fight or flight."

I tried to hang my head he wouldn't let me.

"I can't kiss."

He smirked. "Are you done yet?"

"And I'm a virgin," I blurted. "Now I'm done."

"You're wrong about two things."

His eyes dropped to my lips. "First, you aren't a bad kisser; you just need practice with someone when he's not being a jackass."

"And second?"

His smile didn't quite reach his eyes, but something in his face, in the way his fingers dug into my skin, spoke volumes about the intensity behind his gaze. "You won't be a virgin for long."

I opened my mouth to respond.

Just as his lips slammed against mine.

CHAPTER 26

Awake the pert and nimble spirit of mirth. Turn melancholy
forth to funerals. The pale companion is not for our pomp.
                              –A Midsummer Night's Dream

Sergio

INTUITION TOLD ME to hug her, hold her close, and tell
her everything was going to be okay.

But then I'd be lying.

And I prided myself on my honesty, on my ability
to take the reality of life and deal, even though the days
were filled with horror and bloodshed, because at least
I had that, right?

My truth.

I couldn't hold her close, not the way she wanted.

I couldn't love her, not the way she deserved.

I could offer comfort, physical comfort.

But if she wanted emotional warmth — she was
going to be disappointed. All I had to offer was me.

An empty shell.

With a confused heart.

A broken head.

I kissed her — I was doing that a lot lately, maybe my body was already on board with something my heart wasn't ready for, or maybe…

Just maybe.

It was her.

Not me.

Maybe I'd been looking at the entire situation like a selfish bastard, because it wasn't just my life.

But hers.

And I refused to be the reason that she felt like her life was over. I'd already dealt with that pain, that tragedy, where someone innocent died too young.

There are physical deaths.

And there are spiritual ones.

Only a damned fool would say they were different. They were one in the same. After all, death—

—is death.

She kissed me back, her lips parted as a salty tear met the fusion of our mouths.

In a flurry of sudden movement, Val shoved at my chest and then slapped me across the face.

I was too stunned to do anything except touch the throbbing skin on my right cheek.

Nostrils flaring she gripped me by the shoulders, her mouth nearly touching mine as she said in a clear voice. "First kiss. Remember? And each time it's out of pity. You asked me not to look at you with pity, can you at least do me the same favor? And stop kissing me every time I either piss you off or start crying? We do have to have…" She gulped.

"Sex." I finished for her.

"That." Another nervous swallow. "So you can't go around just… I don't know." Her cheeks turned red.

"Please?"

"Not sure what the meaning was behind that last sentence, but..." I smiled and tugged her body against mine. "I'm going to do it again."

"The pity kiss?"

"Fresh out of those."

"Oh." Her eyes widened. "Oh so, a... yes, that would be..." She bit down on her bottom lip, and immediately my eyes zeroed in on how beautiful her mouth was. Damn it, I wanted to taste her.

And then it hit me.

Almost sucking the breath straight from my chest in one staggering swoop.

I wanted.

To kiss her.

I wanted.

I *wanted*.

Something.

The numbness was leaving, the familiarity of it being replaced by white hot need and damned curiosity.

"This is..." I was barely able to choke out words. "Difficult. For me."

"Me too." She sighed, placing her hand on my chest, against my heart, it was there, but each thump was painful, as if someone was taking an ice pick and doing some serious damage.

"Sometimes..." I stood, pulling her into my arms so we were chest to chest; her soft breasts pushed against me with every exhale. "Not feeling, feels better."

"Still feeling."

"You have smart ass tendencies."

Sighing, Val kept her right hand pressed against my chest, and her left gripping my shoulder. "Yeah well,

213

normally I don't vocalize all my thoughts."

"I think you should." My hands moved to her hair, digging into the chestnut depths, allowing this weird, foreign sensation of touching another woman to wash over me.

And waiting.

For the pain.

And it was there, oh, it was there.

I co-existed with it.

"That feels good." Val swayed forward, her forehead replacing where her hand had been.

Her body was small against mine, and different, but not a bad different, just, different.

"I promise I'll try really hard," she whispered in a sad voice. "To make you happy. I—" She started shaking. "—I'll make it my life's mission, okay?"

And my heart shattered all over again.

"Val, I don't deserve the honor."

She pulled back, a cute frown marring her pretty face. "It isn't about what you deserve." Her face broke out into a beautiful smile, one that had me sucking in a breath and nearly stumbling backward. "It's about what you need."

Never had I been so ashamed of myself.

And I'd done a lot of shitty things.

I couldn't stop myself.

Someone should burst into the room, someone should stop me from doing what I was about to do.

Then again if they did, I'd probably shoot them.

I'd invited anger into my soul and told it to stay.

And it had.

Until an innocent girl made it her mission to make me smile.

That's the thing about pain. You live with it, you embrace the rightness of it, until someone finally reaches through the broken glass, and grabs ahold of the real you, the you that had been lost and hurting. Broken and bleeding, they hold on for dear life, refusing to let go.

They join you in your pain.

And as you watch the blood pour down their arm, you realize, the pain is you, you are the pain, you are the master of your own destiny, you built up the shards of glass.

And now, it isn't just effecting you.

But someone else who isn't deserving of it.

Which makes you pause and take notice — did I ever deserve the same thing?

"I'm going to kiss you now."

"But you said you wouldn't—"

"Because I want to."

"You want to?"

I nodded. "And you're going to say yes."

"I am?" Her eyebrows shot up in surprise as a panicked sound emitted from her mouth.

"Yup."

"Why am I going to say yes?"

"Because practice makes perfect and... because... we can."

"True but—"

I didn't give her a chance to reject me.

This.

Was.

A kiss.

I was going to make her forget all about her regret — and I was going to make it as good as I possibly could.

With a shriek she wrapped her legs around me.

"That's it." I sighed. "Hold on."

Lips trembling, she nearly knocked her head against mine as she clenched my shoulders with her dainty hands, her fingers tugging at my T-shirt like she was getting ready to ride.

Soft legs.

The faint smell of vanilla.

And her erratic breathing.

I stopped trying to pursue her with my kiss and just... listened.

My eyes closed with an inhale as I breathed her in and closed off my mind to the world around me — focusing only on her.

My mouth descended to hers.

Val's breathing was uneven.

My lips met hers tentatively and then again, coaxing them apart, savoring the very different feel of her, of another woman.

In her arms, I wasn't a widower. I wasn't mafia. I wasn't anything but a guy; she made me feel that way, like nothing else mattered.

It was cheesy.

It was beautiful.

It was like breathing for the first time.

The way her fingers danced up my shoulders, the way she clung to my neck for dear life and, even the way she breathed me in as she kissed me back, her tongue sliding against my bottom lip.

With a moan, I deepened the kiss, tried different angles, and pressed my lips against hers again and again, one more time and then I'd stop.

I lied.

Two more times.

Three.

Seven.

Panting, I slid my hand up her side, my skin sizzling with the contact of her smooth skin.

I walked us toward her bed and fell backward with her on top of me, she paused, chest heaving, her big trusting hazel eyes blinking lazily down at me. "You paused."

"People need air." I grinned. "To survive."

"So I was using all your air?"

"Yeah." I swallowed back the emotion that refused to stop building in my throat, my chest, every part of me. Every glance she gave me had me feeling better and worse at the same time, her life was in my hands, and any life, regardless of how bad, was a treasure.

But that was the difference with her.

She was at her core...

Good.

Innocent.

Untarnished.

Undeserving of my bad.

And yet at the same time, it didn't stop me from giving her a tug as she collapsed against my chest, my hands digging into her hair, massaging, exploring.

"Guess we have to get married now."

"Huh?"

"You know since we just had sex."

I froze. "Are you serious right now?"

She burst out laughing. "I was kidding. Holy crap how innocent do you think I am?"

I didn't respond.

She smacked me in the chest. "That's insulting. I read."

"Oh." My eyebrows shot up, "So you read about sex? Is that what you're saying?"

She jerked away from me landing beside me on the bed, her face guilty. "No. I read romance. Huge difference."

"Oh yeah?" My eyes searched both nightstands until I located a book. I grabbed the first one I saw and opened. "He sucked a nipple until she screamed out with pleasure, his arousal pressed against her inner thigh as he moved to the next and—"

"I swear." Val held up her hands. "I had no idea!" She snatched the book out of my hands and read through, her frown growing more and more intense as she read.

"Problem?"

"It doesn't say that!"

"It doesn't?" I grinned. "Sorry, must have been living out my own fantasies there for a moment."

She gasped.

I took advantage of her outrage and captured another kiss.

With a sigh, she pulled back. "Am I allowed to kiss you, too? You know… first? I just I need ground rules if we're going to do this."

"Ground rules," I repeated, my good mood slowly waning.

"Yeah."

"All right." I moved to the edge of the bed and threw my feet over, they came into contact with her white fuzzy rug. "No falling in love." I stood.

"No problem," she said quickly moving to her feet.

Too quickly.

But I didn't have a leg to stand on, so I continued. "We can kiss each other, that's fine."

"All right."

"And, don't pry."

"But—"

"Wife, not therapist. Just, don't pry, don't poke around where you aren't wanted."

Her face fell. Shit. I reached for her hand, but she jerked away.

"Two steps forward ten steps back?"

"I didn't mean that how it came out."

"Yeah, you did." She nodded, another step backward. Damn it. "All right, so tomorrow?"

"Tomorrow." I forced a smile and reached for her, she stepped out of the way.

"I should..." She yawned. "Sleep."

"It's five."

"Nap," she corrected quickly. "Thanks, Sergio. For... the talk."

"No thank you for the kiss?" I asked in a teasing tone.

Her smile was weak. "And that too."

I walked out of the room feeling more lost than I did when I'd charged into it yelling. At least when we fought we figured things out.

Would I always walk on eggshells around her? Would I always say the wrong things and come out of it wondering if I was the ass or if she was just immature and not getting it?

I was still frowning when I made my way into the kitchen. Phoenix was drinking water while Tex chugged wine directly out of the bottle.

"Classy." I pulled out a chair.

He shrugged and offered the bottle. "You want in?

I stared at the bottle then at Phoenix's water and let out a helpless laugh. "Hell yeah, I think I do."

Phoenix's eyes narrowed. "New leaf?"

"Yeah, something like that. What? You want in, too?"

Phoenix held up his hands. "Water's good."

"Pussy," Tex grumbled taking another swig before handing me the bottle.

"Hardly." Phoenix grunted. "You're chugging a cab. Who do you really think has the pussy? Think long and hard." He grinned. "Now, if you were tossing back whiskey like a man—"

Before Tex broke the bottle over Phoenix's head I intervened. "So, whiskey it is, and you're in Phoenix?"

"I'm in."

"In?" Nixon waltzed into the room. "What are we in?"

"Shots." Tex rubbed his hands together just as Chase nearly ran into Nixon.

"No." Chase shook his head. "The last time we had shots I found a horse head in my bed."

Tex grabbed his side and doubled over laughing. "It was a prop, but worth it."

Chase flipped him off.

"You in, Nixon?" I eyed him.

He shoved his phone in his pocket. "Oh, what the hell. It's been years since I've been drunk over a woman."

"Chase." Tex coughed.

"Yeah thanks." Chase flipped him off for the second time. "Let's just roll in giant elephants and family drama. Oh wait, didn't Sergio kiss your wife?"

"Oh, hell." Phoenix rubbed his temples with his fingers.

"Please!" I yelled. "Phoenix attacked Trace!"

Phoenix shoved his chair back. "Are you fucking kidding me right now?"

"Drink!" Nixon stood between all of us spreading his hands wide. When Phoenix didn't attack, he cleared his throat and pulled a bottle of whiskey from one of the cupboards. "Or, we play Russian Roulette with Tex's gun, and we all know he doesn't play fair."

We all sat.

For the first time since Andi's death, we all took a shot together.

And for once, it didn't feel like a tribute.

More of a *what the hell do we do now?*

CHAPTER 27

Lovers and madmen have such seething brains.
—A Midsummer Night's Dream

Valentina

I STAYED IN my room like a complete coward all night. Thank God I had a stash of licorice and protein bars in one of my bags from work.

The piece of red licorice hung out of my mouth as I tore open the next letter. So far, they hadn't given me any clues as to who was actually sending the things.

My money was on Frank.

Until I saw Frank and he seemed more… distant and cold, not the type to send letters from the grave.

Not at all.

There were only three letters left.

Panicked, I went back through to make sure I'd counted right.

Three?

Could that be right?

So what? I'd been given seven?

Frowning, I pulled the sheet of paper out. It looked

223

like it had coffee spilled on it, but it smelled like the Victoria Secret coconut vanilla lotion I wore.

Over and over again the cycle continued, the prince, or the beast, struggled with his demons. His past calling to him while his future was laid out perfectly. But beasts, they are trained to fight against what feels wrong. Emotions can be so fickle, can't they? Patience. Be patient. I imagine you've received your dress, the shoes, something old, something new, something blue. I also imagine that he saw the shoes. So just in case you don't still have them, you'll receive another package tomorrow. Don't open it until ten minutes before you walk down the aisle. Wear everything and give him the other half of the package with his name on it. And remember, it isn't how you start, but how you finish.

All my love,

R

More and more the letters made no sense and bordered on creepy, as if the individual knew me personally or was at least watching me and writing the letters in real time.

Was it one of the guys?

Or their wives?

Ugh, my head hurt.

I guess it didn't really matter who it was, because it changed nothing, right? It changed absolutely nothing.

Something loud clanged from downstairs followed a few seconds later by another loud clanging. Panicked, since it wouldn't stop, I tore out of my room and ran down the stairs.

Yelling and clanging got louder, and when I entered the kitchen I nearly fell over backward.

Sergio and Tex were arm wrestling.

"One way or another bastard, I will beat you!" Tex roared.

"More shots!" Chase yelled slamming a shot glass onto the table and then turning around offering whiskey straight out of the bottle. Phoenix held his stomach as he leaned against the counter cursing Chase to hell, while Nixon looked completely sober.

And yet, he was drinking like it was water.

"Ahhhhh!" Tex yelled using all his strength to slam Sergio's hand to the left, while Sergio leaped to his feet. "Cheating!"

"You never said I couldn't stand!"

Tex stood.

Sergio stayed standing.

"It's amazing how they won't give up." Nixon shook his head. "Guys, call it a draw."

"Shut the hell up!" they said in unison still trying.

"Well, one's going to have a stroke." Chase seemed overjoyed at the idea.

Finally, Tex flinched causing Sergio to switch positioning, but clearly he was bluffing, he slammed Sergio's hand against the table and stumbled back screaming. "Are you not entertained?"

Chase slow clapped.

Nixon took another sip of whiskey.

And my mouth dropped open as Sergio pulled off his shirt, tossed it in Tex's face and said, "Best out of three."

"Great, maybe next time we'll get lucky and I'll detach your arm from your skinny little body."

Skinny?

Sergio wasn't as built as Tex, but he was still massive. Muscles bulged in all the right places, tightening like a freaking cord around his midsection, his traps alone seemed like they were swelling before my very eyes.

Add in his smooth skin and the few tattoos, and I suddenly felt like I was getting a free show.

Tally marks marred his side in the form of a harsh black tattoo.

There were a lot of them.

"What are you up to?" a voice asked behind me.

With a yelp I nearly slammed back against the wall as Frank stood to my right, chuckling out a curse as Sergio and Tex went at it again.

"I, um, was... I heard noise." There, that sounded normal, not like I'd been staring at my future husband with my mouth open. Hey, at least I wasn't panting. See? Progress.

"Eh, they've been at it for the last three hours. Those boys sure can hold their liquor."

Chase stumbled to the floor and started laughing so hard tears ran down his face.

"Clearly." I nodded.

Nixon tried to help him up, but Chase pulled him down with him. I thought Nixon was going to pull a gun on him or something, and then he burst out laughing while Chase made pretend snow angels on the wood floor.

Frank cleared his throat. "They've had a stressful few years. It is good to see them relax."

Sergio chose that moment to slap Tex on the face with his left hand while they still held the same position on the table, neither arm moving.

"Aw, Tex, does that sting?"

"I will literally, LITERALLY..." He screamed, his face turning red. "...castrate you in your sleep."

"Tex likes his dirty work," Chase sang from the floor.

Phoenix stumbled toward Nixon and Chase and slumped to the linoleum. "I need water."

"NO!" Tex roared. "Water's for pussies. You get no water! Hell no H20, hell no H20."

Sergio joined in the yelling, and what was once a battle turned into them shaking hands and doing some weird handshake in the middle of the table while Chase's head bobbed and tried to peer pressure Nixon into snapping his fingers.

"No snaps," Nixon growled. "I think we drank all the whiskey."

"How much have they had?" I whispered to Frank.

"Not much," he said confidently. "I believe they stopped at the fourth bottle."

"Four *bottles*?" I hissed. "They could die!"

"It will never be alcohol that takes an Italian, only a bullet, or perhaps a bomb." He seemed to think about this. "Yes, a bomb seems more likely."

"Great bedtime story, thanks."

He grinned. "It is my specialty. Would you like another?"

"No, no." I offered a polite smile. "I'm good, I'll just head up to bed."

I was maybe five steps away from Frank when he called, "Val."

"Yes?" I didn't turn around.

"Sometimes what we say we don't want is exactly what we need, what we crave. Do you understand?"

I hung my head. "I'm not sure."

"Yes, you are." Footsteps neared, and then his hand was on my back. "Men are stupid. We have our pride, we have what we think is best for everyone. We would rather sacrifice our own hearts and happiness than feel, or have the opportunity to feel and lose. When you mourn love, you never want to repeat that same feeling because it is always worse the second time. Believe me, it is always worse."

"How?" I croaked. "How is it worse?"

A long heavy sigh emitted from behind me as a large hand gripped my right shoulder. "I have loved. I have lost. More times than I can count. And each time, you promise yourself you will not feel as deep, you will not care as much. It is always the times I lied to myself — to the people I loved — that I felt the most. Oh, how I wish I could go back and change words that were said, but once words are released into the universe, they have a way of staying there until we take them back and, even then, the damned memory remains, does it not?"

"Yeah."

"Even those who have accepted the state of being lost… dream of being found."

He patted my shoulder twice before walking away.

But the scent of Frank, my uncle, lingered.

Like cigar smoke and spice.

He smelled of warmth — comfort.

And wisdom.

He reminded me so much of my other uncles, but there was a terrifying strength about him that had me wondering if he would even hesitate when faced with pulling a trigger.

No. He'd fire first, then ask questions, and if he was wrong, simply shrug, and clean his gun.

Was it horrible that I liked his attitude?

Maybe I was changing, growing up, or just coming to accept the fact that I was more my father than I had originally thought.

An hour later, I stared up at my ceiling; thoughts of the next day made it impossible to fall asleep. I was getting married.

I sucked in a breath and slowly exhaled.

I repeated the same process five times before I admitted to myself how useless the stupid calming exercise was.

A knock sounded on my door before it burst open and a very drunk and loud Sergio barreled in. He made a beeline for me and my bed, then with a huge grunt nearly collapsed on top of me.

"Rough night?" I whispered.

"I think that if you ran, I'd enjoy chasing you." He held up his head, it was hard to make out the features of his face because of how dark it was in my room. "I think I would enjoy watching your legs run away almost as much as I would enjoy the feel of them wrapped around me, when you came…" He blinked and whispered. "…home."

"Home?"

"My home. Her home. I guess it's our home now."

"You're drunk."

"I'm inebriated, big difference."

"Spell it and I'll believe you."

"I-n-e-b-r-i-a-ted." He nodded. "Easy."

"You sounded out the last part."

"What are you? The damn grammar police?"

"Or spelling police?"

"Move over." He shoved my little body and then wrapped his right arm around my stomach. "I promise

I won't seduce you."

"Was I in danger of that or something?" Why was I arguing with a drunk person?

"Hah," Sergio shot back. "You have no idea. Every time I see you, I tell myself you're young. You're innocent. You're good. I'm bad. So bad. I keep track of my bad, right here." Before I could stop him, he lifted his shirt over his head and pointed to the tally marks. "I keep track of them here."

"Them?"

"Kills." His voice was muffled by the pillow.

"And that one?" I pointed to the one tally mark that was fresh, larger, and a red color.

"That's what loss looks like." He divulged. "It's red, it's angry, it makes you bleed, it makes you mourn, loss looks like an angry, red check mark, that you can't erase no matter how many kills you have."

"Loss." My mind whirled. What was he talking about?

"Red marks the spot." He yawned. "I told her I'd remember her, I'd give her that honor. I got a tattoo on my arm to honor her. I added the tally mark to give her the respect due."

"What if I died?" I just had to ask the drunk man who refused to fall in love with me. Brilliant. But he was so loose lipped I wanted to at least try to pry some sort of information out of him.

Sergio surged to life as he covered my body with his. I let out a grunt as his stare intensified by the minute. "No."

"No?" My heart sank.

"No, you can't die." His eyes were wild. "Promise me."

"Wh-what?" I stammered.

"Promise me!" His hands moved to my cheeks, and he lightly squeezed my face between his fingertips, and then he rolled to the side, and his head ducked as he pressed an ear against my chest. "I won't let it happen again. I won't."

"Sergio, everyone dies."

"No," he murmured his voice getting quiet again. "I won't make it through again, don't you understand? I don't want another red tally mark. I won't do it, I won't honor or respect your death, because it won't happen. It won't. It can't."

"And if it does?"

"Then I die with you."

"Are you Romeo now?"

He chuckled softly. "I always thought Juliet was hot."

"Go to sleep, Sergio." I patted his head with my hand.

"You didn't promise yet."

I sighed. "I promise I'll try to stay alive."

"Good." He blinked up at me. "Now kiss me."

"You're drunk. And you smell like whiskey."

"You're cranky."

"Gee, I wonder why?"

He refused to budge off of me until I shoved him to the side and even then it was impossible to escape him as he grabbed my body and spooned me. He wrapped one leg over top of me and nuzzled my neck. "You smelled like her, that first day. I hated you."

"Sorry."

"Don't be. Now you smell like you."

"Is that good?"

He inhaled deeply. "And the beast was tamed. For one night, he was tamed."

I froze. "What did you just say?" It was exactly like the story in the letters, and for the second time, Sergio referenced a beast and compared himself.

But the room was quiet.

Except for his snoring.

Of course.

CHAPTER 28

Tongue, lose thy light.

–A Midsummer Night's Dream

Sergio

CLANG, CLANG, CLANG.

What the hell?

I squeezed my eyes shut tighter.

Clang, Clang!

"For the love of God!" I said in a harsh whisper. "Stop banging things!"

The banging got louder.

I opened one eye, and then two.

Val was towering over me, a bat in hand and a freaking cowbell in the other. "Where the hell did you get a cowbell?"

"I was a cow in my first grade Christmas pageant. Dante played Joseph."

"You were a cow," I stated flatly as I tried to get to a sitting position. "And you kept the bell?"

"I'm a pack rat." She raised the bat again to hit the bell.

"No!" I surged toward her, then in a wave of dizziness, collapsed back against the bed. "I think I might puke."

"Oh?"

"Shhh." I lifted my hands into the air in a desperate attempt to gain some silence, but the buzzing in my head continued, and then I burst out laughing for no reason. "Holy shit, I think I'm still drunk."

This time the bat slammed into my shoulder jolting me out of my own amusement. "Ouch!" I leaped to my feet and reached for the bat but she moved out of the way and hid it behind her back. "What are you so angry about?"

"You almost smothered me in your sleep last night and then you…" Her cheeks reddened.

I felt my eyes go wide. "Did I, try to—?" Holy shit. My entire night was blank after the whole snow angel episode where Chase convinced all of us to lie on the floor and pretend we were gazing at the stars at Christmas time. Frank turned off the lights for us. It was beyond ridiculous.

But the last time I remembered laughing that hard with any of the guys was when we were ten and had a slumber party for Nixon's birthday.

"No," Val said quickly. "Well, I mean, you tried to take off my shorts and at one point begged me to flash you, but—"

I groaned, and covered my face with my hands. "I'm such an ass."

"A drunk horny one."

"Well, that was helpful."

She grinned. "Yeah well, this bat really did come to good use where you were concerned!"

I frowned and stared at the bat, really stared at it. "Where did you get that?"

"It was a gift."

"From?"

"A secret admirer."

"Guys don't get girls bats. Sorry, that's not how love works. A bat is a weapon. Someone gave you a weapon?"

"He or she said I'd need it where you were concerned."

My happy mood faded enough for me to feel a slice of pain through my chest as I struggled to breathe. "Just like the shoes, huh?"

Who the hell was sending Val Andi's stuff?

"You should go get ready. It's bad luck to see me before the wedding." Val offered a polite smile. "And maybe try to sober up before you say 'I do.' I've been dreaming about this day a really long time."

Feeling like shit, I hung my head and scratched down my neck. "I'm sorry it's not how you envisioned it."

She grinned. "It sorta is."

"How so?" I frowned, taking the bat out of her hands and pulling her into my arms. "You always dreamed of chasing a horny Italian out of your bed with a bat? Is that it?"

"No." She stiffened a bit then whispered. "But has anyone ever told you… you look like a medieval prince? Or a knight from a story book?"

"I'm no knight."

"No, you're the beast."

I froze. "Right…" The list in my pocket might as well have burned a hole and singed itself on my heart.

I'd gone to Beauty and the Beast but done nothing else to honor her memory.

She'd told me something similar before she died.

"Be the man. Not the beast," Andi whispered one night. "Girls want the guy to storm the castle with a sword and a smile, not all snarling and angry. I would never suggest you become tame, but maybe... not as scary."

"I'm not scary."

Andi's eyebrows shot up as she choked on a laugh. I didn't join in. "Oh, I'm sorry. I thought you were making a joke. Next time warn me when you're trying to be serious."

I rolled my eyes. "Very funny."

"Sergio, girls look at you and see physical perfection. It's intimidating. Don't make it harder for her than it's already going to be."

Anger slammed through me. "We aren't discussing this."

"But—"

"No." With an angry kiss I stole her breath and tried to make us forget, make me forget, that she was dying and yet cheerfully talking about the next girl who would warm my bed.

"Sergio?" Val exhaled against my chest and stepped back. "Are you okay?"

No.

"Sure," I lied. "I just — you're right, we don't want bad luck. I'll see you at the church."

I frowned the entire way down the stairs, my head throbbing between my temples.

"Morning, sunshine!" Chase yelled from the kitchen.

Phoenix groaned and covered his head with his arms.

236

Chase snickered. "He's not used to drinking as much as us."

"Because I like my liver." Phoenix fired back in a tired raspy voice. "Never again."

"Cheer up!" Tex yelled loudly in Phoenix's right ear. "We'll have you feeling great in no time!"

"Let me shoot him, Nixon," Phoenix begged. "Just once."

Nixon glared at Tex from behind the newspaper. "No violence, it's Sergio's special day."

"And we had the best bachelor party ever..." Chase nodded. "Good thing, since we didn't get one last time."

It didn't even occur to me that I hadn't had one before.

Had they planned it?

Chase slapped me on the back. "Stop trying to figure shit out and just say thanks man for the best night of my life."

"The best night of my life doesn't include making snow angels with you on the wood floor while Tex sings Home on the Range."

"Amazing baritone." Chase nodded. "Too bad Nixon's harmony wasn't on point or we could have made a killing on the street corner."

Phoenix groaned. "You don't sing on corners you strip on them."

"And he would know," Tex added.

"Is everyone ready to—" Frank stopped in his tracks. "You have exactly one hour until you need to be at the church."

I glanced down at my wrinkled clothes and just barely managed to hide my yawn while Tex cut loose with a loud burp and pounded his chest.

Things got progressively worse when Phoenix actually slumped out of his chair onto the floor.

Chase died laughing while Nixon shared a humored look with the rest of us.

"Dear God, not only are you mafia, but you'll be in a church still drunk!" Frank made the sign of the cross over his chest. "Your occupation is bad enough; better send some prayers to the saints so you don't get struck by lightning once you enter holy ground."

"We'll send Phoenix in first just in case," Tex said seriously.

"Why do I have to be the martyr?"

"So all the secrets die with you." Tex shrugged.

"Man has a point," Phoenix grumbled. "But I'm not going first, Sergio's the one getting married, he gets to walk in first. If he doesn't die, then we all go."

"Happiest day of your life, yeah?" Chase met my gaze and chuckled. "Just remember, we all do shit we don't want to do for the Family. But something tells me it's more about wanting to do her and feeling guilty about it."

I blinked, and opened my mouth to defend myself when Frank yelled. "Could you women stop bickering and get dressed! It's like herding a bunch of toddlers with weapons!"

"I support gun control." Tex placed a hand over his heart. "How dare you!"

"Oh hell," Frank muttered curse after curse. "Just — go."

Two HOURS LATER and I was in the exact same spot I'd been in over six months ago. Only this time, it wasn't with as much trepidation as it had been then... just an eerie sense of *déjà vu*.

But she was nothing like Andi.

Nothing.

There were over a hundred family members present. Dante made his way to my side and tapped me on the shoulder just as the last few shuffled to their seats. "She needs to talk to you."

"What?" I tried to force a smile. "Is she okay?"

Dante didn't answer right away and then rolled his eyes. "Just come with me, all right?"

My heart did that thing, where it jolts in your chest but you aren't sure if it's out of anxiety or sadness. Was she really going to back out? Holy shit, why did that bother me so much? Not that it was an option anyway, but I felt sadness.

Actual sadness at the thought that she would take the easy way out.

That she wanted a life away from what I could give her.

Not that I'd offered her much.

But still...

I went out the side door and followed Dante to the room she'd been waiting in.

"Val." Dante knocked loudly on the door. "I got him."

The door opened swiftly, Val pulled me in and slammed it shut again.

I stumbled back and swore aloud as she wrapped her arms around her mid section. "I can't do this."

"You're wearing a table cloth."

239

"I know what I'm wearing!" She snapped.

"Okay…" I took a cautious step toward her. "Was that the plan? Put on a white tablecloth and pretend to be the ghost of Christmas future?"

"Hilarious," she said through clenched teeth.

Damn she was beautiful. She'd put on makeup.

Not that it made her prettier, just older.

A lot older looking.

I swallowed my nerves.

How had I never noticed how big her eyes were? Or her lips?

That mouth.

I instantly hardened as she pursed her lips together and gave me an angry stare. "It's bad."

Shit she was fierce when she was angry.

Her eyes flashed. "Sergio, are you even listening to me?"

"Honestly?" I winced. "No, but you look beautiful."

"I'm wearing a table cloth."

"I like your hair."

"Thanks." She reached up to touch the simple white veil causing the table cloth to fall to the ground and pool at her feet.

"Holy mother of God!" I whispered in a hoarse yell.

It was her turn to wince. "That bad?"

Words. Damn I needed a lot of them. A shit load of them. "No."

"It was in the stupid package! And I ruined my own dress so I was like hey, what do I have to lose? I brought a back up simple white dress just in case but it made me look like a first grader, and then I opened the box and it's my size and—"

"Stop talking." My hoarse voice sounded foreign

as I took two steps toward her then tugged her body against mine, capturing her lips in a searing kiss. Her arms went around my neck, there was no hiding my arousal as it pressed against her core.

And for once, it didn't bring me shame.

But this fiery, tempting need to toss her over whatever object I could find and lift up that damn lacy skirt. Shit. Who the hell would buy her something like this?

Val pulled back. "I look like a prostitute."

"A very highly paid one." I kissed her again and again. I couldn't help it, something had snapped, I was hungry for her, starving for another taste.

Shaking, she pulled away. "What will the uncles say?"

"They'll probably try to shoot anyone who stares."

"Right, so the table cloth happened soon after Dante saw me."

"What did Dante say?"

"It was more what didn't he say," Val admitted.

"You're going out there, in this dress, it looks gorgeous on you."

"I feel naked."

"Nobody sees you naked…" I said in a harsh voice. "…but me."

Her eyes went wide. "Getting territorial."

I gripped her ass with my hands and jerked her body against mine. "You were mine before you even knew you were mine. So yes. I'll be damned possessive about you. And I don't give a fuck what anyone says — you've belonged to me forever — and it's going to sure as hell stay that way."

She nodded slowly and then looked down, drawing

my attention to the completely see through bodice, literally the only piece of fabric that wasn't see through was covering her nipples. The lace gave the illusion that there was more than skin — there wasn't.

The skirt wasn't any better, it was a long satin that had a giant slit up one side showing an expansive shot of thigh.

I instantly gripped her thigh with my hand.

She let out a little moan as her head fell back, exposing her long neck. I kissed my way down as someone pounded on the door.

"You guys ready?" Dante poked his head in.

"I'm ready." I crooked my finger into her lace underwear and gave a little tug. "You?"

She licked her lips and nodded as I moved my hand over her tight ass.

I needed to stop before I took her next to the altar.

That probably wouldn't go over well.

Finally, I released her, and took a deep breath.

With shaking hands Val pulled a note out and handed it to me. "I was instructed to give this to you right before I walked down the aisle."

The white piece of paper looked pretty non-threatening. Plus I needed a distraction.

"Val!" Dante pounded again, then barged in. "Oh hell, where's the table cloth."

"No table cloth," I barked. "See you in a few, Val."

She gave me a nervous look and sauntered off with Dante cursing after her.

I followed and made my way toward the front of the church.

Thank God people were still shuffling in.

Curiosity finally won out as the last of the family

finally found their spots in the back pews.

I pulled the paper out and unfolded the sheet. People would probably think they were my vows, nothing else.

Italy,

Remember, I never wanted our love story to end with tragedy. I'd like to think that there's a bigger plan out there for both of us, otherwise, what's the point?

I love her.

I more than love her.

In the times I've spoken to her — I adore her, just as much as you will.

She doesn't know she's met me.

Maybe she never will know.

There will be no going back after you read the next line. One last promise. Can you do that?

Promise me you'll fall in love.

Promise me you'll have children.

Promise me you'll try to make her happy as much as she's going to try to make you happy.

Promise me you'll give everything to her.

Promise me you will give her the chance we never had.

Until death do we part.

Well, Sergio, I died.

We parted.

Now it's time for a new promise.

A new vow.

A new beginning.

A new story for my prince.

There is beauty in life, beauty in death, you just have to look for it.

Sergio.

My love.
I release you.
Be happy.
From Russia, With love.

With a shudder I dropped the note to the floor just as the organ started playing the bridal march.

And I was faced yet again with a choice.

Make a promise.

Or run.

CHAPTER 29

The best in this kind are but shadows; and the worst are no worse, if imagination amend them.

–A Midsummer Night's Dream

Frank

THE BRIDAL MARCH began just as Xavier entered the church. Val frowned, then moved so she was nearly behind me. I helped matters by shoving her toward Gio.

"What is this?" Xavier grinned. "No invitation?"

He'd been a bastard then. He was still a bastard now.

I'd always had good dealings with the Russians. Hell, Nikolai Blazik, or The Doctor as he was nicknamed, was like blood to me, and I didn't take statements like that lightly.

With rings on every finger on his right hand and a cell phone in his left, he looked like he'd Googled how to dress like a hit man and taken it to heart.

From his head to toe black ensemble to the black trench coat. I shook my head. "Must have gotten lost in the mail. You know how things are."

"Yes." His teeth may as well have gnashed in my direction. "These things—" he eyed Val behind me "—are quite delicate."

Gio let out a low growl, while Papi made a move to my left, reaching inside his jacket. They'd been out of the fold for so long I expected them to forget their manners when it came to scum.

They instantly took up their positions, just as they had back when we ruled over the streets so long ago.

Gio behind, Papi flanking the right, and Sal to my left.

Years ago, between us and Luca, even talking to an Alfero without an invitation, without permission, would get you killed.

And now, we had the one man I'd left in charge, the man I'd trusted while I'd gone into hiding, deciding it was his turn for a handout.

What had he done? Other than run my family into the ground?

Had Luca not been keeping track of my family's dealings, had he not kept Xavier quiet with hush money — I would be dead.

By Xavier's hand.

And now that I'd taken control of my family, both in Chicago and New York, I had taken the very last ounce of strength he'd had and made it my own.

"I thought I was blood." Xavier's eyes narrowed.

"Things changed." I crossed my arms. "And I did promise a meeting with the Cappo did I not?"

"About that." Xavier held out his cell phone.

I hesitated then grabbed the phone, the screen was filled with a picture of a cut-off hand, and a finger flipping him off, in a nice donut box.

Barely able to keep my laughter in, I frowned and handed the phone back to him. "So it seems you've been given your answer."

"That, was my right hand man."

The irony wasn't lost on me.

"Clearly, not anymore," Sal said with a chuckle.

Xavier's eyes flashed with hatred. "This is not over."

"Has it just begun then?" Papi answered before I could. "Is that what you were about to say?"

"And where is your army?" I asked in a cool voice. "Your loyal men, the ones willing to die for you — and for what, so you can gain more power, more control, more money? The Nicolasi family paid you off and gave you a street corner. Be happy, go home, make love to your wife, kiss your two children on the head and know this day, if you choose to threaten me or what is mine one more time, I will take that wife. I will take those children. I will take this life from you, and I will do it slowly." I took another step. "Painfully."

Xavier's brown eyes moved into tiny little slits as his jaw clicked shut.

"I'm assuming by your silence, that you understand." I straightened my tie. "Now leave."

He didn't move.

With a sigh, I snapped my fingers, two of my men surged forward and grabbed him by the arms carrying him out of the church.

"Guard the doors," I ordered the minute they shut.

I motioned to one of my trusted associates, he stepped forward. "Hank, follow him."

"Yes, sir."

With an exhale I whispered, "Thank you."

Sal slapped me on the back along with Gio. Papi nodded his head and declared, "We are Family."

"We are." Emotion clogged in that old throat of mine as my heart sank with a wild realization that Xavier would keep coming back, wanting what he considered his due, and he'd either use me or someone I loved to get it. I would need to kill him.

And I would need to kill his entire line.

Something about that truth cracked my heart.

After all, I was a grandfather.

An uncle.

But also a businessman.

Yes. I straightened my shoulders. And a businessman, who loved fiercely, would do just about anything to keep those he loved safe.

Anything.

"Shall we?" I offered my arm to a silent Val.

With a nod, she looped her hand and then whispered, "Thank you for protecting me."

Anything. I would do anything. For her.

CHAPTER 30

Oh hell to choose love through another's eyes!
—A Midsummer Night's Dream

Valentina

IT WAS REAL. The mafia was real. And that man had hatred rolling off of him in waves, it was nearly impossible not to feel the chill in the air as he was carried away.

I must have surprised Frank by thanking him, because for a few seconds his façade cracked, and all I saw was a man who had already seen his prime and wanted nothing more than to put the past behind him.

It was like he was trying to banish the ghost only to be haunted over and over again.

"Does it ever stop?" I asked before taking my first step down the aisle.

"Yes." Frank kissed me on the top of the head. "It ends when, for just a few brief moments of respite, you are in the arms of someone who, despite all the bad, chooses to see only good. That is when it ends."

"Only to start over again?"

"Life." Frank blocked my view of Sergio as he grasped my face with both hands and kissed my forehead. "Is a never ending cycle of good and bad, it is what you do with those moments that define how the cycle ends."

He turned and walked in front of me, much like a flower girl would, but really, it was more meaningful. He was showing his protection by walking ahead of me, blocking me from view, allowing me these last few moments to gather myself as Gio took my right arm and Sal took my left.

Papi followed in the back.

Had someone told me that I'd have four uncles as my wedding party, I would have died laughing.

Instead, it had me near tears.

That the old hands holding mine, had always been willing to fight for me, to die for me. For me!

Like I deserved it.

Because to them, I was precious. I was a promise. I was everything.

I think in that moment, I shed the last part of my innocence, knowing fully that I was entering into a sacred bond, not just with Sergio, but with The Family, with the idea that my father had left behind.

One of peace.

Love.

One where blood was only spilled out of necessity.

Dante was at the front of the church with the rest of the men; they waited near Sergio.

Once Frank stepped out of the way, I noticed I was nearly at the end of the aisle.

Sergio's eyes were closed like he was in pain.

My heart sliced in two.

Because even though I wanted to understand, how could I? He'd lost the only woman he'd ever loved after a ceremony like this — and there I was. The exact opposite, young, innocent, everything he didn't want, but had to take.

Because of his honor.

I respected him for it.

And I knew I would end up loving him.

I was already halfway there.

Yes, it was time to shed the old me and step into a new reality, a new life, because some stories aren't filled with instant love or happily ever afters where all it takes is one kiss to seal the affection between two people.

Sometimes it's work.

Sometimes it's painful.

Our love would be ugly, deformed, awkward. It would be so many things, but I hoped, that in the end, above all else, it would be good enough.

Not just good.

Not even amazing.

But good enough, so that at least I was in a marriage where we had respect, friendship, it was all I felt right in asking for.

Sergio's hands shook at his sides.

Frank turned and lifted my veil from my face kissing each cheek and then whispering a blessing in my ear.

Sal did the same, followed by Papi. When it was Gio's turn, he hesitated.

I grabbed his hands as tears filled his eyes.

I was close to all of them, but Gio... Gio had always been my rock. He'd held my hand when my first real friend in high school moved away.

When she stopped writing me emails, he told me I'd find better friends at college.

When Dante was being stupid, as brothers are prone to be, he talked me through the most traumatic conversation I'd ever had, to date, about guys and hormones.

He thought if he just brought in movies and drew pictures, I'd be okay with the fact that my brother was acting like a jackass.

Halfway through our "talk" we were both so traumatized we swore never to speak of it again.

Gio made sure I ate.

Gio was like an Italian grandmother stuffed into the body of a lean, seventy-year-old man with a secret addiction to Cuban cigars.

His hair was nearly completely gray, his face had aged better than the rest of him, but the worry lines around his mouth deepened as he leaned forward and whispered near my ear, "Just say the word and I'll get you out."

Surprised, I pulled him in for a tight hug. "No. This is what my father would have wanted."

"That does not make this choice easier," he said in a pained voice as he hugged me tight and then kissed both cheeks. A single tear splashed onto his lips as they trembled. "You are my girl."

"I am."

"Be strong."

"I will."

"You are my girl," he repeated. "I die for you, yes?"

"Yes." My voice quivered.

"He treats you bad, I come with the gun, capiche?"

"Capiche." I half sobbed half laughed.

With a grunt, he kissed my nose and joined the rest of the men.

Phoenix, Tex, Nixon, and Chase were to the left with the rest of the Alferos while Dante was to the right with Sergio.

When my gaze finally fell to the man I was going to marry, I expected him to still have his eyes closed — after all, he didn't want this, maybe that was the only way he could go through it.

Instead, his eyes were fixated on me.

White-hot intensity radiated off of him in waves.

When our hands touched, his were warm, not clammy. Strong fingers wrapped around mine.

This is happening.

This is happening.

As the priest made a cross with his incense, he began reciting scripture in Italian. I picked out a few words.

The greetings and prayer flew by, and suddenly the Priest was asking in English if we were of sound mind.

Hah, probably not.

Sergio's lips twitched as we both stated that we were in fact, sane and were not entering into the holy sanction of marriage lightly.

"Sergio..." The priest's accent was so thick even his English was hard to decipher. "Do you take..." I was going to hyperventilate, he talked so fast, it was happening so fast. "Till death do you part?"

Blue eyes blinked at me, slowly, methodically, intensely as Sergio answered. "I vow... till death—" his voice cracked "—do we part."

It was my turn.

My voice was small when I answered the same, I felt odd saying yes, when Sergio actually repeated the last part.

Till death do we part.

Terrifying, to think, it would actually be a very real possibility that one of us would die before the other — chances were most likely him, considering his line of work.

I didn't like it.

Thinking about death when I should be thinking about life.

I clenched his hands tighter.

"And now a blessing." The Priest raised his hands. "From a friend."

Sergio's composure slipped, just barely, as the priest walked away and someone else replaced him.

A tall, dark, and extremely good-looking man with tattoos on his knuckles, and a very familiar face stood before us.

He cleared his throat. "May this new union provide the two of you with the love and laughter you both deserve, may God keep you safe, may God unite our families for as long as He will allow it. May you honor each other, respect one another, die for one another, live for one another. This is the wish of my family, my friends." His hands shook, just once, then he cleared his throat and continued. "This is the final wish and will from Andi Abandonato as read by Nikolai Blazik."

Sergio's eyes filled with tears.

I wasn't worthy.

I would never be worthy of a man who was loved that much.

But suddenly, I was okay with it, because her love

and devotion for him after only a few months showed me *he* was worthy.

Sergio was worthy.

And so deserving.

Of everything I had to offer him.

And I'd give all.

Because she had died wishing she could.

And it was my privilege to be able to pick up where she left off.

Nikolai nodded at both of us and joined Nixon's right side. The men shook hands as the priest held his arms above our head and continued the ceremony in Italian.

We exchanged rings — rings I'd never seen before. On repeating the words, they took new meaning for me; my life had a new meaning.

"Friends, let us bless the unity of these families, may they strengthen and protect us, forever." The priest spoke in Italian again.

"Amen," rumbled the collective murmur through the sanctuary.

"I now present, Mr. Sergio and Mrs. Valentina Abandonato, may our Lord and Savior Jesus Christ bless and keep you, forever and ever. Amen."

"Amen." Everyone made a quick sign of the cross then stood and kissed their right hands and placed it on their heart.

I didn't know what I felt as people started clapping.

Sergio gripped my hand in his then turned me to face him, his lips met mine in a brief kiss before he led me down the aisle.

I was married.

Married.

At nineteen.

To a killer with gorgeous eyes and a burdened heart.

Not necessarily how I had envisioned my story going.

"Be well!" Gio met us in the back of the church with tears in his eyes. "I will miss you."

"Miss me?" I repeated. "I don't—"

"Have fun!" Frank winked.

"Fun?"

Dante elbowed me then tossed rice into the air, a handful of it landed in my hair. "For the record, she's still my sister." I think that was directed at Sergio.

"Adios!" Tex winked. "Make sure to relax, Serg."

Sergio said nothing.

We were rushed toward a waiting limo, and nobody was talking, other than telling me to have fun. Were they talking about tonight?

Heat rushed into my face until I felt like I was on fire.

My embarrassment must have been noticeable because under his breath Sergio whispered, "Don't worry."

My view of the limo was suddenly blocked as a man stepped in front of us. The same one who had read the letter from Andi. He was the type of guy who oozed power and sexuality, but in a totally obvious and over-the-top way. I felt like if I looked at him directly in the eyes I'd lose my soul or something, like he'd see too much, see my insecurities, and tell everyone within hearing distance.

Finally, not wanting to be rude, I stole a glance at him, a real long glance.

He looked vaguely familiar.

But I couldn't place him.

Frowning, I stared harder.

Nikolai's eyes met mine, and then he quickly averted them and held out his hand to Sergio. "She would have been happy."

"I know," Sergio said in a low voice.

"My offer still stands." He gave me a pitiful stare before looking back at Sergio. "It will always stand."

"And I'll always say no." Sergio slapped him on the back then pulled him in for a hug. "Go back to the wife."

"The wife." Nikolai chuckled loudly. "Never thought I'd see the day."

"And we did?" Sergio countered. "By the way, Xavier's been giving us a bit of trouble."

"Shall I hurt him for you?" Nikolai asked.

Sergio paused, his hand gripped mine hard. "He's fine. For now. Perhaps later we'll have dinner."

"You know where to find me." Nikolai shook his hand one last time then walked off.

I frowned after him.

"Sorry," Sergio apologized. "He has no bedside manner."

"No... that's not it." I swallowed, my gaze still stuck on his disappearing form. "He looks familiar."

"Well he won the Pulitzer as a teenager, that could be it. Was on the cover of Time."

"No, not that kind of familiar, but—" I shook my head, "—never mind. So, why do people keep telling me to have fun?"

Sergio opened the limo door and pointed inside. "If I told you, I'd have to kill you."

"Very funny."

"It's kind of funny." His smile was small. "Did you say your goodbyes?"

"Yes, but—"

"Good." He shut the door before I could keep talking. Irritated, I rolled down the window as Sal, Papi, and Gio walked over. "Where am I going?"

"It would be a horrible surprise if we told you." Gio winked.

Papi's eyes shone with tears. "You be a good girl, Val."

"Eat!" Sal added. "You must eat!"

"Sweet potatoes," Gio said in a serious voice. "They help the eggs."

"Eggs?" I repeated. "What eggs?"

Papi blushed and whispered, "Yours."

"Mine?"

"For the children," Sal explained. "We pray for a fertile womb."

Oh please don't. "I'm only nineteen! Let Dante pop out kids!"

"That is not man's job." Gio frowned and then snapped his fingers. "After the act is done, be sure to wait at least five minutes and then drink carrot juice. You will be pregnant in no time!"

Note to self, jump out of bed and stay away from all vegetable juice. "Right. Well, thanks."

Sergio got in on the other side and slid across, then he reached for my hand and didn't let go.

Gio poked his head through the limo window. "I almost forget. Men, they sometimes have minds of their own. He scares you with his..." He didn't say the word. I thanked God. "...manliness, you just kick him.

It may — it may not feel good—"

"Okay!" I practically shoved him out of the window. "Bye now, love you!"

"But Val this is very important, this talk! We must have this talk! Remember the pictures I drew!"

I hit the window so it would go up and blew them all kisses. "I love you guys!"

Once the car started to pull away, Sergio turned to me and smirked. "Pictures, huh?"

"Shut up."

"Do you still have the pictures?"

"Sergio," I warned, face prickling with embarrassment.

"Did you help draw the pictures or were you simply an observer?"

"Are you done yet?"

His blue eyes twinkled. "Oh, I don't think I'll ever be done with this conversation. Ten years from now I'm still going to ask. Fifteen years from now, I'm going to damn well demand you show me what has you looking like sex is the most terrifying thing on the planet."

I didn't respond.

We sat in silence as the limo drove through Manhattan.

"A year ago, sex with me would have been terrifying," he said quietly. "I would have taken you hard."

A part of me was intrigued while the other part was still so embarrassed I was tempted to jump out of the moving vehicle.

"And now?" I just had to ask.

He didn't speak for a few minutes. Maybe I hadn't

said it loud enough. I turned to ask again, only to find him staring intently at me.

Licking his lips he leaned forward, his left hand reached for my face and then stopped as his fingertips danced across my bottom lip. "Slow."

"Wh-hat?"

He pulled back. "I felt like the villain today."

"You're not—"

"I am." He looked away. "In a way I always will be. But, that doesn't mean you have to play hero to my villain, Val." His eyes met mine briefly. "I'm going to try… and though you may never have my heart… I promise you one thing."

"What?" My voice was hoarse.

"You will always have my body."

CHAPTER 31

I am slow of study.

> –A Midsummer Night's Dream

Sergio

YEAH, ROMANCE WAS lost on me. Didn't Andi say those very words a few months ago, when I offered to shoot her twenty-four hours before our wedding? Damn, I was a dick.

I wanted to do better.

It wasn't a second chance, at least not in the way that a person would think. Hell, *I* would have said no if I was offered to me, and I actually had the option of *saying* no, but since it was a forced yes, I wanted to do right by her.

And after reading Andi's letter, I had felt ashamed at the way I'd been acting, but my emotions refused to stay in check where Val was concerned. She confused me, tied me up in knots, and oddly, had me feeling the most vulnerable I ever had in my entire life.

I hadn't deserved Andi.

I sure as hell didn't deserve Val.

Was God insane? Was this some cruel joke to make me change my ways? Give me two of the most incredible women in existence? But make it impossible to love them. Take the first away, and create a pain so swift, so strong, that I had nothing left for the next.

I glanced at Val out of the corner of my eye.

In another life, I could love her. Truly love her.

It wasn't fair.

Bitterness threatened to take over as we took the exit for JFK.

The privacy shield slid down. ""Sir, we've had the same car tailing us for the last ten miles, thought you should know."

I gritted my teeth. "How close are we to the airport?"

"A few miles out, but with this traffic…"

The shield went back up. We came to a screeching halt as the light turned red; cars were jammed all around us. I turned around. Two large men stepped out of a car and started jogging toward us.

"Well, shit," I muttered, quickly peeling my jacket off and undoing my cufflinks.

"Sergio?" Val's eyes were wide. "What's going on."

"Remember?" I flipped up the seat cushion on the left and pulled out two smaller Glocks. "When Chase showed you how to point a gun?"

"Yeah, but—"

"If something happens, you point the gun and you shoot, you shoot until you're sure, got it?" I shoved a gun into her hand and knocked twice on the shield. It rolled down.

And I was already too late.

The sound of gunfire filled the car.

Our driver, a newer associate in his twenties, had

just been shot in the head. I barely had time to push the screen back up before more shots were fired.

We weren't in a bulletproof car, I wasn't a boss, I hadn't thought it necessary. If I died, so what?

But if Val died.

Damn it.

A war.

More war.

When would the families ever learn?

What the hell was wrong with wanting peace?

A bullet hit the side window by Val's head, I pulled her down to the floor of the limo as more bullets went flying above us. Glass crashed all over my body.

I motioned for Val to be quiet.

The shooting stopped.

The guys were amateurs at best. You never stopped, only when the car was a hole. You stopped to set the car on fire. You stopped to place a bomb, you didn't stop because you thought you hit your targets. You never stopped.

The passenger door opened and I fired a shot out.

A rough curse was emitted, and then more shots were fired at the car.

Val didn't cry.

She didn't scream.

She was deathly silent, her eyes locked on mine, afraid, but so trusting my heart ached.

Her eyes said, *you'll get us out of this.*

It's going to be okay.

I trust you.

While I was at a loss of what we could do, of what I could do without injuring myself or putting her in more danger.

Shit.

A bullet grazed my arm, tearing flesh and part of my shirt. Val's eyes watered.

"Stay still," I mouthed, my body pressed against hers. I would die before I let them take her, whoever they were.

We were stuck.

Trapped.

If it was just me, I'd hop out of the car guns blazing, die in the process, and my family would just have to deal with it.

But I had a responsibility, and my responsibility trusted me to stay alive, needed me to stay alive if she was going to stay alive.

The shooting stopped again.

"Do you trust me?" I whispered.

"Yes," she whispered, her voice shaking.

"You want the girl?" I yelled so they could hear.

"Dead. We want her dead!" The man yelled back at me. "Bring her out to us and we'll let you go."

"No you won't." I laughed. "But what if I bring the girl because I've already had her and I'm sick of her? Can I at least choose the way you shoot me? Seems only fair."

Silence.

"You want to choose how I shoot you?"

"I'm dead either way, I have a thing about body shots, too much risk of suffering, bleeding out too slow, collapsed lungs, suffocation. Who wants that? A quick death, that's what I say."

"Fine," another man barked. "Bring her out, but she goes in front of you."

"All right, you can kill her or take her, do whatever

you want with her."

"We take her and then we kill her."

"Take her?"

"The boss will never know."

"She's not that great." I laughed coldly. "You may need to be drunk to appreciate what she has to offer."

Val's eyes narrowed.

But she said nothing.

The men chuckled.

"I'm coming out now." I pulled Val to a sitting position and whispered. "I'm sorry." As I ripped the bottom part of her dress and wrapped it around her hands like a rope. "When we get out I'm going to push you to the ground, it's going to hurt, you're going to get scraped. Flash boob."

Her eyes widened.

"Hell, flash both of them." I grabbed my knife and tugged at her corset. "Your life depends on your ability to make those guys hesitate, got it?"

"Got it." Her voice was clearer, and then without hesitation, she pulled her dress down an obscene amount. I nearly choked on my tongue as she moved ahead of me. True to my promise, I shoved her out of the car, she fell to her knees pulling the top of her dress with her.

The minute she landed on the pavement, both men glanced at her, both men hesitated.

It was all I needed.

Two shots.

One in the head, one in the chest.

Both hit the ground hard.

People screamed around us as sirens sounded, and police finally managed to make their way into the circle of jammed cars.

I put the gun in the back of my pants and helped Val to her feet. I would be lying if I said my gaze didn't linger, because fuck, she had a nice body.

One made for sex, hips begging for a man's grasp.

I tugged her dress up. "Are you okay?"

She nodded, but she didn't cry. It freaked me out. Girls that weren't in our life, hell girls that were, they cried.

"Val?" I wrapped my arms around her. "Use your words, please."

"I'm..." She frowned, "Are we going to get arrested?"

"That's what you're concerned about? Not the dead bodies? Being shot at?"

She chewed her lower lip. "It's louder, the gunshots are louder than I thought, they vibrate, making you th-think you've been shot when you're simply an observer." Another sigh. "I'm not sure tears are the right emotion, or sadness, I—" She shuddered. "Thank you. For keeping me safe."

Damn, I could feel my heart growing as I held her close and kissed her head. A police officer whistled as he walked over to the bodies then to me.

"Accident?"

We owned this town. Plain and simple.

And we were still near our neighborhood.

Hell, we didn't just own the town, we owned the mayor. They were in deep, ever since the economic crash; they'd been taking money from both the Abandonatos and Alferos for the last ten years.

And the police had known we were in town.

From the very day we arrived.

Frank was kind like that.

Hell, it was like writing a freaking press release. "The bosses are here, keep them safe at all costs."

"You're a little late." I spat.

"Clearly." He tapped his chin and glanced over at the bodies. "I'll let the Chief know that there was a... situation."

"We need a ride."

"Right away, sir. Were you headed to the airport?"

"Same airport." I sighed. "Different destination."

I ducked into the back of the limo and grabbed my jacket then quickly grabbed our bags out of the limo's trunk and headed over to the waiting police cruiser as the rest of the cops arrived along with the coroner.

I wrapped my jacked around Val. She snuggled into it then surprised me by turning her face toward the collar and inhaling deeply, a half smile playing on her lips. That little movement, almost as though she were savoring my essence, did a number on me, but I had no time to analyze what it might mean.

People were snapping pictures.

News reporters showed up.

And I'm sure the city would spin the story well — but that wasn't my job, my job was to keep my wife safe, and right now, we were sitting ducks.

"To the airport, officer...?"

"Sherman." He tipped his hat.

"Thank you for the help."

"It's an honor." He looked at us through the rearview mirror. "My pops knew the Families, had Christmas drinks with a few of the men every year during his shift in the neighborhood."

I smiled back at him. "I bet he enjoyed those times."

A grin split across Officer Sherman's face. "He still talks about it."

"Tell him to stop by sometime… I'm sure the Family would love to see him."

"Will do." Sherman pulled up to the curb. "Enjoy your honeymoon? I'm assuming you were just married."

"Our honeymoon was unfortunately just cut short," I said feeling more sad than I cared to admit.

Val gripped my hand as we made our way to the ticket counter.

"Two first class tickets to Chicago on the first flight out, please."

The lady nodded and then frowned. "We don't have any flights that—"

"Thank you for your time," I interrupted her and grabbed my phone as I stepped away from the counter. "Nikolai, I need your plane."

"What is this? No 'Hi? Long time no see?'"

"I saw you a half hour ago and since then have ended two lives and been shot at with more rounds than I could count. Give me your damn plane."

"Done," he said without hesitation, all humor drained from his voice. "Need that favor yet?"

"Hah!" I rolled my eyes. "This is it."

"This is a plane. I own six. Hardly a favor. Call me if you need more… man power."

"Workaholic."

"Yes, sounds so much better than masochistic murderer."

"Doesn't it?"

"What airport?"

"JFK."

"You're in luck, my jet is getting refueled for my flight back. I'll stay an extra night and visit with the Family."

"You're sure?"

"I'm sure."

"Thanks Nikolai."

"Of course, and Sergio?"

"Yeah?"

"Love her well tonight."

I sighed. "I'll do my best."

"Do better than your best."

I pressed *end* and held out my hand to Val again. "We've got a plane, let's get you some clothes."

CHAPTER 32

A lion among ladies is a most dreadful thing.
                    –A Midsummer Night's Dream

Valentina

I WAS BARELY hanging on.

Trying desperately to be the type of woman Sergio needed, the kind that didn't scream when getting shot at — the kind who could kill spiders without cursing and point a gun at someone without shaking.

He needed strength.

But what he needed and what I was able to offer were two very different things.

I didn't speak as he grabbed my hand and led me to a nearby store.

"Val?" he whispered gently. "Jeans or leggings, you don't get much choice."

"L-leggings," I whispered, my voice weak, my body even weaker, my vision blurred as I tried to focus on the task at hand. "And um, just a T-shirt or something is fine, flip flops." I reached for a long T-shirt while Sergio grabbed a pair of flip flops.

271

Sergio frowned, "It's Chicago, I'm not so sure you want flip flops."

I swallowed, and found my voice. "I'm on a plane though."

"Size?" he called over to me, apparently letting me win that one.

"Eight-and-a-half." I took the flip flops and walked over to the cash register, then nearly burst into tears because I realized I didn't have any money on me.

Panicked, I let the thought sink in.

I literally had no money.

I mean, I had made money at the flower shop, but I typically just deposited it and used the cash my uncles gave me because they bought me everything.

And my debit card was back in my room.

Because this morning I'd woken up thinking I was getting married and then returning back to my room to change.

Instead, I woke up. Got married. Was swept away in a limo. And was shot at, nearly killed.

And I had no money.

Shame washed over me as I turned around, ready to ask Sergio, but he was already handing his shiny black card to the sales lady.

She swiped.

He signed and thanked her.

And off we went.

Still not talking.

I think a part of me was afraid that if I talked I'd burst into tears or maybe all the screams I'd been holding in would suddenly explode out of my mouth and I wouldn't stop — screaming that is.

A loud bang had me nearly climbing up Sergio's

body.

"Shh, it's okay." He kissed my head. "Someone's suitcase fell over."

"Oh," I croaked. "Sorry, and I'll pay you back when I get my stuff. I do get my stuff later, right? I mean, if we're going to Chicago?"

Sergio's expression grew concerned as he pulled me close and led me to a nearby door. Once we were on the other side, a man in a black suit motioned us over. He typed in a code and escorted us down a long hallway. When we reached the end, he typed in another code, and we were outside.

In front of a private jet.

A huge private jet.

It was black, sleek.

And loud.

"Let's go." Sergio handed our luggage to the same man and then grabbed my hand and pulled me up the stairs and into the warmth of the plane.

"Mr. and Mrs. Abandonato," the captain greeted us with a warm smile. "I'm Captain Parker, I'll be taking you into Chicago. I've been told you want your privacy so there will be no cabin attendant to help you get settled in. My co-pilot and I are only a phone call away." He pointed to a phone attached to the wall. "If you'll just get seated, we'll taxi and take off."

"Thank you." Sergio shook his hand.

"My pleasure." Captain Parker tipped his hat and closed the plane door, then went into the cockpit while I managed to slip out of the jacket Sergio had given me. A chill ran over my arms as anticipation hit me square in the face.

"Val?" Sergio braced my shoulders with his strong

hands. "Look at me."

I was looking at him.

"No, sweetheart, not like that."

"I am looking at you," I whispered. "Aren't I?"

"You're staring through me, you're not really here, your thoughts are definitely not here. We can talk about it, sometimes it helps."

"I'm fine," I lied, the smile that tugged at my lips was worthless, as the sting of tears threatened to take over. "Really!"

Sighing, Sergio refused to release me. "Your things are already packed. You won't be going back to New York. Not until things calm down."

Funny how it would be the simple fact that I wasn't going to see the only family I'd ever known that would cause the tears.

I could hide my terror at what I'd seen an hour ago.

I could force a smile through the violence.

But take away what I love — take away my security? And I was broken.

With a sob, I fell against his chest. "It was so loud!"

"I know." Sergio rubbed my back. "I know."

Shivering, I tried climbing into him, craving security. "And they wouldn't stop and then you just… shot them. That one man… in the head!"

"He felt no pain."

"I don't care about his pain!" I yelled. "I care about the fact that we were nearly killed! And for what? Is this normal?"

He didn't answer.

"Silence isn't helpful. It makes me assume you get shot at all the time." I hiccupped and let more tears fall as I jerked away from him and hugged my stomach.

"Oh, God! We have to go back! Sergio!" I was beyond hysterical. "What if they go after my uncles? Frank! Dante! We have to warn them, we have to—"

"They already know. They'll be fine. I'm more worried about your safety than theirs."

"I'm young! They're feeble and old, and you know Sal has a cane!" I jumped to my feet and pounded against his chest. "Don't do this! Please, please!"

He closed his eyes and held me tightly as I continued to fight against him, not once yelling back, or returning any of the violence, just taking it while I cried.

"Val," Sergio whispered once I'd calmed down. "Believe me when I say, this is not what I had planned for you. I was going to take you on a real honeymoon right after the wedding. It was a surprise. I had your uncles pack as much as they could, we all figured you needed to get used to being married and deserved some time away, but..."

"But," I said with a sniffle. "We got attacked."

"It's not safe." Sergio tilted my chin toward him, the pad of his thumb rolling across my lower lip. "They expect us to be in Mexico. So we're going to Chicago to buy some time and see what the next move will be."

I pushed away from him again and stumbled into one of the seats as the plane started to taxi.

Warm tears streamed down my cheeks. "I'm sorry I'm weak." Admitting it sucked worse than thinking about it. And it only made me cry harder. I'd been married over an hour and I was already a failure.

"What?" Sergio charged over to me, his handsome features barely containing his rage. "What the hell do you mean you're weak?"

"I'm absolutely terrified that I won't ever be able

to get that image out of my head. All of the images actually. Or that every time I hear a popping noise I'll think I'm getting shot at. I'm a failure. Not a true mafia wife. I know... I know I'm young." I took a deep breath. "And innocent, and from what you've said, Andi was... the exact opposite of me." It hurt saying the words out loud; it hurt more than I realized, admitting my own inability to meet his expectations. "I just... I need to be braver. I'll try harder."

"Are you fucking kidding me right now?" Sergio roared, he fell to his knees in front of me and grabbed my hands. "Val, look at me."

His blue eyes locked on mine. He was so beautiful. Just like the story. And that was another thing. My uncles didn't know about the letters.

Meaning, they were forgotten.

I had two more.

And they were lost to me now.

My stomach sank even more.

"You aren't a failure." Sergio cupped my face. "It's a bit presumptuous of you to assume what I do and don't need in a wife. What if I like the idea of finally having someone to protect? Someone to save? Someone who's vulnerable," his voice cracked. "Sometimes Val, it's nice to be needed. Sometimes, it's nice to be someone's hero. Just for once."

I reached my arms around his neck. "I didn't call you a hero."

"You didn't have to."

"That's presumptuous."

"Well, I'm fairly confident in my damsel in distress saving abilities."

"Cocky."

"Eh, do we want to call it arrogance or just the ability to be a bad ass? I mean, call a spade a spade, Val."

I burst out laughing.

He'd made me laugh.

The same guy who looks at people wrong and makes them burst into tears and confess all of their sins.

He'd made me laugh.

"Thanks." I pulled back, our noses almost touched. "For being my hero."

"All in a day's work." His eyes darted to my lips then back up to my eyes as if asking permission.

So I gave it.

By kissing him first.

With a groan he slammed his lips against mine, meeting me halfway. Strong hands dug into my hips pulling me almost completely off the seat as my legs dangled across his lap. Sergio fell back against the floor, tugging me the rest of the way with him. He stayed in a sitting position as he wrapped my ankles around his waist and continued his wicked assault on my lips.

His mouth was hot.

And it felt — dangerously tempting.

Like I was in danger of falling and never being able to get back to where I had the upper hand — then again, I never did have it, not where he was concerned.

His hands slid up my sides causing my body to rise above his, he guided me back down.

I squeezed my thighs around him, with each squeeze more and more sensation built, his movements were slow. And every time my body collapsed against his, I felt him pushing into me.

Too much dress was blocking our bodies from joining.

Well that, and the fact that he still had clothes on too.

But I wanted it.

Fear wasn't attached to the way we kissed — only hot exploration on my part, and need on his.

"Please prepare for takeoff," the captain said over the speaker.

"Damn it." Sergio pulled away from me, eyes wild. "We should..." He pointed at the chairs.

I hadn't even noticed how nice the inside of the plane was, I was too busy noticing how sexy he was, well that, and having a nervous breakdown.

Cream-colored leather captain chairs and couches were decorated sparsely around the main cabin. A small kitchen and mini bar with a flat screen TV was on the opposite side, and a door that I imagined led to either the bathroom or a bedroom was at the far end.

"I won't pressure you." Sergio kissed my mouth again. "Tonight."

"What about tomorrow? Will you pressure me then?" I just had to ask.

"No." He grinned smugly. "I don't think I'll have to."

"There you go with that arrogance again."

"I'm cocky." He thrust against me, then chuckled darkly against my neck. "What can I say?"

The plane started picking up speed, so I hurried off him, adjusted my dress as best I could, and buckled up in one of the seats nearest him.

Once we were airborne, Sergio took off his seatbelt and walked over to me, he leaned over, his mouth hovering near my ear as he whispered, "Don't move."

CHAPTER 33

And sleep, that sometimes shuts up sorrow's eye, Steal me awhile from my own company.

–A Midsummer Night's Dream

Sergio

I WAS BEING cruel.

Well, not cruel.

But using her fear against her.

Chest heaving with each breath she took, Val froze, her entire body going rigid as I stood in front of her, bent over and slowly unbuckled her seat belt.

I kissed her right cheek, then her left, my lips hovering over her mouth. Her innocent kisses had become addictive in the worst way.

I'd forgotten.

It was that simple.

I'd been so lost in my own sadness and mourning that I'd ignored every single carnal thought — thinking it almost a betrayal against *her* memory.

But each kiss with Val brought me closer and closer to the edge until, finally, I took the leap, only to realize it wasn't guilt I was met with.

But lust. Need. Desire.

I remembered that I liked sex — hell, I loved it.

I wanted it, I could taste it, taste her arousal in the air every time my tongue touched her lips and her innocent little hands reached for my body.

I was hard before I had even touched her.

A virgin.

A girl who hadn't even been kissed.

Which meant I couldn't just slam her against the wall and toss up her skirt, or tell her to bend over and take me.

Damn, just imagining all the different positions had me wound up all over again.

I needed to lock her in the bedroom so I didn't strip her bare and sink myself into her inch by inch.

"Come on." I lifted her into my arms and carried her back into the bedroom. She wasn't as light as Andi had been.

More muscular.

More curves.

And for the first time in a while, it didn't feel like I was making a comparison, where Val fell short and Andi won.

It was more of an observation. She was heavier.

And I liked it.

Her lips were fuller.

And they tasted different.

But they were wicked — tempting.

And when she kissed me, my body buzzed with awareness, my tongue nearly going numb with adrenaline as I felt my blood surge.

I sat her down gently on the bed and crossed my

arms. "Why don't you change into the clothes we bought since yours are packed. You can take a nap." Val was staring at me. And for the first time since I'd met her, I couldn't for the life of me read her expression. So I kept talking, my voice getting louder as if to quiet my thoughts, the dangerous thoughts that pointed out how sexy she was sitting on the bed, and how her right thigh was exposed all the way up to her hip crease.

"And." I coughed and turned around in a semi-circle, trying my damndest to find the light. "Here's the light switch."

Val's eyebrows rose.

"For…" Another awkward cough. What the hell? "Turning… the lights off."

"That is what switches tend to do," Val said sweetly. "Turn off things."

I swallowed, my body completely on board with the whole turn off turn on scenario. "So…" I found my voice, thank God. "Maybe sleep off all the trauma."

"Okay," Val agreed quickly and stood. "But first can you help me with my dress?"

"What was that?" I asked hoarsely, my hands shaking at my sides.

She turned her back to me. "My dress, the back few buttons are impossible to reach. It's a bodice after all, and I don't want to rip the rest of it from the front."

Was she sure about that? Because I was pretty sure I could get on board with said ripping. Instead, I moved toward her and quickly undid the twelve torturous buttons, my fingers trembled as I found the zipper and slid it down the rest of the way.

The sound was more erotic than it should be.

The rustling of her dress as it fell to her feet.

My heavy breathing as I placed my hands on her shoulders.

Only to look up and realize.

She literally had no bra on.

At all.

But she did have on a white lacy thong, nestled between the sexiest ass cheeks I'd ever seen in my entire life.

No comparison necessary.

Just simple truth.

Her ass was more than nice.

Staring at it made me dizzy and jealous at the same time, that the simple scrap of fabric was going to get more action than me.

I slid my hands down her smooth arms then took a step back. "Done."

She turned, hands on hips. "Are you?"

"Hell."

"Sergio?"

"Don't tempt a sinner, sweetheart."

"Funny, I always thought you were more saint." She was like a goddess before me, all curves and smooth skin. My eyes had trouble focusing on one general thing. Funny, how before it had been my goal to focus on just legs, or just her hips, or just her eyes, hell even her ears.

And now, it was laughable. Completely ridiculous how blind I'd been, how I hadn't seen it sooner.

How gorgeous she was.

Because what made Val... Val... what made her beautiful — had everything to do with all of those features. By themselves, they were perfection, they painted a picture of such deep-rooted beauty that, had

I looked at her, truly seen her the first day I met her.

I would have been screwed.

And most likely jumped off a building to keep myself from feeling — from taking — from following through.

"I don't know how to do this," she confessed in a soft voice. "Your move, Sergio."

I wasn't worthy of that type of trust.

"Are you sure?"

"No."

Her answer surprised me. "You're not sure, and yet you're standing in front of me topless?"

"I don't think a virgin is ever sure. That would be lying. You want truth in this marriage? You promised me your body." She took a step forward. "Now give it to me."

Her hands shook, it was barely noticeable. My girl was being brave. Hell, she could cry over gunfights all day long — but bravery in the bedroom? It was all I needed.

And something I never even knew I was desperate for.

Permission to be *with* her.

Minus the guilt of withholding the best parts of me.

Two steps and my hands connected with her lush body, pulling her against me, her breasts pressed against my chest, teasing, taunting.

I moved my hands to cup them both. Damn it, she might be young, but she was all woman.

The power she had over me was humbling and terrifying all at once. Our mouths met in a frenzied kiss. My hands dug into her hair while she gripped my ass.

Where the hell did virgins already know how to please a man before he's even inside her?

Her nails dug into my slacks.

With a curse I pulled back and jerked my shirt over my head tossing it to the side. The plane hit a patch of turbulence sending her into my arms. I fell onto my back pulling her with me, just as we hit another bump.

The seatbelt light flicked on in the bedroom.

"What do you say?" I grinned. "Live dangerously?"

"Oh, I've got that covered." Val smirked. "I married the mob."

"Yeah, you did." I burst out laughing.

In bed.

With my new wife.

Crazy.

Impossible.

But there it was.

She licked her lips then trailed a finger down the middle of my chest. "I want to…" She looked lower. "Please you."

"I want that…" I grabbed both of her hands. "Later. But right now, let's make this more about us than about me."

Her eyes widened.

Probably like mine did.

My admission scared me.

Because I was no longer thinking in the singular — but as a team.

With a new partner.

One I'd never asked for.

One who'd been forced upon me.

Again.

Her eyes searched mine as if to say, "What now?"

I tugged her head down, our mouths meeting somewhere in the middle as I tasted her over and over again, then hooked my foot around her legs, flipping her onto her back. The plane bounced, causing her to jerk up toward me.

I was going to use the turbulence in my favor.

With a sly smirk, I kicked off my pants then crawled slowly up her body, leaving no patch of skin without attention from either my lips or my tongue.

Her eyes closed, and opened, closed again. "I feel…"

"Everything," I said for her. "I want you to feel everything."

CHAPTER 34

My heart is true as steel.

-A Midsummer Night's Dream

Valentina

STEAL HIS BODY — his heart will follow.

The note on my wedding day, the one that came with the dress, had very specific instructions. Steal his body, his heart will follow. Along with the dress and my note was the one for Sergio.

I didn't know what it meant. What any of it meant.

And I'd been too traumatized to think about it until the kiss.

Would I have been as brave without the encouragement? Probably not. But something about the way he was mumbling about turning the lights on and off was cute, like part of his alpha attitude had somehow taken a detour and revealed a nervousness and vulnerability I'd never seen in him before.

It set me at ease.

And had me wondering — did he want me as much as I wanted him?

Worst case scenario, he rejects me and slams the door. Been there, done that, only this time it would suck worse because I'd be half-naked.

The words from the note still haunted me.

Steal his body — his heart will follow.

So I did the only thing I knew how — after all, it worked with killers right? Flashing boob? That's how we'd survived earlier.

I figured if it worked on those killers.

It would work on my husband.

And it did.

Too well.

Sergio's mouth was so wet and hot that I had trouble not squirming beneath him each time his sizzling lips met my skin.

I grabbed a fistful of his hair as he lowered his mouth to my thigh, so dangerously close to kissing me in a place I wasn't sure I was ready for.

My body tensed with nervousness and maybe a bit of dread — it was the unknown, and everything felt good, but it was new. And scary.

He pulled back abruptly, his expression one of concentration. "Get up."

"No!" I shook my head. "I'll do better? See? Not tense!" I tried relaxing as much as I could, while his lips twitched with a smile. "Are you laughing at me?"

"On the inside," he said in a serious voice. "Does that make it better?"

I pouted. "No."

Sergio tugged me up to a sitting position then pulled me to my feet, taking my place at the foot of the bed. He still had boxer briefs on, but they hid nothing. If I was intimidated before. I was freaking the hell out now.

"Sit here." He pulled my body down so I was facing him, my legs straddling him like before. The plane jolted, my body slammed against his, the friction, the feel of our bodies was hot. And good. So good, that if I just moved a little more, a little faster.

"Ride me," he whispered in my ear. "Hard."

Was that what I was doing?

"And get out of your damn head." His mouth met mine in a long, languid kiss. I was dizzy with the sensation of him pressed against me, along with his tongue in my mouth.

He deepened the kiss, moaning as I moved against him more.

The turbulence hit again. I fell against him harder.

"Fuck." He breathed against my neck. "Just like that, let your body take over..."

"But—"

He gripped my hips, his teeth nibbling on my neck between kisses as he thrust me against him. The turbulence, or maybe the universe, agreed because each time we hit a bump it was like our bodies fought to join one another.

Sensations built up within me, impossible to stop the need to move faster, harder against him.

"That's it," he urged, his voice hoarse. "Let go, sweetheart."

The plane jolted.

And so did I as something broke around me, maybe it was my body, my heart, a mixture of both. It felt — too good to be true.

Without giving me any time to think about what just happened, Sergio picked me up by the butt and tossed me onto the bed, kicking off his black boxer briefs, and then very slowly tugging my thong down my legs.

This was happening.

The sensations were gone.

Replaced with a bit of trepidation as a man who I'd seen snap other men in half, hovered his powerful godlike body over me.

He was both beast and prince.

The lines of his body were breathtaking. He wore scars of his battles on his perfect skin, his strong jaw clenched as he lowered his body, closer, and closer, until finally we were skin to skin.

I let out a gasp as he slowly teased my entrance. "You're ready for me...."

"How do you know?" Pressure built inside of me again, an intense need for something I didn't know how to vocalize.

"Trust me." His lips grazed my ear, and then he was kissing me again. This kiss was different, almost violent in nature, so easy to get caught up in, all consuming. Our breathing was one. And then he sank into me.

Completely.

I gasped and then let out a pathetic whimper.

He covered my mouth with his then pulled back. "I'm sorry, it's never easy the first time."

"That's it?" I frowned, slightly disappointed.

He grinned as his body moved in and out, building up a slow cadence, allowing me to get used to the fullness. "Hell, no."

I nodded.

Once.

Twice.

He shifted so he could reach between our bodies. Everything about his body was heavy, massive, sweaty, as his calloused palm pressed firmly against my core, the aching sensation intensified as he thrust into me again and again.

My mouth fell open with a moan as he kissed the side of my neck, and whispered, "Open your eyes."

"Don't want to."

"You do."

"I don't."

"Watch me fuck you."

Maybe I was scandalized, or shocked, or a mixture of both, but I opened my eyes and what I saw wasn't what he described.

He thought he was.

He wanted it to be simple.

But there was nothing but tenderness as he slowed his pace and lengthened each thrust so deep I thought I was going to combust.

"Yes," I whimpered clawing at his back. "Please."

"Please what?"

"Please..." I tugged his mouth down to mine and kissed it tenderly changing the way I clung to him, embracing him, showing him with my body that this was more — we were more than what he was making it. "Make love to me, Sergio. Make me forget everything but us."

A pained expression crossed his features as he thrust one last time, his body pressing mine into the bed as his mouth found mine in a punishing kiss.

Something shifted in that moment between us when I cried out and he collapsed against me.

Something epic.

But I didn't have time to figure it out, because as soon as he collapsed against me, jerked away, scooped his clothes from the floor and stomped out of the room, slamming the door behind him.

CHAPTER 35

For never anything can be amiss, when simpleness and duty tender it.

–A Midsummer Night's Dream

Sergio

ANGER.

Always attacks in two different ways.

Either it's a slow burn, a swirling bitter madness pumping into your veins until you feel like you're going to explode.

Or it's sudden.

Like getting shot in the chest with acid, but being paralyzed, unable to move, and in that moment, you like the feeling, you accept it.

You deserve it.

Madness.

Anger.

Uncontrollable anger.

For the first time in my life.

Both happened simultaneously as I threw my clothes against the wall. Not enough. It wasn't enough.

It still hurt.

The anger still pumped.

I slammed my hands against the bar and shoved all the crystal glassware off. It flew through the air and hit my bare feet then spread around the floor of the plane.

Chest heaving, I punched the mahogany bar with my right fist over and over and over again.

"Sergio." Val's voice was calm. Why the hell was she calm.

"Leave!" I yelled without turning around, not trusting my own violence, my inability to turn on her. "NOW!"

A quiet "No," was whispered.

And then her arms wrapped around my waist.

I tried to pull her away but it was like all of my strength had abandoned me.

"Fuck." I slid to the ground, through Val's arms and pulled my knees to my chest. "You need to go."

She didn't argue, but she still wouldn't leave.

"Val, I'm warning you."

Was she stupid?

I refused to look at her.

I already felt like shit. The last thing I needed to see was the anger in her eyes, the rejection, the vulnerability. I'd just taken her virginity and ran out of the room like demons were chasing me.

They were.

They clawed at my bleeding body, laughing, taunting, shaking me until I wanted to burn in hell — right along with my sins.

I wanted to be more than my past, more than the all consuming darkness, and for a few brief moments, I'd felt happy, the happiest I'd been in a long time.

But as soon as the happiness occurred, the guilt followed. Being inside her, knowing her in that way, it was like I was being forced to let go.

In order to accept her.

I had to let go of Andi.

I refused to do that.

I couldn't do that.

"Damn it." I rubbed my face with my eyes. "Val, I need to be alone. I'm sorry I'm being a jackass. But, can you please just leave?"

"No."

"What the hell is wrong with you?" I barked, irritated that she wouldn't just give me one minute to myself. It was all I needed. Just one damn minute to think things through. To process what had just happened.

To re-live the way she tasted.

The way she felt.

Even though it was wrong.

So damn wrong to feel — a completeness with her that I'd…

My fists shook. She was different from Andi, I knew that. What I didn't expect.

Was for my feelings for her, after one encounter.

To be stronger.

And I hated myself for it.

Had I even loved Andi?

My chest ached.

And it wouldn't go away.

She was the problem.

Val.

She needed to be the one running — there'd been a reason I kept a distance, and now I knew.

Oh, I knew all right.

She was dangerous — the power she already had over me was palpable, like something had changed even in the air between us, the swirling tension of sex, lust, hurt feelings... love.

"Get some sleep, Val," I whispered. "I'm not good company right now."

I tried to sound more gentle, more in control of my words.

"I think you need someone... maybe, even if that someone doesn't do anything except sit next to you in broken glass."

I glanced down, my feet were cut up, my hands were bleeding and bruised, and she was sitting on glass next to me, like it wasn't piercing into her skin, like she was okay with the pain, because it was shared with my own.

With a sigh, Val held out her hand to me.

I stared at it like it was a foreign object. "It's just a hand, Sergio."

"No." I bit down on my lip tasting blood. "It's not."

Val gripped my bleeding hand in hers and held it tight. "For now. It is. Make it simple, Sergio. I'm holding your hand because you're upset. That's all there is to it, okay?"

I didn't trust myself to speak, so I nodded as I found myself squeezing her hand back as if it was a lifeline.

THE PLANE LANDED.

And I still hadn't spoken more than a few sentences to Val. She'd changed into her clothes and started cleaning up the mess of glass.

I was dressed in my slacks and white shirt from the wedding, but my clothes felt dirty, tarnished. And I had no idea why.

After thanking the pilot, I sent a quick note to Nikolai to warn him about the mess and offer to pay for the damages. Not that he'd probably care, but still.

A Mercedes-Maybach waited on the tarmac, its engine running, and one of the Family associates, Darin, in the driver's seat. The minute we stepped off the plane, he got out of the car and opened our doors.

"Did you have a nice flight, Mr. Abandonato?"

I dared not look at Val.

"It was turbulent," she answered for me. "But a quick trip."

Darin nodded his head, pieces of salt and pepper hair fell over his forehead. "Good, I'll take your bags."

His eyebrows shot up as he moved by me and grabbed the bags from the plane. I'd known him since I was a punk kid, his expression said it all.

She was beautiful.

Yeah, message received.

And she looked like the Family — like Luca.

"Get in," I barked to her. "We're out in the open." It was a lie, nobody would dare touch us in Chicago, on our turf, but I didn't want Darin making any more comments or looking at her for that matter.

Val nodded and slid across the plush leather seat.

I followed, waiting for Darin to hurry his ass up so I could get home and lock myself away from my new wife.

"I've never been to Chicago," Val said in a small voice. "It's colder than I thought."

"It's always cold," I muttered. God save me from small talk.

She shook a bit next to me. "Do you think I can turn the heat up?"

Frowning, I glanced over at her hands only to see both of them clasped in her lap, shaking like leaves. When I met her gaze, her face was pale, like a ghost.

Hell, the last thing I wanted was to feel like shit about it, but I did.

Because this was all new to her.

On top of everything that happened on the plane, she was fully entering into my lifestyle.

And had no idea how to do it.

There was no manual.

No directions.

Nothing, but stay alive and watch your back.

I needed the girls.

With a sigh, I reached over to the panel in the back and turned up the heat and flipped on her seat warmer, then grabbed my phone from my pocket and dialed.

"Yo," Mil answered on the first ring. "You land?"

"Yeah." I was suddenly exhausted. "Look, can you bring the girls over to the—"

"Dude, we've been at your house for the past two hours. I'm a mind reader. You can thank me later."

"Or not at all," I joked.

"You're an asshole. Why do we keep you around?"

"I'm too expensive to kill?" I offered.

"Eh, nobody would even find your body. Mo's got that shit locked down."

"Word!" Mo yelled loudly.

"Are you guys watching gangster movies again?"

Silence and then. "They're Trace's favorite, and apparently you get special treatment when you're pregnant."

"Hear, hear!" a voice yelled in the background. I couldn't tell if it was Bee or Trace, but did it really matter? The women were adjoined at the hip; it would be annoying if it wasn't so necessary in our lives.

Family was everything.

Sighing, I said, "We'll see you guys in about fifteen."

"'Kay, and Sergio?"

"Yeah?" I croaked out, my vision blurring from exhaustion and stress. "What?"

"It may not be okay right now. But one day it will be."

"That's the problem, Mil, that's the damn problem, isn't it?"

She was quiet.

Mil and I had always gotten along. Being Phoenix's stepsister hadn't been easy for her and, on top of that, she was married to Chase of all people, she was quick, a fast talker, terrifying, and the only female mob boss in the history of the Cosa Nostra. She saw things other people didn't see.

So my response probably wasn't a surprise to her.

Because I knew, the day when everything was okay.

Would also be the day — that I let Andi go.

CHAPTER 36

That would hang us, every mother's son.
                    –A Midsummer Night's Dream

Valentina

I WOULD BE lying if I said I was okay, that I wasn't feeling humiliated, angry, frustrated, confused. And yet, I was also sad.

Sad for him.

Because the battle was so evident in his face, in the way his shoulders slumped the entire ride through the city. He was upset.

And for good reason.

I was an interloper.

A stand-in for what he really wanted — what he'd always needed.

I would never take the place of what he'd had — but part of me wondered if that was how these things worked. I mean, I was a completely different person, I would never be her, but saying that out loud to him just seemed like a really poor life choice.

He had a gun.

And he'd punched the crap out of a wooden bar.

Nearly sliced open arteries with glass shards.

Yeah, he needed space.

But when you're hurting — at least in my small, innocent mind, what you said was usually the opposite of what you wanted.

So I'd held his hand, terrified that he was going to turn on me. His wild eyes were more exhaustion than anger, now that we'd been driving for a few miles.

I felt lonely.

I missed Gio, Sal, and Papi, and my heart hurt when I thought of Dante being all by himself. Even Frank had grown on me, and now it was like I was ripped away from my old life and given a new one without anyone ever asking me if I was okay with it.

I knew Sergio was hurting, God, I could feel his pain, it was a tangible thing, his sadness, his anger, but, part of me just wanted someone to ask if I was okay.

I needed my hand held too.

I needed a hug.

Or even just something familiar.

We took an exit then drove down a long road that led to a huge iron gate. Something buzzed, and the gate opened.

The house was massive.

Two stories.

With a fountain in the middle.

Huge.

Fairy tale huge.

Hah, ironic, that I'd get part of the fairy tale, at least let there be a library or something.

Since I'd married the beast, give me books.

I gulped as a few men in suits shuffled out of the

house and nodded toward the car.

Our door opened.

Mouth still gaping, I took a step out of the car and toward the stairs leading up to the house, just as a girl shot out from the double doors and ran at full speed toward us.

I backed up.

She stopped right in front of Sergio and winked. "I see Tex didn't kill you."

"Sadly, no." Sergio smirked. "Your concern is noted, Mo."

"Eh, what can you do?" She pulled him in for a tight hug and then turned to me. "Fresh meat?"

I opened then shut my mouth.

"I was kidding," she said in a softer tone. "You're young."

Was that really what everyone thought about me when they saw me?

"Hell, Sergio, I could have sworn I found a wrinkle on my right eye, look." She pointed to the side of her face while Sergio rolled his eyes.

"Mo, you're twenty-three."

With a sigh, she looped her arm in mine and leaned down. "You look like him. Like Luca."

"I look like a man?" I blurted out.

Mo burst out laughing. "And you're adorable, has anyone ever told you how sultry your voice is? It's really low, deep, but sexy as hell. Don't you think she's sexy as hell, Serg?"

It was his turn to pale.

I turned into myself, nearly leaning on Mo as rejection threatened to choke the life out of me.

I was embarrassed.

Ashamed.

Did I smell like him?

Like sex?

Could she tell?

Every movement I made was a reminder that we'd been intimate, my thighs still buzzed with pleasure, I was sore, and my mouth was swollen.

"Not awkward at all, jackass." Mo glared at him. "Leopards really don't change spots do they?"

"The girls?" Sergio ignored her. "Inside?"

"Yeah, we were fixing up her room."

I frowned. "Her?"

"Yours," Mo said softly. "We figured after spending a few days with Sergio you'd want your own space away from the beast, so we made up a bad ass room, with enough clothes to drive any girl mad with envy. We got your sizes from Phoenix."

"Phoenix!" Sergio yelled, "Where the hell did he get her sizes?"

Mo just grinned.

I was too tired to be upset that I wasn't sharing a room with Sergio. He needed space, right? Maybe I did, too.

Maybe it was just too much.

Mo kept chattering about the clothes in my room, she was about two inches taller than me, which wasn't anything new since I'd always been somewhat short. Her long, silky black hair met her waist; it was gorgeous.

She was gorgeous.

The sound of laughter filled the house as Mo led me toward a room and announced, "Look who I have!"

All laughing ceased.

The girls all turned their heads. They all had dark features, and were absolutely mind-numbingly stunning. To the point where I wasn't sure who was prettier.

All of them?

One was at least eight months pregnant. She glowed more than the rest; her eyes twinkled in my direction as she elbowed the girl to her right, whose smirk looked like she'd won a bet or something.

"Hi." I managed to get out and then, like a total loser; I burst into tears.

"Oh, honey!" One of the girls rushed forward and suddenly I had five women hugging on me and bringing me over to a large white couch.

"Pour her wine!" one yelled. "Get the chocolate!"

Within minutes, I had a huge glass of wine in one hand and a chocolate bar in the other. Stunned, I stared at all of them as more tears streamed down my face. "I'm so sorry. I swear I'm normally not a crier. Well, I mean if you count lately I am, but—"

"Everything okay in here?" Sergio knocked on the open door.

One of the girls jumped to her feet and marched over the door. Without answering, she slammed it in his face and locked it.

I gasped. "Did you just slam the door in his face?"

"Eh, he's fine." She grinned.

My eyes narrowed. She looked familiar, like really familiar. And suddenly everything clicked into place. "You!"

Her grin widened. "Me?"

"YOU!" I nearly jumped out of my seat. "You were at the bank!"

"Nice to meet you Val, officially." She put her hands on her hips. "The names Emiliana, but you can call me Mil. I'm Chase's wife."

One of the girls made the sign of the cross over her chest next to me as if to say good luck with that.

"I don't..." I took a deep breath. "I don't understand, what were you doing at the bank? And who was that other guy?"

"Robbing it?" Mil offered with a sly smirk. "I'm good with my hands."

"Stop, you'll give her weird Chase sex nightmares." One of the girls to my right started rubbing my back, her smile was captivating, trusting. "I'm Trace by the way, Nixon's better half."

"Hear, hear!" Mo laughed, while the rest of the girls lifted their glasses in the air, the pregnant one held a water bottle to her lips and winked at me.

"Mo, which one are you married to?"

"The tall ugly one," she said in a completely serious voice. "Really loud, yells a lot, often has dreams about using Sergio as target practice."

"Tex?" I guessed. "Th-the Cappo?"

Mo snickered. "Please don't stutter his name around him, he'll be impossible to live with, already is."

The girl with the water bottle sat near my feet. "I'm Bee."

"You're due soon?" I was glad that the conversation wasn't about me anymore, because I knew if I talked about me, about my situation, I'd feel sorry for myself, and I'd probably cry again, and the last thing I wanted to do was cry in front of new friends, new family.

She nodded. "Yeah, any day now. I can't wait to get this little monster out of me. Phoenix is stressing the life out of me as it is. If he was here he'd probably send me to bed."

Phoenix seemed the darkest to me, but something fit about their situation, he would be protective about his pregnant wife, because without even knowing me, he'd acted that way toward me, as if I was important, even though I was a complete stranger.

"So." Mil sat cross legged in front of me, bringing her wine to her lips. "Did you find what you were looking for?"

"Huh?"

"With the key you had, did you find what you were looking for?"

"Did you…?" I tried to piece the timing together. "How did you know I would be there that day?"

"We have our ways." She didn't say anything else, just drank more wine as her eyes locked on mine over her glass. When she set it down, she raised her eyebrows. "Well? Did you?"

I wasn't sure how to answer. "Yes and no."

The girls got quiet.

A loud knock sounded on the door. "Son of a bitch, Mo! How many clothes did you buy?"

"You can afford it, you jackass!" she yelled back.

"You demo'd the entire room!"

"It needed it!"

The girls all fell into fits of laughter as he stomped off swearing.

I made a face. "What did you guys do?"

"Eh." Trace waved me off. "You needed a room that was close to Sergio's but didn't have ghosts of the past, so we basically remodeled one of the bathrooms and upstairs living areas into a giant master suite. It's gorgeous and there's a connecting door to his room just in case."

Hah, just in case.

I looked down at my hands and mumbled, "Thank you. I don't know how to repay you guys."

"Give him hell," Mo said as my head jerked up. "That's how you repay us, Nicolasi, give him hell."

"I'm an Abandonato now," I said in a defeated voice. "I was a Nicolasi all my life and didn't know, and now I have a new name, one that doesn't even—"

"—fit." Trace grabbed my hand. "I would say to give him time, but, he's had it. And Andi wouldn't want him to be this way. In fact, she'd probably kick his ass if she could. Wouldn't surprise me at all if she found out a way to haunt him."

The girls laughed.

"What was she like?" I asked. "He doesn't talk about her much."

Trace exchanged a glance with Mil who shook her head slowly and said, "Not yet."

"Huh?" I frowned. "Am I missing something?"

"Wait until you read the last note. And then we'll show you the room."

"My room?"

It was silent and then Bee whispered, "Hers."

Later that night, when I was settled into bed with the same glass of wine on my night stand, I realized.

They had known about the notes.

All of them had.

What game were they playing?

Were they the ones writing them?

Not that it mattered, since the notes were long gone by now. I shivered under the blankets, then finally tossed them over and went to the suitcase that had been packed for me.

I unzipped it and started rummaging for something warmer when my hand touched paper.

Frowning, I gave a little tug.

Every single note was wrapped in a little package, including the last two.

I dropped the package like it was fire.

Phoenix had packed my bags.

Was it him all along?

Mil was his sister. Was that how he knew?

My head hurt. It was going in complete circles.

I grabbed a Henley and pulled it over my tank top then started walking back toward my lonely bed, only to hear a knock at the door.

"Come in," I called.

"Thanks." Sergio walked in two steps and looked around, his eyes taking in the giant open concept room with a walk-in closet that was bigger than my entire room back in New York.

The clothes were all designer.

All new.

And all in my size.

I had a moment of rage when I wanted to tear them all off of the hangers and set them on fire, not because I wasn't thankful, but because gifts weren't the way to my heart — if he knew that, he'd know it didn't matter if I lived in a shoe box with one good pair of shoes and a T-shirt, or had a mansion. He'd know that nothing material mattered. Even though for the most part the gift was more the girls than it was him.

Please hug me. I silently begged.

Or at least look at me.

Tell me it's going to be okay.

I shivered, hugging my body close as Sergio's icy eyes finally landed on mine.

He might as well be in another country with the way he looked at me, physically putting distance between our two bodies, refusing to move any closer. "So," he said, and did a little half circle. "By now you know the girls are insane."

I offered a small smile. "Yeah, I kind of love them."

"Terrifying, the fact that they're reproducing carbon copies."

Small talk? Really?

"Did you need anything?" I asked.

He opened his mouth then shut it, his eyes conveying a deep-rooted sadness and pain that I knew he refused to share with me, which hurt even more than being left alone, because I wanted to help him.

Seeing him in pain hurt me.

He just didn't know it yet.

"Well." He rocked back on his heels. "Sleep well."

"Thanks. You too."

CHAPTER 37

I know a bank where the wild thyme blows, Where oxlips and the nodding violet gowns, Quite over canopied with luscious woodbine, With sweet musk-roses, and with eglantine.

–A Midsummer Night's Dream
TWO WEEKS LATER

Valentina

"Sleep well." Sergio nodded.

"You too."

It was our thing.

During the day, he avoided me, slamming doors, running errands. And I caught up on every TV show known to mankind. After a while, boredom won out, and I asked one of the girls to teach me how to do something useful.

Bee came over on Mondays to help me cook, though she had to sit the whole time since she was due any day now.

Trace taught me how to shoot out in the fields, she always had funny stories about Wyoming and made me feel like it was okay to be scared. I cried with her a few times, broke down to where I was so embarrassed I cried more.

But Trace didn't say anything. She just held me and told me it would get better.

Mil helped with the anger. Fridays I did kick boxing sessions, and she'd taped a picture of Sergio's face on the punching bag. At first I felt horrible.

And then Sergio walked by the home gym and just kept walking.

The guilt disappeared, and anger replaced it, a red-hot anger. How dare he ignore me!

I stopped reading the notes too. I had one left.

I didn't want to stop but they made me hopeful.

I was hurting.

I was lonely.

And Dante wasn't texting me back.

Gio had answered the phone when I called and said Frank was busy with Dante and that I'd get to talk to him soon.

The rest of the guys had returned from New York shortly after I arrived in Chicago but they didn't stop by right away.

I think it was their way of letting Sergio and I have time together.

Little did they know, there was no time.

Scratch that, there was time, it was just all spent on my own.

Mo visited the most often, sometimes every day. She always tried to get me to go shopping, and when my own black shiny credit card arrived with my new last name and a credit line with no limit, she said we should buy a car and put Sergio in it, set it on fire, and roll it off a cliff. I laughed, but she didn't.

I wanted to defend him.

But I was tired of lying for him.

Tired of forcing smiles when he was around, when we were in front of people, I knew my moment was coming. When I wouldn't have any energy left.

When I'd snap.

It was only a matter of time, before he sucked the life out of me, because he couldn't get over a death.

I flicked off the light and stared at the door, my mind wandering, my heart hurting.

Sergio Abandonato, my husband, was not living.

He wasn't even dead.

He was a ghost.

And only he could set himself free.

CHAPTER 38

I'll put a girdle round about the earth in forty minutes.
—A Midsummer Night's Dream

Sergio

I WAS TORTURING myself.

I figured if I purposefully remembered everything about Andi, going as far as to even keep her room in perfect condition with all the memories of us together — that maybe I would remember what it was like to be with her and only her.

During the day, I forced my thoughts to Andi.

But nights were completely different, because at night I lost complete control. I couldn't guard my thoughts.

At night, I yearned for Val.

I thirsted for her.

So many nights I'd stand by her door, my hand lifted to knock, only to back up and return to my bed, to sleep, dreaming of the way she responded to me, the way she kissed me, accepted me, was willing to say yes to me.

I knew she was angry, too.

Hurting.

It was a vicious cycle, each of us only focusing on ourselves, refusing to take that first step. And it was my fault. How the hell was I supposed to expect a girl so young to continually put herself in the line of fire when every single time she did, I took a kill shot?

Frank was still in New York, but he was sending Dante, apparently things had gotten more dangerous, so I was to hide the other twin, put him under the protection of all of our families while Frank flushed out Xavier.

Though he still wasn't sure if he was going to simply hire a hit on him and offer an abhorrent amount of money, or take him out himself.

Frank had sounded tired, broken down.

Join the club.

I was exhausted already, and it was only six at night, family dinner night. Everyone invited themselves over to my house since Dante was expected to arrive.

Which meant one more night where I had to force a smile and make everyone think everything was okay between me and Val when really I'd never felt more distant from another human being.

The doorbell rang.

I shuffled over to answer, but the door burst open before I had the chance. Tex was carrying balloons, while the rest of the crew filed in after him, each of them carrying presents.

"VAL!" Mil shouted, piercing my ears with her loudness. "Get your ass down here! We have presents!"

Frowning, I watched as each couple went into the kitchen, wine was pulled out, dishes were shuffled around as food was set on the counter.

It was Chase's turn to cook, which meant we were probably getting some sort of difficult pasta dish.

My breath hitched the minute Val stepped into the kitchen. Her hair was pulled back into a high ponytail, she was wearing tight jeans and a sweater, and she couldn't have looked more beautiful. Her fresh face was shining as she hugged each of the girls and kissed the guys on the cheek.

Since when had she gotten over her fear of them?

Where the hell had I been?

"Hey!" Tex held out a fist to her, she bumped it. "How's the car engine sound now?"

"Good." She sagged in relief. "Thank you so much for coming to my rescue yesterday."

"The hell?" I barked. "Rescue?"

Tex blinked over at me. "You still live here?"

Nixon smacked him in the back of the head and addressed me. "She had a flat tire on her way home from getting some groceries, and you know how Tex can't turn down an opportunity to ride in like a white knight."

"Damn it!" Chase yelled. "Phoenix just tell me where the white horse is!"

"Nope." Phoenix poured a healthy glass of wine and lifted it in Tex's direction. Ever since Phoenix had left a note about a white horse for his sister, Chase had been on the hunt.

Sad bastard.

"Why didn't you call me?" I just had to ask.

Val's gaze met mine. "I did."

"But—"

"You didn't answer." She gulped as her cheeks

319

burned red. "Anyway, thanks, Tex." She gave him a small hug then went over and started talking to Phoenix about Muay Thai.

The hell?

She knew what that even was?

I was still frozen in the spot when I saw another wrapped gift make its way to the table via Nixon, who slid it next to the others. Five gifts. For what?

"Why all the gifts?" I asked, completely confused.

All talking ceased.

Shit. What now?

Val couldn't get any redder if you dumped her in a tank of tomato juice.

"It's Val's birthday," Mo said, her eyes flashing with venom.

"Fuck." I rubbed my face with my hands.

Tears filled Val's eyes as she slowly walked backward and then turned on her heel and ran out of the room.

I chased after her.

The scene was too familiar for words, chasing after my wife as she ran out of the house and into the field.

The same field Andi had died in.

Was the one that Val chose to run through.

Of course.

Because that was life.

She stopped suddenly, her body going rigid, before she turned on her heel and marched toward me.

I felt like I needed to back up, but I wasn't sure why.

Until she punched me in the face, sending me to the ground.

"Shit!" I hissed. "Since when do you punch people!"

"You're not even a person!" she yelled. "You're

not human! A human, a decent human would ask if I was okay! A decent human would make sure there was food in the house! A decent human would come to my rescue after I was followed home with a flat tire! You don't even remember my birthday? I told you yesterday! I told you at dinner! And you said okay!"

That brief conversation flashed through my mind. She'd been wearing short shorts, and I'd been having fantasies about picking her up by the ass and screwing her on the counter.

And then the guilt happened.

Because I saw a vision of Andi on the counter.

And the memory was faded, not as strong. So I'd said yes to get her to stop talking and then excused myself.

I was still in my position on the ground, cheek throbbing. "I'm sorry."

"No, you're not." Val's eyes blurred with tears. "I've tried!" she yelled louder. "I text you. I try talking to you at night. You ignore me! All the time! I just... the only reason that I'm not on antidepressants is because of the girls!" She pointed back at the house. "Even the guys talk to me more than you do!"

I opened my mouth but she held up her hand.

"No," she seethed. "You don't get to talk to me. In fact, I don't want you here. At all. It's my birthday, right? Did you get me a gift?"

"I would have but—"

"Here's the perfect opportunity." Tears streamed down her face. "Give me the gift of your absence. Because looking at you hurts too much, and I want to be happy on my birthday."

"You want me to leave?" My chest cracked open.

Hell, I was bloodied, bruised, dying inside. "As a birthday present?"

"Yes."

I had no choice. I stood and nodded slowly. "Okay, if that's what you want."

"You lost the right to ask what I wanted a long time ago, and the sad thing is, I'm easy, Sergio. I'm a really easy person to please. Really, it's pathetic, being so starved for any sort of affection that had you even smiled at me once since we got here I'd want nothing more than to have you at my side."

She might as well have picked up a gun and fired direct hits into my heart, I was dead, flailing, falling.

How had I messed up so horribly?

Not seen her hurt?

Because I'd been so focused on me.

On keeping a memory alive that was long ago dead.

Shame. Shame was worse than anger.

I swam in it, I embraced it, I was shame.

The anger was gone.

And what replaced it was worse, because at least you can justify anger, but shame?

There's no justifying shame.

It is what it is.

Horrifying.

Val stomped off and rejoined my family —her family, and I numbly went to the garage to grant Val her wish.

CHAPTER 39

Over hill, over dale, thorough bush, thorough briar, over park, over pale, thorough flood, thorough fire, I do wander everywhere. Swifter than the moon's sphere.

–A Midsummer Night's Dream

Valentina

I WANTED DANTE.

And Gio.

And Sal.

And Papi.

And oddly enough, at times like this, I wanted my best friend from high school, the one who'd moved away without a word. She'd always understood me and had been so kind when I was frustrated, almost like she knew me better than I knew myself.

But people get busy.

And we lost touch.

I stared at the door to the house and took a deep breath only to have it open before I even had the chance to touch the knob.

"So." Nixon smiled. "How are things in Jackass

Land? Do I need to bury a Sergio sized body?"

Nixon never really spoke to me much, I mean he did, but not like the rest of the guys; he was constantly watching, calculating. Funny how I used to be afraid of Phoenix and now it was Nixon that had me uneasy, probably because the girls talked way too much, and I learned just how brutal he could be, how brutal he wanted to be when he was angry.

He reminded me a lot of my twin.

Hah, maybe because he was a twin himself. Who knew?

I shrugged.

"Not the shrug." Nixon sighed, and opened his arms. "Anything but the shrug. When Trace shrugs, I hide the guns."

I smirked.

"Ah, a smile?"

"I didn't kill him."

Sergio's car peeled out of the driveway, making my ears hurt, but my heart hurt worse.

Nixon swore under his breath. "What did you say to him?"

"After I punched him?" I offered.

His eyes widened. "You punched him?"

"It felt right."

"Atta girl!" He rubbed his scruffy chin and laughed harder, his lip ring drawing attention to his young face. Even though they were twins, he and Mo looked nothing alike. She was gorgeous, but there was a harsh beauty about Nixon, one that told people like me that we could look all we wanted but to touch was taking our lives into our own hands. "So what happened after the punch, Rocky?"

"I yelled… a lot." Slumping my shoulders, I moved forward into his embrace and pressed my head against his strong chest as he rubbed my back. He wasn't Dante, but again, it felt like Dante. "And told him that since he didn't get me anything for my birthday, my present could be his absence."

"Harsh," Nixon whispered.

"Necessary," I fired back.

"Pain has a way of wrecking us from the inside out, Val. Physical pain is nothing. Damn, shoot my leg, slice my throat, but when it comes to loss?" He shook his head. "I remember when I thought I lost Tracey to Chase."

"Lost?" I stepped back. "What do you mean lost?"

"The point is." He avoided my question. "Emotional pain scars but never truly heals. It's like a scab that refuses to stop bleeding. You think you're fine, until you bump into something and the bleeding continues. It's confusing as hell, and it hurts. I'm not saying to give it time, but know that I know my cousin." He looked out at the road. "He's not fighting you. He's fighting himself. If he didn't like you, if he didn't care for you, he'd keep you close."

"Well that's… confusing."

"If I were him," Nixon said as he opened the door and led me inside. "I think I'd be stuck in a place where I was forced to lay my past to rest in order to accept my future, and because guys are idiots, he probably thinks he has to release the only woman he's ever loved, in order to accept one he isn't even sure likes him. Tell me, would you take that risk?"

"No," I mumbled hoarsely. "I don't think I would. Because I'm not a sure thing."

"Love is never a sure thing." Nixon hugged me again. "All right, enough sadness, go open your presents. Chase made lasagna."

And that was it.

Nobody talked about Sergio.

And there was laughter.

Mainly because Tex bought me a pink gun and a teddy bear that said killer. I'd confessed I was lonely at night.

"You need children." Chase tossed a chip at Tex's face. "And soon, I mean pink guns? Teddy bears? Isn't that a sign?"

"Maybe for you." Tex glared.

A loud knock at the door interrupted the conversation.

I was out of my chair before anyone could say anything, running toward the door as though my life depended on it.

When it swung open, I burst into tears.

Dante had two suitcases in his hands and a smile on his face. "Happy birthday, sis."

I launched myself into his arms and kissed his face. "I missed you."

"Clearly." He chuckled wrapping his bulky arms around me and squeezing me tight. "God must love me because I smell lasagna, and I'm starving." He set me down and made a beeline for the kitchen. Maybe that was just part of being a guy? If there was food, you knew where it was. Period.

I smiled and walked after him.

The minute he entered the kitchen, the girls eyes widened. I went to grab a plate from the table while Bee started choking.

"Are you okay?" I asked concerned.

"Holy shit," Mo said under her breath. "Is he for real?"

"Who?" I frowned then looked at Dante. "My brother?"

Trace and Mil had huge grins on their faces.

Mil shook her head. "No wonder Joyce had an affair. No offense Trace, but I second Mo, holy ever loving shit, he's hot."

"I'm right here." Chase raised his hand. "Sitting right next to you."

Mil swatted his hand away and kept staring while Bee took a large sip of water and cleared her throat. "I almost choked to death. You should warn people, Val!"

I burst out laughing. "Um, he's my brother."

"But not my brother," Mo joked while Tex flashed her a glare.

Dante was in deep discussion with Phoenix, I tried to see him through their eyes. He was tall, just like the other guys, and had a similar body type to Nixon and Chase. Bulky, but lean at the same time. His biceps were clean of tattoos though.

He had baby skin.

Geez, and they were all still staring at him like he was a stripper!

He laughed out loud, his crystal blue eyes twinkling as he ran his fingers over his buzzed jet-black hair, his shirt lifted, just slightly, showing an amazing set of abs. Gross.

One of the girls, I didn't know which, sighed, while another cursed.

So, he looked like a model. It wasn't like they were married to hunchbacks, I could make a killing off of a mafia-themed calendar.

"Where's Sergio?" Dante asked the room, while Phoenix elbowed him and slowly shook his head.

But Dante, being Dante, wouldn't drop it.

"Val." His nostrils flared. "Where the hell is he?"

Trace started fanning herself while Mo poured wine and leaned forward.

"I punched him then asked him to leave," I said in a quiet voice. "How many helpings did you want? Of Lasagna?"

"I'm going to kill him," he hissed.

"I'll help!" Tex said in a cheerful voice.

"Put your hand down." Nixon sighed sounding bored. "Nobody's killing Sergio."

"Clearly he needs to be killed if he made my baby sister punch him. She's the least violent person I know!"

That was true.

I winced. "Well, to be fair, I've been taking lessons from the girls so…"

His eyebrows shot up. "Lessons?"

"Baking." I nodded. "Shooting. Fighting."

Dante cursed. "You're twenty."

"I'm an Abandonato," I said proudly.

"Hear, hear!" Nixon lifted his whiskey into the air and winked while Chase clinked his glass.

"Damn it, I hate being outnumbered." Tex pouted.

"Enough gossiping." Phoenix eyed me. "I say we initiate our two new members… family style."

My eyes widened. "I can't kill someone."

Everyone was silent and then burst out laughing.

"Capture the Flag," Nixon said, through his laughter. "Paintball style."

"In the dark?" I was excited just thinking about it.

Then again, they were trained killers so maybe I'd just hide in a dark hole and rock back and forth.

"Suit up!" Chase stood. "Tonight, we war!"

CHAPTER 40

I will roar you as gently as any sucking dove.
                    –A Midsummer Night's Dream

Sergio

I DROVE IN circles and then drove to her grave.

For the first time since her death, it felt like a grave. There was nothing alive about the marble headstone that stared back at me, just a marker of the life that was lived, and the body the dirt contained.

It started to rain as I fell to my knees in front of the marker and yelled at the top of my lungs. Lightning flashed across the sky, matching my mood.

I'd fucked everything up. And for what?

This?

This grave.

This grave that I'd put a soul into.

That I put a heart into.

A memory that I wound up like a robot and played over and over again in my head until I was bordering on insanity.

Having sex with Val had changed everything.

I craved her.

And, to make matters worse, two nights ago she'd left her door open, and I'd snuck in and just watched her sleep like a total maniac coming off a drug high.

I was worried about her.

I wanted to talk to her, ask her how her day was, see her face light up when she told stories.

Damn it, I really just wanted to hold her hand.

Pride kept me hesitant.

And fear kept me distant.

Because the more I *fell* for her, the harder it was to remember Andi.

To *still* love Andi as if she were alive.

Because that's what I was doing, loving an object that didn't hold me at night, didn't comfort me, didn't do anything except lay peacefully in the ground like bodies are supposed to do. The grass touched more of her essence than I still did.

And yet, the memories they kept her living, breathing, a walking ghost right along beside me.

Maybe that's how people who are left behind by loved ones go insane; they carry on as if the person is still there, until it becomes their reality, even though there isn't anyone next to them in bed, they still arrange the pillows as if there was.

I would always love Andi, but it was like Val was fighting for a position in my heart, a position I didn't even know was vacant, it didn't feel vacant, not when I closed my eyes and forced myself to think about Andi's lips, her touch, her laugh.

But the laugh? Wasn't as strong.

The touch of her lips no longer made my mouth buzz with awareness — because it was air — I was kissing air.

"You're gone." There, I said it out loud. "You're not coming back."

I closed my eyes as rain poured over my face mingling with the hot tears. I didn't know what to do or how to fix things.

So I found myself asking. What would Andi do?

Life was beautiful.

Death was beautiful.

She'd be pissed I was wasting away.

Her note said she released me.

What I hadn't realized, was I'd never needed her permission.

Because first, you need to release yourself.

An hour later, I returned to the house. I caught a glimpse of one of the girls dressed in all black, with a pink bandana around her head. I parked the car and got out when I saw Phoenix pop out from behind a bush, face smeared with camo war paint. I barely had any time to run for cover when a paintball hit me in the stomach causing me to double over with a curse.

"Got ya!" Tex yelled thrusting his gun into the air.

"Bastard!" I hissed. "Do I look like I can defend myself?" I held out my hands and waited.

He shot me again.

"That's it!" I charged him but it was dark, and I couldn't locate him fast enough before he ducked behind a tree.

"Need someone to save your sorry ass?" Nixon ran up to me and tossed a paintball gun, I caught it midair with one hand. "Also, if you could take out one of the girls, that would be super helpful, we're losing."

"The hell!" I yelled. "We haven't lost in five years!"

"So you see the seriousness of this situation?"

"I'll take care of it." I found myself smiling despite the fact that I'd had one of the worst nights of my life since Andi's death.

"Good man." He jogged off and called over his shoulder. "By the way, your girl took out Chase."

My footsteps faltered. "Seriously?" Chase was one of the best, bastard knew how to sneak up on a person, which should be surprising knowing his loud personality, so the fact that she got him was more than slightly impressive.

"Her aim was a bit low, he didn't cry, but his eyes watered."

Pride swelled in my chest as I ran after Nixon and hid behind the first tree. I had enough land that it was easy to set up a paint ball field. It was professional to say the least.

We had several trees strategically planted around the house for protection. The field to the left near the garage was usually empty unless we pulled out all of our obstacles for paintball, creating a huge competition field for Capture the Flag that ended up making most professional fields you paid money for look like a cheap ass circus.

I didn't have time to change.

We were losing, and Abandonatos were competitive by nature.

So I quickly tossed my jacket to the side and started moving stealthily through the trees leading to our group's flag. We always had two base camps, one for the other team, one for us; the flag was always visible. Getting there was the problem.

"I will cut a bitch!" Phoenix roared as a paintball sailed past his ear. "They're taking head shots!"

"Then duck," I offered in a dry tone. "Be the bigger man, Phoenix."

He flipped me off then jogged to the left while I made a beeline toward the girls' camp.

It was about eight hundred feet away, visible, with a spotlight in the window that ran across the landscape back and forth over the course of twenty seconds.

I ducked behind a tree as it landed near me and passed.

Exhaling, I moved again, careful to keep my eyes peeled for pink.

A flash of color moved to my right and then, behind me, as leaves crunched.

With a sigh, I pointed the gun behind me without looking and shot two rounds.

"Son of a mother fu—"

"You got Mo!" Tex shouted just as I turned and gave Mo a little wave. She shook her head and marched toward our base camp while Tex gave me a nod and pointed forward with his fingers.

I was already ahead of him.

I moved to the right while he went wide left.

A shot went off.

Another girl yelled.

I waited in the crisp night air as the wind picked up around me, but nothing. She didn't scream again, which begged the question, was she down? Or was it fake?

Two more steps.

Tex let out a loud curse as rapid fire sounded.

"I hit you first!" he yelled.

"Bull shit!" Mil tossed back. "I got *you* first."

Glaring daggers, he stepped backward shaking his head toward me, just as I fired at her side.

"Aw, bummer Mil, that sucks balls. Guess you just got hit too."

Her eyes narrowed in on Tex while she gave me the finger and slunk off.

"Get the flag, man." Tex's eyes were like laser beams. "The only girl left is Val."

I didn't want to insult her by asking how out loud. But still. How the hell was she the last girl standing up against mob bosses and their wives?

Maybe she'd hidden after hitting Chase.

Not that she seemed like the type.

I took a cautious step toward their base camp and then hid behind a tree when I heard the sound of someone breathing.

My heart started to race as the breathing got louder and louder.

The minute I realized where the breathing was coming from, was a minute too late, as a gun was pointed at my back, I dropped my hands to my sides and turned around, right pointer finger still on the trigger. "Val."

"Sergio." Her cheeks were flushed, her face dirty like she'd been crawling through the mud.

"Did you trip?" I mocked, because really, playing nice with her would just be suspicious at this point. I left because it was her birthday and she'd rather shoot me in the dick then look at me for another two minutes.

Val's eyes narrowed into tiny slits. "I was army crawling."

"Through the poison ivy?" I nodded my head toward the leaves. No chance in hell was she going to fall for it, but I had to try.

Her eyes flashed, and for a brief moment she glanced down at her arm, just as I held up my gun and pointed it at her chest.

"Oldest trick in the book." I shrugged. "Sorry."

"Wow, I don't hear that word often from you."

"It's hard to pronounce."

"Maybe for you..."

I held back my smile. At least she was talking to me, even if every single word was dripping with insults and sarcasm. "Hands up, Val, I'm taking your flag."

"I bet you say that to all the girls before you pull the trigger."

"You have to admit, it does relax them a bit before they meet their maker." I gripped her with my free hand and pushed her toward the base camp where the flag was held. Once we were inside the tiny fort, I pushed her to the side, not hard enough to hurt her, but so she knew I wasn't going to play nice just because she was my wife.

Or just because I'd forgotten her birthday.

Or pissed her off.

Holy shit, I was a jackass.

I grabbed the flag and turned just in time to see her holding another paintball gun and aiming it at my face.

"Surprise." She grinned cheerfully. "I stole Trace's gun before she got taken out."

"But—"

"The rules never said I couldn't take someone else's gun. They just said we had to have an equal amount of weapons."

"Now, Val." I held out my hand, the one containing the flag, just as she fired rapid shots at my chest. Seven.

Not that I was counting.

And when she was done.

And pain seared me from the inside out.

She fired one last shot.

"Son of a bitch!" I yelled, falling to my knees. "I don't have gear on!"

"Sorry." She shrugged. "It's really dark in here."

"Yeah, amazing how that works, you hit me square in the chest, in nearly…" I exhaled shakily. "…the same damn spot, and you did it blind. Impressive. I thought you couldn't shoot."

"I've had some free time."

"Remind me to send you to boarding school." With great effort, I rose to my knees just as she shot me again in the leg. "What the hell, Val! Fuck!"

"Boarding school? I'm not your damn child!"

"Then stop acting like one and shooting me just because you're pissed!"

"Of course I'm pissed!" Val yelled. "You're an asshole! I don't deserve to be talked down to or ignored or just—" Her face twisted with hurt. "You could say hi. You could at least say hi once. Just once a day Sergio, what's so horrible about hi?"

I stood for the second time and hung my head. "What's so hard about hi?" I rubbed the back of my neck. "It's the start of something. You say hi when you open a conversation, it's a simple greeting with thousands of meanings behind it. Hi… always leads to how are you, how are you leads to what are you doing today, and that leads to do you want to hang out? Do you have plans? And honestly Val, if I say *hi*, I'm going to follow through on the rest, I'm going to ask how you are, I'm going to want to die inside when you say you're sad. And when I ask if you want to hang out, you're going to say yes, and when I ask about plans, we'll make them. And if we make plans—" My voice hitched. "If we make plans. I won't have the energy to keep myself from taking you. From stripping you bare. From demanding every part of your body, your soul. I won't stop. I'll keep going, and I'll lose myself, and if I lose the only part of myself that contains her — I lose her too. All because of hi."

Val slowly lowered her gun to her side. "So this is it." Her lower lip wobbled. "It's a little ironic, right?"

"What?" I stood and took a cautious step toward her. Damn it, I was drawn to her even though I didn't want to be.

She backed up, away from my touch. "You said goodbye to one wife, the hardest word in the human language to utter. Because of that ending, you've refused a beginning. You've done that. Goodbye was hard, but why is it, do you think, that Hi is harder?"

I opened my mouth to answer her, but nothing came out.

"Sergio." This time Val walked slowly toward me, her paintball gun fell to the ground out of trembling fingers. "When you move on with your life, when you find that person, whoever she may be, she isn't going to remove every last remnant of Andi from your heart. She isn't going to take over and squeeze out memories.

She's going to fit with them. Live with them. Laugh with them. It's not a matter of *replacing*, it's a matter of joining."

It looked like she was going to hug me.

But she must have thought better of it, because she stepped backward again, picked up her gun, and ran out of the fort.

Five minutes later I heard cheering.

The girls won.

And I was still frozen in place.

Because my young, innocent wife. Was absolutely startlingly.

Right.

CHAPTER 41

....and maidens call it love-in-idleness.
–A Midsummer Night's Dream

Frank

I DIDN'T WANT to meet Xavier any more than I wanted to cut out my own heart and slam it onto the table, but he needed to be contained.

And I needed to be the one to do it.

Not Dante.

Not Sergio.

Not Tex.

Wisdom told me that if I were to die, they would be just fine, but if they were to pass on? It would be tragic. They had so much life yet to live, and I knew that my time was slowly coming to an end, not that I wanted it to. I wanted to see great grandchildren; I wanted to see my family back on the right path.

There were many things I wanted to see.

But that didn't mean I deserved to see them.

I knew that more than anyone.

Mistakes have a way of jarring your sense of reality,

of right and wrong, because in making mistakes, or choices, your constant companion is the need to justify the rocky path you're on in hopes that at the end of the day you'll be able to close your eyes against your soft pillow and sleep.

I have not truly slept in over thirty years.

I wasn't about to any time soon.

Sal fidgeted next to me. "This… this will not work."

"It will work." It might not work, but we could try.

Papi and Gio were on my left, each of them with guns trained on the door just in case Xavier made things difficult.

One knock sounded at the door.

My associate, Joe, answered and paused.

Joe rarely paused.

After looking back at me, he opened the door wider.

And four people stepped through.

Xavier, his wife, and his two children.

"Shit," Gio said under his breath.

Either Xavier was bluffing or he was about to make our jobs a hell of a lot harder.

He wanted to be boss.

Well, if you want something, you need to take it.

No more threats.

No more guns.

No more war.

I dropped my gun to the floor and stood. "So it is to be like this?"

"They mean nothing to me. A means to an end. Kill them right here, right now. I still want what I want. Nothing will change that."

"You could be bluffing." I tilted my head. No, his eyes flashed, this was the look of a man crazed with greed. This, sadly, was the look of justification in its truest form.

The type you do not come back from.

Like a sickness, it poisons the blood until all you want is more — until you are less than human.

He was finally at the point of no return.

And because of his choice — I was going to send him to hell.

"No guns." I waited while Joe patted him down. "You kill me. I will give you what you want." I held out my hand while Sal slowly stood and approached, contract in hand. "Signed with my blood. Stamped with my ring. I will hand over the entire Alfero empire to you. But you must take it."

"Old man, you're about to regret saying that."

I grinned. "We'll see."

"Yes." He slowly rolled up his right sleeve and then his left. "We will."

"First." I handed him a pen. "You sign the dotted line."

"I haven't read it."

"You didn't read the last contract either. Do you not trust me?"

"Does it matter?" He scribbled down his name. "You'll be dead in a few minutes, and if you lie, it is of no consequence. I'll still take your money, your home, your name, I may even take that granddaughter of yours."

"Hah!" I fought to keep myself from laughing out loud. "I'd like to see you get through Nixon. Hell, I'd pay to see that."

"He's a child."

"No." I sighed. "If you need an example of a child,

simply look into a mirror. You think you deserve power, yet you don't know what to do with it. You think you want money, but it only lasts so long. You think you want my name? When the identity does not fit any better than my shoes? You are an errant child, angry at the world, angry at me, angry at Luca." My eyes fell to his wife.

She was young, maybe twenty-five. Her makeup did nothing to cover up her bruised face. The children were too old to be hers, meaning, she was raising bastards, but the way she hovered over them said it all. She would die for them, blood or not. Pity, for we needed more women like that in this world, women willing to lose lung and limb, for another human being simply because it was the right thing to do.

"You are even angry at your wife. Tell me, do you also beat your children? Kick your dogs?"

Xavier rolled his eyes and sneered. "None of your damn business what I do."

"There is a code," I said in a cold voice. "One you have not once followed. One you will die knowing even if I have to shove it down your throat as you choke on your last breath. Never…" I approached him, nearly touching his chest with mine, I had three inches on him in height alone. "Touch another man's wife or your own in a way that is disrespectful." I reached for his right hand before he could pull it away and twisted as hard as I could. His wrist snapped. "Or you lose the hand used to create the trauma." He tried to lunge for me, but Joe grabbed him from behind.

"You lied! You said no guns!"

"Do I have a gun?" I looked around the room. "Do you?"

"I assumed—"

"Ahh." I nodded thoughtfully. "Most children do. They assume they know what the parent will do. But I am not your damn parent, thank God. Nor am I your friend." I grinned slowly. "I am your executioner."

SEVEN HOURS LATER

"If you're going to kill me, you should get it over with," Xavier said a few hours later. I'd kept all water, sunlight, and food away from his body as his wrist continued to swell.

His wife and kids had been given a place to stay that was safe.

That was all that mattered. That victims were safe while the monster was chained.

"Tell me." I sipped my coffee. "What do you think the punishment should be for your... sins?"

He spat at the ground.

"Well." I took my napkin and dabbed my mouth then nodded my head at Joe.

Joe left the room, and then reappeared with the sledgehammer.

Xavier didn't move.

But I could taste his fear.

It was impossible not to see the way his eyes focused on the hammer like laser beams, hoping that the vision was merely a mirage and not his future.

Joe pulled the wooden table over to where Xavier sat then freed his left hand and placed it on the table. Xavier struggled but he was too weak to put up much of a fight.

I eyed his hand.

"Did you know, if I let you live, you would lose all function in your fingers? The bones will splinter into tiny shards, puzzle pieces that can't be glued back no matter how much money you throw at the doctor. A broken wrist and a broken hand."

Xavier glared.

"Unless." I toyed with the hammer, weighing the end of it as I flicked off some rust with my fingers. "You give up all associates who are vital to your plan. Names, addresses, social security numbers. I will allow you to live, with your two broken hands, if you give them to me."

"If I don't, you kill me?" Xavier said in a cold voice. "Is that it?"

"Yes, and I can promise you this. It will not be quick." I took a step forward. "I need an answer."

"I'm thinking!" he yelled.

"Think harder!"

"I'm dead either way." He straightened. "He will kill me either way."

"Who?" Hell, I had no idea he was in deep with someone else. But that would explain why he wanted money and power. Maybe it wasn't about him but about escaping from underneath the thumb of someone else entirely. "Who will kill you?"

"Petrov," he spat the name.

I laughed. "He has been taken care of. Haven't you heard? He's dead. The FBI found some interesting information about his prostitution rings. He didn't... survive prison."

Xavier shook his head hard back and forth. "Not that one."

My eyes narrowed. "What do you mean, not that one?"

"His other son."

"His. Other. Son." I took a deep breath. "His other son would be barely twenty-two. If that."

"His other SON!" Xavier shouted. "Is in league with Satan."

"Aw, he can't be so bad." My eyebrows arched. "Tell me, how does he kill?"

Xavier swallowed and looked down at his feet. "He drowns you. And then revives you, only to repeat the process. And then, he lets you eat and drink. Only to slowly singe the skin off of every single square inch of your body with a torch and, when you are in so much pain he is afraid of your impending death, he injects morphine to keep you alive. But it does nothing, so when he turns the lights on, your skin begins to smoke or what is left of it. There are crowds set up, bets take place, if you survive, it is only to bring you out the next day, allow more bets to take place, and finally when you don't think you can take it anymore, you beg for death. He tosses a gun into the ring," Xavier's voice shook. "And you take your own life."

"Give me names," I repeated. "And I will kill you before he does."

Xavier glanced at me, his eyes, for the first time, betraying his fear as he slowly nodded. Joe released his hands.

He unbuttoned his shirt two buttons then pulled a

necklace from over his head and tossed it onto the table. A thumb drive in the shape of a shark was attached to a string. "I wear it at all times. To keep my secrets close to my heart."

"And now they are my secrets."

"You may kill me now."

I hesitated. "Do you not trust that I can protect you?"

Xavier sneered. "Protecting me would be giving me the title of boss. Already his patience wears thin since I haven't brought him the twins. He needs them."

"You never did," I stated.

"He did and, by giving them over, I could negotiate with you. Everyone would have won. Well except you. Then again, you're old, why do you care? I'm a free man, the twins go to the Russians, and I become what I should have been long ago, the boss of the Alfero family."

"How many?" I ignored his insult. "How many associates have you stolen from my family?"

"Ten." He didn't even blink. "And they will follow me to the death."

"Good." I reached into my back pocket and pulled out my knife. "Because they will have to." One slice across his neck, quick, swift, he grabbed his neck but his wrist was broken, improperly working. Blood oozed from his fingers as I leaned down and whispered in his ear. "May you find peace as the saints drag you to hell." His eyes widened; the Russians always were superstitious. I smirked as he collapsed against the table, eyes open and full of fear.

"Now what?" Gio walked in, half of a sandwich sticking out of his lips. "We go after Petrov?"

"Hah." I shook my head slowly. "No, we eliminate the ten associates who defied us."

"Well, hell," Sal said from the doorway. "Sounds like a vacation."

"Highest body count buys dinner." Papi nodded seriously. "I want cannoli."

CHAPTER 42

...Such tricks hath strong imagination.

–A Midsummer Night's Dream

Valentina

I WOKE UP in a haze. Sergio hadn't said goodnight to me after the paintball war.

It was the first night since I'd been at his home that Sergio hadn't said goodnight. Then again, maybe that was just as hard as hi now that he'd gotten everything out into open.

I didn't want my heart to hurt, any more than I wanted to still be drawn to him, the impossible mourning man who had the most gorgeous blue eyes I'd ever seen.

His pain made it impossible to hate him, because he wore it like a cloak over his muscled body. Pain does that. It makes people feel sorry for you and it does create anger, but it doesn't create hate.

I really wish it did.

After putting on a pair of jeans and a long-sleeve pink shirt, I slowly walked down the stairs and made my way into the kitchen.

The coffee was brewing.

Breakfast was on the table.

And more importantly, Sergio was at the table, reading a freaking newspaper.

I hesitated, maybe he was having a meeting and I wasn't invited?

My stomach grumbled, and my eyes darted to the coffee. Desperation won out, so I wordlessly went to the cupboard and grabbed a mug.

I'd had to locate every fork, every plate, every scrap of food, on my own. Had I not gone to the grocery store we would have starved.

So maybe I slammed the cupboard harder than I should have, and maybe I stomped over to the bar and sat, but I did feel slightly better about the fact that at least he could hear my irritation.

Just as I brought my cup to my lips Sergio blurted, "Hi."

I nearly spewed my coffee all over the table in surprise before I gave him a sharp look. "Um… hi?"

He set the newspaper down and leaned his bronzed forearms across the table. "How are you, Val?"

I turned away. "Tired."

"Yeah well, shooting the shit out of your husband has a way of exhausting a person."

I would not smile. Or laugh. Or turn around.

"So." The sound of the chair scratching against the floor made my heart pick up like a hummingbird. And then footsteps. "What are you doing today?"

"It's Monday," I said in a bored tone. "Grocery shopping and a cooking day."

"Can I come?"

The olive branch may as well have been a bomb going off in that kitchen. My hurt feelings demanded I turn him down, they demanded I say something mean, something that made him feel as hurt as I'd felt. I wanted to hold on to the anger, I wanted him to feel hurt. It shouldn't be easy for him to just come waltzing back in, because in my experience with Sergio, he almost always panicked after we got close.

One more time.

If he did it one more time.

I think, no, I knew, it would completely break me.

Shaking, I put the coffee cup down and stared into it. "No."

There I'd said it.

But I didn't feel better.

"At least let me drive you," he pushed, his voice gentle.

I nodded, not trusting myself not to take it back, take it all back and launch myself into his arms — I was so starved for affection from him that it was hard to keep myself from crying into my morning cup of coffee.

He'd become my friend.

And something more.

I felt him.

I didn't want to feel him.

It would be so much easier if he was just another human body in that giant gourmet kitchen.

But I felt him.

And I had no explanation why, other than, when I was near him, it was never close enough.

"Yeah." My shoulders slumped in defeat. "You can drive."

Sᴇʀɢɪᴏ ʜᴀᴅ ᴛᴏᴏ many cars.

Way too many cars.

It was like going to a dealership and going *hmm which shiny vehicle with a max of fifteen hundred miles on its odometer do I want to use?*

I picked a shiny red Tesla — a car I'd heard about but never ridden in and tried not to look too impressed when he started the engine.

My hands gripped the leather seat as Sergio hit the accelerator as hard as he could sending us sailing down the mile long driveway at breakneck speed.

"Um, Sergio." I grabbed the handle to the door, my hand getting sweatier by the minute.

"Hmm?" He didn't look at me.

"Kinda fast."

"You need fast."

What the heck did that mean?

He peeled out onto the main road. It was the strangest thing, knowing how fast we were going — and accelerating, but not hearing any of the road noise.

Were all electric cars like that? Or just ones that cost more than most people's houses?

Faster, we were going faster, but I couldn't tell by the sound. I felt it, though, like we were soaring without straining to get to that place.

Like I could do anything.

Slowly, I released my grip on the handle and the seat as Sergio kept breaking all speed laws. "How fast do you want to go?"

It seemed like a loaded question. Like there was meaning behind it, although I couldn't figure out what. I glanced over and noticed we were hitting over one hundred and twenty.

"How fast can we go?"

He grinned, shifted, and I watched in amazement as we topped out at one sixty.

I couldn't hold it in any longer, I burst out laughing. "This is insane! Slow down!"

Sergio joined in my laughter. "Now you want me to slow down? Where's your sense of adventure?"

"I think I left it back there with that squirrel you took out."

With a low chuckle, he slowed the car down to around fifty and drove us the rest of the way into the city.

I was still smiling when we parked at the grocery store.

"I want you to have it."

"Have what?" I frowned looking around the car in confusion. What *"it"* was he referring to?

"The car." He pulled off his sunglasses and tossed them onto the console. "Technically, all of the cars are yours since we're married, but this car, I want this car to be yours and only yours. I got it right before I came to New York. The only other time I've driven it that fast was right after she died." His voice cracked. "I took a corner way too fast. I should have rolled, but I didn't. I was so angry. So frustrated that life wouldn't just take me. So I drove as fast as I could, I got the car up to one-sixty and just drove, thinking if I just get fast enough, maybe my heart will stop. Maybe I'll hit a tree, maybe..." He shrugged. "This car at one point, felt like a means to an end. Nobody cares if a man like me gets into a car wreck as long as he doesn't hurt anyone else. It would be an easy out. For everyone."

My heart broke for him. "What made you change your mind?"

He reached into his pocket and pulled out a tattered piece of paper. "I always kept it close to my heart, in my inside pocket, but when I was driving, for some reason it was on the dash, I wouldn't be so careless to leave it there. To this day I have no idea how it got there."

"What is it?"

"Read for yourself." He handed it over to me and pointed at the grocery store. "I think I'll go inside."

"But—"

His door shut, blanketing me in silence as I glanced down at the piece of paper.

99 Things to do on my honeymoon!
1. *Go to Tokyo.*
2. *See the London Eye.*
3. ~~*Learn how to cook!*~~
4. *Pet a giraffe—feed one too.*
5. *Learn Origami.*
6. ~~*Twirl in the rain—as many times as I can.*~~
7. ~~*Get kissed in the rain by a handsome man (doesn't have to be Sergio!)*~~
8. ~~*Jump out of a plane*~~
9. *Bake a cake and jump out of it.*
10. *Get a really kick ass tan.*
11. *See the Swiss Alps.*
12. *Pet a dolphin.*

13. ~~*Sing karaoke.*~~
14. ~~*Have lots and lots of sex.*~~
15. <u>*Go to a Broadway show and sing along even if it sounds horrible.*</u>
16. <u>*Sing at the top of your lungs — badly.*</u>
17. *Make a baby.*

Tears splashed the page as I kept reading. Some of the tasks were crossed off but most of them were still waiting to be accomplished. A few had been underlined like maybe she thought they were more important or she wanted to do them next. Or… perhaps that meant Sergio had done them or was getting ready to do them? There were only ninety-nine different things she had wanted to do, sex was listed more often than necessary

It might have been titled honeymoon list.

But it was a bucket list. Anyone with two eyes could see that.

My heart hurt — for this girl — for the one that Sergio loved, for the time they didn't have, hadn't had. But most of all, I was thankful, because this small scrap of paper had saved his life.

Probably more than once.

She'd saved his life — even without being here to do it.

Maybe it was my turn to pull the weight.

Not that I was going to make it easy on him, but it did help me understand just a little bit more — why he did what he did.

And why it was necessary that I help him stop the cycle of madness and live.

I left the note in the car and made my way into the grocery store. I finally found Sergio in the baking aisle looking about as confused as I'd ever seen him.

"They're chocolate chips," I said from behind him. "Not ammo."

"But there's a billion different flavors, and this one says soy free, this one says dairy free, and it just..." His frown deepened. "...stupidly occurred to me that I know nothing about you, do I?"

My stupid heart melted a bit. "Well." I reached for the dark chocolate chips and slammed them against his chest with a small smile. "Now you do."

He grabbed the bag and looked at it. "Dark Chocolate?"

"I like the way the bitter taste makes your mouth water. No matter how many times you eat dark chocolate, your mouth *always* waters."

His eyes hooded. "Does it, now?"

Oh, crap. He was looking at me. I take it back. He shouldn't say hi, he shouldn't even be near me, because he was dangerous when he was nice, and I was defenseless.

"Promise me something," I blurted.

"Anything," he said without hesitation.

"Don't run."

A pained expression flickered across his face. "I won't."

"Swear to me."

With swift movements he pulled something metallic from his pocket and made a quick slice across one of his fingers, then grabbed my hand, the one not holding chocolate and pricked my pinky. My breath caught when he pressed his bloodied finger against mine. His grip tightened as he pulled me against him. "I promise. I won't run."

"Blood oath, huh?" I whispered. "Aren't those serious? Like deathly serious in the mafia?"

"This means..." His eyes searched mine. "...that if I run a second time, you have permission to kill me or send someone to do it for you."

"Maybe that's what you want," I countered. "You know, part of your plan."

"Sorry, sweetheart." His breath fanned my face as he leaned forward, his lips grazing my ear. "You're stuck with me. Till death do we part. And it won't be because I'm stupid enough to turn my back on you a third time."

I exhaled in relief, but he didn't release my hand.

Instead he took a step back, lifted my finger to his lips and sucked the blood from the tip, his eyes locked on mine.

Paralyzed, I dumbly watched him — and most definitely felt him as his tongue swirled across my wound, his lips closing over a part of my body I'd never given a second thought to — until now.

When he was done, I was breathing so heavy that it was embarrassing.

"You completely and utterly undo me," he admitted. "It's not a comforting feeling, knowing I have spent this much time with you without ever even finding out your favorite color, and one look from you sends me into a fit of rage, lust, anger, passion — it's unsettling and even more horrible admitting it out loud — admitting the truth, that when I touch you — I will always want more."

He sighed and linked our hands tightly together.

"So." He grabbed two more bags of chocolate chips. "What are we baking?"

I finally found my voice as I shook my head out of a stupor. "Well, I'm baking cookies. You're just the driver."

"Ouch, not even sharing with the help."

"I may give you a crumb."

"Tease."

I smiled, unable to help it. "I don't think I've ever been accused of that."

"Probably because guys never got close enough to you to say it." His shoulders straightened. "What else do we need?"

"You aren't going to let go of my hand are you?"

"Nope."

"And you're going to keep pestering me until I feed you?"

"I'm a guy. Next to sex, food will always be a close second."

We rounded a corner. "So if I just give you sex, I can eat all the cookies?"

Sergio stumbled into a lady passing us with her shopping cart and cursed while she scurried out of harm's way. "Don't tempt me. I know exactly what I'd rather eat and it isn't a damn chocolate chip."

His grip tightened and didn't loosen until we were back in the parking lot.

CHAPTER 43

A lover, that kills himself, most gallant, for love.
—A Midsummer Night's Dream

Sergio

I LET HER drive.

She was horrible.

As in, one of the worst drivers I'd ever had the misfortune of meeting; even worse than Bee, and that was saying something. She'd already taken out three mailboxes since being married to Phoenix, may they rest in peace.

It takes some scary shit to scare that man.

Every time she asked to drive, he would go horribly pale, like it might be the last question he answered.

"So." The car jolted to a stop as Val put it in park. "Thanks for letting me drive!"

Poor car.

"Yeah," I managed to croak out as I opened my door and touched the ground with both feet. Solid ground. Thank God. "Anytime."

Val burst out laughing. "You're such a liar!"

"Hmm?" I turned to face her, my face carefully void of emotion. "What do you mean?" I casually leaned my arms across the top of the car and folded my hands.

"I'm the worst driver ever."

I fought to keep my laughter in. "What makes you say that?"

"You made the sign of the cross over your chest, and had you had rosary beads, you would have been clutching them and mumbling prayers."

"No," I lied more. "No, it wasn't that bad."

Her eyes narrowed. "So you don't mind getting back in."

"Cookies," I blurted. "We have butter in the back seat and we don't want it to melt."

"Huh, butter does that? In a temperature controlled environment."

"Yup." I nodded and moved my hands to show her. "All over the seat, impossible to get out, like bacon grease, so…"

"I think I've finally found someone who's a worse liar than I am."

"I don't think I've ever been accused of being a bad liar. Oddly it feels offensive."

"That's how you know you're mafia. When someone says you're bad at lying or killing, you actually get upset and feel the need to prove yourself."

I smirked. "Fine, you drive like hell. Blind grandmas with blue hair drive better than you do. A horny tom cat who couldn't reach the pedals would be a better choice."

Val grabbed the bags from the back seat. "He's horny why?"

"All tom cats are horny." I shrugged. How did that

slip? Because I was pent up with aggression toward her, and all the wrong kind of aggression, the kind that had me thinking about stupid shit, like chocolate chips.

And them melting on different parts of her body.

A wave of heat boiled beneath the surface of my skin, sizzling, warning me that I was in danger of seducing her again. I gulped, the need to run was so strong, so intense that I nearly doubled over.

My body's physical reaction was that terrifying.

Forget guns.

War.

Blood.

Torture.

Dismemberment.

Val. Was. Terrifying.

Fingers shaking, I grabbed the last bag and stood as she walked briskly into the house.

I stared.

At the house.

My fingers clenching the plastic bag. I gave myself a few seconds to just breathe without the choking sensation of her nearness taking over. Because at times, that's what it felt like, as if she was everywhere, and I couldn't escape her, and the more I felt her, the more I was driven to want to be near her.

Running. It sounded easier than walking into that house.

Running. It would always be easier.

If I ran, would she get over it? At this point, my attachment felt stronger than hers, but I had no idea of knowing. All I knew is that I had made her a blood oath, a promise, and it was one of the hardest things I'd done, because I wanted to do the opposite.

I wanted to be the liar.

The one who betrayed her again.

Because easy had swiftly turned into comfort. And I was so damn sick of feeling discontent.

Over Andi.

Over my changing feelings toward Val.

Co-exist. That's what Val had said. By taking a step toward my house, by going into my kitchen, I wasn't pushing Andi out.

I was simply… letting Val in.

With a deep breath, I walked in through the still-open door and slammed it behind me then made my way into the kitchen where Val was already pulling out a shit load of stuff I'd never once in my life used.

From measuring cups.

To a bad ass pink mixer I don't remember buying.

To cookie cutters that were in the shapes of guns. Huh, who knew?

"Where did all of this come from?"

Val froze, her body hovering over the sink and she washed her hands. "The store." She turned off the water and grabbed a towel.

"The store." I nodded slowly. "Could have guessed that. Did you buy it?"

"Maybe?" Her face scrunched up and then her face turned threatening, I took a step back. "Look." She pointed her finger in my direction. "You wouldn't even talk to me. I almost starved to death! Once my credit card came, I went… shopping."

"Let me get this straight." I ignored the starving dig since it made me feel like shit. "You just turned twenty, and your very first purchase with your shiny new card — the one without a limit — was a pink mixer?"

"And cookie trays," she grumbled.

"And—" I pointed "—measuring cups?"

She huffed. "I live dangerously."

"Yes. That was my exact response, in my head, holy shit, she's a risk taker. How much did that mixer set you back? A hundred dollars, two?"

"Six." She grinned, while I nearly choked on my tongue.

"For that?" I pointed at the pale pink contraption. "That's—"

"What?" She cupped her ear. "You don't want any cookies?"

I glared. "It's a beautiful... cookie maker."

"Mixer."

"Whatever."

"Okay slave, I'll bake, you get the super fun job of cleaning up." Her grin widened as she sidestepped me on the way to the fridge. "And I'm really, really messy."

I swallowed.

Twice.

And then counted to ten so I wouldn't tug her backward and kiss every inch of her exposed skin.

"Noted," I finally coughed out. "Do you need an apron or—"

"Nope." She thrust the egg carton into the air. "The dirtier, the more fun. Baking should never be clean, Sergio."

I couldn't look away from her vibrant face as she started tossing ingredients into the mixing bowl, humming to herself while she bobbed her head around, every few minutes she'd stop and turn in a circle around the kitchen like she was confused.

I had work to do.

Correction, I had work I *should* do.

Important work.

Life and death work.

Hacking work.

Instead, I stayed glued to the barstool and watched while more and more flour made its way onto her cheeks rather than the mixing bowl. As she dumped in chocolate chips, she started swiping handfuls until it was apparent that at least half of the bag was never going to make it into the dough.

When she turned around, I dipped my finger into the mixing bowl, and swiped a glob of dough and licked. Damn, it was amazing.

She turned back around and narrowed her eyes. "You did something."

"Nope."

She crossed her arms as a piece of hair fell across her face and kissed the flour on her right cheek. "I think we've established you're a horrible liar. Did you steal dough?"

Shit. I gulped. "Define steal."

"Really doubtful that I need to explain stealing to someone who's a part of organized crime."

"That's harsh." I smirked. "I'm the good guy, remember?"

"If the good guy kills people then marks them on his body, sure, you're the good guy."

"They deserved to die."

She shrugged and examined the bowl. "Fingerprints."

"Those aren't mine," I kept lying. I don't even know why the hell I would lie about something so stupid, maybe I liked her reaction. Holy shit, who was

I kidding? Arguing with her was better than being ignored any day of the week.

Folks, Sergio Abandonato has officially reverted back to the first grade.

Up next watch how he steals all her goldfish and stuffs them in his mouth then pushes her down by the merry-go-round.

"Right here." She pointed with a knife. "One very large finger, accompanied by two scratches from the lazy knuckles on the side."

I rolled my eyes. "My hands aren't lazy. Believe me."

"If memory serves..."

My jaw dropped. "Are you shitting me right now?"

Her expression was complete innocence. "What?"

Was she talking about sex? Or was I just reading into things. Did it matter? I narrowed my eyes as I slowly made my way around the counter and dipped two fingers into the dough and shoved them into my mouth.

Her face quickly went from innocent to horrified. "You don't put your fingers in food!"

I burst out laughing. She didn't.

"Val..." I tried to keep myself from laughing harder. "Do you have a food thing?"

"I d-don't." She crossed her arms. "I just. It's gross when people shove their fingers into fresh food. I mean who knows where your hands have been?"

"They've been on you." I moved a hand to her hip. "Is that gross too?"

She glared. "Yes."

"Now who's lying?"

"Still you."

I moved my other hand so both were bracing her hips. "So, you don't like people touching your food while you bake. Anything else I should know?"

"I like to wait."

"Hmm?" I was beyond distracted by the way she felt between my hands. "What do you mean?"

"I don't cheat. I never taste my own cooking until the finished product. It builds up the taste more... it gives you something to salivate over... something to be anxious for."

Shit. I was so screwed where she was concerned.

"I promise, I won't do it again without permission."

Her smile about knocked me over. "Thank you." She reached up and kissed my cheek, then jerked back as if suddenly realizing what she'd just done.

I gripped her wrists holding her right in front of me so I had easy access to her lips.

"Please don't," she whispered.

"Why?"

"Because you're going to kiss me. And I'm going to forget to be strong, because your kisses make me forget. And I'm already having trouble remembering why I hate you. It was only a day ago that you forgot my birthday. You can't just kiss me and make it all better."

"I know that."

"No, you think you know that. I can't... we can't." She jerked her hands free. "From here on out, your kisses have to be earned."

"Are we going to get some sort of sticker chart for this, or am I on my own?"

Her lips twitched with a smile. "I haven't figured that part out yet."

"Let me know when the cookies are ready…" I wiped some flour from her nose. "And Val?"

"Hmm?" She touched her face where my fingers had grazed.

"What's your favorite color?"

Her cheeks blushed bright red. "Pink."

"Pink," I repeated. "Okay."

"Sergio?"

"What?" I turned back around.

"What's yours?"

"Pink."

She tossed a measuring cup in my direction while I dodged out of the way laughing.

"Be serious!" Her color returned to normal.

I eyed her up and down, not realizing until today that my favorite color had a lot to do with her. I'd never really given much thought to it. Andi and I had joked but I'd never seriously considered the question.

Until now.

I locked eyes with her and whispered, "Brown." Then turned around and left the room.

CHAPTER 44

...A lover is more condoling.

—A Midsummer Night's Dream

Valentina

I LEFT THE mess for Sergio and went to my room to grab some books. I wasn't sure if he was going to actually want to hang out the rest of the day or if his little moment of peacemaking was over.

When I finally made it back down to the kitchen it was to see the man himself washing dishes.

If I thought Sergio kissing me, hovering over me as his lips found my neck over and over again was sexy — I was wrong.

Sergio bent over a sink.

I gasped.

I didn't mean to.

He quickly turned, water splatters had part of his white T-shirt sticking to his abs in all the wrong places. Places that made my control slowly crumble into tiny little pieces of dust.

I needed a blindfold or something.

"I stole two cookies," he confessed after turning back around and scrubbing the next dish. "But they were finished, so…"

"I don't police the product once it's done, so you're safe." I smiled as he hunched his shoulders as though he was gearing up for a heated discussion where I would cut him off from all sugar. "Thanks for cleaning up."

"Yeah well, it was part of the deal." He put the last measuring cup on the towel and dried it off then turned around in a semi-circle.

"Third drawer to your right." I pointed.

"I knew that," he said gruffly, grabbing the cups and tossing them in the drawer only to stare extra hard at the cookie trays.

"Do you know where anything in your kitchen is?"

"I don't bake."

"Nooooo." I grinned then grabbed the cookie sheets and put them in the big drawer underneath the oven. Then I opened the pantry and went over to grab the heavy stand mixer.

"I got it." He had it in one hand like it weighed nothing.

I pointed at the bottom shelf.

The smell of cookies clung in the air.

I had no other plans for the rest of the day except to read. I'd left my books on the kitchen bar.

"Are you going to read?" He grabbed all three and handed them over.

"Yeah." I mean if I had a choice, I'd probably rather have a heated makeout session with him, but reading, I could read.

"I've got a better idea instead, if you're up for it."

I hugged my books like a shield. "Let's hear it."

"Swimming."

"Swimming," I repeated.

"Swimming." With a nod at the window, he confirmed what he'd already said. "That is, unless you can't swim."

"Why swimming?"

"It's one of my favorite things to do, and I figure that if I piss you off you can just drown me and put yourself out of your misery really fast without having to use any sort of murder weapon. Really, it's a win-win."

"Why would I drown you?"

"I missed your birthday. I abandoned you. Took your virginity then smashed the shit out of some glassware. Embarrassed you in front of new friends. Betrayed you. Lied—"

I held up my hand. "Repeating all of your sins doesn't really make me feel like forking over forgiveness."

"That's the whole point, Val. I'll keep reminding you until you trust me enough to know... it won't happen again."

"I don't," I said in a quiet voice. "I wish I trusted you, but I don't."

His voice fell to a rough whisper, "You will."

"I don't think I can... not until you show me everything, not just the pretty parts."

"Did you just call me pretty?"

"Yes. You're beautiful. Like a girl. Wow, what skin products do you use?"

He cursed. "I deserved that."

Another nod.

"So, swimming?"

I was stuck between a rock and a hard place, because he really was trying to spend time with me, but the more I let him in, the more it would hurt when he eventually fought his way out, breaking every part of me until he was free, and I was left picking up the pieces.

"Yes," I found myself saying. "But no touching of any kind."

His lips pressed together as he hung his head. "All right."

"All right." I took a deep breath. "Now I need to find a swimsuit."

Sergio sighed. "Follow me."

I did.

He took the stairs too fast, making it nearly impossible to keep up with him. He stopped at one of the first guest rooms and reached for the handle, then pulled his hand back like it was going to burn him. "Just… wait here."

Something felt off.

Wrong.

He moved into the dark room and quickly returned with three swim suits, each of them with tags still intact.

"Any of these work?"

The only reason my shaking hands took the suits from his hands was due to the fact that each had an expensive price tag hanging off of the material, meaning they'd never been worn.

He wouldn't be looking at me, comparing me to a ghost.

"Yeah." I tried to sound excited. "I'm sure they'll be fine."

About fifteen minutes later and I knew there was a huge difference between me and Andi.

She'd clearly been wasting away to nothing.

Because my boobs were barely covered by the thin scraps of white. What was worse, the swimsuit bottoms were extremely low and revealing. They fit. But I looked like a complete hooker. I'd never worn anything so revealing and, that was saying a lot, considering what my wedding dress had looked like.

And just like that I remembered.

I had another note.

One last note.

Sergio was probably already wondering if I'd fallen into the toilet or something, I'd just have to check later that night.

I positioned the bikini over my breasts as best I could and prayed I wouldn't flash him as I slowly descended the stairs, careful not to add even a little bounce lest one of the girls pop out.

"Sergio?" I called.

"Kitchen," he answered right away.

I slowly walked in and nearly passed out. He was shirtless. Of course he was shirtless, why, in this scenario, did I not think of that? That he would be without a shirt.

And that I'd see massive amounts of olive skin as he moved gracefully through the water. The marks on his side were a glaring reminder.

He was dangerous.

But his danger was no longer in what he could do to my body.

But to my heart.

"You don't mind getting wet?" He didn't turn

around as he grabbed a bottle of wine and two glasses.

"Um, we are swimming right?" I awkwardly crossed my arms over my chest then huffed out a mild curse as I realized it only made the situation worse.

"It's raining." He pointed to the windows.

"Eh, it's okay."

"Great." He turned around and swore a string of curses that had my ears burning red and my arms itching to grab a towel, blanket, muumuu — anything.

"This one fit the best," I said, voice shaking.

"Clearly," he choked, quickly turning around and bracing one hand against the counter before pushing off and walking briskly past me. "Follow me."

I couldn't tell if he was angry with me or just dealing with memories of swimming with Andi.

Was that reaction good or bad?

I had no idea, because I didn't know men the way I should, and I really didn't know Sergio the way I should.

Again, it was hard to keep up, so I started doing a slow jog after him, not watching where I was going until I turned a corner and slammed into his back.

"Sorry!" My arms flew around his midsection as I steadied myself, he was warm, cut, he was everything.

With a sigh he bowed his head, shoulders tense, he grabbed one of my hands and held it firm against his rock hard stomach. "We aren't in the pool yet."

"No." My voice sounded weak, breathy.

"So touching is allowed right?"

"R-right." I should have said wrong, but he felt so right, and his closeness was exactly what I'd been craving. I needed it more than I ever wanted to admit out loud, especially to him.

Carefully he set the wine glasses on a nearby table along with the wine and turned, his one hand still holding mine against his stomach.

Once we were face to face, he released me only to cup my face with his hands and whisper, "I want you."

I didn't know what to say. I know what I wanted to say, what my body was screaming for me to say, but I stayed silent instead.

"But I don't deserve you. I'm not sure I ever will," he finished, his eyes hooded. "Do me a favor?"

"What?" It was impossible not to be drawn in by his icy blue eyes and smoldering body heat.

"When I can kiss you again… tell me. I can't read minds. I'm a guy. I need you to come out and say it. I need you to declare it out loud, so I know."

"Okay." *Kiss me, kiss me, kiss me.* "I can do that."

"Good." He swore. "Great." Another curse. "Out we go." He quickly turned and opened the door to the outside patio then reached back inside for the wine glasses and wine.

The rain wasn't too bad. At least not yet.

"The pool's heated." Two towels were already placed under the pergola, on one of the chairs. "Last one in—"

I surged past him and jumped into the pool — and immediately flashed the wall. Luckily, I was able to adjust my suit as he jumped in.

We swam for an hour. He asked me about life with the uncles.

I asked him about life in the mafia.

From favorite foods, to animals, movies, drinks, books, we covered everything, until I realized we weren't even swimming at all. We were sitting on the stairs in the shallow end, talking.

That was it, just talking while the rain continued to pour on our heads.

Eventually I told him I was freezing, so we moved to the hot tub.

"Did you have any best friends growing up?" He leaned back on his elbows as he lazily swirled the wine in his glass.

"One." Shivering, I scooted closer to him. He naturally lifted his arm as I scooted in his direction. "She was amazing."

"What was her name?"

"Ara." I shrugged. "She was gorgeous." I don't know why I said it, but she'd been stunning, so beautiful that you wanted to hate her, but in the end couldn't help but love her.

"What happened?"

"Hmm?" I glanced up.

"You seem sad, what happened? Did you guys have a fight?"

"Oh, no." I shook my head vigorously. "We only ever fought about things like books and movies. Her dad was a real piece of work. She never came out and said it, but sometimes I wondered about his treatment of her. He never yelled, but he hovered, in a really weird way." I frowned. "One day, she came to my house and said she had to go, that her father had important work and she had no choice but to follow."

"And she didn't keep in touch? Your best friend?"

"She did." I swallowed the lump in my throat. "Until suddenly, it just stopped. I've written her since then, but everything came back saying the address was no longer valid. We always thought it was more fun to send real letters instead of emails. It was kind of our thing. I tried texting a few months ago but it was undeliverable."

Sergio pulled me close and kissed my head. "I'm sorry. Do you want me to look into it for you?"

I paused then pulled away. "What do you mean look into it? Is that code for kill someone?"

Sergio's lips twitched. "I don't shoot everyone, Val."

"Coulda fooled me."

His eyes locked on mine. "I'm serious. Do you want me to find her?"

"Maybe." My stomach dropped. "Yeah. Yeah, I do."

"Consider it done. By the end of tomorrow I'll have every known location and alias."

"Alias?" I laughed. "She's not a spy."

"True." He grinned. "Sometimes I forget not everyone wears masks."

"I don't."

"No." He swallowed. "You don't."

The rain started coming down harder as the silence between us grew. I wanted to kiss him.

I wanted him to kiss me.

There were so many things I wanted.

In a perfect world, I'd make him suffer for weeks, months. I'd make him realize that he'd hurt me. In a perfect world, he'd come crawling back and confess undying love.

In a perfect world — he would earn it, but painfully, slowly.

But the world I lived in — the one where Sergio existed — it was a different world, full of broken dreams, shattered expectations, and betrayal. It was a world consumed by doubt, lust, fury, anger, want.

It was a world that didn't care if I didn't want to give in, because it demanded it anyway.

"Sergio," I whispered.

"Yeah." His jaw twitched as he leaned in, rain slid down his perfect cheek bones.

"Kiss me."

He didn't ask if I was sure.

He didn't hesitate.

He didn't miss a beat… before his mouth collided with mine… his tongue sliding its way past any physical barrier… before I had the chance to put them up.

Hot hands moved to my breasts as he untied my swimsuit and tossed it outside of the hot tub, his mouth moved down my neck as he pulled me against his already aroused body.

I let out a moan as water splashed around our bodies, pushing us together, pulling us apart, moving with us as his teeth grazed the skin by my ear. His breath was hot as he whispered, "Tell me I can kiss you anywhere."

"You…" I panted. "…can kiss me anywhere."

He sighed in relief. "Thank God." Without warning he slid his hand down my leg and tugged my swimsuit bottoms off then tossed them in the same direction my top had gone.

I didn't have time to cover myself as he lifted me by the hips and set me up on the edge of the hot tub. All I saw was a sexy as sin dark head bob down and start to suck. I braced my hands against his shoulders as my body arched under the pressure of his mouth.

Back flexed, I dug my fingers into his muscles,

trying to balance my body so I didn't fall backward, whenever I felt like I was going to backflip over the side, he'd grip my hips so hard it almost hurt.

But the pain of him keeping me there.

Was completely forgotten as he moved his tongue, and kissed, and sucked, only to repeat each slow movement with a fast one, followed by tricks I didn't even know existed.

I felt too much.

The cold rain, as it hit the top part of my body, gave me enough of a chill that I shook each time he took me deeper and deeper with his mouth.

"Sergio." I pounded his back with my fist. "That's…" I couldn't form words, I didn't know how.

"You taste perfect," he whispered reverently — but didn't stop, no, he never stopped. He tortured me until I was panting and then screaming his name at the top of my lungs. It was too much — he was too much.

Heaving with exertion, he pulled my body back into the hot tub only to kiss me over and over again, his hands going from cupping my breasts, down my back, and tugging me against him.

He cursed as I moved against his hardness.

And cursed again when I locked my arms behind his head and did it again. Driving him crazy might just be my new favorite thing.

When I slid my hand into his swim trunks, he bit off such a violent curse I wasn't sure if he was angry or just at his tipping point.

"What the HELL are you guys doing out in the rain?" a voice yelled.

I stopped moving and ducked my head into Sergio's shoulder as he panted out, "Go back inside before I shoot you, Tex!"

"The door was open!" he yelled.

"One! Two!" Sergio started counting.

"Fine, fine." Tex laughed loudly. "You two heat that water on your own? Nixon would shit himself if he saw all the steam coming off your bodies."

Sergio flipped him off and blocked me with his body.

"We have news," Tex yelled. "Five minutes to get decent, Serg, or I'm joining."

"The hell you are!"

"Four minutes!"

"Son of a bitch." Sergio slammed the water with one of his hands while the other held me against him. "Tell me the truth." His swollen lips met mine in a punishing kiss. "Would you be terribly disappointed if I killed him so I could have sex with you?"

"Well, it's human life," I whispered. "Then again..." I glanced down at the water, even that didn't hide evidence of his arousal. "It's really a toss-up isn't it?"

"You have..." He kissed me fiercely, tugging me by the hair as he growled out. "...no idea."

CHAPTER 45

...the juice of it on sleeping eyelids laid, will make man or woman madly dote.

–A Midsummer Night's Dream

Sergio

TEX GAVE ME a middle-finger salute about fifteen minutes later. I was dry. Decent. But extremely turned on, as in, if my jeans were any tighter, the friction from my zipper would be a serious issue.

"So…" Tex put his hands behind his head as I closed the door to my office and then opened it just to slam it again three more times. "How's the married life?"

I opened my mouth then shut it and pulled out my chair. "What? What is so damn important you needed to interrupt?"

"Interrupt?" He cupped his ear. "Kissing? Damn, you move slow. I would have already been working on the baby-making part. Oh, wait." He snapped his fingers while I envisioned my hands around his neck.

I wondered on a scale of one to ten how horrible it would make me as a human that I'd smile while killing him.

"Tex."

"Frank killed Xavier."

I sighed and leaned forward, my elbows on my knees. "So he's no longer a threat?"

"He's no longer a threat, nor are the ten associates that were working for him."

I jerked back. "Because?"

"Because..." Tex sighed. "A hit was ordered on every last one and rather than share, Frank carried them all out himself, with the uncles, of course. Dirty bastards probably had the time of their lives."

"Hmmm." I licked my lips and leaned back in my chair. "So, I'm assuming there's more."

"There's always more." Tex tapped his temple. "He left his wife and two kids, and when I say wife, I say girl he was given by Petrov in order to keep his mouth shout, and two kids who lost their parents."

"Petrov is dead."

"Not his son."

"Damn it, why is he alive?"

"Because up until last year he wasn't a threat."

"Where are you going with this?"

"Frank offered her protection."

I exhaled a curse. "Of course he did, he's turning into a damn saint in his old age."

"Yes, I'm sure that's exactly what Xavier thought right before Frank broke his wrist, starved him, then slit his throat and cursed him to hell. Hey!" Tex paused. "This old man's gone soft!"

"You've made your point."

Tex stood. "He's flying back with her later this week, just thought you should know since Frank's got it in his head to bring another stranger into the fold."

"Splendid," I muttered. "Let me guess, I'm the new hotel?"

"Nah." He laughed. "Actually Nixon gets dibs on this one, lucky bastard, I heard she screamed for one hour straight before Frank could finally calm her down and when he did, she bit him."

"Hell. Good luck with that one."

"She's eighteen."

"Shit."

"Right."

He was quiet. I didn't mind. Tex did that a lot to me and, for the most part, I needed that quiet time to process whatever bomb he had the tendency to drop out of nowhere.

"Tex?"

"Shoot."

"How do you know I'm going to ask you a question?"

"That's what you do. You're a numbers and questions guy, so ask."

"Val mentioned a best friend she used to have, I didn't really..." Shit. "I didn't get her anything as a wedding gift, and I thought that locating her might be a good place to start."

Tex froze. "Really?"

"Yeah." I sighed. "Or is stalking some random stranger and then buying them a plane ticket to your house frowned upon these days?"

Tex burst out laughing. "Look, I think it's a solid plan, just..." He hesitated, like he was actually thinking before speaking, which was a rarity. This was Tex. Not Nixon. "Prepare yourself for bad news, people disappear all the time, you know? Without rhyme or reason, and although you have creepy as hell computer skills, you don't even know her last name."

"I didn't say that," I said slowly. "I never once said I didn't have her last name."

"Well, do you?" he countered, avoiding the question altogether. "Have her last name?"

"No." I sighed. "But, I'm sure if I track Val's bank account history along with her uncles, look through school records, it'll be easy."

Tex rose from his chair and slapped me on the back. "You're probably right. Good hunting."

"Thanks," I muttered while he walked out, leaving the door wide open. Minutes later Val knocked.

"Can I come in?" she asked.

"Sure." Thank God she'd changed into sweats. All bets would have been off if she still had that bikini on. It had fit every luscious curve, every expanse of skin. Shit, there I went again, losing control.

"I was going to make dinner, anything you want?"

"Cookies?"

Laughing, she started to walk out. "Those are for dessert."

"Or," I added, "We eat them now and come up with our own dessert for later?"

"I think a pot roast," she said, completely ignoring me as she headed out the door. "Sounds... mmm... juicy."

"You're killing me!" I yelled after her.

"Get used to it!" she called back.

Damn it. Round two went to Val.

THREE HOURS LATER, Val brought food into my office,
I was hunched over my computer typing vigorously
away and I still hadn't located any info on her best
friend. It was literally like she didn't exist. But she'd
have to be brilliant to wipe her own school records,
unless someone did it for her.

"Hey." Val plopped down in one of the chairs. "I
already ate. I didn't want to bother you, but here's
some food." She pointed to the plate. "I have cookies
for you when you're done."

I forced an exhausted smile. "Great, thanks."

She frowned, then stood and walked over to me,
leaning over my shoulder. Normally it pissed me off,
people looking over my shoulder at my own shit. That
was my domain, my world, but, for some weird reason,
I wanted her to see it, the code, the hacking, the weird
numbers and algorithms.

"Wow." She sighed and pointed at the screen.
"What does that even mean?"

"It's a type of language. If you know it, you can use
it to your advantage." I typed in a few keys and hit
enter. A picture of Val in high school appeared.

She burst out laughing. "Tell me you love the
braces."

"My very first thought. Next to the One Direction
shirt of course."

I received a pinch in the side.

"Show me another," she whispered, her words

kissing my neck with their nearness. I was powerless to say no, so I typed something else in and found another picture, this one from Facebook.

She was laughing hard, Dante was trying to steal her Kindle, and suddenly, my world did a little flip.

It was the exact picture from my folder.

Without thinking I grabbed the black folder from the other side of my desk and flipped it open.

It was the exact same picture.

"What!" Val hissed out a little yelp. "You have pictures of me."

I nodded, unable to speak. "It's the first one I saw of you."

"But that..." She frowned. "That wasn't recent at all. I mean it was taken easily over a year ago."

Which was why, when I met her, I was shocked, nearly brought to my knees.

"I'm not sure." Because usually the mafia was better than that. Hell, Luca was better than that.

He would have updated information, or asked someone to update my folder, right?

Or was it just laziness?

I frowned.

Torn between wanting to call Phoenix and dig some more on my own.

"Sergio?"

"Yeah?"

I hadn't even realized Val had my folder until it was too late, with shaking hands she pulled out a picture of Luca and frowned. "I hate him."

Tears streamed down her face as she ran out of the room and up the stairs.

Her father?

I understood. I really did, I hated it, but a part of me got it — understood her anger. So I sighed, and slowly followed her up the stairs just as her door slammed shut.

CHAPTER 46

...grows, lives, and dies in blessedness.
–A Midsummer Night's Dream

Valentina

WITH SHAKING HANDS, I grabbed the last note and started to read.

> I'm sorry.
> It's really all I can say.
> I think if I explained myself, it wouldn't make sense, not yet anyways. So, I leave you with this.
> Ask him to show you.
> Ask him to show you us.
> But only after you show him a picture of you and me.

The picture fluttered into my lap.

I read the note again and again, then picked up the picture, just as Sergio burst into the room, making a beeline for my bed.

"Val." His voice was cold. "Why are you in a picture with my dead wife?"

He was wrong.

Completely delirious with his anger and sadness, and it was finally breaking him, making him hallucinate. Irritated, I shoved him away. "It's my friend, Ara."

"No." Sergio jerked the picture from my hands and stared. "That's Andi."

"No." I shook my head, unable to believe what he was saying. "That's my best friend. She's—she's fine, and she's happy, and you're just confused because you're sad." Tears streamed down my face. "Everyone has a doppelganger you know? Everyone! It's not her!"

Sergio's eyes closed briefly before he held out his hand. "There's something you need to see."

I wanted to climb under the blankets. I wanted to ignore him, ignore the pain in my chest at his expression, ignore the world, but his eyes had changed, transformed from this deeply rooted sadness to something worse.

Pity.

I grabbed his hand and followed him down to the guest room where he'd grabbed the swimsuits.

He opened the door wide.

And turned on the lights.

It wasn't a huge room.

Still pretty in its own way, even though it was smaller than mine, less new. Then again, it could be the fact that the blinds were drawn, a choking sensation wrapped itself around my neck as I tried to inhale through the staleness of the room, with shaking hands I touched my neck in an effort to free up the air.

"This…"Sergio grabbed a framed picture, held it close to his chest, and closed his eyes briefly. "This is Andi."

I reached for it, but he didn't hand it over, instead he eyed me up and down with suspicion as if I knew some great secret.

"What?"

"You really have *no idea*, do you?"

"What are you talking about?" I think, deep down, I suspected, maybe I even knew, but I didn't want to know, I wanted to turn on my heel and run out of the house, out into the field, I wanted to run, and I had no idea why, other than the look on his face told me my world, or the world I'd known up until then, was going to be shattered one last time, maybe for good.

He sighed and bowed his head, then handed over the frame.

The minute my hands locked on it, it was like a physical shift in my body as I turned it over and stared.

My friend Ara... was Andi.

The same smile, lips, posture, eyes.

Shaking, I nearly dropped the picture until Sergio held my hands, gripping them in his.

I should be confused, scared, angry, so many things, instead, all I felt, was such a horrific sadness that I collapsed to my knees and sobbed.

Because it was she who had helped me.

She who had, at one point, made me feel alive.

She had who rescued me when nobody knew I needed saving.

It was his dead wife.

Who had brought me into the land of the living.

And I couldn't even thank her.

I couldn't say thank you.

And worst of all — I hadn't even known she was gone — until it was too late.

"No." I pressed my hands against the carpeted floor and tried to breathe through my tears. "No, it's not true. You're lying! It's a trick!" I didn't recognize my own voice as I screamed at him.

"Breathe." Sergio ran his hand down my spine and whispered urgently, "Breathe in and out."

"I am!" I choked out a breath. "Breathing! Leave me alone!" I tried to swat his hand away but all of my strength was zapped the minute I locked eyes with her.

It had to be her.

It had to be her.

"Why?" I finally croaked out once I was able to form the words. "Why would she do that to me? Befriend me then leave?" And die. I didn't say the last part, maybe I didn't need to. It was a selfish thought, but I was feeling selfish, and more than abandoned, tricked even.

Had our friendship been real at all?

Or had she used me?

With a sigh, Sergio joined me on the floor. A sliver of sunlight peaked through the curtain drawing a line on the carpet between our bodies.

"I wish I had answers. I don't." He sighed. "I had no idea, Val, believe me. If I had…"

"What?" I gasped. "What would you have done? Anything different?" Please say no. It was hard enough being rejected by him, but being married to the man my best friend had loved with her whole heart, knowing he had felt the same way about her.

It was impossible not to feel angry and hurt, but what was even worse, was I could see it, how easily she fell even if it wasn't on purpose, and how much she must have loved him.

"What were you holding earlier?" Sergio asked. "In your bedroom?"

I stared down at my hands. "Letters."

"Letters," he repeated. "From Andi? Or Ara?" he corrected.

"No." I frowned. "I have no idea who sent them, I was given a key to a security box at the bank and —"

"And you're just telling me this now?" His voice rose an octave as he scooted closer to me. "Seriously! It could have been a trap! You could have gotten hurt. Need I remind you that there's a pissed off Russian who wants to kill you?"

I shivered at the thought. "It was before I met you."

"And that makes it better?"

"Stop!" I shoved at his chest. "I was lonely, okay?" Tears streamed down my face. "My best friend had all but abandoned me, Dante was distancing himself, and I was bored! I had nobody to talk to, and then suddenly I get this letter, assuming it's from Ara, FINALLY, you know? Because she just stopped writing and I tore it open without thinking, and then, I don't know." I shrugged. "I don't know what happened, suddenly I was in front of the bank and —" I frowned.

"And what?"

"And Mil was there…. and this other tall guy, who was really good looking and —" I vaguely remembered the guy with the easy smile. I blinked at Sergio and then let out a little gasp. "He looked… like you."

Sergio tensed next to me. "A really good looking guy with Mil who wasn't Chase and looks like me?"

"Yes. No. Maybe." I pressed my fingertips to my temples. "But he was lankier."

"Oh, that's helpful." He bit back a curse and shook

his head.

"I'm sorry!" I snapped. "I didn't know I was going to be getting profiled later!"

"Shit," Sergio whispered out the curse. "I'm sorry, it just, none of this makes sense, and if I'm right, which I typically always am, that means my brother Ax has been in on this since the beginning."

"Y-your brother?"

He clenched his jaw and then asked, "May I see the letters?"

"You've already seen one, on our wedding day, it came with the dress."

The silence was tense.

"If you show me that one, I'll show you mine."

"No." He didn't even pause or hesitate.

So much for trusting each other.

Another curse escaped between his full lips before he pulled out his phone and pressed a button then barked out, "Mil, tell me what the hell is going on now, or I'm going to point a gun at your husband's temple and pull the trigger."

I didn't hear what she said on the other end.

"Phoenix? What do you mean Phoenix?" Sergio's eyes widened. "Frank too? Fine, send him over now."

He tossed the phone onto the carpet and groaned.

"Good news?" I sighed, tugging at the carpet fibers.

"She said to ask Phoenix since it was he and Frank who were given the instructions."

"Instructions?" I shook my head. "For what?"

Sergio hung his head. "Our love story."

"I'm sorry, what?"

"Exactly." He rose and held out his hand. "Phoenix was with Chase anyways, so Mil relayed the message, they're on their way."

"They?"

"Everyone."

I suddenly wanted to crawl into the bed and hide, but not my bed, not even Segio's, hers.

My best friend's.

Because I knew if she were here, she could explain the method to her madness, and she'd also laugh with me and tell me everything was going to be okay.

And maybe, after she did that, I could apologize.

For falling in love with the same man.

Only I wasn't sorry.

I would never be sorry.

And that made me the worst sort of best friend, the worst sort of person, because every time I thought about her touching him, a pang of jealousy shot through my chest. Cancer or not, if she were here, I'd still fight for him.

And I hated myself for it.

CHAPTER 47

If we imagine no worse of them than they of themselves, they may pass for excellent men.

–A Midsummer Night's Dream

Sergio

It was raining again.

I was angry again.

I was frustrated.

I was irritated.

And as much as I wanted to comfort Val, I was livid that she'd kept such a secret from me — for so long. How could I trust her in the future?

The division between us grew along with the silence as the gang slowly started to arrive.

They knew something.

And it pissed me off that they'd kept it from me right along with Val, then again, she was as much a victim as I was. What the HELL had Andi been thinking?

Maybe she'd been delirious, and Frank hadn't the heart to tell her no, maybe Phoenix was desperate, maybe they were all worried I would jump off a cliff the minute she passed.

They'd had good reason to be worried.

As much as I didn't want to admit it.

Phoenix was the last to arrive, and when he did, he slammed the door behind him with such force; the aftershock pierced the tension in the house with a knife, causing an explosion of emotion to boil in my chest. I surged to my feet and started to charge him, only to be intercepted by both Tex and Nixon.

"Stop," Nixon hissed in an angry tone. "You attacking him accomplishes nothing, let him speak."

I took a deep breath and nodded as Nixon shoved me back toward the couch where Val was curled up. The girls had stayed home. I really wished they hadn't, because Val needed someone, something, and I couldn't give it to her, not now, maybe not ever.

How do you comfort someone in this type of situation? I'm sorry that I was married to your best friend and didn't know it? I'm sorry she abandoned you, may have betrayed you, and hurt you? I'm sorry that I loved her?

I'm sorry that I'm falling for you too?

Shit, it was messed up. And for the first time since Andi's death, I felt anger toward her, actual anger.

I hated it.

Phoenix walked over to the sound system and popped in a DVD then grabbed the remote and pressed play.

The screen was black.

And then it was filled with Andi.

I bit out a curse as she smiled, her body so frail and worn from the cancer that she was almost unrecognizable. She had put on makeup, but the dark circles under her eyes were still noticeable, the glassy expression that she wore during her last two weeks, one where you could almost swear they were caught between heaven and hell. It was an expression of sadness and waiting, but it was also an expression of peace.

"Surprise!" she said in a loud voice as she spread her arms wide. "And don't be mad," she coughed out. "Sergio."

And God I wanted to be mad, but she made it damn near impossible.

"First…" She shrugged. "I need to explain myself." She bit down on her lip and frowned. "I was sent to New York first. I worked for your dad, Val." Tears filled her eyes. "He saved me. I know you didn't know that, but he saved me from my father. He used to work for the FBI, but my real dad was Russian Mob. Sergio can fill you in. Those details aren't really important. What's important is that you know, the moment I met you, I was jealous. Insanely, out of this world jealous. I knew who you were, and I knew who you were going to end up with. It was the perfect setup for the families, and while I worked for your father, I was supposed to be gaining intel on Xavier, who, newsflash, is bat shit crazy, so you guys better shut down whatever he's brewing over there. Anyways, I was under cover, but as things started brewing between my family and the Italians, I was sent to Eagle Elite to start school, with the goal of infiltrating, so basically I'm like a bad ass double agent. That was around the time I found out my leukemia was back, and I knew it was kind of like one of those missions you go on where you know you'll never make it back." A tear escaped, sliding down her cheek.

She wiped it away and shrugged. "I didn't want you to remember me like this." She pointed down at herself. "Frail and diseased. You were and still are my best friend. The plan was never for me to end up with Sergio, I'm sure you know that by now. But my father was coming after me, and it was the only way. And I'm so sorry." More tears fell. "I'm sorry that I stole his kisses."

My heart clenched in my chest.

"I'm sorry I stole those moments from you, moments you should have had first." She smiled. "But I can't be sorry I had him. And I know you well enough to know, you probably feel the same way. If I was in that room right now, you'd slap me then hug me, then slap me again. I know you. You're good. So maybe you'd just shove me or something, since good girls don't slap." She winked. I scooted closer to Val and wrapped my arm around her as she started to sob into her hands. "Please don't be mad, Val. You were one of the best friends I've ever had. I wish I could have stayed in touch, but Luca made me swear to keep your identity a secret, and once he died, everything kind of... came to the surface. I did write you, just so you know. The letters were supposed to be delivered right before your first meeting with the beast." She laughed. "Oh, by the way, Sergio, that's you, both beast and prince, because if I know you well, and I'd like to think I do, you were all bark with very little bite. You had moments of tenderness and then regret. A process I'm sure you're still struggling not to repeat over and over again."

I squeezed Val's shoulder as shame washed over me.

"So, the letters. There's one more for you to read, Val. Phoenix will give it to you, and by then, I think you'll know what you need to do. Please don't be mad. This was the only way... the only way I could think of to give you guys a chance."

Her eyes clouded with tears. "Sergio. I wrote you a letter on your wedding day releasing you, I hope you finally understand that you never needed my permission, you already had it, you have it. I want happiness for both of you but mostly, I made this video to ask for forgiveness, my intention was never to hurt anyone but to help heal." She shrugged. "Sergio, you're a smart man, kiss the girl, it's so much easier then pushing her away and making her cry. And Val, let him love you, his love is great." She sighed. "He has so much to offer, and I'd like to think this life right now, between you two, is just the beginning of something beautiful. Wouldn't that be great?" Tears rolled down her cheeks as she smiled brightly. "Because, my ending, my favorite ending would be one where my best friend marries my best friend. I can't imagine anything better than the love of my life falling for the only best friend I'd ever had. That," She nodded. "Is pretty spectacular."

With a heavy sigh, she hung her head and stared directly at the camera.

"I love you both. Be happy."

The screen went black.

I didn't know what to say, how to feel.

Because my concern was for the girl sitting on the couch with me, the girl quietly sobbing into her hands whispering over and over again, "She's dead, my best friend is dead."

With a curse, I wrapped my arms around her while

she sobbed for my dead wife.

Not how I imagined the first few weeks of marriage between us, not at all.

I glared at the guys from over her head and nodded toward the door. I imagined they all came just in case they needed to keep me in check. I didn't blame them. I'd been losing my shit a lot lately.

"Val." I kissed her head. "Do you want me to call Dante?"

She shook her head.

The front door shut, blanketing the house in silence.

"Do you need anything to eat?"

What the hell? Like that would make her feel better? A hamburger? Her best friend just died, and I offered to make a McDonald's run? I mentally slapped myself and hugged her tighter, trying to remember what had made me feel better after Andi's death.

The door opened and shut again.

"Go away," I barked.

Phoenix held a white envelope in his hand. "The last letter."

Val pulled away from me but didn't look up.

A clap of thunder shook the house as the sound of rain started pattering against the roof.

"Thanks, Phoenix," I said gruffly, snatching the envelope out of his hands and handing it to Val.

Phoenix nodded and left.

And once again, it was just us.

Only this time the angry storm was our background music, like a reminder that everything had been ravaged, destroyed, tossed around.

"Can you read it?" Val asked in a small voice.

"Yeah." I licked my lips, opened the letter, and read

aloud. "Life is full of two-twirl moments — don't allow her to settle for only one."

Val frowned. "I thought it was for me? The last letter?"

I sighed, chest heavy, stood and held out my hand. "It was."

"What?" She grabbed my hand as I pulled her to her feet and started walking us toward the front door. "What are we doing?"

I didn't answer.

Instead, I pulled her out into the rainstorm as thunder bellowed. I kept walking.

Val followed.

I stopped once we were in the middle of the field and lifted my head toward the sky as rain splashed across my face, the cold both numbing and reviving me simultaneously.

"Sergio?" Val ducked her head into my chest.

"She died here." I pointed to the ground. "Watching the sunrise. Smiling. Happy. Peaceful."

Val choked back a sob.

"So this is where we dance." I announced turning toward her. "This is where we twirl."

"But—"

"Life..." I couldn't believe it, but I was channeling Andi. Something snapped inside my bitter chest, like a crack that finally allowed the sun to break through. Val needed to mourn, but she also needed to see that Andi's life was a celebration. I'd been given that chance. She hadn't. "...is meant to be lived — felt — experienced. Why spend your life walking — when you can dance?" I gripped both of her hands and started dancing with her in the field as memories of Andi's life flashed through my mind.

Her smile.

The way she laughed.

Slowly, I held up my hand as Val twirled once beneath my arm, her face finally breaking out into a smile as rain poured down her face mixing with her tears.

"Again," I whispered as I held her close. "Two twirls, you deserve two twirls."

She twirled three times and then wrapped her arms around my neck, her warm lips touching my skin with a sizzle. "The last letter was for us."

"Yeah, it was."

"I'm not sorry."

"What?" I pulled back searching her eyes. "What do you mean?"

"I'm not sorry that I'm falling for you. I should be sorry, but I'm not. I'm torn between wishing my best friend was here — and feeling guilty that I'm glad it's me..." She shook her head. "Glad that it's me, dancing with you, twirling, because not having you in my life terrifies me more than death."

"Val—" I cursed. "I don't want you to be sorry for that."

"No?"

"I'm not sorry either," I whispered. "I miss her more than life itself... and she'll always be here." I placed Val's hand on my chest. "But the really great part about being human is our hearts grow, they make room, they have no parameters for how big or how much they can love, and even though I'm not worthy, I'm honored that you're willing to share space with someone I loved — I'm falling for you too, and I'm not sorry for it. I'm only sorry that the road was marked with so much pain for you — and for her."

"Kiss me." Her hands tugged greedily at my shirt. "Please. Because, that was really romantic, and I'm still sad, and I don't want to be sad, I don't want to be sad..."

"It's okay to be sad."

"I know."

"It's okay to cry."

"I know."

"Val..." I brushed a kiss across her lips. "What do you want? Just tell me."

"You." She sighed. "I want you."

CHAPTER 48

What is Pyramus? A lover, or a tyrant?
—A Midsummer Night's Dream

Valentina

SERGIO HAD ALWAYS been beautiful — masculine in the way the lines of his face met each other. Everything from the contouring of his cheeks to the fullness of his lips had me wondering if he was some sort of misplaced knight from a storybook.

What made it worse was his hair.

Just slightly past his ears, it curled near the nape of his neck, just begging for a girl to give it a little tug.

But wet.

Sergio. Wet.

Sergio. Wet and strong.

Sergio being my rock.

That was sexy.

Never in my life had I needed him to step up to the plate more… and never in my life had I doubted so much — that he'd fail to do it, after all, it was his dead wife.

I expected him to cry with me, to run off, to blame me, to pull at every ounce of bitterness he still had and toss it in my direction.

"Let's go." He tugged me against his chest as we walked side-by-side back to the house.

Once we were inside and the door was shut, he peeled off his shirt and tossed it to the ground, then shrugged out of his jeans and repeated the process until he was completely naked.

I went from sobbing to gaping. From cold, to sizzling.

"Here." With a gruff curse he tugged my shirt over my head and moved his warm hands to my hips as he slowly rolled down my leggings, then pulled my boots off, tugging the leggings over my stocking clad feet.

How unfair.

He was naked and beautiful.

And I had on my bra, panties, and ugly wool socks.

"I think my grandma had a pair of those." He pointed at them and smirked. "Which means they need to go."

"Chicago's cold," I said with a tremor in my voice.

"Maybe if your husband wasn't such an ass, you wouldn't have to wear wool socks." He leaned down, his muscled thighs tightening as he gripped one foot and tugged the sock off, then grabbed the other. "Because you'd be sleeping with him instead."

"He's only an ass sometimes." I felt the need to defend him.

Sergio looked up at me from underneath dark eyelashes. "You don't need to butter me up with compliments, Val. I'm already going to sleep with you."

"Like now." I grinned ignoring the way my foot felt in his hand, and how my skin buzzed with his tender touch. "Right now you're only kind of an ass."

"You smiled." He stood to his full height then cupped my face. "Which means I'm doing something right."

Sighing, I wrapped my arms around his naked body. "You do a lot of things right, it's the whole after you do the right thing that really pisses me off... you know. Kissing, then running away, sleeping with me then slamming doors, sharing fun intimate details, then threatening to kill me—

"I get the point." He held up his hand.

"Are you sure? Because I think I have more examples."

"I'm good." He nodded. "Thanks though, makes a man feel good that you have all of those incidents stored right up here." He tapped the side of my head. "Now... you said something about not being sad."

"I'm not sad," I lied as a choking wave of anxiety washed over me. She was his first. He was my first. "I mean I am. I'm sad. I miss her. And it makes me feel like I can't breathe and then, when I'm done missing her, I'm angry."

"Okay." He picked me up as though I weighed nothing and carried me up the stairs. "I know anger, we're practically best friends."

"And here I thought you didn't have friends."

"I have you," he whispered. "Now, stop attacking me, I'm not the one you're angry with, at least this time."

"That's true, it would be easier if it was your fault."

"Would you like me to take the blame? Be the

punching bag? I can do that, if it helps. I'd be more than happy to be on the receiving end of a black eye; I imagine I'd be your first recipient."

He walked us into his room then placed me on the bed and went into the large marble bathroom. There was glass everywhere, no privacy whatsoever. How did he live that way? I shivered at the raw sexuality he emitted by merely walking, the muscles in his legs shifted and tugged all the way up his tight as sin ass.

My body broke out in a cold sweat at the sound of water, and then he was walking back toward me. It was almost impossible to keep my eyes on his face when there were other parts of his body fighting for my attention.

At least it was a distraction.

He was a distraction.

Yet, every time I looked at him, I saw her touching him, loving him, pleasing him, and it made me sick to my stomach.

I wanted to scream with jealousy while at the same time sob with the unfairness of her death.

"Hey." Suddenly Sergio was in front of me. "You're still angry."

"Yeah." I gripped the comforter with my fist and twisted, afraid that if I used my words, said all the horrible things I was thinking, he would hate me. I felt bad enough for even thinking them, let alone speaking them out loud.

"It's a new bed." He pointed down at my hand. "So you don't need to take out your aggression on the pillows and down." He gently grabbed my hand releasing my fingers from the comforter. "Do you really think I'm that much of an ass? That I'd bring

412

you into my room, strip you naked... on the very same bed? With the very same scents?"

I didn't trust myself to speak and not scream. "I wasn't sure."

"Val." Sergio frowned. "I'm trying here, but you have to meet me halfway. Normally, you speak what's on your mind, normally you're only quiet because you're pissed at me, and I can fix that. But I can't fix this unless you tell me what's going on inside your head."

I sighed.

"Fine." He grabbed my hand and tugged me off the bed. Once my feet hit the bathroom tile, they immediately warmed, heated tile? A giant old-fashioned claw-foot bathtub waited in the corner. "I'll go first."

"Go?" I frowned.

"I'm angry," he whispered, "that she didn't tell you who she was."

"Me too." My voice shook.

"I'm angry..." His mouth met my ear in a wet whisper as he unhooked my bra and slowly pulled it free from my body. "That I'm torn between missing her and being pissed at her for making you sad."

That made two of us.

His hands moved down my hips, fingers hooking into my underwear as he slid them down to my ankles, his lips met the back of my thigh. "I'm angry that for the first time in weeks, I have you naked, and you aren't blushing."

I blushed, basically, on cue as it dawned on me that I was completely without clothes in front of him, with every single bathroom light shining on my body.

"That's better." He stood and pulled me back against

413

him. "Anger isn't bad, Val. It's normal to feel anger. Anger turns deadly when you allow it to control other emotions, because then you go from having a natural response to a supernatural reaction that manifests and eats its way through every positive area of your life."

Tears welled in my eyes, I held them back, because they weren't the sad kind, they were the angry kind, and I knew if I let them fall, I'd do something stupid, like yell, or say all the things I shouldn't say.

"In the tub." Sergio sighed heavily and turned off the water. "Unless you'd rather I take advantage of your nakedness."

I hurried into the tub and sat, only to be immediately joined by him.

"What are you doing?" I asked.

"Isn't it obvious?" His deadly smile deepened as the water swished around our bodies. Slowly, with cat like precision, he moved until he was kneeling over me, almost chest to chest. "I'm seducing you so you'll tell me all your secrets."

"Oh," I squeaked, unable to escape. "Isn't that cheating?"

"So is that one of your things, Val? You like people to play fair?"

"Good looking people, people like you... they should always play fair."

"Why?"

"Because you already have all the advantage!" I pushed back against the tub, water sloshing into my hair as he looked down at my breasts and breathed out a curse.

"I have all the advantage?" He raised his hand to one as it overflowed his hand and cursed again. "Yeah,

I'm going to have to disagree."

His other hand danced along my collarbone and then slid down my stomach until he reached the apex of my thighs.

I squirmed beneath the pressure of his touch.

"Talk to me," he demanded, one deadly hand was massaging my breast while the other skillfully wreaked havoc on the lower half of my body. "Now."

"No," I moaned, nearly rising out of the water as he toyed with me over and over again. The bath water felt too hot, sweat started pouring down my face, and just when I felt like I was ready to lose my mind, he stopped touching me and leaned back. "What are you doing?"

"Oh, I'm sorry, were you expecting more?" He tilted his head. "Relationships don't work like that Val. You can't just take. You have to give too."

"Is this your way of asking for a sexual favor?"

"I don't want sex."

"Right."

"I want you to talk to me."

"And I want to forget about today."

"And when you're done using me, using us, what then?" Sergio asked, his tone was scary calm. "You'll go back to being angry and sad and eventually you're going to resent me, resent us, resent the whole situation. No, we deal with this now."

"In the tub?" I threw up my hands and splashed the water, angry that he was making me talk when all I wanted to do was go curl up in the corner and rock back and forth.

"In the tub."

"Now?"

"Now would be good."

"You really will keep me in here won't you?"

"I think you know where I stand when it comes to my threats." He leaned forward again submerging his fingers beneath the water, I tensed at the first touch and then relaxed as a slow rhythm built within my body, images of her, images of him, images of everything flashed in my mind. One last touch.

One last vision of them holding hands.

In bed.

Married.

"I hate her!" I yelled slamming my hands against the water. "I hate that she ruined this! I hate that she left me! She abandoned me! My best friend! She lied to me! She betrayed me!" My voice was going hoarse. "And she had you!" I sobbed. "She had you, all of you! And I get the pieces! I don't want the pieces, I know I said I'd try to make you happy and I'd work to make everything okay but I can't function that way, I tried, and I can't do that. I can't live in constant comparison with a girl that up until today used to be my idea of perfection! You were married to the perfect girl, and now you have me, and I'm angry, so angry, that selfishly I hate being second best. I want to be first, Sergio. You were my first and…."

His mouth fused against mine as he gripped my body and pulled me against him, water spilled out onto the floor as his frenzied kiss had my arms flying around his neck, my legs fighting to wrap around his body as fast as I possibly could.

With one hand holding me, and the other pushing against the tub he stood and took a step out of the tub, pulling me with him, he didn't let go as he pushed my

416

body up against the tile wall and slid into me.

It was painful at first and then, my world split into two, like I was watching myself get completely taken by this man, this man that I was falling for, this man that I could love, this man that I wanted to love, this broken man.

He thrust his hips slowly, painfully slow, and then dug his hands into my flesh as he angled my body down onto him, his eyes locked on me, and I was lost, completely without armor as I let him see how I felt about him, allowed him in, his mouth found mine again.

And I knew that I was a liar.

I would take the pieces.

I would search for them.

I would keep them close.

I would mend them back together.

I would cut myself on them when he hurt me.

And the process of scattering them would repeat.

Only for me to collect the pieces all over again and continue the torturous cycle of being Sergio Abandonato's wife — of being second.

Muscles bulged as he reared back, his eyes wild, like every ounce of control he'd held onto was slipping.

"Please," I whispered.

I needed him, all of him, just this once. I lied again, because I'd always want all of him.

"Yes," he hissed, punishing me with a harsh kiss only to thrust deeper, harder, until I thought I was going to pass out from the intensity of the feeling.

I clenched around him, holding on for dear life as my body collapsed against his, completely worn out, the tension in his shoulders released, still connected he kissed me tenderly and whispered, "I vow to never make love to you…"

My breath caught as anxiety built up.

"Where I made love to her."

I sagged in relief.

"Val." He kissed me again and again. "You aren't her. I don't want you to be her. I want you to be you. Just like I want us to have a chance to start with something good, something new. She would expect your anger, in fact, I'm sure she probably planned for it. Allow yourself to grieve, allow yourself to be angry, but don't hold back from me out of fear."

"I'm afraid I won't be enough for you."

"Want to know what I'm afraid of?" His eyes closed and then opened again, glassy. "Losing someone else. I can't do it again, Val. I can't—" He shook his head. "You get one chance. If you leave now, I'll let you. I won't chase you. I swear it. But if you stay in my bed tonight, you are mine. Wherever you go, I'll find you, no matter what you say to push me away; I'm going to push right back. I don't care if living with me is a version of your own personal hell. I want you. Here. Because I care. Because I see myself falling faster than I should. Because when I hold your hand, the world goes from gray to color. Because when I kiss you, I forget all about the pain of loss and remember the joy in being found." He kissed my lips softly. "Because when I'm with you…I don't want to be anywhere else. And that's my confession, my truth. This, here, you, us, is what I want. No do-overs. No should haves, would haves, no if onlys. Just. Here. Now."

"I want that too," I said in a shaky voice. "I want us."

"About damn time you start making sense, Val." His smile was back. "Now, get in my bed."

I must not have moved fast enough, because the minute he pulled away from me he was grabbing my arm and dragging me back toward the bedroom.

"Put on clothes and you'll be punished," he said in his threatening voice. "I'll be back in five minutes."

CHAPTER 49

Here come the lovers, full of joy and mirth — Joy gentle friends! Joy and fresh days of love! Accompany your hearts!

—A Midsummer Night's Dream

Sergio

I STARED AT the empty kitchen for a few minutes before grabbing two glasses of water and a few snacks.

Memories of Andi flooded my consciousness, but it wasn't sadness I felt, it was peace.

Finally.

I felt at peace.

Like her ghost was no longer following me around yelling at the top of its lungs for me to get my head out of my ass. I smiled as I remembered the dinner table where she used to bother the hell out of me. It was also the same table she had collapsed against when she almost passed out.

I made my way into the entryway and the sitting room, the table where I'd ripped off her clothes with my knife.

Where she was nearly killed.

I did a slow circle around the room and smiled to myself.

"Thank you," I whispered to both nothing and everything. Andi's death didn't just teach me how to love. She'd taught me how to live, how to survive through the darkness, how to make it to the other side and not feel horror at my broken state but celebrate the victory of making it out alive in the first place.

Without Andi, I don't think I would have ever fully appreciated Val. Andi helped me become a better person for Val. Had it been Val first, I would have ripped her to shreds, terrified the shit out of her, and most likely ended up getting shot by one of my family members. Andi had been able to handle me when I was my cranky bitter self.

And Val had come along when I needed healing, when I needed to talk, when I needed a friend.

I'd had both.

And like a self-proclaiming prophecy, Andi's words came back to me.

She'd said she loved me, but that I'd find someone who would set my world on fire, someone who would be more than my friend, more than my lover, she would be my other half.

My soul mate.

I thought it had been Andi.

But, as I started making my way up the stairs, I wondered, if I had it wrong all along.

Andi had been my best friend.

My partner.

My first real love.

The first person in my life who loved me back, who

saw me as loveable, who reached past the darkness and flipped on the light.

And Val.

Val was …

I paused.

I had no words for Val.

No way to explain to another human being how deeply she'd uprooted every single vulnerability I'd ever had and planted herself in its place.

I saw her coming.

I studied her.

I still wasn't prepared.

Val wasn't Andi.

And I didn't want her to be.

I was thankful, that as I took that last step into my bedroom, it was Val waiting for me, Val shaking with nervousness even though I'd already seen every inch of her naked body twice by now.

Val, blushing from her rosy flushed cheeks all the way down to her toes.

Val, smiling like she saw me, marks and all, and embraced them.

Val, who, in a complete act of selflessness, didn't ask me to push Andi away, but simply asked if I could make room for one more.

"I lied," Val admitted once I walked back into the room with our glasses of water.

I set them on the table and joined her on the bed, pulling her into my arms. "About what?"

"Well, I mean, at the time I made a promise, but I'm going back on it."

"What promise?"

"Not to kiss you."

"You broke that a while ago."

"Right." She sighed, pressing her palm to my chest. "But you also said that you didn't want my love, that you wouldn't do it again, you told me not to fall for you, you warned me." Another big sigh. "And I fell anyway."

"I know."

Val smirked. "Well that was arrogant."

I kissed her forehead. "I know, because I feel the same way."

"Please don't." Her eyes filled with tears. "Don't say it unless you mean it."

"Okay." I nodded. "I don't love you."

Her eyes widened.

"I've known you less than a month."

"True."

"I will."

"What?"

"I will love you," I whispered against her lips. "Because I'm halfway there and I found out your favorite color a day ago."

"And I know yours," she whispered. "Brown."

"The exact color of your eyes. A Valentina brown."

Her breath hitched as she kissed my mouth softly. "I want to show you something."

She quickly jumped out of bed. I would be an idiot not to watch as she charged out of the room, still naked, and then came right back in with a stack of paper.

"Here." She thrust them in my face. "These, were from Andi."

I started with the first letter.

And burst out laughing.

"Is she comparing me to the beast in Beauty and the

Beast?"

"Yeah." Val smiled. "Though I didn't know she was talking about you at first…"

We talked about each letter late into the night, until I finally found the last one and frowned. "You didn't open it?"

Val snatched the letter and turned it over. "I swear this wasn't in my pile the other day."

"You're sure?"

"Positive." Val stared at it like it was going to eat her.

"Open it."

"But—" She sighed. "What if it ruins what we have and—"

"Val." I kissed her soundly across the mouth. "Open the damn letter."

"Okay." She ripped it open as I peered over her shoulder.

Make sure he performs one of those numbers, you know which one, at least seven times a week.

Give him hell.

Find the one imperfection, left ear, you're welcome!

Love him well.

Love her well, Italy.

In a way, you guys are more perfect for each other than we ever were, and if I know Sergio the way I think I do, I'm going to assume he's already drawn that same conclusion. Best friends to lovers and now, Sergio, you have your soul mate, the one you're inexplicably drawn to.

The one you would die for.

Silly boy, you were never meant to be with me in the first place. It's me who should feel guilty, not you guys.

Enjoy this life you have been given.

And, Sergio, for the love of God, take the woman on a honeymoon!

All my love, to my two best friends, my two favorite people...

Andi

Val didn't cry.

I didn't cry.

We both smiled at the letter and then burst out laughing.

"You know." Val crossed her arms. "I've never been out of the country."

"I think I'll have to fix that."

"I think you should."

"You think Dante would house sit?"

"I think if you want your house to be still standing you'll have someone else babysit him while he house sits, but yes."

"Next week." I shoved the letters onto the floor and pressed her back against the mattress. "We leave next week."

"What about all the drama and hiding out and—"

"I'll bring my gun."

She smirked as she looked down.

"Both of them."

"Oh good, I was worried."

"I could tell by your laughter."

She wrapped her legs around me and kissed down my neck. "I'm ready for more seduction."

"Are you sure?"

"Yes." She nodded. "But this time, can I—" Her hands got all fidgety as she blushed and then covered her face with her hands.

"You're too innocent for your own good. You're going to end up killing me, aren't you?" I groaned as she reached for me and started exploring, slowly, so slow that I was ready to scream.

"Yes, but, I'm a fast learner."

"Yes." I jerked up off the bed. "Yes, you are."

"Sergio?"

"This is my punishment, isn't it?" I groaned aloud. "I asked you to talk to me and now you won't stop. Meanwhile, I'm ready to explode and—"

"For an older man you're kind of hot."

"I'm not old!" I yelled, completely offended. "I'm barely ten years older than you."

"Old." She licked her lips and then me.

And I forgot all about her teasing as I was reminded yet again, how perfect she was, how right it felt, to be in her arms.

EPILOGUE

Love is love. There is no explanation, no reason, no path.
It is what it is, and as it should be.

—Valentina

FIVE MONTHS LATER

Sergio

"Holy shit!" Nixon roared as he ran down the hall nearly tripping over his own feet in an effort to grab me. "Sergio! Upstairs NOW!"

Val pulled away from me and winked while her fingers grazed my ass. I let out a pitiful groan and tugged her into the corner, capturing her lips, I couldn't get enough, I would never get enough. I loved her more now than I ever thought possible.

"Sergio!" Nixon roared.

"In a minute!" I yelled back.

"She's in LABOR YOU JACKASS!"

"WHAT?" I jerked back from Val and took the stairs two at a time. "Where is she?"

"Her water broke and then she said she felt like she needed to push! I don't know what the hell to

429

do!" Nixon's eyes were crazed as yelling commenced downstairs.

Soon Tex, Chase, and Phoenix were all in the room with me while Trace braced herself against the bedpost and screamed.

"I think I'm going to pass out," Tex whispered to Chase. I could have sworn he was leaning heavily on him before Mil marched into the room with Frank and announced that someone was going to have to deliver the baby.

"Hurts so bad!" Trace said through clenched teeth and then turned her face in Nixon's direction. "YOU!"

"Oh, hell." Chase stumbled backward while Tex held up his hands in surrender.

Phoenix yawned. Then again, he'd already been through the whole process with Bee and was one of the best dads I'd ever seen — he actually hummed songs when he changed the little dude's diapers.

"You're on your own man," Tex mumbled as they ran out of the room.

Frank mumbled something to Phoenix then pulled out his phone; I hoped to call the medics, because I sure as hell wasn't a doctor.

"Sweetheart," Nixon said calmly. "This is a completely normal reaction to—"

She threw a shoe at his head then started pacing.

Nixon, poor man, went a shade paler. Aw hell, looked like I'd have to step up after all, or at least offer to keep the guy from fainting like a girl.

"Nixon." I shook my head at him and made my way over to Trace. I'd never finished medical school but I was pretty confident I *could* deliver her baby if the ambulance didn't make it on time.

"I feel like I need to push. I feel..." Trace's exhaled. "Pressure, so much pressure, and if I hold back it hurts." Tears streamed down her face.

I looked to Nixon for a decision.

After all, he was about to be a father.

And for the first time in my life, I saw fear in my cousins eyes.

Because he would kill for this woman, over and over again; he would protect her with his life, and now it was my turn to protect her for him.

"Trace, I'm going to examine you okay?"

Nixon clenched his fists, but he didn't move.

Val swiftly walked into the room and began pulling the comforter back and getting it ready for Trace, while Nixon stood frozen in place.

Once Val was finished, she went over to Nixon and grabbed his hand. "She's going to do great."

Nixon squeezed back and stood, paralyzed as Trace lay down on the bed. "Trace." I cleared my throat. "I'm going to—"

"Ahhh!" She punched the bed. "Just do it already!"

It felt weird, checking my cousin's wife to see how dilated she was. What was even weirder, seeing a baby's head. "Oh, shit."

"Oh, shit?" Nixon yelled. "That's what you say?"

"Head." I took a deep breath. "There's a head."

"A baby's head?" Nixon gasped for air, then pounded his chest.

"No. A grasshopper." I glared. "Yes, you asshole, your daughter's head. Okay Trace, on this next contraction I need you to push." I eyed Val. "Get some towels."

The sound of the ambulance became her symphony

as Trace pushed twice and then rested.

"Good work." I was touching a head. Holy shit. I was the calm one. Thus the whole medical school track, every mafia family needed one, I just quit before I could actually become one; that's what I reminded myself as I asked her to push again.

Soon EMT's were waltzing into the house. I could hear their muffled voices then the stomping of feet on the stairs.

"One last push, Trace," I encouraged.

"So tired." She sighed. "It hurts."

"Sweetheart." Nixon finally moved from his spot on the carpet and ran over to her, kissing her forehead. "You can do this."

"I can." She grabbed his hands and pushed.

"Almost there!" I said, injecting calm confidence into my voice. "Come on, Trace."

With a scream, she pushed one last time, and a baby's wail pierced the tension in the room. I held the little girl in my arms, shocked to the core as paramedics finally made it into the room and went to Trace's side.

"She's beautiful." Val's eyes shone with tears as she wrapped an arm around me.

"She's so small," I whispered, picking up a towel and wrapping the tiny infant. "So defenseless. Innocent."

"She's perfect." Val kissed my forehead. "And so were you."

One of the paramedics applied a plastic clamp to the cord and snipped it.

I stood and walked over to Nixon and Trace, carrying the child like she might break. With shaking hands Nixon took his little girl and gaped, tears streamed down his face.

It was one of the only times I'd ever seen him cry.

"My God, she's beautiful like her mama," he whispered reverently. "Thank you." He brought her to Trace and kissed every inch of her face over and over again. "Thank you so much."

Val and I quietly excused ourselves. She followed me to the bathroom and shut the door behind her as I washed my hands.

"What." I smirked as I grabbed the towel. "You're awful quiet."

Arms wrapped around me, and then a mouth was sucking down my neck from behind. "You would have been a sexy doctor."

"You're really making me re-think medical school right now." I groaned as she stepped in front of me and her hands moved to my pants and started undoing them.

Giggling she pulled my shirt over my head and kissed me harder.

"Have I told you how much I love you?" I whispered between kisses, "Because I do. A little more, every day."

"Say it again."

"I love you, Val."

"I love you too, Doctor..."

I rolled my eyes just as a loud knocking sounded on the door. "You better not be taking advantage of my sister!"

"Go away, Dante!" Val yelled. "Don't you have school today?"

"Don't call it that!" he fired back. "It's college, not school!"

"School is school!"

"I'm not going… not with *her* in the car."

Val froze, her face falling as I took a step back and took over the conversation. "You will get your sorry ass in the car with her."

"She's a whore."

"That's it." I pushed Val aside and opened the door to face Dante. "You are a serious pain in my ass." I threw on my shirt and buttoned my pants then faced the guy who I was seriously itching to punch in the face.

"You married my sister, doesn't make you my father, makes you my brother-in-law, so if we're done here…"

He tried walking away, so I grabbed him by the shirt and slammed him against the wall.

But it was Dante.

He wore his anger like a badge of honor. It didn't help that he'd been fighting again. I could see it in his eyes; they gleamed with the need to punch something.

And for being only twenty years old, he had more muscle on him than sense, which made my job that much harder since we were equally matched. Though his immaturity made me want to pull a gun on him and use his body as target practice.

"It's fine," Ella said in a quiet voice. "Really, I can go by myself."

Her face was flushed red.

Frank had brought her home after his dealings with Xavier. Though she had been married to Xavier by force after he'd murdered her parents, it still made Dante feel like she was our enemy. That was made worse by the fact that she refused to come under our protection unless she was allowed to bring both of

Xavier's bastard kids.

They were easier to deal with than Dante.

I pinched the bridge of my nose. "Look, why don't both of you just stay home?"

"Home," Dante snorted. "I'm sorry, I don't have one of those." With that, he shoved past me, ran down the stairs, and slammed the front door.

"Give him time." Ella always went to Dante's defense even though he treated her like shit. "He's just angry."

Val watched everything in silence.

"Sorry." I pulled her in for a hug.

"It's his fault, not yours."

"It feels like it's mine."

She sighed. "What are we going to do with him?"

"Well I'm sure as hell not going to keep training him with weapons. Last time he nearly took my head off — and was upset he missed."

"I don't know why he's acting like this."

I didn't say anything.

Because it wasn't my place.

Nor was it my story to tell.

No. That was another story entirely.

About carrying the weight of a legacy you never asked for, never wanted, and don't feel like you deserve, only to discover that you're alone in the world.

I knew his anger. His hate. His resistance.

I just didn't know how to break through to him — and was afraid that by the time I figured it out — I'd be speaking them to a corpse as they lowered his lifeless body into the ground.

"Hey!" Val elbowed me. "Think we can go back into the room? I want to hold the baby."

"Yup." I steered her away from Ella and the drama of Dante and followed her into the room. She made a beeline toward the baby and everything felt right in my world again.

Because soon, that would be us.

A family.

Want to read ENRAGE, Dante's story?
Be looking for it Summer 2017!

ENRAGE
COMING SUMMER 2017

EAGLE ELITE BOOK 8

Enrage: To anger, incense, infuriate, madden—to make very angry, ie; the man was enraged at his family for taking everything—and offering nothing but death. He lived his rage, he fed his rage, and in the end, the man fell in love with the rage, because that is what's done when you feed the beast.

It grows.

PROLOGUE

Dante

THE FAMILIAR SMELL of blood invaded my nostrils as it ran down my wrists, its hot wetness fueling the anger inside.

"Again." Nixon screamed, his face flashed with fury as blood caked his face. "Do it again."

So I did.

And again.

And again.

And again.

"Finish him." A cold voice whispered.

"Give me one good reason why I should." I didn't recognize my own voice, it may as well have been a stranger talking for me.

"I'll give you the only reason." A gun was held in front of my face — pointed directly at her. "Now finish him."

ABOUT THE AUTHOR

RACHEL VAN DYKEN is the New York Times, Wall Street Journal, and USA Today Bestselling author of regency and contemporary romances. When she's not writing you can find her drinking coffee at Starbucks and plotting her next book while watching The Bachelor.

She keeps her home in Idaho with her Husband, adorable son, and two snoring boxers! She loves to hear from readers!

Want to be kept up to date on new releases? Text MAFIA to 66866!

You can connect with her on Facebook www.facebook.com/rachelvandyken or join her fan group Rachel's New Rockin Readers. Her website is www.rachelvandykenauthor.com.

ALSO FROM
RACHEL VAN DYKEN

Eagle Elite
Elite
Elect
Entice
Elicit
Bang Bang
Enchant
Enforce
Ember
Elude
Empire

The Bet Series
The Bet
The Wager
The Dare

Seaside Series
Tear
Pull
Shatter
Forever
Fall
Strung
Eternal

Seaside Pictures
Capture

Waltzing With The Wallflower
Waltzing with the Wallflower
Beguiling Bridget
Taming Wilde

London Fairy Tales
Upon a Midnight Dream
Whispered Music
The Wolf's Pursuit
When Ash Falls

Renwick House
The Ugly Duckling Debutante
The Seduction of Sebastian St. James
The Redemption of Lord Rawlings
An Unlikely Alliance
The Devil Duke Takes a Bride

Ruin Series
Ruin
Toxic
Fearless
Shame

The Consequence Series
The Consequence of Loving Colton
The Consequence of Revenge
The Consequence of Seduction

The Dark Ones Series
The Dark Ones
Untouchable Darkness

Wingmen Inc.
The Matchmaker's Playbook

Other Titles
The Parting Gift
Compromising Kessen
Savage Winter
Divine Uprising
Every Girl Does It
RIP

RACHEL VAN DYKEN BOOKS

www.rachelvandykenauthor.com

Made in the USA
Las Vegas, NV
23 April 2023

71019965R00252